A Novel of Murder in Ancient Egypt

YEAR
OF THE
HYENAS

BRAD GEAGLEY

Simon & Schuster

New York   London

Toronto   Sydney

SIMON & SCHUSTER
Rockefeller Center
1230 Avenue of the Americas
New York, NY 10020

For information about special discounts for bulk purchases,
please contact Simon & Schuster Special Sales at
1-800-456-6798 or business@simonandschuster.com

Book design by Ellen R. Sasahara

Manufactured in the United States of America

2 4 6 8 10 9 7 5 3 1

Library of Congress Cataloging-in-Publication Data
Geagley, Brad, date.
Year of the hyenas / Brad Geagley.
p.   cm.
1. Egypt—History—To 332 B.C.—Fiction. 2. Ramses III, King of Egypt—Fiction.
I. Title.
PS3607.E35Y43 2005
813'.6—dc22   2004058979
ISBN 0-7432-5080-X

For my mother,
Adell J. Geagley

GATE OF HEAVEN

PLACE OF BEAUTY
(VALLEY OF THE QUEENS)

PLACE OF TRUTH
(WORKERS' VILLAGE)

DJAMET TEMPLE
(MEDINET HABU)

RAMASSEUM

RULER OF RULERS
(TEMPLE OF AMENHOTEB III
COLOSSI OF MEMNON)

WESTERN THEBES

SEMERKET'S

EASTERN THEBES

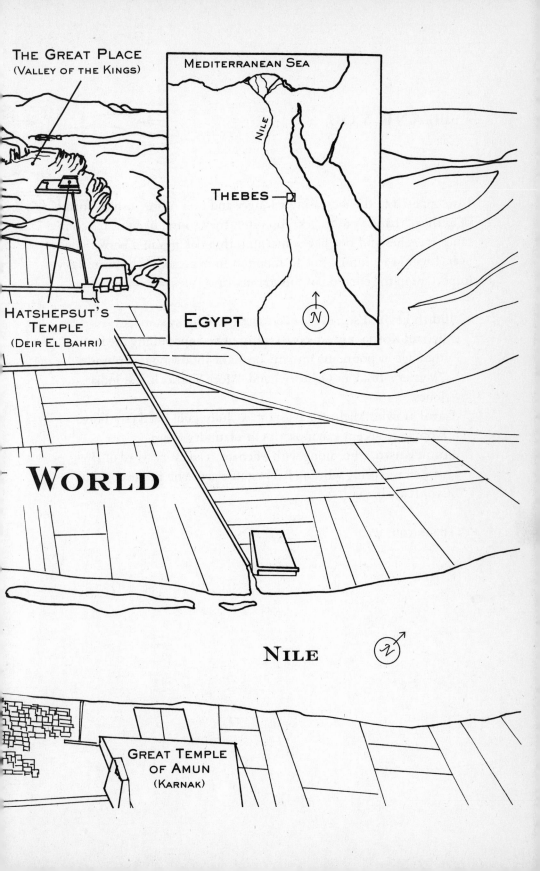

THE GREAT PLACE
(VALLEY OF THE KINGS)

MEDITERRANEAN SEA

NILE

THEBES

EGYPT

N

HATSHEPSUT'S
TEMPLE
(DEIR EL BAHRI)

WORLD

NILE

GREAT TEMPLE
OF AMUN
(KARNAK)

THANK YOU

I am opposed to the increasingly longer and ever more gushing forms of author "thank you" pages. Too often they sound like Oscar acceptance speeches and not like something that belongs in a book. However, I would be remiss not to mention four persons who were very important in the creation of this manuscript:

Judith Levin, Esq., my lawyer, agent, and lucky star.

Michael Korda, my esteemed editor, who kept pulling me from the edge by pounding into my head the following two phrases: "Mystery, Brad, not history," and "More Sherlock, less Indiana Jones."

Carol Bowie, Michael's assistant; as Judy said, it takes a brave woman to accept a manuscript in a laundry room.

Frank Russo, who, along with Michael, read every word of *Hyenas* as it was being written. Real estate may be his profession, but words are his art.

Thank you, all.

INTRODUCTION

THOUGH *Year of the Hyenas* is a work of fiction, the mystery depicted in the book is based on history's oldest known "court transcripts," the so-called Judicial Papyrus of Turin, the Papyrus Rifaud, and the Papyrus Rollin.

The year is 1153 BCE. The pyramids are already fifteen hundred years old, King Tut-ankh-amun has been dead for two hundred years, and Cleopatra's reign will occur over a thousand years in the future. To the north, Achilles, Ajax, and Menelaus are battling the Trojans for the return of Helen.

Most of the characters in this book are modeled after those people who lived at the time and participated in the events. Ramses III, "the last great pharaoh," ruled Egypt with the aid of Vizier Toh, while at the Place of Truth the tomb-makers Khepura, Aaphat, and Hunro lived in homes that can still be visited today. We even know that one day Paneb really did chase Neferhotep up the village's main street.

Though I have simplified Egyptian spellings and names for the modern reader, I have chosen to call certain temples and cities with the names used by the Egyptians themselves. Medinet Habu thus becomes Djamet Temple, Deir el Medina becomes the Place of Truth, the Valley of the Kings becomes the Great Place, and so on. The exception to this is the city of Thebes, a name too magnificent in itself to change to the more correct Waset.

Brad Geagley

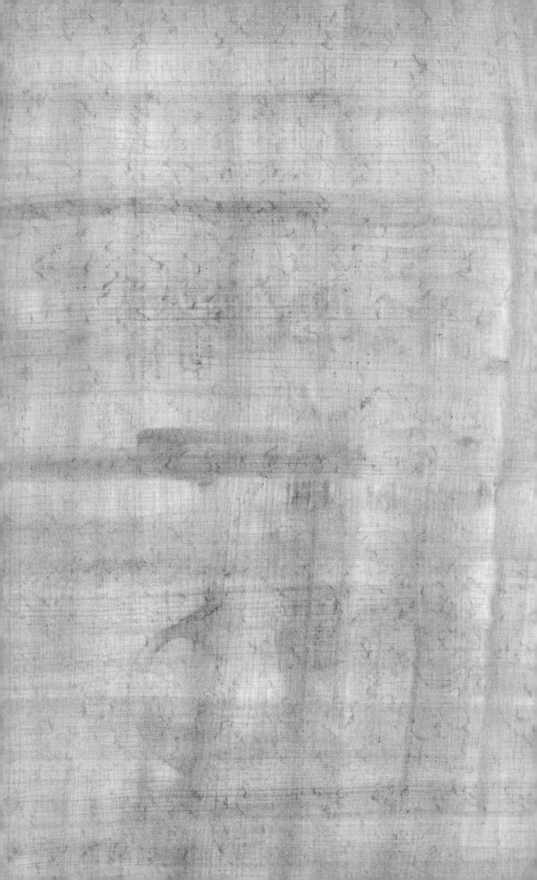

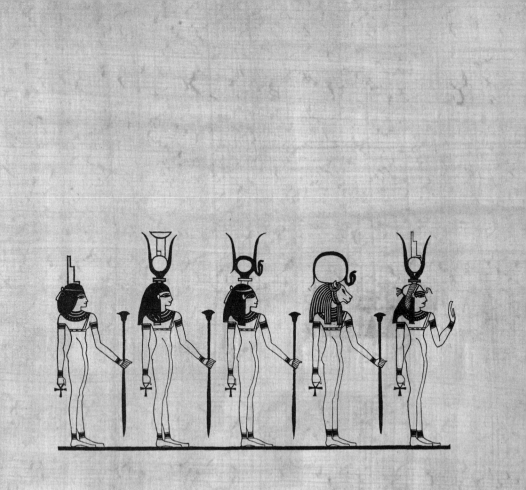

THE GODS
WILL NOT WAIT

HETEPHRAS LIMPED FROM HER PALLET TO THE door of her house like an old arthritic monkey. She pulled aside the linen curtain and squinted to the east. Scents of the unfurling day met her nostrils. Sour emmer wheat from the temple fields. The subtler aroma of new-cut barley. Distant Nile water, brown-rich and brackish. And even at this early hour, someone fried onions for the Osiris Feast.

The old priestess's eyes were almost entirely opaque now. Though a physician had offered to restore her sight with his needle treatment, Hetephras was content to view the world through the tawny clouds with which the gods had afflicted her; in exchange they had endowed her other senses with greater clarity. Out of timeworn habit she raised her head again to the east, and for a moment imagined that she saw the beacon fires burning in Amun's Great Temple far across the river. But the curtains fell across her sight again, as they always did, and the flames burnt themselves out.

She pitied herself for a moment, because as priestess in the Place of Truth she could no longer clearly view the treasures wrought in her village—decorations for the tombs of pharaohs, queens, and nobles that were the sole industry of her village of artists; pieces that lived for a smattering of days in the light of the sun, then were borne to the Great Place, brought into the tomb, and sealed beneath the sand and rock in darkness forever.

Hetephras unbent her thin, bony spine, firmly banishing self-pity. She was priestess and had to perform the inauguration rites for the Feast of Osiris that morning. At Osiris Time, the hour for speaking with the gods was at the very moment when the sun rose, for it was then that the membrane separating this life and the next was at its most fragile, when the dead left their vaults to gaze upon the distant living city of Thebes, girded for festival.

Though she had been a priestess for over twenty years, Hetephras had never seen any shape or spirit among the dead, as others said they had. She was an unsubtle woman who took her joy from the simple verities of ritual, tradition, and work. She believed with all her heart the stories of the gods, and put it down to a fault in herself that never once had they revealed themselves to her. Her husband, Djutmose, had been the spiritual one in the family, having been the tomb-makers' priest when he married her. When he died in the eleventh year of Pharaoh's reign, the villagers chose Hetephras to continue his duties; they had seen no reason to search elsewhere.

Hetephras sighed. That was many years ago. Soon her own Day of Pain would come, as it must to all living things, and she would be taken to lie beside Djutmose and their son in their own small tomb. Perhaps it was only the morning breezes that made her shiver.

She limped to a large chest in her sleeping room. On its lid, flowers of ivory and glass paste entwined, while voles and crows of pear wood worried the curling grapevines of turquoise and agate. It had been made by her husband. In addition to his priestly duties, Djutmose had been a maker of cupboards, caskets, and boxes for Pharaoh, and he had fashioned these simple images knowing they would please his simple wife. She cherished this casket now above all else she owned; it would be buried with her.

From this chest Hetephras plucked her priestess garb: a sheath of linen, white; pectoral of woven wire, gilded; and a bright blue wig of raffia fibers in the shape of vulture wings. Then she carefully packed the oil and sweetmeats the gods so loved into an alabaster chalice. Thus attired and burdened, she waited at her stoop for Rami, the son of the chief scribe. It was Rami who had been appointed to guide her to the shrines on these feast days.

But there was no sign of the boy. Hetephras stood waiting patiently for him, skin prickling against the cool air of morning. Her thick wig made a comfortable pillow as she leaned against the doorframe. Her eyes closed, just for a moment . . . and the old lady was carried away into nodding forgetfulness by the quiet and the breezes. She was brought awake again by the subtle warming of her skin.

She looked around, startled, sniffing the air. Irritation and panic made her heart beat faster. It was fast becoming full dawn! She would miss the appointed time for the offering! The gods would blame her, and in turn would become churlish with their blessings.

Damn Rami! Where was he? Sleeping with the shroud-weaver Mentu's little slut, no doubt. She had heard them together before, her ears keen to catch their shared laughter and, later, their moans. The youngsters of the village often used the empty stable next to Hetephras's house as a trysting place—as did some of the adults. The old priestess murmured dismally to herself that a generation of sluggards and whores was poised to inherit Egypt.

Hetephras decided to go alone to the Osiris shrine. It was the most distant of all the shrines and chapels she tended, and when she thought of the effort it would cost her, half-blind as she was, her heart thumped with fresh anger toward Rami.

Damn him! She would give him a tongue-lashing in front of his parents, that's what she would do—in front of the whole village!

This satisfying thought propelled the old woman up the narrow avenue as if she were young again. So what if Rami were not with her! Didn't she know the Great Place better than anyone? She had traveled between the shrine and her home every Osiris Day for almost a quarter of a century; she would find her way. But as she passed through the northern gate, Khepura's voice called out to her.

"Hetephras—you're not thinking of going up to the Osiris shrine by yourself, are you? You, who can't see a cubit in front of your face."

"The rite must be performed, Khepura, and I've no time to wait." The smell of onions was stronger, and the squinting Hetephras could almost see the dark form of her neighbor bending low over an outside griddle. "Rami never came to fetch me this morning, wicked boy."

"Then *I'll* go with you." Khepura's voice was insistent, as always. Wife to the goldsmith Sani, she had been chosen head woman of the tomb-makers' village in the last election. To everyone's regret, she had become quickly used to the habit of command. "I've gotten enough of the feast organized here for the servants to take over. I'll just get my shawl. It's brisk this morning." She turned to go back into the village.

"No time, Khepura, no time—the gods will not wait! And you're so fat, you'll only slow me down!" The old priestess hurried on impatiently, leaving Khepura to sputter ineffective protests.

The path up the Gate of Heaven was narrow, bounded on either side by limestone chips. The bright shards, remnants from carved-out tombs, served to prevent the unwary traveler from straying too far to the edge, where a sheer drop of some twenty cubits waited. By keeping to the center of the path, Hetephras was able to ascend quickly. Near the crest of the pathway, however, a cascade of stones suddenly blocked her way.

"These were never here before," Hetephras thought in wonder, curious not to have heard the stones tumble in the night. All the tomb-makers were keenly alert to the sounds of shifting rock. Landslides had been known to bury the village—along with many of the villagers—in distant eras.

Hetephras edged forward and gingerly felt her way across the unfamiliar heap of stones. She looked up toward the sky, fearing that the time for the ritual was long past. But she felt no light on her face; it was as dark as ever on this side of the mountain.

She thought again of Rami, how he should be helping her, and muttered aloud, "I wish my husband could see how this pathway has been neglected, and how children no longer heed their elders." She pulled herself forward across the heap of rubble. The irregular limestone rocks shifted beneath her feet. Hetephras steadied herself, then took a step forward. Another few cubits and she would attain the smooth, narrow path once again. She placed a sandaled toe tentatively upon a rock and took a tiny leap—

The unsteady rocks gave way. The alabaster chalice flew from her hand, smashing to pieces on the valley floor below, spilling its lode of oil and sweetmeats. Hetephras pitched forward, a scream caught in her mouth. The wig saved her from dashing her brains out on the sharp rocks as she rolled swiftly downward. The landslide that had caused her accident now served as a kind of steep, sloping causeway to the floor of the valley. Her shoulder twinged as she tumbled, and she tasted blood. A rib cracked, and the sharp rocks stabbed her thin shanks. She landed with a soft thud on the valley floor.

Hetephras lay gasping. Aside from her shoulder and rib, she felt no other injury. She laughed weakly, weeping too. "I am not dead!" she said in giddy relief. "I'm not dead!" She moaned as she sat up. She would be horribly bruised, crippled even, but indeed, she was still alive.

A rustling from behind silenced her. Dark shapes began to emerge from the earth itself. Dark, animal shapes—beasts with ears and snouts. She gasped. Hyenas and jackals, even the occasional lion, were known to prowl the Great Place at times. All around her the animals sprang up, and fear cleared the clouds from her eyes. She opened her mouth to scream—

Yet before she could utter a sound, the first true rays of the sun reached their length into the valley and she saw—*she saw!*—no pack of slavering beasts but the golden faces of the gods themselves! Anubis the jackal god, Thoth, Set . . . Horus the hawk! And everywhere, everywhere the flash of gold emanated from them as the sun's rays caught their unblinking eyes.

The old priestess was seized with a holy rapture, which drove away all her pain. Here, today, after so many years, she was graced at last to meet the gods of Egypt in their incorruptible flesh of gold!

"Ay-aa!" she cried out in reverence.

"It's Hetephras!" one of the gods said. He seemed to be in as much wonder as the old woman.

"Yes! Yes! I see you, August One! I know who you are!" Hetephras burbled. "My eyes see everything now!" But somewhere at the rim of her consciousness another thought nagged. Curious that the god—she believed it to be ibis-headed Thoth—curious that he reminded her of someone she knew, someone against whom she held a recent grudge . . .

"What will we do?" Thoth faced the other gods, his youthful voice querulous. For gods they seemed extremely perplexed. But Hetephras had not much time to wonder.

It was the god Horus who walked decisively to where Hetephras lay.

She raised her face to him with a smile so completely believing, her cloudy eyes turned so joyously upward, that for the briefest moment the god hesitated. And then he reached into his belt. He held something high. Hetephras could vaguely see the flash of cold blue metal in the sun's rays before it came down.

The axe bit deep into her neck, tearing across her throat and spilling blood down the front of her linen sheath. Her blue wig was knocked from her head, and it tumbled down the rest of the sloping valley like a weed in a windstorm. The bald old woman raised her hands in feeble supplication. The axe raised high again, and once more descended.

Hetephras, without further sound, entered the Gates of Darkness.

IT WAS THE LAST NIGHT of the Osiris Festival, and bonfires lit every street corner in Thebes. The avenues overflowed with riotous Egyptians. Foreigners were there, too, invited by Pharaoh from tributary nations to attend the Osiris festivities. They were easily distinguished from the Egyptians—their dress was barbarously colored, the men were bearded, and their women did not even shave their heads. The fastidious Egyptians averted their noses at the outsiders' oily reek. The foreigners were barefaced, too, not intelligent enough to know that during the Osiris Festival one went about sensibly masked. It was the only time of year when Osiris allowed his dead subjects to revel with the living. Practical Thebans wore masks lest a resentful spirit, the enemy of some ancient ancestor, had come to the festival to harm them. Unconcerned, the foreigners instead gazed at the wonders of Thebes, barefaced and unprotected.

They pointed, amazed by the size of the glittering temples and by the long blue and crimson pennants that undulated in the night breezes, flying from high poles whose spires were tipped with crystal and gold. They were stunned by the vastness of the temples' gates, sheathed in silver and bronze, encrusted with gems. They marveled at the height and girth of the temple pylons on which painted carvings depicted Pharaoh's greatest triumphs—triumphs over their own peoples.

Down at the harbor, crowds of families carried tiny reed boats to the Nile, each containing a wax candle shaped like an enthroned Osiris. In each miniature barque, according to ancient custom, the families had placed a limestone chip or piece of papyrus bearing a written prayer asking Osiris to grant their most cherished wish. At the Nile's edge, where the tall reeds grew, each family's eldest child lit his or her candle and launched their little ship. The current took the fleet of offerings north, to Abydos, where Osiris's body resided in a magnificent tomb. The entire breadth of the Nile was choked with thousands of the glittering miniature craft. Slowly the gentle Nile god gathered them up in his arms and bore them northward until their lights drifted out of sight at the bend in the river. At the river's edge families gazed at the little ships with avid eyes, for surely the good god would grant them their wishes.

One family, that of the stonemason Kaf-re, had at last reached the river after a tiring walk from the masons' quarter. Kaf-re's wife, Wia, held their baby girl in her arms, while their son, four years old, gripped a tiny reed barque in both hands. The children's eyes glowed from behind their palm-bark masks, entranced by the sights they had seen on the way here, and their bellies were full of the honeyed cake their father had bought them with a precious copper.

"Light the candle, sweetheart," Wia urged her son. She pointed to the charcoal brazier placed there for the purpose.

"No," the child said. Wia saw the stubborn line to his jaw harden beneath the palm bark. She knew that line; it was his father's.

Her voice became a little sharper. "Go ahead, silly, or the god won't grant our prayer!" The family had asked for a larger wheat ration from the temple guardians, for Wia was again pregnant.

"No."

"But there's nothing to it! Just hold the wick to an ember, and set the boat free by the reeds over there. The river will do the rest. Then we can go home. You'd like that, wouldn't you?"

"No."

"Light . . . the . . . candle," his father said between clenched teeth.

The little boy screwed up his face. "Don't want to! Not while *she's* there!" He pointed to something in the dark water. "Scary. Ugly." The child exploded in tears.

"A crocodile!" screamed Wia. Kaf-re lunged forward and caught his son in his arms so swiftly that the child's mask was knocked from his face. Now the boy wailed in earnest.

Wia's panicked screams attracted the attention of a guard at a nearby wharf. He ran to where the family stood, holding high a long spear as he made his way through the throng. At the water's edge, peering into the dark reeds, he aimed the spear carefully. Then he looked closer, slowly lowering his arm.

"Why do you just stand there?" Wia shrieked. "Kill it! Kill it!"

The guard did not answer immediately. "It's not a crocodile," he answered almost apologetically. "And it's already dead."

He called for a torch, and someone brought one from a nearby stanchion. The crowd gathered round and stared. The guard held the torch close to the water . . .

The linen-clad body of Hetephras bobbed before them, face down, caught in a thicket of reeds. She still wore her gilded pectoral, but her skin was a ghastly, puckered white. In the wavering torchlight, the second gash made by the axe at the back of her skull was clearly visible. Blood and matter oozed from the wound, and a small cloud of tiny minnows darted in and out, feasting. One of her arms was outstretched, seeming to point accusingly toward the city itself. A chorus of gasps and screams filled the quay.

Though no one knew it at the time, the Year of the Hyenas had begun.

FOLLOWER
OF SET

A FEW STEPS AWAY FROM WHERE HETEPHRAS'S body floated, a man stumbled from a waterfront tavern, oblivious to the screams from the nearby quay. Slim and long-limbed, he roughly shoved aside those trying to make their way to the river's edge to see why people were yelling. The hardness of his black eyes and the determined line of his mouth were enough warning to those in his way to step quickly aside. He seemed to tempt someone, anyone, to cross him.

"A follower of Set," they whispered to one another as he passed, meaning that he looked as if he loved the chaos and recklessness of that god whose kingdom was the fierce alien desert.

Hot-eyed women in the crowd shot him glances from beneath their lowered lids. He refused to notice them, despite the provocative messages they sent him. As he staggered past, the women turned to stare.

The man was not handsome. Neither was he plain. His narrow face was arresting, the more so because beauty was not a part of it. It was the intensity of his black eyes that overcame the women. They were a luminous jet in which lights moved and swirled, where intelligence warred equally with passion. The swarthiness of his skin, the height of his cheekbones, and the drawn set of his full lips met in tense collision; the man's emotions were as apparent as a bloody gash on his face.

Soon the dark-eyed man reached the boulevards of outer Thebes. Here no festive bonfires lit the streets, only the odd meager torch. He plunged fearlessly into the dark, however, heedless of the thieves who might be loitering in the shadows.

He strode past long stretches of whitewashed walls that encircled the estates of the nobles and gentry. Only when a group of private guards emerged from an alley, loud and boisterous, did he stop, withdrawing into a statue's niche. When they had passed he set out again, the hilt of his gleaming knife a comforting weight in his hand.

When he reached the Boulevard of the Goddess Selket, he slowed his pace. Peering around a corner, his face a study in stealth and craftiness, he paused to stare at a bronze gate across the square. Fresh torches on either side of it streamed droplets of fire onto glazed tiles. No doorman guarded it—the servant had probably deserted his post to slip away to the festival.

The man's movements suddenly became as balanced and predatory as a stalking leopard's. He moved quickly to the gate. Looking furtively to the left and right, checking for any hidden guard, he took hold of the handle and pulled.

It did not move.

The man shook his head in muddled confusion, as if this eventuality had not occurred to him. He pulled harder. The gate scraped loudly at its hinges but did not budge. It was locked.

A distant pounding came to him through the dark, and he realized that his own hands were beating desperately on the bronze plates. Over and over again they smote the doors, and there was wailing, too. He seemed almost surprised to realize it was his own voice that he heard.

"Naia!" he screamed into the night. "Naia!" His grief-stricken yells merged with the clamor of his own frenzied fists on the door. "Naia! Come out to me!"

When there was no response, he backed into the middle of the street, standing on the hitching stones near the well, howling even more forlornly, "Naaaiiiaaaa!"

He beat again on the gate and shrieked the name for what span of time he did not know. Finally he heard the noise of wooden shutters opening in the house. A line of distant torches on the balcony came toward him amid a scuffle of feet and muffled shouts. Torches now shone in the forecourts of the other houses on the small square.

He heard the voices working their way from the house to the street, and he smiled joyously. Naia was coming to him! He would hold her in his arms again, feel his lips on hers again, the press of her body—

Servants wielding cudgels and whips burst from the gate, led by their foreman. They fell on him instantly. His curved knife slashed out. The servants began to fan out and encircle him. One of the younger men lunged at him with a club, and the man slashed the servant's arm to the bone. Seeing their comrade's blood flow so enraged the others that they fell on the black-eyed man in earnest.

Though he fought back, slashing a nose or cracking a skull with the dagger's hilt, some part of him disengaged from the fight to observe the event from afar. Small details came to him as odd fragments of time amid the frenzy. He saw their hard, brown eyes like those of desert jackals circling him. He pondered their fists as they came nearer, and when they connected, there was an almost delicious taste of blood inside his cheek. A club caught him in the side of the head and he crumbled before the well. He fell to his knees, the dagger dropping from his hands. Seeing their advantage, the servants resorted to kicking him with their hard, hempen sandals.

He no longer felt their blows. He curled into a ball waiting for his death, smiling a little, calm overtaking him. He suddenly heard from far away the voice of a man yelling at the men to cease their punishments, to raise him to his feet and hold him.

The man who spoke was hastily throwing a linen wrap over himself. He was young, like the black-eyed man, but in his handsome face lurked the indefinable essence of nobility—or fortune.

"I've told you before, Semerket," the man said in a clipped, toneless voice, "that if you disturbed my wife again, I'd thrash you."

Semerket struggled in his captors' hands. "*My* wife, Nakht! Mine!"

"Hold him!" commanded Nakht. "Strip off his tunic."

The foreman moved to rip the cloth away from Semerket's shoulders.

Seizing a whip held by another servant, Nakht spoke into Semerket's face. "I'm going to beat you worse than I beat my horses—worse than even my servants. I'm going to show you that if you dare approach my wife again, the next time I won't hesitate to slit your peasant throat."

"Brave man, Nakht, when your men hold me."

"Turn him around."

A lash rang out. Even through his wine fumes, Semerket felt the whip strip away a ribbon of flesh from his back. Despite any resolution not to give the man satisfaction, he groaned aloud.

Another lash, and he felt the blood dripping down his back. Then another. He lost count after the sixth blow and fell to his knees. His ears rang from his pain. Dimly he heard a woman yelling at Nakht to stop. Stirring once more to life, he saw the swirl of white linen skirts before him, and smelled her familiar scent of citrus oil even before he saw her face.

"Stop it!" she screamed. "You'll kill him, Nakht! Please, my lord—please! Do not beat him further!"

"He has made our house a place of lamentation long enough. Go back inside."

"My lord, give me a chance with him. I will make him see reason." She saw Nakht hesitate and pressed the advantage. "I promise that if he comes again after tonight, I won't interfere. *Please.* Leave me with him."

Nakht angrily beckoned to his men to withdraw, but loudly told the foreman, who was wiping away blood from a gash on his forehead, that he was to stay and watch over his mistress from the gate. "Don't take your eyes off her!"

The servants retreated into the house. The foreman sent them to their rooms to have their wounds tended and stitches taken. He himself took up the post at the gate, as commanded, hiding in the shadows, ready if his lady needed him.

The woman sat cross-legged, leaning her back against the well. She turned the man over and he groaned as she cradled his head in her lap. She unfolded her linen headdress, crumpling it into a ball, and began to dab at the blood on his face. His eyes fluttered open and he smiled up at her.

"Your perfume . . . sweet."

Her voice was tired. "I'm not wearing it for you."

"Have your servants bring a torch, that I can see you again in the light."

She sighed. "Oh, Ketty, why do you shame me like this?"

He spoke simply, surprised by the question. "I want you back."

She pressed her lips together. "You must stop all this—shouting my name in the streets every night. It can't go on. Look what has happened to you. I could prevent my husband from killing you this time—"

"*I* am your husband! *Me!*" His shout was so fierce that the foreman thrust his head from the gate, his hand clutching a spear. Naia caught the movement in the dark and shook her head. The gate closed a bit.

"No, Ketty. You are not my husband. Not anymore."

"Always."

"We've said the words of divorce. You returned my dowry."

"I didn't know what I was doing! I was drunk!"

"When were you not drunk at the end?"

He looked up at her beseechingly. "I'll give up wine this night if that's what you want. From now on, only water. Not even beer. By the gods, I swear!"

Her eyes filled with tears as she rocked his head gently in her lap. "Oh, my baby, my baby," she crooned to him as to a child. "What am I going to do with you? You know why I left you. Our marriage was cursed."

"It was the blessing of my life."

She looked away and sighed raggedly. "I thought it mine, too. For a while."

Eagerly he pounced on the thought. "It could be again!"

"No. The gods have willed it."

"Gods," he muttered darkly, spitting out the word as if it were poison. He reached behind himself, felt for something, then suddenly clasped the dagger that he had dropped in the street. He held it to her throat, the curve of its blade against her neck's gentle arch. "If you won't come back to me, then he can't have you either. I'll kill you here, now!" There was an abrupt grating noise as the foreman came bursting through to the street, spear raised.

She did not move her head, but her voice was steady. "No!" she firmly commanded the foreman. "Go back! He won't do it." The foreman paused, spear still held high.

Semerket laughed. "How do you know I won't? Our blood will mingle together here in the street and the poets will sing of it for centuries."

She didn't speak for a moment, and her tears spilled upon his face. "Because . . . because, my love, you would kill another with me."

It was a moment before he registered what she had said. Then he winced as if she'd struck him with a blunt object. She nodded.

"Nakht's child is in me."

Very gently she removed the dagger from her throat, handing it to the foreman. "Take it away now," she told the man in a low voice. "Somewhere where he won't find it." Then, looking down at the man to whom she was once married, she took the hand that had held the blade and placed it on her belly.

The tiny movement beneath the linen pleats burned his hand hotter than any fire, cut deeper than any blade. The black eyes in his face became fathomless. Slowly he sat up, not even registering the pain of his beating.

Naia could not meet his gaze and looked down at her own hands instead, aimlessly clasping and unclasping her crumpled, bloodied headdress. "Do you finally understand why you can't come back, Ketty? There is no hope, ever, that I can be your wife again. In the surest way, the gods have decided."

He slowly extricated himself from her lap and stood up. Blood ran from his wounds, and his breathing was shallow. He said nothing. He turned away, put a hand to his forehead, and then shook his head to clear his senses. His lips formed silent words, but none emerged. With a desperate final look at her, he stumbled into a nearby alley. He began to run.

"Ketty—!" Naia yelled after him, standing and calling to the retreating figure. "Ketty . . ." He stopped, but only to vomit against a wall. Without looking back, he began to run again into the dark.

"Mistress—" The foreman hovered nearby. "Do you want me to follow him?"

She shook her head. "No. Tell the others he won't be coming back.

They can relax their guard." She pressed a fist into her mouth to stop the moan that threatened to escape her. She steadied her breathing, and followed the foreman into the house. With great care, he locked the gate behind her.

"HE WENT TO HER HOUSE AGAIN." The woman's harsh voice filled the small courtyard with indignation.

Sitting in his tiled bath, four rooms away, Nenry brought the razor to his skull and drew it across his scalp. The morning sun stabbed painfully into his eyes from the mirror held by his whimpering valet, reminding him he had drunk too much at the Osiris Festival.

Merytra, his wife, continued her tale from the courtyard. "Banging on the door, calling her name over and over again. Of course he was drunk." When her husband did not respond, her voice became even shriller. "Are you listening to me?"

"How could I be listening to anything else?" Nenry muttered.

"What?"

He called out cheerily, "I'm listening, my love."

His wife strode into the bathroom, bracelets jingling as merrily as donkey bells. Her expression was far from tinkling, however. Nenry noticed how his valet shrank from her. Merytra took this as her due and continued her harangue. "It's a disgrace. And if you're not careful, it'll cost you your position!"

She watched him scrape his head ineffectively with the razor. "Here," she said with impatient superiority, "let me do that."

"I can manage." In truth, Nenry did not want his wife anywhere near him with a razor.

"You'll only hack yourself to pieces and bleed all over your linen again—and I'm not going to wash and pleat your robes twice in one week. I said, give it to me." Her voice was firm, and the glint in her eye fixed.

Nenry wanly handed over the razor. Hastily he brought his hands down into the water to cup his soft genitals. She was done in five expert sweeps of the razor. Angry red welts rose burning to replace the stubble, but there was indeed no blood.

"Thank you, my love," he said, moving to the farthest recesses of the tiled enclosure, rubbing the stinging welts with one hand, the other still clasped firmly to his midsection.

"Well?" She crossed her arms.

With great determination, he forced his features into something resembling casual indifference. "Well . . . ?"

She looked with a sideways glance at his cringing valet and grabbed the cloth he held. "Leave us," she ordered. "Bring water from the city well. Two jugs." The man nodded dully and backed out of the bathroom, limping.

"And don't linger!" she called out. She dried her husband briskly with the piece of tattered cloth, as she would a child or a dog. "This is the last time I let you pick a servant. What were you thinking when you chose this one? Better to buy a trained baboon from the temples. At least then we might be able to keep something in the larder for ourselves."

"I don't understand why you're having trouble with him, my love. You're always so clever with servants." This was a lie. Two had run away, and another had hanged herself.

"He's slow, lazy, and gluttonous. What's more, he's a sneak. Last night he left his station and went off to the festival. When the fool finally returned he was so drunk he peed into my lotus pond. All my little fish were belly-up this morning. I had to throw scalding water on his feet just to wake him for his caning."

"So *that's* why he's limping . . ." Nenry moved past her and into his sleeping chamber. He dressed quickly, feeling less vulnerable when a sheath of linen was between himself and his wife.

Relentlessly she followed him into the room, still clutching the razor. "So what are you going to do about him?"

"Enroll him at the servant's school, I suppose. What else can I do?"

"Not the servant. Your brother."

"I thought you were speaking of—"

"I wasn't. Pay attention. Ever since his divorce he's behaved like a madman. Not that he was much of a prize to begin with—not that *anyone* in your family is." Nenry sighed, knowing that she was off on another favorite tangent.

He had married Merytra because she was the grandniece of Lord

Iroy, the high priest of Sekhmet. Glazed with ambition, Nenry had allowed himself to be adopted into Iroy's family and married to his unlovely ward. Though his home life was sour, advancements had come rapidly; only recently Nenry had been promoted to chief scribe to the Eastern Mayor of Thebes.

But the price was terrible. Their first and only child, a son, had been snatched by Lord Iroy to be raised in his own house and named his principal heir. Merytra, torn between loyalty to a powerful uncle and hatred because he had stolen her child, was left embittered and frustrated. Nenry became her natural target.

Nenry hurriedly fastened a sash around his waist and thrust his feet into his sandals. When his wife turned her back, he quietly tiptoed from their sleeping chamber.

Escaping to the mayor's home was the only way to avoid Merytra's tongue on such days. Lately he had been leaving earlier and earlier. In the courtyard he looked unseeing upon the ground, wanting to weep from the unhappiness of his life.

"Ah me," he sighed.

And now this trouble with his brother had compounded his woes. Semerket had always been a trial, his pitiless black eyes forever belittling Nenry's desires for advancement and position. Where the older Nenry followed every stricture and rule in Egyptian society, the younger Semerket had been wild in his ways, intemperate in his habits. Early in his youth people had taken to calling him a follower of Set. He was never easy with words, and the few things Semerket found to say were mostly unpleasant—but always truthful. Truth was, in fact, Semerket's chief mode of warfare against others.

Then, almost miraculously, Semerket had met and married Lady Naia. He was besotted by her, and under her influence Semerket had become almost pleasant in his society. The few words he spoke lost most of their rough sting. Naia had even prevailed on him to accept a post in the courts' administration, for like Nenry he knew how to write.

Semerket had become the clerk of Investigations and Secrets, a position in which he was used to ferret out the truth in confusing criminal cases. He was even praised by the judges for whom he toiled, though grudgingly, for he was not above hurling a few truthful observations in their direction when he thought the need warranted.

For a while it seemed that such pleasant times might endure. But Semerket's marriage was cursed; Naia failed to conceive. Physicians with their poultices and bitter brews; priests with their chants and prayers, incense and candles; even Nubian witches with their amulets and eerie rites of magic had failed to kindle Semerket's seed in his wife's womb.

More than anything Naia desired a child of her own body. In despair of ever becoming a mother, she had convinced Semerket that divorce was the only solution. Soon after, she married Lord Nakht, a nobleman who was responsible for the upkeep and provisioning of Pharaoh's royal harem in Thebes.

Semerket's reaction to his wife's desertion had been characteristically simple. He had fallen apart. Never at peace with words, he found his tongue at last through drink. For weeks he had howled his grief and rage into the night, pounding on his ex-wife's gate, pleading in vain with her to return to him. Many nights embarrassed Medjays awakened Nenry, whispering that his brother had been arrested again. Nenry paid the bribes to keep the policemen quiet, but Merytra was correct—such behavior could not go unnoticed much longer. In Egypt, when a family member committed a crime, all the family suffered the resulting loss of status—and status was the one craving shared by Nenry and his fearsome wife. Something indeed had to be done.

"Nenry!" He jumped when he heard Merytra's voice in his ear. He'd been so wrapped in his own misery he had failed to hear her jangling approach.

"I was inspecting the lotus pond, my love. Yes, I can see how all your little fish have died. Why don't I give you a few copper rings and you can buy some new ones . . . or anything you choose . . . ?" He searched desperately about in his sash.

"I want something done about your brother."

"But what can I do?"

"Use your influence, however small it might be. Get him a position somewhere."

"How can I? People know him. They'd think I was trying to foist him off on them."

"I don't care what they think. I won't have what little we've managed to seize for ourselves ruined by your brother's sordid behavior. . . . Are you listening to me?"

"It seems I do nothing but listen to you." In his misery he had spoken the words aloud, without thinking. He had gone too far. Nenry saw her arm drawing back, her right hand forming a fist, the expression of rage on her face. He closed his eyes, waiting for the blow.

A burst of rapid knocking at the gate made them both jump. He and his wife stared at one another.

"Who could it be?" he whispered.

"The police, who else?" she hissed back. "Here about your brother again!"

Nenry slowly pulled open the gate. A Medjay was indeed standing there, black skin gleaming in the morning sun, dressed in the uniform of the Temple of Justice. His insignia proclaimed him to be a bodyguard of the high vizier. Nenry felt his knees swimming beneath him. The high vizier! How could his brother's scandal have reached that high?

"Are you Nenry, scribe to Paser, the Eastern Mayor of Thebes?" The guard was terse, his manner cold and official.

"He is." Merytra pushed herself forward. "What do you want?"

The man, surprised by the woman's forcefulness, blinked. "An . . . an urgent summons for the Eastern Mayor. I was instructed to give it to his chief scribe."

Trembling, Nenry broke the seal on the wax tablets, eyes becoming wide as he read. "Oh, my," he said helplessly.

"What is it?" Merytra clutched his shoulder, looking from the tablet to peer anxiously into his eyes.

"A priestess has been found dead—possibly murdered. There's to be an investigation. I have to fetch the mayor to the Temple of Ma'at. The high vizier himself commands it."

"A priestess, dead! How horrible!" She paused, and in the interval he saw her face once again harden. "Just remember what I told you. You'll either deal with your brother or you'll deal with me." She strode back into the house, the merry jangle of her bracelets filling every corner.

Nenry glanced at the Medjay, and was comforted to see a shred of pity in the man's eye.

·   ·   ·

WITH HIS WIFE'S WORDS still ringing in his head, Nenry hurried to the poor section of town where Paser, the Eastern Mayor of Thebes, lived. Glancing around at the refuse and rot of the area, the teeming crowds of beggars, he could not fathom why his master chose to reside in such an awful place. Nenry had spent his whole life trying to flee such poverty.

To create the imposing abode of a mayor in so poor an area, Paser had simply purchased all the little houses there and knocked holes through the walls to link them together. Nenry hurried through the compound's many kitchens and storage rooms, past its harem, to finally pace anxiously outside the mayor's distant sleeping chamber.

Nenry glanced past the flapping curtain at its doorway and saw that Paser was already awake and dressed, adjusting his wig. Nenry's ears pricked when he heard other voices in the room. To his horror, he recognized one of the voices as belonging to Nakht, Naia's husband. Nenry's knees buckled, and he leaned against the mud brick wall to steady himself. He would be ruined, just as his wife had predicted.

The other person beside Nakht was someone unknown to him—a large, powerful man with a brutal profile, dusted in the grime of limestone chips and desert sand. Nenry momentarily pitied the man that he should appear before the mayor in such humble attire. Incredibly, as if to confirm Nenry's thoughts, it seemed as if the man were indeed weeping.

Before he could hear what the men said, two slave girls wearing only leather thongs emerged from the mayor's chamber. Seeing Nenry's face, which had furrowed itself into a mask of tortured remonstration, they smirked.

"Is he almost finished?" Nenry asked them. "Will he be out soon? What's he talking to Nakht about? And who's the other man?"

"I thought I heard him say he was going back to bed," the African girl said with a sideways look at the other girl.

"After last night, who could blame him?" the tall one chimed, with a pretty yawn. The two glanced lewdly at each other and burst into laughter.

"How now," Paser said as he pushed his rotund bulk from behind the curtain. "What's all this noise out here?" He casually glanced at his scribe. Beyond the curtains, Nenry noticed Nakht and the stranger departing through a rear door in Paser's chambers.

"It's Nenry, lord," the tall girl answered Paser. "That's why we laugh! When he scrunches his face like that, he's so funny!"

"And I'm not?" The mayor's booming voice filled the tiny room. "I was amusing enough last night, you fickle things!" He feinted at the girls and they fled, trailing behind them their piercing and highly satisfying shrieks. Paser smiled to see them run away, a reminiscent gleam of lust in his eye. Reluctantly, he turned to his scribe.

"What's all this with the vizier, then, Nenry?"

"You know of the meeting, lord?" His surprised manner quickly became honeyed. "But then of course you're so perceptive, so quick. What is there in Thebes you don't know?"

"Nakht told me of it."

"Has . . . has Lord Nakht spoken of anything else, lord?"

Paser didn't answer him. With long strides he left the room and went to his front stoop. "Come on then, Nenry," he called. "Don't dawdle. Mustn't keep the old dear waiting." The mayor did not waddle as most fat men did, but strode like a wrestler. The mayor and his scribe resembled nothing so much as an enormous hippopotamus with its flapping tickbird.

"Apparently a priestess has been murdered." Nenry was breathless, trying to keep up.

"Yes, poor nag. Nakht says it's all over town. Nasty business. But we don't know it's murder yet, Nenry. Mustn't jump to conclusions. More than likely it was an accident of some sort."

The mayor stepped into his waiting sedan chair. "Up!" he shouted. With many a moan and curse, his bearers lifted the chair to their shoulders and then exited through the front gate.

"The Temple of Ma'at," Nenry directed the lead bearer. Sweat already trickled down the man's face, and he merely nodded. There were more strenuous careers in Egypt than being a bearer for the porcine Eastern Mayor—pyramid builder, perhaps; obelisk hauler.

Two mayors were appointed to rule over Thebes-of-the-Hundred-Gates: one for the part of the city on the east bank of the Nile, the other for the section west of the river. Paser ruled the living, while his cohort, Pawero, ruled the dead in their tombs in the west. And though they shared the capital of the world between them, the mayors were so unlike in temperament and philosophy that there could not be found two more dissimilar men in all the rest of it.

Paser was fat, prosperous, quick to laugh, in character exactly like the people over whom he ruled. His true parents had been lowly fishmongers, but the young Paser was so pleasant and engaging that a childless scribe had adopted him into his family years before and sent him to the House of Life to become a scribe himself. There Paser had learned the 770 sacred writing symbols in the shortest time ever recorded in the temple's history—for the one thing that exceeded his girth, it was discovered, was his cleverness.

After graduation into the priesthood, Paser entered the city administration offices and had risen swiftly. At twenty-seven years of age, he now found himself appointed mayor of Eastern Thebes, reporting directly to the high vizier of Egypt. It was a satisfying position to have achieved at so young an age. Paser relished his office enormously and never so much as now, when the gates of his compound opened and the cries of the crowd greeted him.

Paser leaned from his chair to clasp their outstretched hands in his. "Nefer!" he called to an ancient crone. "Still the most beautiful woman in Egypt!" The woman blew him a kiss from withered lips. "Hori, you rascal!" He turned his attention to a legless beggar. "Watch your purses, citizens; he's quicker than a gazelle!" The beggar laughed in glee, taking no offense at his words.

Then, sniffing the air, Paser swore that the fish frying on a nearby griddle was the best to be had in all of Thebes—and who should know better than he, the child of fishmongers? This was the cue for Nenry to toss small rings of copper into the crowd. The mayor challenged them all to taste for themselves and see if he was a liar. The grateful fish vendor sent over a slab of greasy river perch, spiced with cumin, and the mayor gobbled it down, delivering hymns of praise and delight between gulps. By the time his chair was borne to the main avenue along the riverfront, the crowd was chanting hymns to him as though he were Pharaoh himself.

Nenry trotted alongside the sedan chair, all the while trying to answer the sharp questions that Paser put to him.

"Is the Old Horror coming as well, Nenry?"

The "Old Horror" was the epithet by which Paser designated his colleague Pawero, the Western Mayor.

"Yes, lord, the summons included the Old—the mayor of the West."

"What was its tone?"

"Pardon, lord?"

"Come on, come on, Nenry—what did it read like? Angry, threatening, cold, what?"

"No, my lord! It was full of the usual compliments."

"Nothing indicating displeasure?"

"Nothing, lord."

The mayor brooded. "I still don't like it. Why ask the Old Horror to attend? A crime, after all, that occurred in *my* side of the city. What does it have to do with *him*?"

Paser fell to uncharacteristic moodiness and he and his scribe traveled the last few furlongs to the Temple of Ma'at in silence. As luck would have it, Pawero's river barge pulled up to the stone wharf just as Paser and Nenry came to the broad stretch of ramp that led into the temple. Pawero sat motionless as a god's statue beneath the barge's wooden canopy as the boat bumped against the bales of straw cushioning the wharf. Once the tethers were secure he rose, majestic in his starched white robes.

Where Paser ruled the living part of Thebes, Pawero's jurisdiction extended over the tombs and mortuary temples across the Nile in the west. This included the Place of Truth where Pharaoh's tomb-makers lived, the Great Place where the Pharaohs rested, the Place of Beauty where their queens were buried, and the fortress temple of Djamet, the southern residence of Pharaoh.

Pawero was at forty-three a man given to pious readings and long-winded prayers. No wife or slave girl warmed his bed; Pawero was drawn to the lean, hard life of the most rigorous priesthood. He was a zealot, in fact, who secretly disapproved of the increasingly casual way Pharaoh performed his religious duties in his later years. Pawero longed for the day when a more god-fearing pharaoh might rule; perhaps— Amun willing—a pharaoh from his own family, whose lineage was far more ancient than Ramses'.

Such a miracle was a possibility, too, for Pawero's sister Tiya was the second of Ramses' great wives and had borne him four sons. One son in particular, his nephew Prince Pentwere, was commander of an elite cavalry unit and a great hero to the Thebans. He would make a splendid pharaoh. But to even imagine the death of a pharaoh was an act of treason, and Pawero sternly banished such thoughts from his mind.

As Pawero descended from his barge, head held high as the slaves and temple guardians bowed, he crossed in silence to the jetty. The effect would have been grand, indeed, had he not placed his sandaled foot in fresh horse dung left by a passing chariot. Stopping abruptly, gazing down, Pawero murmured a most unprayerful word.

Paser's laugh bellied out across the quay. "That should teach you to raise your sights too high, Pawero. You'll only land yourself in shit."

The Western Mayor's eyes went as flat and deadly as a cobra's. "I must heed my revered colleague," Pawero said as his valet rushed forward to clean his sandal. "For he comes from shit himself."

In the uneasy silence Paser laughed loudly again, as if appreciating a fine jest. Only Nenry recognized the cold, subtle anger that lurked in it. "I've never made any secret about my lack of pedigree, Lord Mayor," Paser said. "Everyone knows your glorious birthright, while I merely had my wits to get me by. But here we are, all the same, equals."

"Equals?" Pawero mused. "Yes. As we all are before the gods, even Pharaoh himself."

"Well, you must tell Pharaoh that, for I don't have the nerve." Paser bade his bearers to set his chair on the ground. After a few false starts he was able to wrench himself at last from the narrow seat and hurtle himself over to where Pawero stood. Their contrast was never more evident than at that moment. Lean and fat. Haughty and simple. Tall as a reed. Compact as a wrestler. Yet they were united in something greater than their differences: their pure and utter loathing for one another.

Paser held his arm for Pawero to lean on. Together, they ascended the long ramp that led into Ma'at's Temple of Justice, each clutching his identical staff of office. To all who saw them from afar, it seemed the mayors were the most cordial of friends. But Nenry privately was reminded of the stilted and wary courtship dances performed by certain desert spiders, where death, not mating, was often the result of such delicate footwork.

The high vizier received the two mayors in the usual temple ante-room reserved for such meetings. Outside, a long line of petitioners and litigants waited. With shouts and pleas they tried hard to catch the vizier's attention, for Toh was not often in Thebes these days, being instead at Pi-Remesse, the northern capital where Pharaoh resided. If the petitioners could not catch the high vizier's ear, or failed to bribe him sufficiently, it might be weeks or months before Toh was again in the south.

The vizier was a wrinkled old man of some seventy years, older than even his friend, the Pharaoh. He tottered slowly to his chair, waving his hand in the direction of the litigants, and exchanged compliments with the mayors. Wanly, he directed a slave to take them a bowl of fried dates and other dainty tidbits. Beer mixed with palm wine—a most heady brew—was next brought, and the old man treated himself to a hefty draft to fortify his liver. He then directed all the litigants to wait outside and wiped his toothless mouth with his hand, ready for the business at hand.

When the room was empty but for the mayors and their retinues, Toh spoke. Gone was the feeble, tremulous voice, the doddering manner. "By Horus's little brass balls," he shouted, "I want to know what's going on." He slammed the goblet down on the arm of his throne and peered at the two mayors. "A priestess murdered. There's not been such infamy in Thebes since the Hyksos left. I want answers and I want them speedily."

"I beg to remind you, Great Lord," Paser began with a broad smile, "that we've no way of knowing whether or not it even *was* a murder. And I beg to inquire why this incident should justify the presence of the *two* mayors of Thebes?"

Toh spat into a bowl at his feet. "Because the crime falls by a technicality into both your jurisdictions."

From his position at the rear of the anteroom, Nenry strained to hear.

Toh picked up a set of wax tablets. "We've learned from this report of Captain Mentmose of the Medjays that the dead woman has been identified as coming from your own village of the tomb-makers, Pawero—the Place of Truth." He handed the tablets over to a slave, who bore them to Paser. "But her body was found on Paser's side of the city. You can see the dilemma."

Paser made a tactical error then, scanning the report quickly. "Surely, Lord Toh, this is a regrettable but trifling matter. It says here that this Hetephras tended only small shrines in the desert hills."

"Are my priestesses any less valuable than yours?" Pawero fumed. He was going to continue in the same vein, but a roar of outrage from Vizier Toh stopped him.

"You think this a minor incident, Paser? I tell you, the people will rise in their anger and demand justice when they hear of it, for the murder of a priestess calls forth the awful rage of the gods. You're young. You've never seen the populace in its fury, or the city after a riot. I remember during the famine that cursed this region fifty years ago, the Thebans rose like a single animal and blamed us, their rulers, for the calamity. We had to flee to the hills for our lives. I'd not be too eager to dismiss this 'minor crime' so blithely if I were you. At such times it's difficult for mayors to cling to their offices." He paused, allowing his aged eyes to flash. "How do you think *I* was promoted?"

The old man spat into the bowl once more. "So what are you going to do about it, I ask you again, so that we can all sleep peacefully in our beds?"

Paser immediately spoke up, hoping to make good his error. "Since the body was found in the eastern part of the city, the crime—if it is one—is mine to solve."

Seeing the vizier begin to favor Paser caused Pawero to speak up. "The case belongs to me. The priestess was a member of my flock, after all."

"And so well tended she ends up slaughtered on your watch," Paser murmured loud enough to be heard by the entire room.

"We don't know that, yet," the vizier remonstrated. "The crime could very easily have occurred at the Osiris Festival, on *your* watch."

"But no tomb-maker is allowed on my side of the city," Paser reminded him.

"Do you quote the law to *me*, Lord Mayor?" Toh narrowed his eyes.

With his advantage ebbing, Paser grew reckless. "But clearly the gods have spoken in their clearest voice, Great Lord."

"How do you mean?" Toh was curious.

"I mean that if the gods had any faith in Lord Pawero's abilities, the body of this Hetephras would surely have been found on his side of the city. Obviously, the August Ones want *me* to handle the case."

"That's preposterous," Pawero gasped, "and heretical as well!"

"You accuse me of heresy?" It was the most serious charge in Egypt. "I can see where you're going with this—don't think I don't. You have some darker purpose and hope to obscure it with these charges against me."

"Darker purpose . . . !"

"That's why you want this case—to hide the truth."

The attendants and temple slaves gasped out loud at this accusation.

"Enough!" yelled the vizier. "This is unseemly, to make such charges as these. I know you have no love for one another, but if these accusations are true, what does that make me, who appointed you both?" Vizier Toh sucked his rubbery lips into his mouth. "We must have a solution to this problem and at once. Who is to discover the truth in this case? And how am I to know that what you will tell me is not some made-up tale to pacify me?"

At the back of the room, a wild thought seized Nenry, and he coughed slightly to be heard.

"Yes, what?" Vizier Toh's filmy eyes raked the room. "What do you wish to say? Who are you?"

"I am Nenry, Great Lord, chief scribe to Lord Paser. If the mayors will forgive me, I think I may have a solution to this dilemma."

"Well?" said the vizier.

"Someone with allegiance to neither mayor must be appointed to investigate this crime," stated Nenry, "to assure that Lady Ma'at's feather of truth is honored."

"Yes, yes. But in all Thebes is there such a person? Surely a man must belong to one mayor or the other."

"My brother, Semerket, is that person, Great Lord."

The name was caught up in whispers, like the rustle of quail wings, and repeated throughout the room.

"And what makes this Semerket so right to investigate this crime?"

"He was once the clerk of Investigations and Secrets in this very place, Great Lord. He knows the laws of Egypt and is very clever—and is devoted to the truth."

The Vizier was intrigued. "But surely because *you* are in Lord Paser's employ, wouldn't your brother favor him out of love for you?"

"Great Lord, my brother has no love for anyone. And since Lord

Paser's good friend is Lord Nakht, who married Semerket's ex-wife, I don't think he would be inclined to show favor to Lord Paser at all."

"Nakht—the keeper of Pharaoh's harem?"

"Yes, Great Lord."

"Better and better," Toh cackled gleefully. "But should he not then favor Pawero, to take revenge on Nakht?"

"Oh no, Great Lord. He'd never do that."

"And why not?"

Nenry gulped. "Because . . . because he has told me he considers Lord Pawero to be a . . ." His voice trailed away.

"Well?" Toh was becoming impatient.

"Well—he calls him a pea-brained old pettifogger, Great Lord."

Laughter erupted in the room. Seated on his stool, Pawero stiffened and color rose in his dark face.

"Silence!" Toh yelled roughly. "I will clear the room if there is another outburst." He turned again to Nenry. "He sounds a very sour man, this brother of yours."

"Oh, yes, Great Lord," Nenry nodded vehemently. "He has respect for one thing only—Lady Ma'at's feather of truth."

Pawero rose indignant from his seat. "I protest. To retain such a man—a follower of Set, as I have heard his own brother describe him—it flies in the face of the gods. No good can come of this."

But Toh ignored him and addressed Nenry. "Bring this man to me." With a gesture he indicated that the audience was concluded.

The high vizier rose from his throne. Stumbling a little from the effect of his beer and palm wine, he went outdoors to relieve himself against the wall. Pawero, glaring at Nenry and Paser, exhaled loudly in disgust and took himself back to his river barge. Nenry and Paser stayed behind in the anteroom. Paser still said nothing.

"I hope you did not think me too forward, lord, proposing my brother as I did . . ." began Nenry.

"I should have you beaten," the mayor stated matter-of-factly. "Don't ever do anything like that again, Nenry, without discussing it with me first."

"Yes, lord. It was wrong of me, lord. Never again, lord."

The Mayor of the East chuckled and clamped his huge arm around his trembling scribe. "Don't be too hasty, Nenry. You were wrong in not discussing it with me. But not wrong with the plan itself."

"Lord——?"

Paser chuckled. "Did you see how angry the Old Horror was? Hee-hee-hee! It was worth it just for that." But almost at once, a look of foreboding swept over him. "I still say it, though——there's a reason Pawero wants to control this investigation. I don't trust him. I never have. Your drunken brother is perhaps just what we need. And I intend to give him all the help I can."

The mayor turned swiftly and strode out of the anteroom. Only after he was gone did Nenry realize, however dimly, that Mayor Paser had referred to Semerket as his "drunken brother." How could the mayor know? Unless . . .

But before he could ruminate further, he was hailing a sedan chair to make his way into the center of the city to begin the search for Semerket. The gods alone knew what sordid places he would have to seek him in.

HE WAS IN THEIR sleeping room, just as he remembered it. Semerket laughed aloud to find himself at home, and he gazed around in delight. The walls were sensible mud brick, whitewashed, and a small window of thick transparent mica was set into a wall. He had purchased the mineral at great price from a passing caravan years ago so that Naia could gaze upon her courtyard planted in fig trees and papyrus. Sunshine poured into the room from the window, and Naia was bending down solicitously to tend him on his pallet. Semerket sighed luxuriously. He'd known, always, that Naia would return to him. They loved each other too much for it not to happen.

Then in the distant fields he saw the birds.

"Naia!" he cried happily, pointing from the roll of bedding. "Naia, look! The ibis chicks are in the furrows!" He knew how dear she found the little birds, probing the ruts with their long, black beaks. Semerket turned his gaze from the sun-besotted window. The corners of his mouth drew down. Someone else——not Naia——was bending down to peer at him.

When she saw his eyes open, she called his name. He heard her as though from very far away . . . and it was not Naia's voice that he heard.

Semerket blinked, trying to force himself back into the sun-drenched room with the mica window. He had only to close his eyes, and he and his wife were again in the little mud-brick house, and hares were nipping at the wheat.

No, not hares. What were they?

"Ibis chicks," he whispered aloud, and smiled.

The woman knelt on the floor where he lay and reached forward to feel his forehead. "Ibis chicks? Semerket, you're scaring me. Please don't say such things!"

He could barely register more than mild shock to see this strange woman again reaching down to stroke his cropped black hair. He shook off her hand. "You're not Naia," he said under his breath.

"Please get up, Semerket. Unless there's another copper in your sash for more drink, they'll make you go home. You should go home anyway."

What was she talking about? He *was* home.

The curtain to the room was drawn back with a sudden rush of dank air. A Syrian eunuch brought another man to his pallet. The stranger was thin and bald, his face a festival of tics and twitches, and he held a kerchief to his nose, repelled by the smell of stale wine and vomit. "Yes," the nervous man said, "yes. This is my brother." Semerket heard the clink of copper exchanging hands.

"Nenry?" He wanted to ask why his brother was here, in his home, but a rising tide of panic drove all curiosity from him. He sat up. Where was Naia? And the window of mica? What had happened to his little house with the sensible mud-brick walls?

From somewhere far away he heard thin screaming. Semerket shook his head, forcing his mind to shut out the terrible sounds. But the shrieks penetrating his head were now so loud he tried to keep them out by clamping his hands over his ears.

The bald man continued to stare at him in horror. "How long has he been like this?" he asked the woman.

"Since early this morning. He couldn't stop screaming, no matter what I did for him."

Tears slid down her face. She brushed them away with irritation. "He's so tortured, your brother," she said. "I've never seen anyone sadder. I'd do anything for him if he'd ask. But he doesn't see me at all. I'm just a tavern wench he sobs to about his wife sometimes."

Semerket's eyes fluttered open. The bald man was speaking to a physician, who was sitting next to him on the cot. The pretty woman was holding Semerket's head in her lap.

"Will you undertake his cure?" his brother asked the physician.

The physician nodded. "Get me some date wine," the man said to the tavern maid.

"More wine?" said Nenry. "Surely more will kill him!"

"He hasn't had much else for some time. To deprive him of it suddenly would shock his body." The physician quickly wrote a prayer on a strip of papyrus in red and black inks. The woman placed the bowl of wine before him. From his instrument box, the physician withdrew a stoppered bottle. When he opened it an acrid smell invaded the room.

"What is that?" Nenry asked suspiciously.

"Fermented pine resin," he said as he poured. "And this," he said, opening another bottle, "is opium from Hattush."

"Will it cost much?"

"You want him to live?"

Nenry nodded.

Five tinctures of the serum were dropped into the palm wine, then a quail's egg was broken into it and stirred. The physician dipped the prayer strip in the bowl and the ink of the spell's glyphs dissolved into the liquid. The physician jammed an ivory plug between Semerket's teeth, then spooned the wine down his throat.

The shrieks stopped almost immediately, and Semerket saw that the beautiful room with the mica window was serene once again. With the ivory in his mouth, Semerket could not speak. He would have filled the darkening room with questions, had he been able. He would have asked the physician if he knew why his beautiful Naia was not there and when she would return . . .

Suddenly, he knew the answers to his questions.

For the first time in many days he lay quietly, and his restless mind did not conjure visions of beautiful rooms and pleasant pastures, everywhere inhabited by the shade of his beautiful wife. And perhaps this was why, occasionally, tears oozed from beneath his bruised and flickering lids.

HE AWAKENED TO the slosh of water and the sound of a scrubbing. When he opened his eyes, sensible mud-brick walls rose before him, and he saw a pane of mica set into the wall.

For a moment he believed himself back in his dream, but the window glared red with late afternoon sun, bloodily picking out unpleasant bits of detail in the small room. He lifted his head and stared, wincing from the heavy, clanging weight of his skull. He lay on dirty, crumpled linen. Broken crockery littered the floor around him. Mouse droppings were everywhere, and above him the palm rafters of the roof glistened with spider webs.

A man with scaled and peeling feet was cleaning up the mess, listlessly scrubbing the floor with a pig-bristle brush. Semerket swallowed, tested his voice, and was able to croak to the man, "Who are you?"

The man whirled around. He dropped the brush into the basin of water with a plop, calling out, "Master! Master! He's awake!"

Nenry appeared at the doorway. "So he is," he said with sardonic disapproval. "Don't be afraid of him. He's only my younger brother, of no account."

Semerket regarded his elder sibling with wonder. "Nenry, what are you doing here?" Then memories of the last few days flooded his mind. The inside of his skull itched like fire, and his throat felt like sand. He turned a plaintive gaze on his brother. "Some wine? Beer?"

"Water is what you'll get." His brother poured some into a bowl and handed it to him.

The bowl went flying across the room. "Wine," he rasped out again.

With a covert look at the servant, Nenry brought out a couple of copper rings from his sash. "Go to the tavern at the corner, and bring us a jug of wine. If I find the seal broken, you'll be beaten with a stick."

The man scuttled from the room like a dung beetle. Semerket noted that he limped, that his injuries were fresh. Instantly an image of Nenry's terrifying wife took shape in Semerket's mind. "Your servant?" he asked.

"My valet," Nenry answered. "I had to bring in someone. This place of yours smelled worse than a nest of river ducks. You can't expect someone of my position to wash down a house by myself."

Semerket laid his head back down on the pillowed cradle. The mere mention of wine had done much to calm him. "What position?"

"Why, I'm the chief scribe to the Lord Mayor of the East! I sent you an announcement when the office was given to me. You didn't receive it?" Nenry's face revealed sad disappointment that his brother apparently knew nothing of his good fortune, for he believed in his heart that all men envied him. Nenry counted on it, in fact.

Semerket spoke with difficulty. "I thought you served at Sekhmet's temple."

"I'm happy to say that my diligence and skills were noted there." A fatuous smile settled on Nenry's lips. "Thanks to the gods, my wife and I are now among the first citizens of Thebes."

"Ah, yes. Now I remember. And you had only to sell a son to do it." Semerket inserted the phrase like a surgeon incises a wound, finished before the bleeding has begun.

Nenry winced. He rose to stand indignant and outraged above his brother. "How can you say that? My son is now a prince because of my selflessness. I gave him to my wife's uncle because of what could be done for him. I did it for the boy, do you hear?"

Semerket became calmly reassuring. "You mistake me, Nenry. You've done well. 'Chief scribe to the mayor'—that's worth two sons, at least."

Nenry looked at his brother, hands falling to his side. "Why do I keep helping you? You're never grateful. You always sneer at me. Why? What have I ever done to you?"

Semerket now directed so level a gaze at his brother that Nenry was forced to drop his eyes. "You sold your son to become a scribe. A *scribe,* Nenry! If you knew how much Naia and I yearned for a child . . . Yet you gave yours away as casually as a woman loans a kerchief."

Tics and twitches laid claim to Nenry's mouth. "I should have let you die today. Everyone would have been better off if I had."

"Yes." Semerket's voice was tired, dull. "Especially me."

• • •

THE SERVANT RETURNED with the wine, and Nenry broke its seal. He poured a bowl and handed it to Semerket, who drank it down in a single draft. Silently he held out the bowl for more. This time he drank it more slowly, and sighed. Strength visibly returned to him. He turned his black eyes on his brother and the serving man. "Join me," he said.

"You're very free with the wine I paid for." Nenry was still peevish, but he nevertheless poured the wine. The three men sipped in silence for a while.

Semerket raised his head from the bowl and looked about the small house. "I never expected to come back here," he said, almost in wonder.

"Why not?"

"Wasn't that obvious? I meant to die."

Nenry remained unmoved. "You mean you'd tired of pounding on Naia's gate at all hours, heaping shame on yourself and the family?" He expected his brother to fly into one of his dark rages, and waited apprehensively for the explosion.

But Semerket said simply, "No. I've done with that, now."

Nenry grunted sarcastically. "To what miracle does Egypt owe this change?"

Semerket inhaled slowly, and the words came out in a long sigh. "She's pregnant with Nakht's child. Did you know?"

Nenry turned a shocked face on his brother. His hostility was forgotten, and he became instantly contrite. "Oh, Ketty!" He drew nearer to his brother, his face inches from Semerket's. "How did you find out? Who told you?"

"She told me herself."

"When?"

"I don't remember. During the Osiris Festival, I think. She took my hand—I felt it stirring . . ."

"When is it due?"

"I don't know. Three months? Four?"

"Ketty, I'm so sorry. Truly I am."

Semerket turned his face to the wall. "Don't pity me. Not you."

"Receive it from one, then, who knows what it's like to lose a son."

It was as near a confession as Semerket had ever gotten from his brother. Semerket's eyes began to smart with tears, and he blinked them away, harshly wiping his face with the back of his hand. "Why did you come today of all days?" he groaned. "Why couldn't you just let me die?"

Nenry raised his head. "I came because I've found you work. We thought, my wife and I, that if you had something to occupy your time, you would forget all this."

Semerket sighed dismally. " 'All this.' "

Nenry pressed on, his voice becoming excited. "In fact, I'll wager that when you've heard what it is, you'll give up this terrible idea of drinking yourself into an early tomb. And the best part—you're the only man right for the job."

The valet brought them a second jar of wine. Whether it was this second jar, or the fact that Semerket had reached the lowest point in his life and had nothing more to lose, he listened to his brother's tale without complaint.

Nenry told Semerket of the murder of the priestess, of how the case by chance fell within the jurisdiction of the two mayors, and how the vizier himself had chosen Semerket above all others to lead the investigation—thanks to Nenry's intervention, of course. What was best, Nenry assured him, was that Vizier Toh had chosen Semerket because of his contrariness and allegiance to none. He was the only one who could do it because he despised everyone.

When Nenry stopped speaking, Semerket was so still that Nenry had to stifle the fearful impulse that his brother had died while he spoke. But he saw his brother blink at last, and Semerket's next words gave Nenry the answer he needed.

"And you say the priestess was found on the city side of the river . . . ?"

"No!" MERYTRA SHOUTED at her head man. "The whole effect is in the balance of the reeds with the lotus. Are you too stupid to see that?"

The head man stood up to his waist in the lotus pool, clutching a dripping bunch of papyrus. During the past few days the pool had been painstakingly cleaned of urine and refilled. Merytra had spent a great deal of copper in the bazaars, buying plants imported from the Nile Delta, and new fish. Inching forward with the reeds in his hand, the man hesitated and looked at her for confirmation.

"Yes—there! Exactly so. Plant it."

Two nights had passed since her husband had last been home. He had told her only that his mission had something to do with his drunken brother, Semerket. There had been no word from him since then. That suited her: she was indifferent to where her husband was, or when he would return.

Her maid, Keeya, stood with her in the courtyard. She was a plain girl (Merytra would tolerate no pretty ones) who sighed and yawned sleepily, holding the pot of expensive, gem-colored river fish far out in front of her. Because she hailed from a town that proscribed the eating of fish for religious reasons, she was in truth appalled by the gulping, gasping creatures.

Merytra noticed that despite the early hour the girl had managed to rouge her cheeks, outline her eyes with kohl, and attach long shimmering earrings of blue faience beads to her ears. Though Keeya knew herself to be plain, she did her best to brighten her appearance with careful attention to her make-up and jewels, cheap as they were.

But the glimmer of Keeya's beads in the dancing light was a constant, irritating distraction. Gritting her teeth, Merytra forced herself to ignore the blue flashes at the corner of her vision. The head man bent down to plant another bunch of green shoots. Unfortunately his backside caught the lip of the pool's stone edge, and he plunged forward. The resulting wave of water completely engulfed Keeya.

The girl dropped the jar on the stone floor of the courtyard, where it shattered. The fish slid across the tiles, writhing and flopping, quickly expiring right at the feet of Nenry's wife. It was the second time that week her fish had been massacred by her servants. "I am surrounded by imbeciles," Merytra said between clenched teeth.

Her observation was interrupted by a shrill scream from Keeya. "Look at my dress!" she shrieked. "It's ruined!"

"Your *dress*?" Merytra fumed. "What about my fish, you little slut? You've killed them all!"

"It wasn't my fault. You saw what he did."

"I swear you'll pay for them. I'll take their cost out of your wages."

"You can't blame me."

Merytra strode quickly over to the girl and slapped her hard across the face. The girl wailed even louder.

"I won't pay for them! I won't!" Keeya obstinately shouted between slaps, shaking her head adamantly, blue beads shimmering like beetles' wings in the sun.

She meant to pull only the girl's hair, truly, but when Merytra reached out, she felt something cold and metallic between her fingers. Then she heard the satisfying crunch of torn flesh.

Keeya abruptly stopped screaming, looking dully at her mistress's hand, now clutching the crumpled blue beads. Hesitantly she touched her earlobe and found her hand bathed in blood. Her dress was saturated in red as well.

The neighborhood was ripped apart by Keeya's shrieks. People stopped their labors to listen. Neighbors climbed to their flat roofs to stare down into the courtyard. They clucked their tongues to witness their neighbor Merytra torturing yet another servant.

It was then that the gate was pushed open by Nenry's dull-witted valet. Keeya fell abruptly silent and she and Merytra turned to stare. Nenry stood beside a large litter.

Nenry blinked, trying to take in the scene. Blood on the tiles, the serving girl weeping, fish flopping all about . . . What could have happened?

Merytra strode to the gate and bowed her arms low in exaggerated homage. "Blessed be the day that brings my lord back to his house!"

Nenry, leery of his wife's sarcastic tone, attempted to speak. "My love—" he began.

But he was interrupted by the invective now pouring from her lips. "So you're safe. What a fool I was to worry that you were dead or wounded by hoodlums! Why couldn't you send your man with a message for me?"

"I needed him to help me. My brother was, *is*, very ill—as you can see."

At this he turned and indicated the man in the litter. The woolen shawl that covered Semerket barely moved with his breathing.

"In a chair with four bearers, I see—better than any I've ever sat in. How much did it cost you?"

"Thirty copper—"

"*Thirty?* God of thieves and wayfarers, hear him! What—does the chair fly?" She hurled an accusing look at the hired bearers. The men instinctively stepped back into the alley.

"It was the only chair I could find, my love. I told you, he is ill. Very ill."

His wife snatched the coverlet from Semerket. "Hungover, you mean!"

There was a slight stirring from the chair. Semerket's bruised lids were fluttering. Slowly he opened his eyes and the lights of jet in them glittered to see the unfamiliar scene before him. He registered the overly decorated courtyard, his brother's cringing expression, the bleeding serving woman—and knew precisely where he was. With a slight moan he closed his eyes again, only half-listening to Merytra's continued diatribe.

". . . good money thrown away!"

"My love, please, he is our guest—he'll hear you."

"Guest?!"

"I thought it right to bring him here, to tend him more easily."

"Without asking me?"

"What was I to do? He's my brother."

"I am your *wife*."

"You said to do something about him!"

"Did I say to bring him here, then, to our home? No doubt he'll just get drunk again and shame us all. Yelling like a rabid baboon into the night for that whore of a wife he was married to, for everyone to hear."

Her torrent of reproach ended in an abrupt yelp. Semerket's hand had reached out from the litter to seize her wrist. She gasped at the pain, tears spouting from her eyes.

Semerket forced Merytra slowly down to her knees so that her face was directly across from his. His voice was low and implacable. "Do you feel this hand," Semerket asked, "its strength?"

"Let go of me," she whispered, eyes wide.

"Another word against Naia and I'll snap your neck like a reed."

She stared into his black eyes and knew him to be a man of Set, generating chaos and disarray—and violence—wherever he went. She could not rule him by her temper or her quicksilver moods as she could her frightened, malleable husband.

"Say what you want about me," Semerket continued in the same level tone. "But nothing about Naia, understand?"

She nodded.

He let go of her wrist so suddenly that she fell to the pavement in an ungraceful heap. She looked from her husband's face, embarrassed and silent, to her servants. Keeya had forgotten her torn ear and gaped at her mistress, sprawled on the courtyard tiles. The head man in the pool stared from behind the grassy reeds. Suddenly, from all the houses that surrounded them, a great cheering erupted. Serving women shrilly ululated and men hooted their approval.

Merytra rose to her feet. Refusing to meet anyone's eyes, she began to walk swiftly into the house. As she reached the doorway, she broke into a run. From the courtyard, they heard her muffled wails.

Nenry, after a moment, turned to his brother. "You really shouldn't have done that, Ketty. She isn't such a bad woman."

Semerket merely closed his eyes and lay back down in the chair, and so did not see the tiny smile that played briefly on Nenry's lips.

IT TOOK SEVERAL DAYS before the wine leached from Semerket's body sufficiently so he could stand without dizziness. During that time he slept on a pallet in a storeroom off his brother's courtyard. Merytra kept to her room, declaring that she wouldn't come out "until that madman is gone from my house." All in all it was a happy arrangement for everyone, and the servants whispered among themselves how they wished their lord's brother would visit more often.

But Nenry's wife was forced to break her vow when Lord Mayor Paser came calling, wanting to pay his respects to the new Clerk of Investigations and Secrets. It was in the morning and Paser arrived with his usual army of admiring citizenry. Nenry met him at the gate, bowing low before him, arms outstretched. Merytra remained in the background, tight-lipped with fury that Paser had not sent word that he was coming.

"No, no," Paser protested, "I only came to see your brother, and will be gone in a trice. But if there should happen to be a haunch of beef about . . . ? Some river fowl might be tasty as well. Fried dates if you're going to the trouble, for I am feeling peckish this morning. Nothing fancy, mind you—please don't go out of your way."

With that Paser strode into the reception hall, while Nenry's wife and servants flew about preparing the light meal for their honored guest. He seated himself on the biggest chair in the room, and Merytra bit her lip to see its thin ebony legs creak in protest beneath the mayor's bulk. Semerket, hastily clad in Nenry's best kilt and collar, soon joined the mayor.

"Well, well, so the man of the hour is here at last, the one whom we all await. Semerket, isn't it?"

Semerket bent at the waist, holding out his hands at knee level.

The rotund Paser smiled. "Nenry here has bragged of your talents to everyone. We're expecting great things from you in this sad business."

Semerket peered at his brother, a doubtful look on his face.

Paser caught the look and laughed. "It's true. You wouldn't be here today but for your brother's having had the courage to speak for you. And let me tell you, when the Old Horror's anywhere about, even I have difficulty speaking up!" He gave a fond look toward his scribe, who stood diffidently at the rear of the room.

"The Old Horror?" Semerket asked.

"Just my private name for my colleague on the west bank. Pawero."

"Oh, yes."

"I'm told you apparently share my opinion of him. What was it Nenry said you called him? A 'pea-brained old pettifogger,' wasn't it? Wonderful!"

Semerket was appalled. "My brother shouldn't have said it."

"And why not? It's only what everyone thinks. In fact, your words were what convinced me the vizier was correct to give you the case." He lowered his voice conspiratorially, leaning in close to Semerket. "Between you and me, I suspect that Pawero knows more about this business than he lets on. Ah, here's the food!" Keeya, her ear bandaged, brought in a platter of meat and bread, while Nenry's valet poured wine into silver bowls. Though Paser's face was always smiling, his eyes never left Semerket. "Please," he said, offering a bowl of wine to him, "have some. I insist."

In the shadows Nenry's face twisted into a mask of alarm.

Semerket disregarded his brother's expression and accepted a bowl of fragrant Mareotic white from the mayor's hands. Nenry was offered none; he could only watch helplessly as Semerket drank, thinking it might undo all his brother's healing.

"Why does the Lord Mayor suspect his colleague?" Semerket asked.

Paser brought a beef rib to his mouth and thoughtfully gnawed on it before answering. Seeing that Semerket's bowl was now empty, he poured again. "It's just my old distrust of the nobility. They're not like us, Semerket, you and me. We've had to play by the rules all our lives while they've had a free ride."

At the back of the room, Nenry coughed. The mayor was mistaken to think that Semerket had ever played by any rules other than his own. Still, Nenry did not rush to correct him and neither, he noticed, did his brother.

"These southern families are the worst," Paser went on. "They're just arrogance and privilege! Can you pass the duck? Excellent. And I'll tell you something else—now that the empire's almost gone, these families have had to endure shortages for the first time in generations. All the wealth's in the north now, not here in Thebes. And they don't like it. I suspect them, Semerket—Pawero most of all."

"Of what?" Semerket accepted a third bowl of wine from Paser.

"Of everything . . . of nothing. It's just an instinct I have, that's all. Nothing more but nothing less, either. And I'm absolutely convinced that Pawero is hiding something sinister. Now"—here Paser's gleaming face became sly and importuning, as he sucked the marrow from the rib bone—"if you were to find anything, anything at all that might justify my suspicions, I could be in a position to . . . well, we don't have to say it, do we?" He let the promise dangle in the air, unspoken.

Semerket's face remained a mask. "I understand," he said, ensuring that his words slurred a little.

Paser, absently wiping his fingers on the ebony chair's cushion, untied a leather bag from his belt and tossed it to Semerket. The bag was full of silver. "I knew you were a perceptive man," said Paser.

With that the Eastern Mayor rose, bringing the interview to a close with a loud belch. "Count on me, Semerket," he said. "I am your friend in all things."

"I will remember, Lord Mayor."

Semerket did not accompany his brother and sister-in-law to the gate to bid farewell to Paser. Instead Nenry found him a few minutes later at the privy, vomiting out the wine he had imbibed.

THE NEXT DAY Nenry made arrangements to present his brother to the vizier. But shortly before dawn a sandstorm began to blow across the desert and into Thebes. Sand drove itself into the wrinkles of old people and dried on the cheeks of crying children. It swirled in eddies and surged into the huts of the poor, into temples and palaces, and ran in streaming rivulets from unsealed cracks in mud-brick walls.

Shrouded in fine-mesh tunics kept for such days, Semerket and Nenry linked arms and made their way through the deserted avenues to the Temple of Ma'at. They did not speak, the better to keep the grit from their mouths. Though it was mid-morning, it was almost as dark as night in the southern capital. When they reached the temple, they were admitted at once into the vizier's presence.

"I've asked around about you," Vizier Toh said to Semerket, gazing at him from his small, raised throne. "You are well remembered here."

Semerket inclined his head.

"But not with fondness."

Semerket, arms crossed at his chest, merely continued to stare at the vizier from his own low backless chair, placed below the old man's dais.

It was Nenry who spoke instead. "Great Lord," he said, his face wreathed in tics, "I informed you that my brother was a plainspoken man, not given to flattery or sweet words."

"Plainspoken?" the vizier interrupted. "They told me he was rude. Insubordinate to his superiors. Bad-mannered and bad-tempered. Some even call him vulgar."

Nenry tried another tack. "My brother has one virtue, however, Great Lord—he speaks the truth."

Toh leaned back in his throne, sighing. "That, too, I have heard." He groaned—all his joints ached when a sandstorm raged. He peered irritably from beneath his wig in the general direction of Semerket. "I have heard your brother tells the truth like a woodcutter wields an axe."

Toh called for beer sweetened with honey. His scribe, sitting on the floor next to him, put down his pens and poured from a jar beside him.

"So," the vizier said, "let me have a sample of this truth-telling of yours. Tell me something that none dare say to my face."

Nenry was instantly alarmed. "Great Lord!" he began, sputtering. He feared the outcome of such a request.

In the dim light, Toh held up his hand to quiet him. "Go on." He continued to level his piercing gaze on Semerket. "Amaze me."

Semerket seemed to be considering what words he would use. "The Great Lord's bones are a misery to him today."

"Aye," Toh agreed with a suspicious sigh, "my bones are indeed an agony to me. I am old, old."

Semerket's voice was clear. "Why do you not retire, then, and leave the rule of Egypt to a younger, more vigorous man?"

The expression on the vizier's face at that moment caused Nenry to fling himself from his chair to the floor, trembling.

"What?" Toh rumbled in a low, dangerous growl.

Semerket continued, "You've made the mistake of believing what every long-lived despot does—that what is good for you is good for the country."

Toh's lips quivered. "Insolence. I should have you beaten!"

Semerket shrugged. "How can you know the truth about a priestess's murder, then, when you want only to silence it with beatings?"

"By the gods—!" Toh began to rage, then stopped. The mention of the priestess had quieted him. He sat back on his throne, breathing hard, and his fingers drummed the filigree of its inlay. "They spoke correctly about you. Your manners should have gotten you killed long ago."

Quietly, Semerket said, "I will never lie to you, Great Lord, no matter how unpleasant the truth. Nor will I again make sport in truth's name."

So the man had been joking, Toh thought. This realization soothed his wounded pride—somewhat. "How long will it take you to solve this crime, then?" he asked.

"There is no guarantee that I *can* solve it, Great Lord. I don't know how long it will take. Weeks, months perhaps."

"I suppose you will soak me in expenses."

"My keep; the usual bribes . . ."

"You will take this badge proclaiming you to be my envoy." Toh gave him a necklace of jasper beads from which hung the vizier's insignia. "You may draw from my treasury all that you need. Travel will be unrestricted. All access will be granted. Spare nothing and no one in finding the truth. I expect reports, but only when you've something to tell me." The vizier snapped his fingers and his scribe handed him a leather sack. He threw it to Semerket. "This should get you started."

Inside were rings of gold and silver, and bits of snipped copper. Semerket felt the bag's weight. "It's enough."

"If you need anything else while I am in the north, you will see Kenamun here. He is my eyes in the south." At this he indicated the scribe who sat cross-legged on the floor next to the throne. The man rose politely and bowed to both Semerket and Nenry. He had an intelligent, kindly face.

A sudden scent of musky perfume made them cease their conversation, and Toh sniffed irritably in its direction. At the doorway to his chambers stood five ladies, each covered from head to toe in gauzy vestments, protection against the storm. The lady at their center was the only one of them to pull away her net covering.

The woman who emerged into the dim light was older in years, but her dark-skinned beauty was very pronounced. She was dressed simply, almost to the point of severity. Only the asp in her wig caused Semerket to instantly stretch his hands out at knee level; none but members of the royal family were allowed the insignia of the sacred cobra. Nenry also dropped face down on the floor.

The vizier had a sour look on his face. He moved stiffly to genuflect. "My lady," he said.

"Forgive me for disturbing you, Vizier Toh."

Her voice, thought Semerket, was one of the most beautiful sounds he had ever heard, light but resonant with warmth and maternal concern.

"Queen Tiya's presence is like the sun after a storm," said the vizier stiffly.

Strange that the vizier's words of homage sounded so cold on his tongue. Semerket glanced surreptitiously at the renowned but rarely viewed queen.

"Please sit down, old gentleman," she said, crossing to Toh and assisting him back to his small throne. "I will be only a moment. It's Semerket I've come to see."

Nenry hiccoughed in shock. How had Semerket come to the notice of so high a personage as Queen Tiya? From his vantage point he could see only her gilded sandals as she moved to his brother and touched his shoulder.

"Please," she said in that magical voice, "I dislike ceremony. Come sit beside me, that we may talk together as people do."

Semerket moved to do as the queen said. He hesitated before sitting, and she smiled and patted the seat of the bench beside her. He sat, though only on the edge, his back rigid.

The queen held out a hand and one of the shrouded figures came forward to place a metal object in her palm. The queen turned to Semerket, seized his own hand, and placed the object into it, closing his fingers around it.

"I came here today to give you this. It will protect you, and also assist you in this terrible . . . this awful crime that has claimed the life of that lovely old lady."

Incredibly, Queen Tiya began to weep. Semerket's tongue immediately fused to the roof of his mouth, and he could only stare at her. She still clutched his hand in hers.

"I looked on Hetephras almost as a mother," she said after she had taken a moment to gather herself. "We met as sister priestesses, but became far more than friends over the years. When I think . . ." her lip trembled again, but she firmly composed herself. "When Paser told me you had been chosen to solve the mystery of her death, I knew I must do everything I could to assist you."

"Thank you, lady," said Semerket, prying his tongue loose.

She laid her wet cheek upon his hand, and kissed it. "I know I am only a weak woman, but you must believe me when I tell you that this amulet is very powerful. I have also sent such charms to the Medjays guarding the Great Place as well. You must keep it with you always."

Semerket nodded.

"May the gods bless and keep you, Semerket. Know that if you need anything, you are to come to me at once."

He nodded again.

She rose from the chair then, saying that she must not be late for her choir practice at Sekhmet's Temple. Once again she draped the shroud around herself. The men all bowed low again as she and her ladies silently withdrew.

"Hmmmph. Females and their magic!" said Toh after the women had gone. He gestured wanly, wearied by the sudden appearance of the queen. "I am tired," he said, "and the sand is chafing my eyelids. You may leave me now as well." The vizier's voice took on a bemused tone and he regarded Semerket with something akin to mischief. "I really must bring you to see Ramses. It would do him good, hearing the truth from you."

Outside the justice building, where the spiraling sands were intensifying to a furious crescendo, Nenry and Semerket took shelter behind an alabaster sphinx of the great god Ramses II, a distant ancestor of the present pharaoh. He yelled to Semerket through his shawl, "You play a dangerous game, brother—tweaking Toh like that about his age!"

"I play no games," Semerket shouted back. "I only use the least time necessary to achieve an end." Semerket suddenly grasped his brother's arm in the howling winds, and Nenry felt its strength. Even in the swirling sands, Nenry saw his brother's black eyes glittering. "Can I count on you, Nenry?"

Nenry looked at him unwillingly but at last said, "I know I am a coward and a fool, of no use to anyone—for my wife tells me this—but you are my brother. Yes, you can count on me. For what it's worth."

Semerket nodded. "I'll send word when I can," he said. Then in the churning sands, Nenry thought he saw a flash of his brother's teeth. "Tell your wife she can come out of her room now."

Nenry was suddenly alone. He saw only his brother's shrouded form disappearing into the waiting vortex of sand.

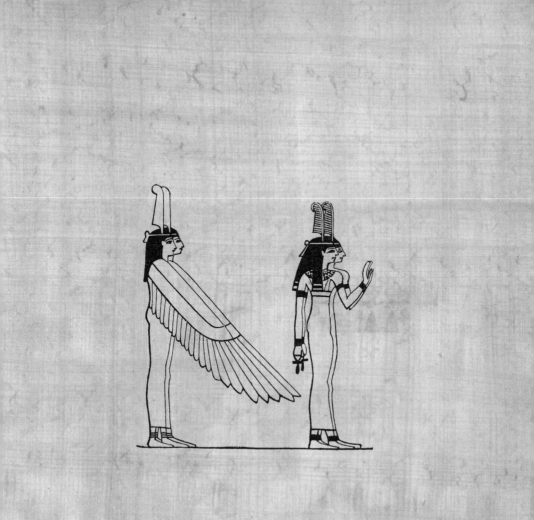

THE SERVANTS OF
THE PLACE OF
TRUTH

"WHAT DO YOU WANT?" THE BOY HAD OPENED the large wooden door with a sullen grunt. He used a finger to dislodge a seed caught between his molars, then casually wiped his hand on his filthy loincloth. He stared at Semerket, or rather at the jar of strong beer he held.

It was midday. The air was heavy with fine sand left over from the storms, and summer-like heat baked the landscape, trapped by the lingering haze. Semerket had deliberately chosen noontime to visit the House of Purification, knowing the priests and their servants would be taking their rest. But he also knew that this was the time when the smell in the house would be at its sharpest.

"Does Metufer the Ripper Up still live?" he asked.

"He's old, and his hands shake, but, yes, he's still the Ripper Up."

Semerket held the beer up to the boy. "Take me to him."

Eagerly the boy seized the jar. He tore off the soft clay seal and smelled the brew. "Ah! Fresh, too. Not like the piss they normally bring us." A suspicious look shadowed his face. "But you bring no one to be purified. What is it you want with Metufer anyway?"

"I'm his friend. Semerket is my name."

The boy snorted. "A friend who doesn't know if he's alive or dead. Maybe you bring him trouble."

"If you don't want the beer . . ." Semerket shrugged and reached out to take the jar. The boy quickly stepped back, just out of Semerket's reach.

"I'll take you to him. I'll take you," he said in a wheedling tone. "We don't get many visitors, is all. I'd be beaten if I brought someone Metufer didn't want to see."

The boy opened the door a fraction wider. Semerket took a last breath of fresh air and crossed the threshold into the dim interior of the House of Purification. The boy closed the door.

Slowly Semerket's eyes adjusted to the gloom. He was in the entry hall where Osiris's shrouded limestone form loomed, blackened with generations of oily incense. The god was still garlanded from the festival, though the flowers were limp. An equally filthy Anubis stood to Osiris's right. Windows set near the roof admitted the hall's only light. Beneath his sandals Semerket felt the soft crunch of natron, the fine granular soda quarried in the desert.

"Wait here," the boy said. "I'll fetch the Ripper Up." Semerket realized he had not taken a breath since he entered the house. Steeling himself, he exhaled. Even before his nose drew in its next breath, he could smell the cloying spices. Heavy resinous myrrh clashed with the effluvia of sweet floral attars. Juniper resin, salts, and above all the salty smell of natron conspired to make his gorge rise. But it was the intense underlying odor of rotting meat that made him gag—a pervasive stink the perfumes failed to mask.

Semerket fumbled in his sash for the bag of cedar chips he'd brought and inhaled deeply of the aromatic wood. Though he could still smell the rot, it was fainter now.

With knowing steps he made his way through the entry hall, cedar bag held resolutely to his nose, finding his way through the gloom to the rear of the compound. A wooden shutter was propped slightly ajar, noon sun streaking through its slats. He pushed it farther open and stared, blinking, into the gauzy light of the yard.

The sheds were to the left of the yard, as he remembered them, placed tightly next to one another, each monotonously alike. Built to the fringes of the desert, with layers of tight shelving, every level was covered in mounds of yellow natron.

At the far end of the yard, Semerket saw furtive movements at the desert's red edge—pariah dogs nervously worrying the rim of the estate. The dogs eyed the sheds avidly, ears pricked in their direction. The boldest of them, his scrawny beige flanks a moving carpet of ticks and fleas, crept toward the farthest shed. The sentry boys had withdrawn to sleep through the hottest part of the day. Only one youngster was on guard at that hour, and he ran forward to fling stones and yell at the curs.

The lead male dog stood his ground, head down and snarling. When struck by a piece of broken pottery, the dog ran at the boy, barking ferociously. The young sentry instantly turned and fled, screaming for the other boys to help him.

Seeing the sheds temporarily unguarded, the dog immediately seized his chance and ran to the nearest one. He pawed furiously at a mound of natron, the dust flying up in yellow clouds between its legs. In seconds, his quarry was exposed—a thin, shriveled, human arm.

Seizing it by the wrist, the dog yanked. The rest of the body soon emerged from the yellow dust, a woman in the last stages of her purification. Her hair was bleached yellow by the natron, her body a thing of leather, taut, dry, and stringy.

With a sharp crack the dog snapped the arm off at the elbow. Two ragged bones and a hand with blackened nails were his reward. The pariah dog ran as fast as he could back into the desert, growling fiercely at the other hounds who now hurled themselves at him, tearing at the arm for a morsel of the desiccated flesh.

Semerket saw other sentry boys emerge from the house to bury the woman once again under the heaps of natron. The woman's relations, if she had any, would never know she lacked an arm, for the embalmers in the House of Purification would supply her with one of clay, or perhaps a palm frond whittled to the correct shape. Under her tight wrappings no one would be able to detect the forgery.

Semerket returned to the reception hall to wait for Metufer on a rickety bench. The heat, together with the nauseating smells, combined to form a kind of narcotic vapor. As he waited for the Ripper Up to appear, his eyelids began to close against his will. Soon he was oblivious to the omnipresent droning buzz of black flies that swam lazily around him.

A distant laugh that erupted into a wracking cough exploded in Semerket's head. "By Anubis's shiny red pizzle, it's Semerket! After all these years!" The dry hacking filled the gloomy hallway. Semerket awoke, almost choking as he swallowed his wandering ka once again into his body. His eyes opened calmly, and he beheld his old friend and former mentor, Metufer.

"But here you are," the old man coughed out, "snoring away in my house, when I expected you to be up and amazed that I am still alive!" Metufer was grotesquely obese. Though it had been ten years since they had last seen one another, Semerket was surprised to find the Ripper Up so little changed. His hands did indeed shake a bit and his voice seemed a trifle querulous, but Semerket marveled that not one line or wrinkle creased his face.

"Metufer." Semerket clasped his arms as far as they could reach around his friend. "You look fit."

The old priest threw back his head and laughed, which again induced a fit of savage coughing. "Never . . . better . . . in my . . . life," the old man managed to gasp between breaths.

As long as Semerket had known him, Metufer always had the cough; he claimed that natron irritated his lungs. But if the cough had robbed him of clear speech, it had somehow enhanced his powers of intellect. Metufer in fact was regarded as something of an oracle in the House of Purification, both for his intelligence as well as his skill with the basalt dagger. It had been the reason he was appointed the Ripper Up.

Something of the oracular seized Metufer at that moment. As he regarded Semerket, he ceased laughing. "Something troubles you," he remarked, his mouth drawn down. "But if I remember correctly, that's nothing new. You were always a surly youth."

"Trouble does bring me here, Metufer," Semerket answered. "A priestess is dead. If it is murder, I am to find her killer."

"So once again you are the clerk . . . of . . ." The old man clutched his wide stomach and bent double to retrieve his breath.

"Investigations and Secrets," Semerket finished for him. "Vizier Toh appointed me." He lifted his mantle and revealed the badge inscribed with the vizier's insignia. It hung about his neck on the long chain of jasper beads. "I must first determine if the priestess's death was accidental," he said. "Her body was found in the Nile. She might have drowned. A crocodile might have made the wounds, or perhaps they were made after her death; I don't know. I only know that you, Metufer, are able to hear the dead speak long after their lips have ceased to move."

"Your timing is fortuitous," Metufer said. "Hetephras's body has been here in the natron baths, as the tradition prescribes. I was just about to open her up when you came along. Come and help me, then, as you did in the old days."

The room to which he followed Metufer was the largest in the compound. Like all the others, it nestled in gloomy, torch-lit twilight. A large pool, filled with Nile water stained yellow with natron, took up most of the southern corner of the chamber. Here Semerket could pocket his bag of cedar chips once again, for the smell of rotting meat had been replaced by the harsh medicinal smells of juniper resin and bay.

Beyond the pool, in neat rows, were large stone tables upon which lay bodies in various stages of purification. Boys, wakened from their noon naps, began again to sweep the floor, sluicing it down with jugs of water. This was a necessary chore, for drains on the altar tables carried a constant stream of fluids from the dead. Other youngsters carried baskets of natron that they scattered about on the floor, which helped to absorb the runoff from the tables.

Metufer went to a table that was free and from there directed a man to fetch the body of Hetephras from the pool. Seizing a pole with a large bronze hook at its end, the man began to poke through the cloudy water. One by one he dredged bodies to the surface, hooking them beneath the chin, bringing them into the dim light to be identified. Semerket watched closely, peering with his black eyes.

"There!" Semerket said when an old woman's body bobbed to the surface. Instinctively he knew Hetephras. He had imagined her in his mind since he'd received the case, and felt a pang on seeing the old lady. Though he had once labored in the House of Purification, and knew what to expect, he had nevertheless imagined her a living thing—not this poor rubbery piece of flesh being hoisted to the table.

Then he saw the gash across her throat. It gaped open, as clean a wound as priests make on the victims of temple sacrifices. No crocodile could make so clean a gash. Still, there was the possibility that Hetephras had been mutilated after her death. That question, too, must be asked and answered, though Semerket was dismally sure that no such thing had occurred.

Metufer and three of his assistants had disappeared into an anteroom. They returned, each wearing a leather mask of Anubis, the jackal-headed god. Metufer held a gleaming knife of basalt, its finely polished edges catching what little light there was in the room. Muttering a last prayer for forgiveness, Metufer abruptly thrust the knife into Hetephras's side and slashed toward her midsection.

As quickly as a fowler filets a duckling in the marketplace, the Ripper Up opened a long, bloodless incision. Semerket winced, surprised to find that after all these years his toughness had gone. As Metufer eased his knife down Hetephras's side, Semerket felt his stomach twitch rebelliously. Silently he bade it behave, as if it were an unruly dog, but a light sweat nevertheless broke on his forehead.

When Metufer at last withdrew the knife, the other Anubis priests began wailing, raising their hands in feigned outrage and grief. Using phrases of archaic Egyptian that had been spoken for a thousand years at the moment of this ritual "re-murder," they chased the lumbering Metufer from the room with shouts and curses. As he left the room, Metufer surreptitiously directed one of the boys to bring Semerket a box.

Semerket saw that the box contained a linen sheath. He took the garment out, unfurling it. From the bloodstains cascading from its collar down the front and back, he recognized it as the dress the priestess had been found in. Despite the time she had floated dead in the Nile, all its water could not wash away the blood. Farther down in the box was a wire pectoral, studded with amulets and some glass jewels. She had not been killed for her riches, Semerket thought grimly. He folded the sad relics and placed them in the box. Metufer returned to his side.

"Was that all there was on her? No wig? No sandals?" Semerket asked.

"Nothing more."

Semerket considered. More than likely the wig and sandals rested at the bottom of the Nile—a lamentable possibility. But if they were elsewhere, and if he could find them, they might indicate where the lady had met her end.

Metufer stood again at the altar table, beckoning for Semerket to join him. "What is it you want to know, Semerket?" he asked. Remarkably, his cough had vanished.

Semerket approached the table. "Did she drown?" He knew the answer, but the question still had to be asked.

"Let us see what this dead woman wants to tell us," Metufer said. He thrust his large hand into the incision. Semerket saw the flesh of Hetephras's body roll and heave with the hand's searching movements. With practiced touch, Metufer found what he was looking for and pulled. His hand emerged into the light, trailing a lung that was brownish and distended.

"She was not drowned," Metufer whispered. "If she had been, I could have wrung water from her lung as from a sponge. Look what comes now when I squeeze." His hand clutched the flesh. Blackened blood poured from between his clenched fingers. "She was on dry land when she was killed, and blood filled her lungs from the wound to her neck and windpipe. This is what makes the tissue so brown."

"Then she did drown—in her own blood," Semerket said.

"No." Metufer shook his head. "There's not enough of it here. She was dead before she could inhale more." He handed the organ to his assistant, who packed it in a jar of natron. Later, when thoroughly drained of moisture, it would be sealed in hot juniper resin and bandaged for burial with Hetephras's other organs.

"Could the wounds have been made after her death?" Semerket asked.

Metufer instructed the Anubis priests to turn Hetephras onto her stomach. "See the color of her flesh, Semerket? What do you know of blood, when a person dies and it lies within, undrained?"

"It pools, drawn down toward the ground, however the body lies."

"And Hetephras's flesh is white. No pooling blood has turned her black. What do you learn from this?"

"That all her blood ran from the wounds before she died."

"Yes!" Metufer clapped his hands at Semerket's cleverness, as if he were once again his student and Metufer his teacher.

It was then that Semerket saw the second wound at the base of Hetephras's skull, a depression in the bone and flesh, revealing the brain within. Metufer's old but keen eyes saw it, too. He seized a small wire hook and began to intently probe the wound. "I would usually make an incision through the sinuses and remove the brain, but since there is such convenient access here . . ." He began to withdraw bits and pieces of the brain without much finesse, large and small chunks quickly extracted. The brain was not to be preserved, being a useless thing, so Metufer was thorough rather than neat.

Then, without expecting to, both he and Semerket heard a slight ping of metal against metal. They looked at one another. Delicately, Metufer moved the hook back and forth within the priestess's skull. Again the small metallic noise sounded. Gingerly, Metufer probed further, homing in on the object of his search.

Semerket barely breathed.

Metufer found his quarry. Semerket bent closer to look. The Ripper Up manipulated the hook a final time, and withdrew it slowly from the skull. At its curved tip, a piece of dark metal shone, glued to the hook by serum and bits of brain.

It was unmistakably the tip of an axe blade, made from the rare blue metal of the Hittites, broken at its corner. Metufer held it between his fat thumb and forefinger. With great deliberateness he placed it at the edge of the second wound at the back of Hetephras's head. Allowing for the natural slackening that had taken place within the Nile, it fit exactly.

Metufer handed the piece of axe to Semerket. "Obviously our priestess wants you to know something. She has seized this metal, even though it is the strongest in the world, and clung to it in death. Not even the Nile waters could take it from her. Find the owner of the blade this piece fits, and you will find her murderer."

Semerket was doubtful. "If it hasn't been melted down already, or hidden from sight. But at least we do know the poor lady was murdered."

Metufer merely nodded, and very carefully bent to rinse the bit of blue metal in the pool of milky natron. He wiped it with great care, then gave it to Semerket. Semerket pocketed it in the folds of his sash. Turning once again to the fat, old priest, Semerket placed a grateful hand on Metufer's shoulder. The dry hacking cough erupted from the old man, filling the chamber to the rafters. With a last lingering look at Hetephras, Semerket put the bag of cedar again to his nose and left the way he had come.

• • •

DAWN CAME WITH a formidable, glinting brightness. Semerket stepped from the reed craft that had ferried him across the river and tossed the boatman a copper. He turned to face the Gate of Heaven, the pyramid-shaped mountain protecting the Great Place, where the pharaohs lay. The newborn sun dyed the mountain a vivid shade of melon; as it rose, the shadows on the mountain visibly flattened so that its rock face soon took on its usual hue of dusky pink.

Semerket strode quickly from the boat landing to the causeway that led west. The raised paving stones were not crowded; he saw only a few fishermen heading for the river. Semerket's walking stick smote the stones with a steady rhythm that echoed through the clear, cool morning.

A few minutes later he found himself passing the temple of the great god Amenhoteb III. The decrepit building was guarded by the former pharaoh's twin colossi, which the local people called the Rulers of Rulers. The seated statues were still vividly painted, though now flaked and peeling. No pharaoh—not even Ramses II—had built larger. The temple they guarded, however, was inhabited by only a handful of priests. The main structure had crumbled years before, for the ambitious architects had located the building near the river so that the Nile waters surrounded it at flood time. Thus the temple became the symbolic mound of earth that had first emerged from the waters of primeval chaos. Unfortunately, years of Nile flooding had undermined the temple and it had collapsed in on itself. Later pharaohs—particularly Ramses II—had used its vast ruins as a convenient quarry. The remaining temple complex was overgrown by grasses and seedling palms, and the chirps of larks and katydids were the only orisons sung there now.

Even in its ruined state, its priests were offering up platters of onions and loaves of bread to the statues' spirits as Semerket passed. They returned Semerket's stare matter-of-factly. Semerket walked on, turning his face resolutely toward the Gate of Heaven.

The causeway soon diverged. The southernmost road, he knew, would take him to Djamet Temple. Crowded and noisy, Djamet was the hub of all industry and wealth in the area, being the southern abode of the current pharaoh, Ramses III. To Semerket's right, the northern path led to the mountains, and beyond that into the fierce, red desert where the god Set resided.

Semerket hesitated. The Western Mayor's offices were also at Djamet. He knew he should present himself to Pawero as a gesture of courtesy, for the mayor was the absolute lord of Western Thebes. Semerket was technically violating the mayor's jurisdiction by treading there.

Yet some force drove him to seek the harsh silence of the cliffs and desert. It was where Hetephras had tended her small shrines and temples. He must go there in any case, if only to get a sense of where the priestess had lived, what she had seen and heard during her days on earth, even to smell the air she had breathed.

Semerket made the decision that Pawero could wait. He turned north onto the road that led to the Gate of Heaven.

Peasants still harvested the fields, gathering the last of the emmer wheat. None hailed him. They hurried in their labors, for soon the inundation of the Nile would be upon them. In the fields several bonfires were lit to consume the chaff, and the black smoke rose thickly upward. It was a smell that caught him unaware, abruptly reminding him of Naia. He remembered how their home, built at the edge of similar fields, had been filled with these same earthy smells, and how he and Naia often joined the peasants in their harvest festivals . . .

Semerket stopped. His great bitterness suddenly engulfed him, and he could feel again how his ka shriveled to nothingness. Her name was a scream in his head. He did not know whether he actually cried her name aloud or if he remained silent, but it seemed the entire countryside rang with it.

Some demon or evil genie must have taken possession of him, he decided. How long would it take to forget her and become himself again? How long before this crushing sense of loss would lighten? At that moment he wanted nothing so much as a long draft of soothing wine.

Resolutely throwing his gray woolen cloak over his shoulder and setting his feet firmly one ahead of the other, he continued walking. The paved causeway became a dirt road, and then narrowed into a small pathway bordered by tufted grasses, barely wide enough for a single person to tread. As the minutes elapsed, the scream in his head that was Naia subsided to a whisper.

The harvested lands abruptly stopped. He could actually place one foot in the black land where the Nile had crested in last year's flood and another in the red sands where the desert began. A well was there, and he drank deeply of its cold water, not knowing when he would drink again.

The sun was overhead now, the morning chill vanished. The trail rose, ascending sharply through cliffs of sheared red sandstone. Ahead of Semerket was a Medjay tower. He reckoned that these Nubian policemen would surely stop him, to challenge his identity and review his credentials. The Nubian Medjays were fierce in keeping all unauthorized persons out of the Great Place, or so he had heard.

But as Semerket advanced, no one called down to halt him. Drawing nearer, he heard the faint but unmistakable sounds of snoring from high above him. He shook his head in disapproval. The wealth of the generations of Egypt was buried in tombs not more than a few feet away and no one was guarding it.

"Medjay!" Semerket shouted up to the tower.

There was no answer. The snores continued.

"Sergeant!" he called louder, picking up a stone and throwing it through the tower window. It struck something soft, and the snores were abruptly choked off. Semerket waited patiently for the policeman to appear, but soon the sounds of heavy slumber again wafted down to him.

Shrugging, Semerket turned away and headed once more into the mountain gorges. Such laxity was a sad example of how poorly Pawero governed this side of the Nile. Semerket's disdain for the Western Mayor honed itself to a keener edge.

By now Semerket had penetrated deep into the Great Place. The red of the sandstone cliffs had gradually given way to the dull white of weathered limestone. The silence was so pervasive that it assumed a noise of its own, an eerie primordial roaring. He discovered that if he stood very still, the noise was actually caused by the beating of his heart.

Somewhere beneath these rocks Egypt's most important crop was sown: the mummies of the dead pharaohs. The tombs were in fact the forges that sparked eternal life in the kings. Magical inscriptions painted on the walls ensured they awakened to life, to eternally labor for the good of Egypt. In return, the people worshipped them in perpetuity and kept their names alive.

Something at the corner of his vision made him cease his musings. What had he glimpsed? He peered again at the horizon and then saw it—the remains of a small encampment littering the valley floor. Instantly he was striding the mountain pathway that led to it. The thin road twisted in and out of the jutting crags, and as he followed its serpentine path around a cliff face, he was suddenly blocked by a mound of limestone chips. He had not seen it before, located as it was in the shadows and crevices of the mountain. Semerket looked about for any sign of a work gang, for limestone rubble was a sure sign of tomb-makers laboring at their profession.

But no workman's chant reached his ears, nor any mumbled word. Not even the wind blew. High up a hawk wheeled, the only evidence of any living thing. On the tops of the cliffs surrounding the valley, Semerket saw other Medjay towers, identical to the one he had passed before. One reason the kings had chosen this desolate place for their burials was that it was so easily observed and protected. But this pile of limestone rubble was somehow hidden from the Medjays' view, he noticed, obscured by crags and their long shadows.

Even so, the distant lookout posts seemed deserted; as before, no one shouted at him to explain himself. Gingerly Semerket stepped onto the pile of white rubble. Its gentle slope allowed him to half-walk, half-slide to the floor of the Great Place.

The rubble deposited him directly at the deserted campsite. Whoever had been there had attempted to hide the remains of their fire with a light covering of sand. Throughout the day the winds had blown the sands away to reveal its dark circle of ash.

Haphazardly littering the camp were the shattered pieces of an earthen pot, the shards blackened from long use over a fire. Apparently the pot had broken from the intensity of the heat, then been discarded. Semerket noticed that no residue of food caked the interior surfaces of the shards. But traces of gilding could be discerned upon it, and on one of the pieces he was almost certain he recognized a rudimentary glyph, perhaps the name of the pot's former owner. Idly he began piecing the shards together. He dug around the camp, looking for more of the earthen remains. It was then he struck a wooden rod with his fingers.

From the sands he withdrew the blackened end of a sycamore branch that had been the stick of a torch. Whoever had used it had been working too quickly to refuel the torch with a wax-soaked cloth. He thrust the branch aside and began to kick at the surrounding sand. Five more of the crusted sycamore torch ends emerged: at least six persons had camped there.

Semerket asked himself what kind of labor in the Great Place required such light? Medjays camping outside would have made do with only a fire. Perhaps inside a tomb? Dimly he remembered that tomb workers used a special mixture of expensive sesame oil and salt that supposedly made a torch smokeless. These in the sands were only ordinary torches.

As he puzzled the conundrum out, Semerket began to quickly amass as many pieces of the shattered clay pot as possible, not knowing why he did so. Tying them into his cloak, he was fastening the ends when he heard the voice.

"God-skin is made there . . ."

From where he sat on the desert floor, the voice seemed to assail him from all directions. Semerket whirled around, peering up and into the crags. He at last spied a young boy astride a donkey. The boy stared down at him. His head was shaved, and he wore the plaited sidelock of a royal prince.

"What did you say?" Semerket called up to him.

"It's where they make it. The god-skin."

Semerket began to clamber back up to the pathway, finding it difficult to retrace his steps up the mound of limestone shards. He spoke to the boy as he ascended. "I don't understand what you're saying!"

"Every month they come."

"Who?"

"The ones who make the god-skin. When Khons hides his face." He was smiling.

"When there's no moon . . . ?"

The boy said nothing. Semerket remembered that there had been no moon for the past two days.

"Who are you? Wait there, please! I want to talk to you."

Semerket reached the pathway and ran in the direction the boy had gone. He followed the twisting road, hoping to catch a glimpse of the boy in the fissures ahead. "Please!" he shouted into the air again. "Wait!"

There was only silence. When Semerket reached the jutting corner of a crag, panting, the boy was gone.

In his place stood a Medjay, spear lowered. His angry, red-veined eyes glared at Semerket from his black face. Semerket had no choice but to slowly raise his hands over his head.

WESTERN MAYOR PAWERO fingered a fan of short plover feathers. He kept his face slightly averted as if loathing the idea of having to speak directly to Semerket. "You broke the law by going there," he told Semerket, "particularly without first presenting your credentials to me. You're lucky to be alive—the Medjays are instructed to kill intruders on sight." Pawero condescended to level a withering glare at the Medjay standing at the back of the room, as if to accuse him of failing in his duty to see Semerket standing alive before him.

The Medjay was blinking, heroically attempting to keep awake. Tears of fatigue oozed from his eyes. Pawero plucked at the fan, oblivious to the Medjay's drowsiness. He continued his harangue, "If every commoner were allowed to roam—"

Semerket held up the vizier's insignia on the chain of jasper beads. "The vizier has granted me unrestricted access."

Pawero's cold eyes barely registered the badge's existence, but his nervous fingers continued to tear at his fan. "I shall tell Vizier Toh there cannot be two authorities here in Western Thebes. I shall tell him the harmony of Ma'at will be disturbed."

Semerket shrugged. "As the mayor wishes."

Pawero was irritated by Semerket's indifference. Then he remembered what this Semerket had said about him, and the laughter that had risen in the vizier's chambers when others had heard: "a peabrained old pettifogger."

Flushing deeply at the memory, pulling at the fan's feathers, the Western Mayor tried another tack. He smiled, his thin lips drawn back from his long, narrow teeth. "I'm curious, clerk, how you managed to slip past the Medjay's tower?"

Semerket saw panic in the Medjay's red-veined eyes. Sleeping on duty incurred terrible punishments for the Medjays, even dismissal from service.

Semerket quickly considered what his answer should be. "I . . . climbed to the high pathway above the tower, lord," he said after a moment. "I had seen a boy—a prince—and was curious to meet him."

Relief visibly flooded through the Medjay's face. But Pawero's next words made the black policeman once again quiver in fear. "Then if this is true, Medjay Qar, under your watch two strangers have been allowed entry into the Great Place. What are we to think about this, eh?"

The Medjay fell to his knees, hands crossed against his chest. "There was no such boy, lord. All the way from the Great Place this man told me how a prince appeared to him. Yet when I examined the trail there were no footprints other than his own. I thought he must be lying, or mad, and so I brought him here."

Pawero turned to Semerket with the same toothy smile. "I agree with the Medjay, clerk. You don't know the desert as we do; it's a mystical place, able to conjure hallucinations and mirages in naïve folk such as yourself."

"It was no mirage. The boy and I spoke."

Pawero was unused to being contradicted; his lips grew thin with suppressed rage. He fanned himself furiously, only to find himself in a shower of floating plover feathers. He threw the fan to the floor. "And what did this young 'prince' say to you, then?"

"That god-skin was being made there."

The Medjay stood up, pointing an exasperated finger at Semerket. "I tell you there was no such boy!"

Pawero made a slashing movement with his hand and the Medjay was silent. "God-skin?" Pawero asked, looking directly at Semerket for the first time.

Semerket nodded.

Pawero was momentarily taken aback and dropped his head to gaze at the floor of black basalt, considering. After a moment, he looked up. His voice was doubtful. "The skin of gods is gold," he said. "Incorruptible. The purest material in the universe. I cannot imagine what the boy meant—god-skin, gold, cannot be 'made.' "

"At least the Lord Mayor now acknowledges the boy spoke to me."

Pawero bristled. "I do no such thing. It's obvious you were merely under the desert's spell, nothing more. You imagined this so-called 'prince.' "

Though Semerket remained silent, he radiated contempt for the mayor—for his overly elegant garments, his elaborate wig whose tiny braids were woven with droplets of gold, and most of all for his unrelenting hauteur. As far as Semerket was concerned, Pawero was the essence of the empty-headed nobleman.

Pawero's patience broke at last. "I am well aware of your hostility, clerk. The feeling is mutual. I know I'm just a 'pea-brained old pettifogger' to you—oh, yes! I know that's what you called me, don't deny it—"

Semerket silently cursed his brother for having burbled that story.

"Nevertheless," the Western Mayor continued, "on this side of the river I make the rules, and you will do what I say."

"I labor for the vizier, Lord Mayor. What you command does not affect me." Semerket's voice was low.

This was too much for Pawero, who rose from his chair of state. "You! You with no family to speak of—you will not talk to me this way! I shall not help you, sir. No supplies will I give you. All whom I rule will be instructed to tell you nothing. And when you die, may it be without shroud or tomb."

Semerket was unfazed, and the black lights in his eyes were dancing. He understood human beings well enough to realize that when Pawero threatened to inform the vizier about him, the mayor had in fact exposed his greatest fear. Semerket was quick to use the weapon. "Then I shall inform Vizier Toh I suspect you of complicity, as Mayor Paser himself does. That you must in fact be questioned more closely."

Medjay Qar regarded Semerket with stupefaction. This was either the bravest man he'd ever met, or insane. The Western Mayor was brother to Queen Tiya, the great wife of Pharaoh. Did the clerk understand what he risked with his unguarded tongue?

Pawero glared at Semerket. He rose tall from his chair, his face becoming even redder than before. But he could not sustain his wrath;

his expression suddenly crumpled. He sat down to perch shakily on his chair again, his rage burnt out as quickly as it had ignited. He sighed for a long time before he spoke, looking at Semerket sideways from beneath his lids, as if to gauge his effect on him.

"Paser is wrong. This crime troubles me—you don't know how much. He uses this case to make me look like a fool, particularly now that he's caught my sister's ear. Even she, the great wife, clamors for justice. Tiya is convinced catastrophe will come to us all because of this death, and urges me to make an end of it. But what am I to do?"

Semerket looked at him evenly. "If you would solve this crime, then I must be allowed to accomplish my task without interference from you or the Medjays."

Another heap of sighs emanated from Pawero. He nodded. "Find who did this, clerk." But his kohl-rimmed eyes still glowed with a tired hatred.

Semerket bowed. As he turned to leave the room, Pawero spoke again. "Where will you go next?"

"To the tomb-makers' village they call the Place of Truth. I will question the old lady's neighbors."

"After you have questioned them, I would know everything they tell you."

Semerket shook his head. "I cannot. What I learn must be a secret thing, to catch a killer."

Pawero considered for a long moment. Then the Western Mayor waved both Semerket and the Medjay away with a weary hand. The last Semerket saw of him he was slumped in his chair, staring at nothing.

Through the vast, high-ceilinged halls of Djamet the two men walked. Semerket stared, never having been in a king's residence before. The turquoise faience tiles that lined the walls were luminous in the sun's afternoon rays, and the brightly painted pillars that supported the high ceilings were too many to count. Gold and silver glinted from hammered vases full of the last of summer's blossoms. At the doorways and windows, fine netting flowed with the afternoon breezes, keeping the swarms of black Egyptian flies outdoors.

Djamet was a temple devoted to the worship of Amun-Ra, it was true, but it was also the center of government for Western Thebes. Scribes, soldiers, servants, and nobles hurried about, intent on their important tasks. Honor guards formed from corps of Libyan mercenaries marched in formation, or stood at the doors to Pharaoh's private chambers, preventing entry. Semerket was momentarily disappointed to see no women on the premises, for the beauty of Pharaoh's wives and their maids was legendary. He had imagined a court full of pretty females, decked in flowers . . . sheer muslins . . . musky perfumes . . .

"Where are Pharaoh's women?" Semerket asked Medjay Qar. They were outside the hall of audience, well into the outer alcoves where the craftsmen and priests lived.

"Our pharaoh is a soldier and has a horror of allowing women to meddle in the affairs of men. He confines them up there—in the harem—or in the gardens."

Semerket looked up to where the Medjay pointed. On an enclosed balcony, high above the ground, he saw the gauzy figures of Pharaoh's wives peering through the window slits. The harem was the responsibility of Naia's husband, Nakht, who because of his noble name had been appointed the steward of the king's royal wives. Semerket shuddered, remembering their last meeting. Seeing the movements of the women behind the grating, Semerket flattered himself that he was the object of their gazes. As if to confirm this impression, faint, high-pitched laughter pursued him as he made his way under the harem's balcony to the temple's entrance.

At the Great Pylons, Semerket spoke to Qar again. "It's not true, you know, that I avoided your tower this morning. I stopped there to present myself when I went into the Great Place. Whoever was on duty was asleep; I heard the snoring."

He did not wait for Qar's explanations or protests but started once again on the path that led to the Gate of Heaven. Qar, his lower lip thrust out in shame, hurried after him, saying nothing.

As they walked the stone road to the north, Semerket asked, as if idly, "Tell me, were you Medjays on maneuvers last night in the Great Place?"

"No."

"Any party of mourners . . . officials taking inventory? Something of that sort?"

"No. I told you. Why do you ask?"

Semerket had not the heart to tell Qar that not only had both Semerket and the boy trespassed into the Great Place, but at least six others had come and gone there as well.

TENDRILS OF DISTANT CLOUDS caught the setting sun as Foreman Paneb emerged from Pharaoh's unfinished tomb. Wearily he climbed the long flight of limestone stairs up to the tomb's door. His team had labored there for their customary eight days and now they would pack up their gear and go home to the village for three days of rest.

A flame flared to his left. Over in the company shed, the scribe Neferhotep was trimming the wick on a candle. It was the scribe's custom at the end of the work period to compose a report to the vizier concerning the tomb's progress, whether he asked for one or not. The scribe casually looked up, inadvertently glancing at Paneb. No unspoken communication was made between them, no gesture of deference or greeting uttered. Neferhotep leaned forward and pulled the curtain shut.

The two men had never gotten along. It was ironic that now, thanks to the tomb and their high rank within the Place of Truth, they were bound together closer than brothers. Paneb admired how Neferhotep never let their current alliance stand in the way of their mutual disregard.

Hearing his men's footsteps on the tomb's stairway behind him, Paneb turned to welcome their paint-splotched forms into the fading light. "Going home to that pretty wife of yours tonight, eh, Kenna? We won't be seeing you for a day or two. . . . Kofi, get some sleep these next days, you're looking tired. . . . Getting drunk tonight, Hori? Good man . . ."

Though his words were cheerful, Paneb was not. Since the day when his aunt Hetephras was reported missing, misery had been his only companion. Nothing cheered him.

Paneb was the foreman of Pharaoh's tomb, a large, solid man of prodigious strength and mercurial temperament. Though by no means handsome, for his nose was smashed from fights with other foremen, his presence was mesmerizing. Paneb's status in the Place of Truth was more like that of a folk-hero than a real person. Seeing him so unnaturally subdued caused his crew to regard one another with concerned frowns.

Many years had passed since the "piercing," or excavation, of the tomb had been accomplished; now the team labored on the lavish paintings of rituals and spells that covered its walls, ceilings, and galleries. Because Pharaoh Ramses III had been blessed with so long a reign, generations of village tomb-workers had lived and died without ever working on another royal tomb. These men, including Paneb, were in fact the sons of those who had started the work.

Inside the large tent where the men slept nights, Paneb sat cross-legged, surrounded by his men. They carefully cleaned their brushes and reed pens, and sharpened their metal tools. This was a nightly chore never entrusted to servants, done even before dinner was prepared; the men's tools were the most precious things they owned.

The boy Rami sat closest to Paneb. Though he was the son of the scribe Neferhotep, he was a large lad, big-boned like the foreman, and shared Paneb's gold eyes and wide, determined mouth.

"Paneb?"

"What is it?"

"Have I done well with the gridding of the figures this week?" Rami was charged with creating large grids on the painted gypsum surfaces of the tomb, snapping strings imbued with red chalk into precisely measured squares. This allowed the master painters to map the designs from smaller test paintings their fathers had created on papyrus years before.

"Yes."

The boy looked at him significantly. "I'm fifteen next month."

Paneb drew a whetstone across the blade of his chisel. "Well?"

"Am I old enough, then, to start outlining the figures? Not the important ones, of course, but those at the edges of the tomb, or on the backs of the pillars? The ones no one will see?"

"But you've no experience in it."

"I've been practicing. Here, I'll show you!"

Eagerly, Rami took some limestone shards from his straw knapsack. The boy had made a variety of practice strokes on them. Some of the lines tapered to fine points, some twisted into curls and circles, while still others ended in sharp, blunt edges.

"Very impressive," Paneb said.

Rami beamed.

"But these are short pen-lengths," Paneb continued. "Can you sustain such a stroke for the span of an entire wall, to keep the reed pen steady all its length?"

"I know I can."

"Can you draw, as Aaphat here can"—Paneb winked at the tomb's master painter—"the line of a pharaoh's lip, to catch only the hint of a smile? Or a god's eye that peers into a world we cannot see? Or the curve of a queen's delicate fingers grasping the stem of a lotus blossom?"

Rami's mouth dropped in dismay. "All I wanted was to outline a few images," he said dolefully, "not to finish the entire tomb."

Paneb's sudden yelp of laughter echoed loudly in the Great Place. It was the first time since his aunt's death that his men had heard any mirthful sound from him. They laughed with him.

Though Paneb had once beaten a tomb-worker to death for insubordination, his men adored him for the thoughtful kindnesses he lavished on them. They remembered the time when his team had completed a task in advance of its deadline and he'd broken into the stores for extra rations of beer and oil, heedless of Neferhotep's protests. Another time, Paneb had traded his own copper chisels for half an oxen because he thought his team deserved it. They had trumpeted with laughter when he had requisitioned new tools the following day from the apoplectic Neferhotep.

In fact, his men loved him as much for his prodigious faults as for his virtues. And chief of these, whether fault or virtue, was his prowess with women. The fact that sometimes Paneb even made a conquest of their own wives did nothing to dampen the men's loyalty; they would lay down their lives for him.

"So you'll let me do some outlining?" Rami continued to press the foreman.

"We'll see," said Paneb, clamping his hand around the boy's neck.

Like any lad, Rami was convinced these words actually meant "yes," and his wide smile was a mirror of Paneb's own.

Then Rami made a mistake. He dropped his head and whispered to the foreman, "I'm . . . I'm sorry about Hetephras, Paneb. I've not gotten a chance to say it."

It was as if a gate had suddenly slammed and locked in Paneb's face. His eyes grew small; his wide mouth became stubborn.

"Damn you!" he growled. "I told you men never to speak of it again, didn't I?"

His angry gaze raked the team so keenly they dropped their heads to stare at the sands in front of them. Still swearing, Paneb thrust his pack of tools onto his shoulders and rose abruptly to begin the journey back to the village. He strode quickly so none could catch him.

Rami was struck senseless. He venerated Paneb, loved him better than his own father. Seeing Paneb trudge angrily down the trail caused the boy's shoulders to sag with grief. As his treacherous eyes began to overflow, he hastily packed up the rest of his tools. Nothing had been right since the morning Hetephras had died. Nothing.

IT WAS DARK when Paneb passed the Medjay tower where Qar was stationed. He waved to the policeman, but did not stop. He wanted no company, for he was by then chastising himself for his mean-spirited treatment of Rami. The boy had been only trying to voice the concern that all his men felt.

Another few paces and Paneb had forgiven the lad. He would make it up to him by allowing the boy to complete a few outlining chores in the tomb. But he chose not to inform Rami of this benediction until the next day. Paneb simply hadn't the strength to endure the lad's glee that evening. Tired in his soul, and sad as death over his aunt's tragic end, he was not cheered even by the welcoming smells of the village's cooking fires.

But at the village walls, shielded by the dark, someone waited at the gateway. He peered closely and saw that it was Hunro, leaning indolently against the lintel. Although she had attained an age when most Egyptian women were beginning to fade, the years had made no inroads on her charms. She was not beautiful in any classic sense, being a tall, thin woman with hair bluntly cropped. But her gaze was bold, full of sordid promise, and her smile with its overbite was enticing. Though he had known hundreds of other women more beautiful than she, all of them had ultimately bored him in time. Their breasts and lips became dulled by familiarity, their movements, however artful, predictable.

But Paneb had never tired of Hunro. As they aged, their passion was revitalized by her constant inventiveness, which in turn became dangerous in its recklessness. He felt his loins stirring simply looking at her. It had been more than a month since he'd last had her. Even the memory of his aunt's death could not diminish his mounting lust; Hunro was exactly what he needed that night to drive away the sadness and the demons.

"I should have known you'd be waiting for me," he said, setting his tool sack on the ground.

She hooted scornfully, her voice high and feathery. "Oh? How do you know I'm not waiting for my husband?"

"Because I know Neferhotep sent a servant to tell you he'd be late."

Her laugh was a little, liquid, gloating sound. "I hate it when I'm so obvious."

His voice was a whisper in her ear. "You can't help it. It's your nature."

In the dark her eyes flashed a warning, even as her sharp teeth flashed in her smile. "You're a pig," she said.

"That's *my* nature."

She laughed again, louder than before. He pressed against her. Paneb could feel the heat she radiated, and he seized her in his arms. Hunro had doused herself in a heavy sandalwood perfume, his favorite scent. He brought his mouth to hers. Her lips parted and his tongue began to probe her mouth. Abruptly she bit down hard on his lip. He pushed her away with a grunt, wincing.

"That's for taking me for granted," she said. "And for bringing me no gift."

He ran his tongue over the torn flesh of his lip, tasting blood. Tempted to strike her, instead he bent down to his sack, feeling in the dark for something inside. He found what he sought, and drew forth a small object wrapped in soiled linen. "Who says I bring nothing?"

Her eyes were greedy as she reached for the thing. Quickly she undid the cloth that bound it, gasping when she saw it, for it gleamed brightly even in the dark.

"Oh . . . !" she breathed. "Where did you ever get it? In the bazaars of the eastern city? Have you been across the river again?"

His eyes became blank. "No," he said. "Old Amen-meses came into camp again."

"The merchant from Kush? It must have been dreadfully expensive."

"Aren't you worth it?"

Paneb slipped the bracelet on her wrist. Its weight made her dizzy, and Hunro held it up to the feeble torchlight shining from the village parapets. The thing outshone even the fires, a magnificent cuff of gold covering most of her wrist, inset with cabochon rubies that glowed brighter than freshly spilled blood. Inlaid glyphs circled it, and where the ends joined together, the talons of two vultures formed a clasp.

Even as she draped her arms around his neck, she could not take her eyes from it. Making soft sounds of joy in her throat, she took his hand and led him around the corner of the village building to the work sheds. "I must thank you properly," she whispered.

With practiced steps they hurried to a shearing room and fell onto a pile of freshly cut wool, sinking into its softness. He roughly stripped off his kilt, and she reached to caress him, smiling to herself at finding him engorged and slick with lust. He brought his mouth again to hers, groaning aloud as she expertly kneaded him. His lip throbbed where she had bitten it, but the pain only served to inflame him further.

Then he was roughly removing her dress over her shoulders, slowly inching himself down her body, licking the small of her neck, her ears, the corner of her mouth. He would have lingered at her breasts if she'd let him, but she pushed him farther down. She arched as she felt his tongue intimately caressing her, and her eyes became slits in the dark, half-moons where no pupil showed. He bored into her, and the taste of her on his tongue was mixed with the taste of his own blood. She began to moan, to writhe, and then she groaned aloud, once, then again, trying to simultaneously push him away yet keep him there forever. At the sound of her cries he instantly climaxed, the hot stickiness of him spilling over her. Paneb quickly pulled her toward him, parting her legs so that he could finish within her. He buckled and collapsed on top of her, still thrusting, and his groans became deep, animal cries of pleasure. Then it was over, and their movements slowly ceased. They lay drenched in their own sweat and could not find the strength to part. He moved to say something tender in her ear, but was interrupted by a scratching at the door.

"Paneb!" It was a whisper that might have been the wind.

Hunro sat up. Paneb shook his head, warning her not to betray their presence. He indicated to her through gestures to remove the bracelet.

The voice was insistent. "Paneb! I know you're in there, so don't pretend you're not!"

"Khepura?"

"There's trouble!"

"How did you know I was here?"

"I'm not head woman for nothing. You come out of there, too, Hunro. Your son Rami is already home."

Hunro let loose with a whispered string of invectives that would not have been out of place in a barracks. After wiping herself with some strands of stray wool, she seized her dress and slipped it back over her shoulders. Hunro detested the idea that Khepura was keeping accounts of her whereabouts. Reluctantly, she thrust the bracelet into the cloth that had covered it.

Khepura, the corpulent and intimidating wife of the goldsmith Sani, stood waiting for them at the door, disapproval etched into the folds of her wide, flat face.

"Look at you two," she scolded. "Courting a trial for adultery, that's what."

"Go to hell, Khepura," said Hunro, her sandy voice laced with scorn. She allowed no one to pass judgment on her, particularly this fat, ugly, overbearing woman.

"Be quiet, both of you!" Paneb snapped impatiently, still fastening his kilt around his waist. "What's this trouble, then?"

"At your aunt's house—"

Alarmed, Paneb ran off before she could finish speaking. "Wipe your lip, Paneb!" Khepura called after him. "It's bleeding!"

The two women hurried in his wake as he sped through the village gates. Khepura, who considered it her duty as elected head woman to oversee the morals of the village women, kept up a steady strain of outraged commentary. "Don't think I'm the only one who knows about you and Paneb!" she warned Hunro as they entered the village's narrow main street.

"As if I care," Hunro shot back, avoiding a group of shrieking children playing in the lane. Faster than Khepura, she deftly sidestepped the pack of barking dogs now streaking past them. Like an eel among the reeds she agilely wove through the groups of villagers gossiping together in doorways. Khepura, panting and wheezing, fought to keep up with her.

"You have the morals of an alley cat!" the head woman charged. "I doubt you can name the fathers of your own children!"

"I'm sure your Sani must be one of them."

"Isis hear her!"

The two women were still arguing when they reached Hetephras's home. Stopped from entering by Paneb's bulky frame at the doorway, Hunro strained to peer over his shoulders into the room. Frustrated, she finally pushed him forcibly aside. Khepura thrust her bulk into the crowded room as well.

A man sat at Hetephras's prayer bench. Though he remained silent, his incredibly black eyes glinted when he turned his gaze to Hunro. She had never seen eyes as black as his. For perhaps the first time in her life, Hunro was suddenly bashful, and her hands fluttered to her neck to conceal any love bites that Paneb might have left there.

"I understand why you don't want strangers in your aunt's home," Semerket was patiently saying to the man with the smashed nose who loomed over him. "But the vizier sent me to discover her murderer and bring him to justice."

Paneb's loud threats to evict Semerket dwindled to silence. "Murderer?" he whispered, shocked. The horrified faces of the two women beside him were mirrors of his own.

Khepura stepped forward, hands fluttering. "But we had heard that . . . that she had perhaps drowned, or that a crocodile . . . ?"

"She was killed with an axe."

Paneb uttered an obscenity so foul that even Hunro blinked. He collapsed on the floor, and Hunro bent to drape her arms about his shoulders, murmuring sounds of comfort and pity.

Khepura spoke sharply to Semerket, "How do you know it was a murder?"

"I examined her body myself at the House of Purification."

"But . . . but after being in the Nile for so long, how could you tell—?" Khepura shot Paneb a glance, now rocking slowly forward and back, dumb with grief.

"There is no mistake." Semerket did not mention that he also possessed a part of the axe that had killed Hetephras; he intended to go secretly through the tomb-workers' tool sacks himself to look for the matching blade. This was the chief reason for beginning his investigation at the village: the tomb-makers were more richly provisioned than all other laborers in Egypt. If any group possessed tools of blue metal, it would be them.

Semerket looked up to find Hunro staring at him with avid interest. Their eyes caught for just a moment, and he thought he saw in them an invitation to something more. He quickly dropped his gaze. "Tell the villagers, please," he continued with a cough, "that I will be calling on them for their statements."

Hunro nodded, about to speak, but Khepura interrupted her. "That's impossible. Such a thing . . . it must be approved by the Council of Elders," she said, raising her chin with a trace of defiance.

"Then I will begin with the elders. Tomorrow."

Khepura reacted with alarm. "You're staying overnight? In the village?"

"Yes."

The fat woman shook her head. "No one is allowed in this village at night who is not a tomb-maker by trade—Pharaoh's tomb is a state secret."

"The vizier allows it, as does the Western Mayor." Semerket held up Toh's insignia, fastened to his neck by jasper beads.

Hunro reached forward to take the bar of etched gold between her fingers. Khepura grunted in disgust. Hunro paid her no attention, and continued fingering the vizier's insignia. Though she could not read the glyphs inscribed upon it, she smiled up at Semerket and let it fall back to his chest with a slap.

Khepura looked nervously down at Paneb, silently willing him to say something. Paneb rose to his feet and said gruffly, "Do what you want to, then. But you can't stay here."

"I must, to examine the house for any clues—"

Paneb's instant and unexpected roar of anger was so loud that neighbors came running, abandoning their dinner and gossip. He hoisted Semerket from the stone bench so swiftly that the wind was knocked from him. Flashes of light exploded in his brain as his head cracked against the mud-brick wall. Paneb's hands were tight about his neck.

Both women flew upon the foreman, pounding on his vast shoulders with their fists, pulling at his cloak. "Paneb—let him go!"

"Paneb—no!"

"If you kill him, everyone in this village will pay the price!"

"Paneb, he is the vizier's man!"

Semerket tore at Paneb's hands, clawed at his face, tried to gouge his eyes. Then, with the last bit of strength he had left, he managed to pant, "Why . . . don't you want me . . . to solve your aunt's murder?"

That question at last penetrated Paneb's rage. The demon glaring from his eyes suddenly fled. With a final groan of anguish, Paneb released Semerket, who fell on the floor, choking.

The foreman spoke, panting heavily, "Yes. Yes. Of course I want her murder solved."

A querulous voice demanded entry from outside the house. The scribe Neferhotep eased his way into the room, sliding past the gawking neighbors. He was a slight man, and though still relatively young, was already hunch-shouldered from his long years as a scribe. It took only a moment for him to size up the situation. "Oh dear," he said. "What have you done *this* time, Paneb?"

Paneb still panted. "Tell him—tell him he can't stay in my aunt's house, Nef. Tell him you forbid it."

"Well now, I would—but who is he?"

Together Khepura and Hunro spoke. Between the two agitated women Neferhotep was apprised of the situation. His reaction to Hetephras's death was the same as the others'. "Murder!" he said at last, as if he could not believe it.

Neferhotep bent down to help Semerket to his feet. "Please forgive us, sir. As you can imagine, we're all devastated by this news. Paneb here was her nephew and the shock of it no doubt unhinged him—"

"I don't want him staying here!" Paneb seemed ready to lunge again at Semerket.

"Well now, Paneb, he's the vizier's appointed man. If he needs to—"

"*No!*"

Neferhotep's face was instantly and startlingly transformed. "Listen to me," he said, bringing his eyes close to Paneb's, "I don't think you know what you're saying. I think you're too upset to speak intelligently. I think you'd better not say anything more, or this fine gentleman here

might return to the vizier with terrible stories about our . . . hospitality."
Neferhotep never blinked as he spoke. "Do you understand me?"

Though Paneb's wide mouth was a stubborn line, he dropped his
head and nodded.

"Good," said Neferhotep. "Good. Now I think you should apologize
and then go to your home."

"That's not necessary—" Semerket began.

"I say it is. Paneb?" Neferhotep's voice was calm.

The foreman crooked his head in the direction of Semerket, the hatred on his face plain to see. "Sorry," he muttered, and bolted from the
room. His startled neighbors were quick to jump aside as he shoved his
way through the crowd and down the narrow avenue.

When he was gone Neferhotep exhaled shakily, and smiled at Semerket. "I am sorry for that," he said. "Paneb is our foreman, and a better one you'll never meet. But a foreman around here has to use brute
force sometimes—and, well, Paneb's approach is rather uncompli-
cated."

Semerket rubbed his throat. "I'll bear that in mind."

Neferhotep's tone became cajoling. "I hope you won't hold it
against us, particularly in any formal reports to the vizier."

Semerket said nothing. Neferhotep, now all warmth, went on. "I
am Neferhotep, the chief scribe and head of this village. This lady is
Khepura, who I believe welcomed you here earlier. And this is my wife,
Hunro." To Semerket's surprise he indicated the tall woman who had
stared at him so audaciously.

"This lady is your *wife*?" Had a jackal married a lioness, Semerket
could not have been more surprised.

Neferhotep's cordial smile didn't falter. "Yes, we've been married almost since we were children, though Hunro wasn't brought up here.
Please, let us know how we can make you comfortable, and how else
we can be of service. I want to know we've done everything possible to
assist you."

"Well . . . I'd like something to eat, if that's all right. I'll pay for it, of
course."

Hunro spoke up eagerly. "Our servants here cook for the Medjays.
I'm sure there are some extra rations I can bring you." Neferhotep
watched her leave with an enigmatic expression. A few seconds later

Khepura too slipped quietly from the room. The scribe turned just in time to see Semerket staring after Hunro.

A shadow crossed Neferhotep's face. "Well now," the chief scribe said. He was looking at Semerket in the same way he had regarded Paneb—his eyes unblinking, never wavering, never leaving Semerket's face. When the smile returned to his face, his eyes remained cool.

HUNRO WAS RUNNING TO the kitchens. To her intense irritation, Khepura again caught up to her. Khepura spoke casually, as if discussing the previous night's dinner. "What do you have wrapped up there in your hand?"

Hunro stopped and tossed her head. "My way out of this hole!" Defiantly she slipped the bracelet onto her wrist, smirking at the head woman.

It took all of Khepura's resolve not to strike Hunro's slatternly smile from her face. "You'll bring this village to ruin with your whore's ways. But you'd better know this, Hunro—the women here won't let it happen. We're all of one mind about you."

Hunro's lips curled into a sneer. "Judging from present company, I'm surprised they all add up to one mind." She spoke lightly but her dark eyes were filled with malice. "What's really bothering you, Khepura, is that you can't abide the fact that the chief scribe is my husband, and the chief foreman's my lover. Push me a little further and you'll find out who the real head woman in this village is."

"You won't get away with it," Khepura retorted evenly.

Hunro smiled indulgently. "You rule your way, Khepura," she said, "I'll rule mine." She held her arm up to the torchlight so the bracelet could flash a defiant red, then turned to hurry toward the kitchens.

Khepura did not follow her. She had said enough. There would come a time, Khepura thought, when the gods would demonstrate their disapproval of Hunro. And Khepura silently vowed to herself that the time would be soon.

A FULL HOUR elapsed before Hunro returned to Hetephras's house. Semerket had begun to despair of ever getting any food that night. He yawned despite his hunger, fatigued. It had been a long, disquieting day. Perhaps it would be better to go to sleep unfed and start fresh in the morning. But then Hunro was pushing open the door, bearing beer, bread, and beans.

"I'm sorry for being so late, but the servants just brought it to me. I don't know what kept them." She placed the bowl on the tiled floor of the reception room and unsealed the jar of beer. The aromatic yeastiness of it caressed his nostrils. He was immediately very thirsty.

"Join me?" he said, indicating the beer.

"N-no," she answered reluctantly, "My husband . . ."

"I was hoping we could talk."

Her eyes flickered. "About what?"

He gestured, indicating the village around them. "This place. Hetephras. You."

"Me?" she said with a tiny laugh. "I'm hardly interesting. I haven't left this village since the day I was married." Her voice suddenly sounded old, and she dropped her head. She leaned against the stuccoed wall, staring moodily out the opened door.

He wondered at the change in her. Gone was her former flirtatiousness. He lifted the jar of beer to his lips, and stared at her over the rim.

She turned and watched him drink. "Is it to your taste?" she asked.

He shrugged. "There's a flavor . . . what is it?"

"We add coriander and some other herbs to it. Not as fine as the beers you get in Thebes, I imagine. But then, what could be?"

Semerket shook his head ironically, and quoted the words of the poem, " 'What do they say, they who are so far from Thebes? They spend their days blinking at its name. If only we had it, they say . . .' "

Her eyes became hard as basalt. "I'll have it," she said firmly. "Soon."

Semerket dipped his fingers into the fava beans and tasted the same pungent herb that was in the beer. "What would you do with it?" he asked her, swallowing. "It's a sad place. The people there are angry, grasping—like all cities."

"But the festivals! The bazaars, where you can buy the world if you want. The inns, where people laugh and sing all night long . . ." From the rapture in her sultry tenor she may as well have been saying "moonlight!" or "kisses!"

"And the foreigners . . ." she continued in the same breathless fashion, ". . . from as far away as India and Cathay, I've heard. What excitement!"

Semerket yawned, intensely sleepy. He was feeling the effects of being awake since before dawn. "The beggars, the cheaters and tricksters, the fat greasy priests . . ."

She laughed, and the sound was quivery to him, like oil on water. "You can't discourage me. You've just forgotten how wonderful it is because you've lived in Eastern Thebes always, I'll wager. I'm going to live there, too, one day. See if I don't. I'm leaving this little turd of a place, and I'm never looking back."

Semerket did not dispute her. His head fell to his chest, and he struggled to keep his eyes open. "I'm sorry . . ." he muttered. "So tired . . ."

"Let me help," Hunro whispered. She put his arm around her shoulders and hoisted him to his feet. Semerket found himself leaning on her surprisingly strong frame, stumbling toward the back room of Hetephras's house. Setting him on a bench, she unfurled his pallet. Helping him lie down, she covered him with some light skins that had belonged to the old priestess. Did her lips graze his? He was not even aware when she left . . .

It seemed like hours later when he woke, but not much time could have elapsed, judging from the omnipresent din of the village. Somewhere a child wailed. From around the corner came the sawing of wood, a carpenter working late into the night. Someone doused a cooking fire, its loud sizzle accompanied by clouds of acrid smoke. Words of conversations too distant to be clearly understood floated to him in the dark, punctuated on occasion by the odd, shrill laugh. He heard a group of men, whispering, their heavy tools clanking together in the night. The men were soon gone, apparently going down a side alley.

How did these tomb-makers sleep, Semerket wondered, so tightly packed together for all of their lives? It was a wonder they did not murder each other more often.

And then, from somewhere close by, he caught the sounds of a couple arguing, their voices scarring the dark. He fought to keep slumber at bay, straining to listen, and their angry words came to him in slurred phrases, like screams from hyenas.

". . . gave it to me . . . Why not? You never . . . stingy, good-for-nothing—"

". . . imbecile!"

". . . talking to Khepura again . . . don't care . . . leaving you! . . . across the river!"

There was a sharp slap. An outraged wail in the dark, then the sounds of a real physical fight commenced. Punches and more slaps. Curses. Oaths. Silence. Semerket was about to drift off, but then there came to him different sounds.

The sounds of a couple making love.

He jolted awake again. What strange people these tomb-makers are, Semerket thought. Yet even the sounds of furtive lovemaking could not keep sleep at bay. His ka strained to flee his body. With a long sigh he let it loose and closed his eyes.

WHETHER IT WAS his profound exhaustion or because he was in a strange place, wakefulness and sleep soon became blurred. Sometime after the fifth hour, when the village was at its most quiet, Semerket finally slipped into something resembling slumber.

Only moments later, however, he gave a great start, his ka rushing to rejoin him, his eyes jerking open. He had heard something—the latch on Hetephras's door being opened.

Fiercely he quieted his heart, willing it to beat at a more subdued tattoo. Concentrating, he heard nothing more than the noises he expected to hear at night in the desert. A kite-bird whistled high above. Somewhere a cow lowed in a distant paddock. A vole, or maybe a scorpion, scuttled nearby. He closed his eyes once again, convinced that he had heard nothing out of the ordinary.

But just as sleep began to pluck once more at his eyelids, he heard a different noise—the deep, primordial breathing of some huge beast, too low to even register as a sound. Semerket sat up, staring into the dark, hearing the sonorous panting growing louder as it came into the house through the front door. Semerket's ears grew numb with fear as a feral animal reek oozed into the room, bringing with it the rank and bloody odor of the hunt.

Silently, Semerket threw back the skins. In three strides he was at his small sack of belongings. Throwing it open, careful not to make a noise, he felt about in the dark for his curved knife. The weapon would provide little protection, but it was all he had.

The knife was not there.

Only then did he remember that Naia had taken it from him on the night of the festival, when he had howled his drunken rage and grief at her door.

He tried to call out for help, but his throat was so constricted by fear he managed no more than an absurd croak. Semerket peered into the dark, trying to find a weapon, anything, with which to defend himself. Then he saw her, and froze.

The lioness entered the room, rubbing her spine against the lintel like any ordinary house cat. In the dark, its coat emitted a kind of golden light. Semerket saw her clearly now, muscles taut beneath her fur, long strands of red saliva stringing from her fangs.

Death has come for me, he thought; this is what it looks like.

Though he had sought death so keenly just a short time before, every part of him now shrieked for his life. He didn't want to die like this, torn to pieces by fang and claw. He backed slowly away from her. Her yellow eyes glittered, and the lioness lowered herself into a crouching stance. Slowly she advanced on him.

He ran—to the rear of the house, past the kitchen, to the stairway leading to the roof. The lioness snarled and leapt after him. Semerket climbed swiftly. He was on the roof of the village now, emerging into the most profound darkness he had ever experienced. No moon lit the sky. Taking refuge behind a huge urn used to collect rain water, he waited. His eyes began to pick out bits of detail—the distant torches at the village's southern gate, the outline of a Medjay tower beyond, and farther away the fires of Eastern Thebes, throbbing on the other side of the river.

The communal roof over the village was a patchwork quilt of many differing levels; occasionally a small second story had been added to some of the homes. He thought if he could just sprint to one of them, he could pound on the doors for help.

But then he saw that the lioness had somehow silently scaled the side of the building from below, to perch on the top of the small wall that surrounded Hetephras's home. He could hear the lioness's low, even panting, like the scrape of millstones. Slowly he peeked at her from behind the urn.

She saw him, and dropped to the roof from the wall. She was going to leap—

A prayer suddenly bubbled up to Semerket's lips, one that every Egyptian child spoke upon waking from a nightmare. "Come to me, Mother Isis! Behold, I am seeing what is far from my city!"

The lioness sprang with a terrible roar. Semerket threw his arms over his head, falling onto the roof, waiting for the kiss of her teeth—

The impact of cat and man never occurred. In the ensuing silence, Semerket forced himself to peer from beneath his clenched hands. He was again in Hetephras's house, atop his bedroll. Behind him, there was a slight noise. He whirled around with a gasp. It was a house cat, obviously a pet, for it did not shy away from him.

Semerket, breathing hard, lay back down on his pallet. It had been a dream, probably the trick of wine vapors still festering in his blood. His breathing became calmer, and he laughed out loud.

A dream lion, nothing more.

The cat came over to snuggle beside him on his bedroll. He fell asleep to the rumble of its purrs.

THE KNOCKING WOKE HIM. Dazed, he shook his head to clear it of cobwebs. What hour was it? Glancing up through the clerestory windows to the slit of sky above, he found the sun impossibly high overhead. He sprang to his feet, and the cat leapt away, accompanying him to the courtyard.

Khepura waited for him a few steps down the alley. "I'm here to tell you that the elders are assembled at Neferhotep's house," she said, "to consider your request to question the villagers."

"Request?" he asked. He was still half in the land of sleep. He thought it odd that a directive from the vizier should be considered a request.

"You said you wanted to meet them," she went on accusingly. "I heard you myself."

"Yes, but—" He was irritated. Nevertheless it was probably best not to appear too high-handed. At that moment the cat slipped through the door, heading in the direction of the kitchens.

"Sukis!" cried Khepura. "She's come back!" The cat turned and regarded the head woman with palpable scorn.

"Last night, in fact. She gave me quite a start, too."

"She was Hetephras's cat. We haven't seen her since the priestess went missing." She bent to scratch the beast's ears, but it shied from her hand, backing into a corner and hissing. "Sukis! What's the matter with you?" said Khepura, offended. The cat ran down the corridor.

Shrugging, Khepura turned again to Semerket. "Well, are you coming?"

"I'll be there," he said. The head woman walked back down the narrow main street, in the direction the cat had gone. Then Semerket remembered and yelled after her, "Khepura—?"

She did not turn around, merely saying over her shoulder, "Five houses down, at the end of the alley."

Moments later he was standing in Neferhotep's dark front room. Seven men waited for him, none of them very old despite their designation as "elder." They gravely told him they were the elected heads of the village clans. Khepura as head woman had a place on the council as well, along with Neferhotep as chief scribe. Khepura informed them that she would speak for the absent Paneb, who was at the royal tomb, and proceeded to do so. "Paneb opposes any investigation into the village," she declared.

Semerket raised an eyebrow. "Why should he?"

"It's an insult, that's why," Khepura said flatly. "To believe that any of us had anything to do with such a crime . . ." Her nostrils flared with indignation. Though she meant her expression to connote dignified outrage, she resembled nothing so much at that moment as an irate water buffalo caught in a thicket. "It was some brigand or other criminal who murdered Hetephras—if that's what really happened—not any of us from the village."

"It's strange," Semerket said, almost to himself, "I would have thought that Paneb would be the first to demand an inquiry."

One of the elders coughed, a man smeared with slurry stains. "I am Sneferu, potter to Pharaoh," he introduced himself quietly, leaning forward. "Why do you say that Paneb should desire this inquiry?"

Semerket was surprised the situation needed explaining. "Because Hetephras was his aunt, for one thing," Semerket said.

Sneferu looked sideways at the other elders. They fidgeted uncomfortably for a moment and then broke into soft chuckles. Noticing Semerket's shocked expression, they immediately resumed their sober demeanors. "But we are all nephews of poor Aunt Hetephras," Sneferu said.

Semerket blinked.

Sneferu held his hands wide, attempting to explain. "Oh, he was her true nephew by blood. But as tomb-makers we've rarely been allowed to leave here, and so we marry our cousins. In this village, we're all related in some way or another."

The elders grunted to show their approval of Sneferu's words.

The sun had reached midheaven, and the temperature had climbed with it. Looking away, Semerket spied Hunro at the doorway of a distant room, listening. He nodded a surreptitious greeting. She instantly stepped back into the concealing darkness.

"Yet the vizier sent me here to make an inquiry and I must insist on it." Semerket stood up from the bench, crossing his arms in front of him.

Neferhotep deftly interrupted. "Please, please—don't be hasty. We're not forbidding this investigation. Not at all." He looked around with a glance, letting his sharp gaze rest significantly on Khepura. "But we have our traditions, too. All we're saying is that we must debate the issue together as elders. Even the vizier will understand this."

Semerket was nonplussed. Never before had he encountered so phlegmatic a crowd, particularly one that had only recently learned that a relative had been brutally slain. Usually the victim's relations would be screaming for vengeance at the tops of their lungs in some public place. Suspicion flooded through him.

"How long, do you think," he asked, "before Hetephras's angry spirit howls through this village, seeking vengeance?" A note of incredulity crept into his voice. "Ghosts of murder victims are the angriest spirits of all. They vex your crops, cause illness in your children. They can even stopper the gods' ears against your prayers. Why do you risk it?"

Sneferu was about to say something, but Khepura coldly cut in be-

fore he could speak. "Hetephras's spirit will understand the need for
the elders to debate this issue, even if you do not." Her clipped voice
was dismissive. "Why, she was gone three days before any of us even
knew she was missing, and in that time no ghost—" Khepura's words
dissolved into silence. She had said too much and looked desperately at
Neferhotep to rescue her.

Semerket's eyes were black isinglass. "She was gone three days before you noticed she was missing?"

No one said a word.

"When did you report her disappearance?"

Again, no one spoke. Semerket had his answer. "You mean . . . no
one *did* report it."

Khepura was the first to recover her speech. "You needn't be so accusing," she said. "Hetephras tended shrines all over these hills. It was
commonplace, her being gone so long."

One of the elders spoke up, his enthusiasm getting the better of
him. "Why, before the gods afflicted her with blindness, we often didn't
see Hetephras for weeks at a time."

Khepura winced at his words, her lips forming silent curses. Neferhotep cupped his head in his hand. Seeing their reactions, the elder
who had spoken became confused. "What?" he asked. "What did I say?"

"She was *blind*?" Semerket's black eyes shone harshly.

"But this is no secret," the elder insisted defensively. "Everyone
knew it!"

"I want to understand this," Semerket said quietly. "A blind old
lady—your aunt—wanders the hills for three days with everyone
knowing about it—and not one of you thought to inquire after her
when she didn't come home?"

The elder clapped his mouth shut. He suddenly understood the import of what he had burbled.

"It was Rami's job to accompany her," said Khepura into the void.
"But don't blame him. When he arrived at her house that day, she had
already gone up the mountain. Hetephras could be very stubborn, you
know."

Neferhotep at last spoke up, smiling apologetically. "This is all very
interesting, but I'm afraid I can't allow this line of questioning to continue, friend Semerket—not until after the elders have debated."

Semerket shot the scribe an irritated glance. "When will you have debated?"

"Tomorrow, or by the end of this week," Neferhotep answered. "No later."

SEMERKET WENT WALKING through the Place of Truth, which is what the tomb-makers had named their small town. Though prevented from opening his formal inquiry, he could still do a bit of exploration on his own. The tomb-makers were chary of him, but no one challenged his reason for being there. Nevertheless he let the vizier's seal swing prominently on his chest to discourage any potential confrontations.

He first made a mental map of the village. By pacing from end to end he estimated that it held about a hundred families, each house sharing walls with its neighbor's. He also noticed that some families, including Hunro, had added a second story to their home.

Semerket tried to imagine what the Place of Truth would look like from a hawk's point of view. It would be a single building shaped like an immense tortoise, he fancied, with tapered ends and a wide middle. The crooked main street he stood in, so narrow he could touch both walls, was its spine, and the multiple alleyways that led to the east and west were its ribs. The roofs, being flat and uneven, were the plates on the beast's gigantic shell.

Retracing his steps, he realized that he was being pursued. Hetephras's cat, Sukis, followed him through the streets. When he paused to gaze around at the sights, she paused with him, sitting down to assiduously groom her yellow coat. He bent to stroke her, and she wound herself around his ankles, mewing.

The clack of a shuttle emanating from an alley caught his ear, and he followed the sound. Glyphs painted on the wall above the doorway proclaimed the place to be "Mentu's Shrouds." He and Sukis went to the door. The woman at the loom didn't even look up at him as he peered inside. A young girl, probably her daughter, helped to feed the linen thread from a spool. The shuttle in the woman's hand flew from left to right and back again, so fast that Semerket could not see it clearly. The pure white thread the girl unwound was so fine as to seem nonexistent. The cloth that fell from the loom to the floor was mist.

A cacophony of hammers banging against metal next drew his attention. In a stall farther down the alley he spied Sani the goldsmith, Khepura's husband, carefully polishing the face of a golden mask. All around him Sani's assistants—his sons, by the look of their identical silhouettes—were hammering golden ingots into papyrus-thin sheets. Semerket moved closer to examine the mask Sani polished and was startled to see the face of Pharaoh Ramses III himself. On a table behind Sani stood the nemes crown of striped gold and lapis that would later be riveted to the mask to form a seamless whole. It was blasphemy for Egyptians to even imagine Pharaoh dead in his tomb—but there before him was the mask that would be fitted to his mummy.

Semerket dropped his eyes, overcome, feeling that he looked upon something too sacred, too awful, to be so casually observed. Yet outside the stall, people passed Sani's workshop, intent on their own errands, not even slowing to look inside. Only Semerket was unnerved, it seemed, and he and Sukis hurried on.

From up and down the alley, in every doorway, came the sounds of industry—hammers, the clank of an anvil being struck, the rasp of saws, voices shouting instructions. Semerket felt crushed by all the activity, almost asphyxiated by it. He walked blindly to where the public kitchens were located, near the village gates. As he came closer, a strong aroma of fat and oil overtook him. He followed the swarms of flies that were arriving in great black clouds, drawn to the smell as he was. Sukis disappeared in the direction of the stables, hoping no doubt for a drop of sheep's milk.

Semerket came around another corner and saw servants trussing a side of beef. He was taken by surprise—Pharaoh was indeed generous to his workers if this was how he fed them. To eat roasted beef on a regular workday was rare anywhere in Egypt, and he decided that not only was such richness odd, it was disturbing.

Semerket had seen how the women went about with gold and silver sparkling in their hair, or draped in ropes of precious stones and wearing collars set with jewels. The weave of their dress was of royal quality, tightly pleated and embroidered in dizzying patterns. The men, too, wore rich armbands of copper and bronze, and their work garments were of expensive linen. These villagers would have stood out even in

Eastern Thebes, where the nobles constantly vied to outdo one another in the richness of their dress. There were no beggars in the village, either, and this too was disquieting. Cripples or victims of wars, accidents, and famine, those poor unfortunates who haunted every corner of Egypt, were nowhere to be seen.

The entire village seemed faked somehow, like one of those model towns or farms that people took with them into their tombs, perfect and idealized in every detail. Everyone seemed whole and young, healthy and rich. The paint on their houses was fresh, the walls repaired, and no sorrow was allowed to live there. The village of the tomb-makers seemed a wizard's creation. Any minute Semerket expected the place to vanish, leaving wind-blown sand in its place.

Nothing could be so perfect.

The shadows were very long when he and the sand-colored cat traveled the main street back to Hetephras's house. As usual, the din of the village was deafening, but somehow the plaintive notes of a harp came to him. Following the music, he was surprised to see that it was Hunro who plucked at the instrument. She was seated in her front room with her back to him, nestled on cushions, and Semerket ventured the few steps to her door to listen.

With a painful thud in his heart, Semerket recognized the tune as a favorite of Naia's, an ancient folk melody from the Faiyum, the huge oasis that was at Egypt's center. Hunro began to sing:

> Waterwheels cry to me,
> And seven geese go flying,
> From the dark lands I hear
> That my love is dying.

> Waterwheels cry to me,
> Alone, on an empty bed,
> My love is in the western land
> But still the fires spread.

His eyes blurred as he remembered Naia's lovely low voice, and he backed away slowly. But he accidentally brushed against the door's rattling hasp, and Hunro stopped playing and spun around. Her lips formed a slow smile when she recognized him.

"I didn't know I had an audience," she said.

"I was eavesdropping," he answered, hastily wiping the tears from his eyes. "I'm sorry. I should have said something." He withdrew another step back into the alley. "You play very well."

"There's not much else for me to do around here, really, other than to strum my life away." She stretched, playing a languid arpeggio on the strings. "I don't have a profession like most of the women here."

"Certainly your family occupies your time . . ." Semerket indicated the house behind her, implying with a gesture the grievous amount of work it required.

She shook her head. "Only my youngest, Rami, is left at home now, and he's off with his girl most nights. Now that he's almost fifteen, he'll be married and in his own home soon. As for my husband, he's gone tonight, too."

Semerket raised his brow. "Where?"

"Is that an official question?" Her eyes were veiled, but she laughed, too. "He's across the river, in the eastern city. He'd probably kill me for telling you that, but I don't care." She looked away.

"I thought everyone here was restricted to this side of the river."

"Oh, he and Paneb go over there all the time—in their 'official capacity'—every few weeks or so." She broke off, and took a long breath. "And so I stay here and practice my harp." She began to idly pick out the song again, humming its refrain, "Waterwheels cry to me . . ."

"Sing something else," he said harshly.

"Why?" she asked innocently, her fingers continuing to pluck at the strings. Then she laughed in a heartless way, utterly surprised. "Look at that—you're crying!"

"No."

"Yes!" And she laughed again, remorseless. "I see the tears on your lashes. Imagine, the hard-nosed vizier's man moved to tears by my singing."

"The song was my wife's favorite."

She stopped playing to casually pick at an imaginary flaw in her sheath. "Wife . . . ?"

"Not anymore," he said.

A tiny but ferocious smile played about the corners of her mouth. "Did she die?"

"We divorced."

"Ah," she sighed, as if his words explained everything. "You beat her."

"No."

"You slept with other women, I suppose."

"No!"

"Then what a fool she was."

"She wanted children."

This made her reflect for a moment. "And you couldn't . . . ?"

He shook his head.

"Believe me," she said, "some women might find it one of your strongest allurements." She turned again to her harp. Her cruel fingers picked out the waterwheel tune, and defiantly she sang the words, "'My love is in the western land, but still the fires spread . . .'" She stopped again. "What do you think they mean, those words? They seem silly to me."

"It's a song from the Faiyum."

"I've heard it's entirely overgrown with green there," she sighed. "How I should love to see such a wonder."

"Huge waterwheels carry the water far into the countryside. All day long they creak and groan. Some people think it sounds like a woman wailing for her lover."

"But if there's so much water, then how can fires spread? It's stupid." She plucked out the refrain again.

Semerket suddenly wrenched the harp from her, dropping it on the cushions with a discordant twang. "Some fires can never be quenched," he said roughly. He hovered over her, close, breathing tightly. Leaning slowly back into the cushions, Hunro stared into his black eyes.

"Never?" she said. Then she laughed, picking up her harp again.

IN HETEPHRAS'S HOUSE, he set about to systematically create an inventory of the priestess's possessions, searching for anything that might help him know her better, and by that perhaps determine who her enemies might have been.

He was in the priestess's sleeping room when he found the box hidden beneath a blanket where Sukis lay. Shooing the offended cat away, Semerket took the chest into the reception room and held it up into the shaft of light coming from the high window. On its lid black ravens of agate flew through the vines, snatching at grapes of lapis lazuli. Grape leaves of pear wood lay tattered on the ground, and beneath them mice and dung beetles fought over the grapes the raven had dropped.

Semerket held his breath while he ran his fingers over the inlaid woods and stones. The more he stared at the box, the more awestruck he became, not just at the chest's shimmering colors and the perfection of its workmanship, but at the artist's eye that could conceive such a work.

It was a poem, this box, and a sad one.

More than depicting a simple rustic scene, the work was about life itself, how beauty and perfection are inevitably destroyed by the chaotic evils that assail them. As he turned the box in his hands, he saw glyphs of bone inlaid in the dark wood on its bottom panel. "I, this box, belong to Hetephras, made by Djutmose, cupboard-maker to Pharaoh, her husband."

Semerket allowed himself a moment to imagine this Djutmose stealing a moment or two in the evenings to work on this gift for his wife. It was plain to see that Djutmose had poured all his affection for Hetephras into it, and that he had also foreseen how time would inevitably rob them both of the moment's joy.

Semerket thought of the things he had given Naia over the course of their marriage. Nothing so lovely as this box. He remembered how once she had wanted a rare flowering cactus that grew high on a cliff in the desert, but he had not been inclined to scale the heights for it.

Carefully he placed the chest again in the corner of the room. As the noises of evening came to him in the chill desert air, he marveled how fate had delivered him to this place. It was an enchanted city, where beauty was the legal tender. Strangest of all, the tomb-makers took it as much for granted as other Egyptians regarded well water, or bread.

Semerket almost hoped that he would not find Hetephras's murderer among them. If he did, he could only play the role predicted on the lid of Hetephras's chest, the raven who spoiled the grapes, the defiler of perfection. The tomb-makers lived in an isolation of privilege and confinement; if Hetephras's killer was among them, Semerket was sure to become the breath of air that would burst it apart.

Disturbed, he scooped the cat into his arms, where she nestled, comforting him by her purrs.

SEMERKET WENT TO Medjay Qar's tower after sunrise. He found the Medjay crouching naked at its base, sluicing water over himself from a jug. Semerket had come to realize just how scarce water was in the tomb-makers' village, for no wells or springs were to be found near the Great Place; the whole land was as dry and desiccated as the mummies entombed there. Every day, teams of donkeys bore the tomb-makers' water up the steep trail from the distant Nile.

"I see you value cleanliness over thirst," Semerket said in a friendly tone as he approached the Medjay.

Qar stood up, drying his body with a rag. "Does it surprise you," he asked, "that a 'dirty Nubian' cares to wash himself in the mornings?"

"I didn't say that," Semerket said.

Qar grunted. "But like all Egyptians, you thought it."

Semerket's face was bland. "I envy you, knowing what 'all Egyptians' think. It must make things so easy."

Qar dressed quickly, strapping on his armor and fastening his helmet. When he was finished he regarded Semerket warily. "What do you want of me?"

"To show you something, in the Great Place."

Qar's grin was almost a sneer. "Another invisible prince on a flying carpet?"

"Something far more interesting than that," Semerket said, adding coldly, "and if you're lucky, it might even save your post."

Qar reached for his spear. With a nod he indicated that Semerket should lead the way. Together they climbed the path that snaked around the perimeter of the Great Place. When they had gone past the cliffs of red sandstone and entered the valley, they were met by its eerie hush. Their steady footsteps on the pathway sent the loose pebbles tumbling into the valley below. In the silence the cascading stones sounded like an avalanche of boulders.

The sound evoked immediate response from the Medjay towers around the perimeter of the cliffs. At least seven policemen climbed down, spears in hand, to watch them from various points around the valley, and Qar waved his spear at them. Satisfied that the intruders were not enemies, the other Medjays retreated again into their towers. Semerket and Qar continued walking in silence. Vipers sunning themselves on stones hissed at them as they passed, or crawled for cover into the crevices. Scorpions fled before them.

On and on they walked until, finally, Semerket was forced to confess, "I'm baffled. I thought this was the road you arrested me on."

"It is," answered Qar.

"But . . ."

He wanted to show Qar the campsite he had found at the base of the limestone-rubble mound. Semerket had finally decided that if unauthorized persons were entering the valley, it was his duty to tell the Medjays.

Semerket scanned the place slowly, turning around in a full circle. Nothing was familiar. There was no limestone mound, and certainly no campfire. They had vanished into air, as certainly as had the prince astride his donkey. He remembered Mayor Pawero's warning about how the desert was enchanted, the abode of ghosts and demons, and he was slowly coming to believe it.

"I could have sworn . . ." Semerket began apologetically, then stopped.

"Another mirage?" Qar's voice was flat, the kind used by all policemen when confronted with an unreliable witness.

"Apparently."

Qar knelt down to take up some sand in his fingers, letting it flow from his hands slowly to the ground. He gazed down into the valley. "What is it you thought you saw?" he asked.

"A campfire site. There were six torch sticks buried there, fresh ones. I wanted you to know I wasn't the only one to get in here undetected."

Qar pursed his lips, and continued to stare unblinking into the sands below. "And you think the camp was in this canyon?" he asked.

"I'm not sure anymore," Semerket answered ruefully. "There was a mound of limestone shards—behind that crag, I thought." He pointed to the base of a nearby wall of stone soaring upward to the pathway. "It sloped all the way down to the floor."

"Limestone?" asked Qar sharply.

Semerket nodded. "From an excavated tomb." He knelt beside Qar, scratching his chin. "But it seems I'm mistaken. Perhaps I did indeed imagine it."

Qar continued to stare. Then he abruptly straightened up and pointed to a spot on the valley floor. "There," he said.

In the next breath Qar was climbing down the side of the cliff, knowing just where to place his feet against the jutting rocks and crevices. Semerket did not dare follow him, for fear of injury. Instead he ran down the path to a point where it coursed low over the valley, and jumped the short distance to the floor. When he rejoined the Medjay, breathless, Qar had already unearthed some stray pieces of charcoal from the fire's remains. It was all he could find.

"They were here," Qar said. He used his spear to sift through the sand, digging in certain areas. No torch ends revealed themselves.

"How do you know? These are only charcoal pieces; they could have come from any fire made here in the last fifty years. Where are the limestone shavings?" Semerket asked, looking around.

Qar did not speak for a time. He stood and looked in a semicircle all about him, his keen eyes searching every crevice. "They got rid of them," he answered softly. "Poured them back into the tomb."

"They? You mean the tomb-diggers?"

"No tomb has been dug in the Great Place for over thirty years, Semerket, except for Pharaoh's. And his is on the other side of the valley." He spoke reluctantly, as if he were betraying a great secret.

Semerket did not care for the frightened tone of his voice or the expression on his face. "I don't understand—" he began.

Qar thrust his spear again into the earth, not knowing that he did. "Tomb robbers," he breathed, and the words were carried in the air to echo softly against the stone walls. "Tomb robbers have come into the Great Place. They filled up the hole they made with the rubble you saw. That's why the mound is gone."

Semerket swallowed. Tomb robbery was the most serious offense in Egypt, the highest tier in the crime of heresy. If Qar was correct, and the Great Place had indeed been violated, the delicate balance between life and death would be forfeit. The dead pharaohs, who eternally worked for Egypt's well-being in the afterlife, would harden their hearts against the living. Misery and chaos would be the result.

A small but definite click came from the sands at their feet. Qar's spearhead had struck something metallic. For a moment he and Semerket looked at one another dumbly. Then the Medjay was on his knees, furiously digging. When he saw it he instinctively drew back, as if he had uncovered some hideous burrowing insect. Semerket bent to look, and there on the valley floor, shining like a flame upon the sands, was a golden ear loop.

It was Semerket who reached down to retrieve the object. The loop was of gold, an immense and gaudy jewel from a previous dynasty. All around its hammered edge cabochon rubies were inset, a thing of sunlight and blood.

"I AM TO BLAME," said Qar dismally.

High up in the Medjay's tower, he and Semerket ate the dinner brought them by the village servants. The herbs the tomb-makers used were not so sharp that evening, Semerket noted—or else he was getting used to their pungency.

Semerket raised the jar of beer to his lips. "You don't know for certain anything has been stolen."

"The jewel——"

"It could have been there for centuries."

Qar said nothing, as if considering this explanation for the first time. Semerket chewed some dates. "Even if not, how is it your fault?"

Deeply ashamed, Qar coughed, and began tentatively, "That day you came here——?"

"Yes?"

"I was asleep."

Semerket said nothing. He had known.

"This post," Qar continued, "I'm getting too old for it. I'm so tired it's all I can do just to strap on my armor anymore. I tell you, I allowed these robbers to slip into the valley."

Qar's was a difficult confession to make, Semerket knew. No one, man or woman, wanted to admit they had passed their prime. In Qar's case the admission brought with it the knowledge that perhaps his feebleness had allowed a great crime to occur.

Qar went on, not finished with confessions. "And that morning Hetephras went into the hills—the last morning anyone saw her alive?"

"What about it?"

"I slept through that, too. Usually I would check on her during my rounds. That morning I didn't even know she'd come and gone." His voice was very sad.

Semerket let out a long sigh. "What are you going to do?"

Qar considered his answer. "I'll meet with the other Medjays and show them the site you found, and the jewel. Then I'll resign my post. If I'm lucky, I'll get reassigned to some quiet town on the Nile. Who knows?"

Semerket was skeptical. "Why confess to something you don't even know is occurring? What is there, really, to prove a tomb robbery has happened? A few pieces of crumbling charcoal. An earring. Some limestone chips . . ."

"We'll have to examine all the tombs and make a list of their contents."

"That will take years."

"We'll send notice to the Medjays in Eastern Thebes, then, to raid the bazaars. If royal treasure pieces are for sale there, then we'll know there's been a robbery."

Semerket shook his head. "The minute you Medjays appear in the marketplace, any suspicious goods will get tucked neatly away into sacks of grain or vats of olives. You'll never find them."

"What else can we do?"

Semerket thought. "Send someone into the bazaars as an interested buyer. Someone whom the dealers would never suspect. Have him buy a piece—it should be proof enough."

"Who could do this?"

Semerket thought for a moment. Then he answered slowly, "I may know someone." He grimly smiled to himself. He owed his brother something for getting him this position. It would serve Nenry right.

Semerket then recalled the shards of broken pottery he'd collected at the phantom campsite. For some reason, one that he could not even explain to himself, he did not tell Qar of them. Though he and the Medjay regarded one another more amiably since their trek from the valley that first day, they were not yet friends. Let trust come later, he thought.

"Something disturbs me about all this, Qar. Did you ever stop to think that perhaps you're not the only one sleeping on duty?" Semerket asked.

"What?"

"If tomb robbers are afoot," Semerket said, "why didn't the other Medjays hear them digging during the night? Why didn't they know that I had come into the Great Place the other day? And how is it you alone woke to find me?"

Qar was uneasy, and spoke unwillingly. "A dream woke me—a terrible one. A lioness stalked me. The dream seemed so real I could even smell her—the blood on her breath, her scent. I truly thought I was going to die in her claws . . ."

It was not the chill desert air that caused Semerket to shiver then.

"And as she sprang," he asked in a soft voice, "did you wake and say the prayer to Isis for nightmares?"

It was Qar's turn to look amazed.

To Toh, Vizier of the Two Lands, life! health! prosperity! under Pharaoh Ramses III, life! health! prosperity! From Semerket, clerk of Investigations and Secrets, Greetings . . .

Report to the Great Lord in the case of Hetephras, high priestess in the Place of Truth; This is what I have discovered—

Quickly Semerket wrote of how he had learned in the House of Purification that Hetephras had indeed been murdered, on dry land. He did not tell the vizier that he possessed a piece of the axe that had killed her, for he had no way of knowing who else read his reports. Semerket laid down his reed pen and considered what to tell Toh next. He sat cross-legged on the floor of Hetephras's reception room, Sukis's prone form sleeping next to him, a single tallow candle serving as light. Earlier, he had bought a roll of papyrus from Neferhotep, some new reed

pens, and a pot of lamp-black mixed with gum for ink. Now the paper was unrolled before him, the ink watered, and he had chewed the reed pen to the exact point he preferred.

Semerket trimmed the wick of his candle, and picked up the pen again.

From the Council of Elders here at the tomb-makers' village I have learned that the priestess was semi-blind and that she often went alone to attend the local shrines, even in her debilitated state, and often for a stretch of several days. This happened so frequently, the elders say, that no one thought to report her missing.

His thoughts turned to his own reception by the villagers, and how they seemed more concerned about his right to question them than about actually determining who had killed their priestess. Semerket weighed the possibilities. Perhaps Hetephras had been resented in her village, a crone who had unwittingly engineered her own demise with a cruel tongue. But this did not jibe with the image of the pious mother Queen Tiya remembered. Yet again, he could not write of that impression, because it was not a proven fact.

The image of the large and intimidating foreman Paneb loomed in Semerket's mind. Despite his attack on Semerket, Paneb was the only one of these odd tomb-makers whose behavior was comprehensible. Paneb and his aunt must have been close indeed for him to disintegrate so completely upon learning the truth of her death—but Semerket could not write down such a supposition for Toh to read.

Semerket's hand went unwillingly to the bruises on his throat, remembering the thickness of Paneb's fingers there. The same nagging thought picked at his mind: why would the foreman, like the elders, be opposed to finding the killer of his aunt? It simply made no sense, unless—

Semerket sat up, staring into the dark.

Unless Paneb was—unless they all were—protecting the person who had committed the crime.

Moments later, Semerket found himself striding restlessly around Hetephras's home, his letter to Toh abandoned, his mind ablaze. Conspiracies were everywhere. He despaired that he would ever find his

way out of the mare's nests of possibilities. And now this other mystery had come, more disturbing than all the rest—why was the Medjay Qar dreaming of the lioness?

Perhaps it meant nothing, the lioness being only an apt symbol for the tension he and Qar both felt in their day-to-day lives. Semerket stopped his pacing, and sighed. He wrapped himself in Hetephras's light skins, for the desert air was cool.

A scratching on the priestess's door took him unaware. The tallow candle lit his way to the front room.

Hunro waited in the street for him. She was arrayed as he'd never before seen a woman dare clothe herself. Her sleek shift was dyed the radiant color of pomegranate, a color reserved for gods and goddesses. Her hair was spangled with flecks of gilded wax. Her face was painted like those of the goddesses in temples, her eyes extended by antimony and malachite, and on her cheeks she had daubed circles of ochre. The heavy scent of sandalwood enveloped him.

Semerket's tongue instantly cleft to his mouth, refusing to move.

"Let me in and close the door," she said impatiently. "Or the neighbors will gossip."

Instead of doing as she said, Semerket pushed the door open even wider so that all could see inside.

Hunro smiled defiantly and walked past him into Hetephras's front room. "Can it be you're afraid of me?"

Semerket nodded.

Hunro affected a little moue of hurt. "It doesn't please a woman to hear she frightens a man, because then that thing beneath his loincloth becomes shriveled and useless."

She drew nearer to him, but he backed away again. "I fear your husband, as well," he said.

"Neferhotep?" Hunro chortled. "Don't fear a mouse—rather fear the lion, Paneb." His expression once again made her roll her eyes in exasperation. "How do you think we amuse ourselves in this dreary little place? If it weren't for the sin of adultery, we'd all go mad."

"You more than most, I think."

Her high, sandy voice was laced with defiance. "I'm an honest woman in that respect—more than most, I think."

"Why did you come here?"

"I came to tell you," she said with a sigh, "that the elders have agreed to allow you to question the villagers. You can begin whenever you like."

He looked at her with skepticism. "And you came here to tell me, dressed like that?"

Her brow was knitted with hurt, and her voice was like a small feather. "What's wrong with the way I'm dressed? Most men find me beautiful when I robe myself like a goddess. Don't you?"

Again his tongue became unusable, and he only nodded.

Cooing a little trill, she pressed herself against him. Despite the cool night air, he began to sweat. "If you think me so beautiful, why don't you make love to me then?" she asked, and sought his lips with hers. They kissed for how long Semerket did not know. He was surprised to find himself so aroused. Summoning all his resolve, however, he firmly pushed her away.

The gold in her hair shimmered as she shook her head in disbelief. After a time she said to him, "If you will not have my body, then—for I am obviously only a withered and ugly hag to you—what about my mind?"

"What about it?"

"What if I told you I know things?"

He blinked. "About . . . ?"

"About this place, its secrets."

"If you do know something, it's your duty to tell it officially, for the record."

She laughed again, amused by his naïveté. "Others around here might have a different idea about what my duty is."

"Tell it for Hetephras's sake then, for the old woman that everyone seems to have forgotten."

At the mention of the old priestess's name, Hunro's painted mouth became a gash in her face. "It's true she was kind to me, about the only woman around here who was. And I'm not the sort who forgets her friends, despite what people may say." Semerket was amazed at how quickly Hunro changed when the spark of desire was not in her. She seemed suddenly old and defeated, the paint on her face becoming caked and cracked. "But since I never give away my favors for nothing, I will tell you this, and put it on account."

She leaned forward and whispered in his ear. "Do you know why the elders needed two days of 'deliberation' before you could question the others?"

"Because of your tradition of debating the issue—"

She laughed. "There is no such tradition. But that's all I will say, Semerket. Unless . . ."

He took a step nearer. "Unless . . . what?"

"I am wealthy," she said urgently. "From gifts I made the men give me to sleep with them—every one a stone to make a bridge across the river. Take me there. I don't know the city; you do. You'll never want for anything again, I promise. We can live in luxury there. And I'll give you love like you've never known it before—" She would have brought her lips again to his, but he moved aside, staring into the dark.

"Look elsewhere, Hunro," he said. "Luxury has no appeal for me. And I would never take a man's wife from him, for I know the other side of it."

Hunro stared at him. "What a fool you are. I could drive that wife of yours from your mind. I could turn your skin to ashes if I wanted. And I could make you a rich man in the doing of it." She pushed open the door, looked back at him, and then walked swiftly down the alley.

That night on his pallet he could not rid himself of the memory of her words. But it was not the tantalizing hints and clues she'd given him regarding the tomb-makers that kept him awake. He remembered only the press of her flesh against him, the curve of her belly and the feel of her breasts. He thrashed about in misery for long minutes in the dark, and in the end resorted to that solitary gesture by which Atum begat the entire world.

IT WAS NEAR DAWN when he heard a whisper at Hetephras's door. "Semerket!"

Qar, waiting for him in the avenue, put a finger to his lips. When they had taken themselves inside, away from the street and from those who might hear them, Qar said quietly, "I've just come from a secret meeting of the Medjays."

Semerket nodded, waiting.

"I told them of my sleeping sickness." Instead of being desolate, he was smiling. Sukis leapt to the Medjay's lap, and he stroked the cat idly. "What do you think? It only needed my confession for the others to admit they suffer from it as well. Always on the same nights—when there is no moon."

"How is that possible?" Semerket asked.

"Can't you guess? Someone drugs our food," Qar said balefully. "It would be easy. Our meals are all prepared in the village kitchens by the servants, and then brought to us individually. Anyone could do it."

Semerket's eyes widened and he bent close to Qar, whispering, "But for what gain?"

Qar exhaled in a great, sad gust. Irritated, Sukis jumped from his lap to the tiles and headed to the kitchen, hopeful for mice. "What better time to rob a tomb than when the Medjays are sleeping? What better night than when no moon lights the Great Place?"

Semerket considered, and then said aloud, "'Where the god-skin is made . . . when Khons hides his face.'"

Qar looked at him. "What are you saying?"

"It's what the boy told me there in the Great Place, remember? The prince you said didn't exist. He spoke of gold being made when there was no moon."

Qar shook his head. "It still doesn't make sense. You can mine gold. Hammer it. Grind it into dust if you want. But you can't *make* it." Then in the dark he inhaled sharply. "But you can *re*-make it . . ."

Semerket shook his head, not understanding.

"Long ago," Qar explained quickly, "a series of tombs in the Place of Beauty were robbed. The thieves didn't need to disturb the seals on the tombs' doors—they dug straight into the queens' tombs, from the top, then burned it all. When the flames died, all they had to do was gather the pools of melted gold from beneath the ashes. That's how we caught them—melting the bigger pieces in a jar."

At that, Semerket remembered the shards of broken pottery wrapped in his cape, the blackened pieces shattered by fire—and the traceries of gold in their cracks. He had believed the gilding to be some kind of design, or writing, but if what Qar believed was true, its meaning could be far more sinister.

"We've agreed that on any given night one of us Medjays will not eat," Qar was saying. "He'll raise the alarm if he sees anyone suspicious go into the Great Place. Obviously, someone from the village is behind it."

"Who?"

Qar shook his head. They pondered for a few moments in silence. Then the Medjay spoke. "What I've really come here to ask is this—can you have that person you mentioned begin to search the bazaars for royal jewels?"

"Yes."

"Good man," Qar said. He walked back toward the night-shrouded alley. "And Semerket—be careful what you eat. Your food, too, is prepared in the kitchens. The Medjays agreed that it's only a tiny step from making us sleep the night to making us sleep forever."

Semerket felt his scalp tingle.

"One thing more . . ." Qar's voice was suddenly hesitant, and he sighed again before he spoke. "We dream of lions. All of us."

Noiselessly Qar closed the door behind him.

SNEFERU LOOKED UP from his potter's wheel. Semerket loomed in the doorway with a heavy bundle, which he placed on the ground. Like many of the other artists, Sneferu used a makeshift wooden shed at the village's northern gate as a workshop. It was located next to the cistern where the donkey train unloaded the village's daily supply of water, sparing Sneferu from having to tote heavy jars back and forth from the cistern to his home.

Sneferu let his wheel slow, and squeezed a dripping sponge over the half-formed bowl that was spinning on it. From experience he knew that visits from Semerket were long and arduous, and that the bowl must be kept moist.

"Semerket, good friend," Sneferu attempted a cheery tone, "why have you come here? Have you decided that I murdered Hetephras?"

With a grunt Semerket untied the ends of the woolen sack and up-ended it. Fragments of charred black pottery spilled out in a heap, the ones he had found in the abandoned campsite in the Great Place.

"I've broken this jar that belonged to Hetephras."

"Hetephras? I don't recall her owning any such—"

"Can you fix it? I don't wish to offend her spirit."

Sneferu nodded. "If all the pieces are there, yes, I can mend it for you."

"I thought it would be best to bring it to you, as you probably made it . . . ?" If Sneferu replied affirmatively, then Semerket would know that the campsite had been attended by someone from the village, that the pieces were not from some ancient fire kindled centuries before.

But Sneferu shook his head. "Perhaps when it's together again, I'll be able to tell."

"When will it be ready?"

"So many pieces here, my own business being so full—I've no assistant, you know—"

"How long?"

"A few weeks."

Semerket took a gold piece from his belt and laid it on the counter. "I'll match this if you can make the repair faster," he said.

But the potter let the gold ring simply lie there, not looking at it. "I'll get to it when I can, friend Semerket," he said, "as I've told you." He turned his attention back to his wheel.

When Semerket left the workshop, the potter took the gold into his palm and sniffed.

ACROSS THE RIVER, in Eastern Thebes, the smoke of sacrifice twined silkily into the sky, rising in a thin black smudge from Sekhmet's temple. It was early morning and the temple fires blazed, hungry for the first of the sacrificial victims to be offered.

Nenry's wife, Merytra, waited at the edge of the crowd of acolytes, clutching a piece of crumpled papyrus in her hands. She shifted her weight nervously from side to side, her myriad bracelets jingling each time she did. Her eyes found her great-uncle, the Lord High Priest Iroy, as he prayed silently to Sekhmet.

The acolytes drew apart as the first bull was led to the altar. The beast walked placidly up the stairs to where Iroy and his priests waited. There, the animal nodded its head, signifying that it went willingly to its death. Merytra knew this to be an old trick caused by the priests flicking holy water into the bull's ears.

Just as one priest stunned the bull with a hammer blow to its skull, her great-uncle deftly slit its throat with a large bronze knife. The bull fell to its knees, emptying its bowels convulsively upon the altar, its steaming blood coursing over Iroy's hands. The salty, ferrous smell of blood and the acrid smell of shit rose in his niece's nostrils. At the altar Iroy cupped the blood in his hands; he then carried it to the goddess's garments, patting them down. The robes clung redly to Sekhmet's stone breasts, picking out the goddess's nakedness beneath.

The sun glistened on the altar of white marble, suffusing the temple with a bright, blinding light, and Merytra was momentarily stupefied by it. She began to feel faint. Sickly haloes vibrated at the periphery of her vision, and the reedy music of the piping priestesses screeched eerily in her head.

She stood mutely as Iroy drizzled roasted barleycorns over the lifeless bull, which was the tradition. His attendants began to expertly flay the black hide from its flesh, then hacked the beast's haunches from the carcass with glinting silver axes.

The fatty thighbones were handed to the high priest, who set them upon the sacred fire, when they sizzled and spat as the flames leapt to devour them. The oozing blood ran over the marble altar to pool in a specially contrived font in the ground.

Merytra fainted.

She awoke in her uncle's sanctuary, nauseous, with the taste of bile in her mouth. "What . . . ?" she asked.

She was answered by a long, low growl. A lioness stood over her, sniffing at her suspiciously. She screamed. The cat took a step back, uncertain of this shrieking thing before it, and cowered behind the legs of the man who held its leash.

"There, there, Tasa," the man said in low comforting tones to the beast, scratching its head. "It's only my silly niece."

"Take it away!" Merytra pleaded.

"I would advise you to stop screaming, Grandniece. Tasa will begin to think you're just something to play with, and it's difficult to stop her when mischief is on her mind."

The high priest resembled his niece, down to his wide nose and slanting eyes. But where such features made her seem ungainly and mannish, her great-uncle was handsome, still virile and strong despite his age, though he had begun to run slightly to fat.

Iroy's sanctuary was a small room located behind the Holy of Holies where the goddess resided. On the walls, skins of lions stretched taut. A profusion of votive statues depicting the lion goddess were placed around the room, some cast in gold and other precious metals, some carved in stone, donations of warriors anxious to curry the war goddess's favor.

"So why have you come to see me today?" her uncle asked indulgently. He handed Tasa's leash to a junior priest, with tender instructions for her feeding, and the lioness was at last removed from the sanctuary.

"It's Nenry!" Merytra's words came out in a petulant wail. "He struck me!"

Iroy sat on his throne, cleaning the blade of his sacrificial knife with a soft cloth. He chuckled. "Good for him. You should be struck often, my dear. I told him that when he married you."

She hid her face behind her arm, great tears oozing from her eyes. Her head pounded.

Iroy sighed. He had always been a trifle embarrassed by his dead nephew's offspring, preferring to keep Merytra from his sight. He settled back on his chair, bored by her trivial marital concerns. But his niece's next words made him sit up at attention.

"I know his brother, Semerket, is behind it," she said.

His usually languid voice became very clipped. "What of him?"

"He's investigating the murder of a priestess, over in Western Thebes—"

"I've heard of it. Go on."

"A message came from him last night—this one—" She handed her uncle the wrinkled sheet of papyrus. "He's trying to get Nenry involved in something he shouldn't. When I tried to intervene, Nenry hit me. For the first time in our marriage." Her tears flowed in earnest now. "This morning after he left, I stole the note to show you. I want you to stop him, Great-uncle! I know whatever that madman asks him to do, it will somehow threaten us."

Quickly Iroy scanned the letter, running a hennaed thumbnail over the glyphs as he read.

To my brother, Nenry, health and life be yours! From Semerket, clerk of Investigations and Secrets, greetings:

Brother, I need the help you promised. Go into the marketplace. Wear a noble's disguise. Put it about that you seek royal jewels. Assure them that you care not from where they come. Buy one or two if they are offered. When you have done so, bring them to me across the river. I will explain the rest in person. Semerket, your own brother.

Iroy put the papyrus aside. "Do you know what this says?" he asked in his clipped, harsh tones.

"N-no." She did not know how to read.

"Has Nenry departed from his usual routine?"

"Yes! Yes, he has! He sent a message to the mayor saying he was ill. Then he hired rich robes and went into the bazaar—but I don't know why."

A foul oath escaped Iroy's lips. Oddly enough, when he next gazed at his grandniece it was with an expression that bore traces of appreciation. "It could mean nothing; in any event, it's better if you don't mention to Nenry that I've seen this." He held the letter out for her to take. "Put it back where you found it. Say nothing to him."

"Yes, Great-uncle."

His expression eased a bit. "You've done well."

She smiled gratefully. If she had done as well as her uncle had said, perhaps she could venture to ask him . . .

"Great-uncle?"

"Yes?"

"Have you news of my son?" She swallowed. "Does he thrive?"

"*Your* son?"

She nodded.

His irritation was now full-blown. "I have adopted him as my heir. Nenry was given a worthy post for him. It does no good for you to ask after the child—he certainly doesn't ask after you. Leave him alone. The child has a different life now."

She felt both hot and icy at once. Her heart was palpitating. Her viscera churned. For a moment she felt she was going to faint again. Then a sudden warm flush between her legs explained to them both the reason she had fainted that morning. She looked down in dismay to see a small red stain spreading on her sheath.

The shame on her face was evident, and she blushed to see her uncle staring. But he burst out laughing. "Do you think me so naïve concerning the tides of women?" He laughed again. "You're lucky it didn't happen when Tasa was here. The scent of blood makes her remember her wild ways. Now wrap something around you and come with me."

Together they made their way to a pavilion across the temple compound. Iroy begged an urgent and private audience with the seeress of the temple, and both he and Merytra bowed their arms to knee level when she entered the pavilion.

In whispers Iroy told the woman of Semerket's letter. For a long while the seeress said nothing.

Then in a voice that was a magical instrument of many strings, she spoke. "Bad dreams are no longer enough, it seems. We will require something stronger. A cutting of his hair will do."

She looked at Merytra then. "Come near to me, my dear. Let us discuss this situation between your husband and his brother. We women know how to manage these things, don't we?"

Overwhelmed by the woman's majesty, yet curiously attracted to her all the same, Merytra crept forward.

OPEN YOUR
EYES

"No one here would want to harm her," the painter Aaphat said as Semerket sat cross-legged before him, writing notes. "Her body was found on the other side of the river. Why do you question *us*?"

"She was beloved by everyone," softly echoed his wife, Teewa.

"She was kind," murmured their daughter.

They sat together in their small reception room, which Aaphat had vividly decorated with portraits of his neighbors at work. The figures crowded together on the walls, so lifelike that Semerket half-expected them to voice their own opinions about the murder.

Aaphat rose and pointed to the likeness of Hetephras herself, whom he had painted as she made offerings to the moon god, Khons. "Tell me—does she look like a woman with enemies?" he asked.

Semerket examined the portrait closely. Hetephras had been in her prime when the painting was made. Though she wore a wig of bright blue in the painting, Semerket recognized her from her pectoral and the style of the linen sheath she wore, the kind he had seen blood-drenched and crumpled in the House of Purification.

"Nevertheless," said Semerket, "she is dead and someone murdered her."

"Perhaps a foreigner or a vagabond. No one here. We loved her."

Aaphat and his wife lowered their heads to indicate they had no more to tell him.

A quick surveillance of Aaphat's studio told Semerket that whatever tools the painter used, they were not made of the hard blue metal that matched the small chip he kept always in his sash. He never mentioned the chip directly to the tomb-makers—to do so would ensure the axe's quick disposal, if indeed it still existed. But his eyes were ever on the alert for anything made of the same dark metal.

The morning after Hunro told him of the elders' consent, he began his investigation. From home to home he went, always uninvited, asking questions of even the children. But however he phrased his words, however deeply he probed, the villagers made their eyes into blanks and their answers seemed always the same. Nevertheless, he pressed on, believing that if any villager knew something about the murder, he would find it out through simple persistence and repetition.

The sculptor Ramose was chipping at a small statue of diorite when Semerket came upon him in his workshop at the back of the village. From the figure's distinctively shaped wig Semerket saw at once that it was Hetephras, and he said her name aloud.

"Do you recognize her?" asked Ramose, pleased, holding it up so that Semerket could see how finely detailed the figure was.

Semerket nodded, making a note to himself that Ramose sculpted with only copper chisels.

"It will be placed in her tomb, an offering from her neighbors. She was a great lady."

Behind Ramose an immense stone circle of limestone was being smoothed by his sons, Mose and Harach, who also supervised a host of village men-servants. The stone wheel lay on the ground, taking up most of the workshop's length. From time to time, the sons glanced at Semerket from beneath their eyelids coated in fine dust.

"Had she any enemies?" Semerket asked. "Did she indulge in feuds—exchange unpleasant words with anyone?"

"No." Ramose shook his head firmly. "She was kind."

"We loved her," said Mose from across the yard.

"If you ask me," Ramose said, his voice so low and conspiratorial that Semerket had to bend to hear him, "it had to be someone of foreign birth. Or a vagabond. You're wasting your time here in the village asking all these questions. Why don't you go to the other side of the river? She was found there, after all."

"Do you agree with your father?" Semerket barked suddenly to Mose and Harach. They jumped.

"Hetephras was loved," Mose repeated.

"A vagabond or foreigner," seconded Harach.

The young men returned to their task of polishing the wheel; the pumice scraped against the stone like a scream caught in a woman's throat.

Yunet, the woman who embroidered shrouds and robes for the royal court, plied her needle while she answered him, her eyes cast modestly downward. Her three nieces sat beside her in their reception room, clothed in the same intricately pleated white linen their aunt wore, starched so stiffly they seemed to be wearing egrets' wings. The nieces embroidered on the cloth, too, and Semerket found himself staring fascinated as their bronze needles, fine as hair, quickly stitched a constellation of five-pointed stars along its border.

"Hetephras? Enemies?" whispered Yunet. She was a widow, though young-looking. Her many knotted braids were discreetly drawn back into a heavy ebony cluster at the nape of her neck. She wore no jewelry, but her features were even and her lips red. "I had known Hetephras since I was a girl . . . not so very long ago, though you may not think it. No one was kinder or more beloved." Her voice was a gentle breeze.

"When was the last time you saw her?"

Yunet pricked herself suddenly, and sucked the blood from her finger. She gazed at Semerket, considering. "The last time . . . ?" She looked about in pretty distress. "That would be at the Festival of the New Moon, wasn't it?" All of her nieces nodded their agreement. "Just a day or so before her . . . disappearance. She loved the moon god, Khons, above all the others."

"Can you remember what you said to one another?"

She shook her head. "I can't seem to . . ."

Her niece Thuya spoke up clearly, "I remember, Aunt. You sought her advice about Uncle Memnet."

"I thought you said you were a widow." Semerket again checked his notes.

Yunet blushed to the roots of her hairline. "Yes, that's correct."

"Uncle Memnet's ghost comes to Aunt Yunet at night," Thuya continued in the same forceful tone. "He takes the form of a . . . of a . . ." Even she could not go on and solemnly rose from her seat to whisper to Semerket. The word she uttered into his ear sent him into a sudden fit of coughing. One of the other nieces inexpertly stifled a giggle.

Yunet glanced at Semerket with embarrassment. "I believed that after he was in his tomb, he would make no further demands on me. Yet, alas, the women in my family are desired even by the dead." She leaned forward and placed a tender hand on Semerket's knee to emphasize her earnestness.

Semerket abruptly raised his head from his notes to find Yunet and her nieces gazing at him with limpid eyes. None of them any longer stitched at stars. Quickly he rolled up his papyrus scroll, rising from the brick bench.

"We seldom see men from outside this village," breathed Yunet. "It's very . . . stimulating . . . to us poor provincials." Her nieces' heads bobbed with enthusiasm.

"Do you think," Semerket asked in a croaking voice, ". . . er . . . do you suppose that Hetephras could have been the victim of some vengeful ghost, then? An unhappy ancestor?"

One of the nieces spoke up hesitantly. "I hear," she began softly, "that is, it's been said in the village . . ."

Semerket held up a hand to stop her. "Yes, I know—that a foreigner or a vagabond killed her." He nodded his thanks and hurried out of the house before they could invite him to sample their beer.

In the alley Hunro waited for him. She had listened, and laughed to see him undone. "Are you ready now to pay my price?" she whispered to him. "Do you see now that you can learn nothing from these villagers—that I alone can help you?"

He spoke more harshly than he intended. "I might have the soles of your feet beaten with sticks if I thought you were really hiding something," he said. "I have only to command it."

Her reply was the papery rasp of her jeering laughter.

THE FOLLOWING WEEK, Semerket found himself outside the northern gate. He stepped into the sunlight, and followed the path around the village walls to where the tomb-makers' tiny temple stood. He had no purpose for going there, other than to flee the oppressive atmosphere of the village, for its smallness was beginning to grate on him. That, and the fact that every one of his interviews had yielded the same unshakable opinion that a foreigner or vagabond had slain Hetephras. As he drew near the temple, he realized that Sukis had joined him. Tail erect, she led him in the direction of sounds that he realized came from a classroom in session.

Curious, he followed the children's voices to the rear of the temple. In the open air the village children sat cross-legged before a young priest, each clutching a wax tablet and stylus. They were reciting from a text that Semerket recognized—the story of the Snake King and the Lucky Peasant.

As he watched the students, he was glad to see the young priest was not overly fond of using his stick on the children. Nevertheless, like any good teacher, he followed the ancient maxim that a student "learns through his backside," and occasionally lightly whacked a child who flubbed the lesson.

Hearing the noise of the priest's reed cane slashing through the air brought Semerket instantly back to his own school days, for he had often heard the same sound. There had come a day, however, when the teacher had raised his stick once too often and brought it across Semerket's face, breaking open his cheek. A few minutes later, the neighbors were drawn to the schoolroom by the man's plaintive cries, to find the thirteen-year-old Semerket thrashing the man almost to death. It was the first time that he had been called a follower of Set, and his formal education was over. Soon thereafter Semerket became Metufer's assistant in the House of Purification.

"Did you want something?" the young priest in the tomb-makers' school asked.

Semerket shook his head and hurried away. But at the temple gate he stopped again, hearing the familiar voice of the scribe Neferhotep.

Semerket could tell from the scribe's tone that his conversation was acrimonious, though the persons he spoke to were well hidden behind the temple wall. Treading slowly in the deep shadows, keeping to the taller tufts of brown grass, Semerket approached a large boulder and hid behind it. From there his view was unobstructed.

Astonishingly, Neferhotep was speaking to a trio of beggars. Their leader was brown and shaggy, and, as Semerket peered closer, he could see that the man was shorn of his nose and ears—sure signs that he had once been punished for some terrible offense. Even at a distance Semerket caught the beggars' sour, unwashed scent.

He kept to the shadows. Straining to hear, only the sibilant sound of half a word came to him: ". . . meses," Neferhotep said. Creeping closer, hoping to hear more, he was disappointed to find that the scribe and his unlikely companions had reached a satisfactory end to their discussion. Smiles were shared all around the motley group. At that point Neferhotep brought out a large sack from a niche in the temple wall. Whatever its contents, they were weighty, for the scribe staggered as he handed the sack over to the beggars.

Noseless peered inside, staring raptly, and a slow smile spread across his toothless maw. He nodded to Neferhotep and wrapped a cord tightly about the neck of the sack. A final word of farewell and Neferhotep departed quickly for the cliffs above the village. He was no more than a few feet away from where Semerket hid, but the scribe stared only at the ground as he passed and remained oblivious to Semerket's presence.

The beggars still huddled together at the temple wall, talking in low voices. Once, years before, Semerket had been a familiar figure in the murky world of the Beggar King of Thebes, doing him a service in the course of an investigation. In return he had been taught the secret signal that gained him protection in the king's realm.

The beggars jumped apart as he approached, and stood as a human wall in front of the sack. Though Semerket made the secret sign to them with his fingers, their eyes remained hard and wary and they gave no sign in return.

"A copper piece, my lord?" Noseless implored, thrusting out a monkeylike hand to grab at Semerket's cloak. "Amun's blessings upon you for a bit of silver . . . ?"

"Alms! Alms!" cried the other two beggars in unison.

Semerket fished out a copper from his belt and tossed it to Noseless. "I've not seen you here before," he said. "How did you get past the Medjays?"

"Do not beat me, my lord!" Noseless whined shrilly. "We're only poor beggars looking for a copper, a bit to eat."

"What business do you have with the chief scribe?"

At this the man's face became sly. "I might ask you, my lord, what business is it of yours?"

"I am the new foreman here—tell me at once."

"Forgive me, my lord, but you're not the foreman. You're that one who labors for the vizier. We've heard of you . . ."

The other two beggars began to circle behind him. Semerket pressed himself against the wall of the temple to prevent being attacked from behind. In the fading rays of the sun he saw knives suddenly glinting in the beggars' brown hands. They lunged at him then and he jumped to the side, hearing their blades scrape against the temple wall where he had stood. They mumbled curses beneath their breath at having missed him.

At a signal to one another they separated, one going to either side of him. Noseless, Semerket noticed, remained steadfastly protecting the sack.

The other two beggars were advancing on him from the left and right, to force him away from the wall and make his back vulnerable. He saw the beggar on his left carefully aim his knife to throw it. Semerket was on the verge of yelling for help when he saw a light streak of fur shoot past him. It was Sukis. The beggars stared at her, briefly entranced at seeing a cat so close by. Only nobles or temple acolytes possessed cats. In that moment, Semerket made his move and fled.

He was lucky to encounter a horde of children rounding the corner of the temple. The priest had dismissed his class for the day, and his students were babbling in high childish voices to one another. They stopped abruptly, mouths agape, seeing Semerket. As he sprinted into their midst, the children shied from him, but the beggars did not dare follow.

At a sign from Noseless the trio melted away into the shadows of the cliffs. The last Semerket saw of them, they were headed down the northern trail that would take them over the Gate of Heaven, and from there to the Nile.

Though most of the class had run away, a few children still lingered, staring at him. "Tell me," he said to a boy, "did you see Neferhotep just now?"

The boy's older sister stepped forward to punch her brother's shoulder. "Don't tell him anything!" she said. She was a stringy thing, with the same buckteeth as her brother and the same precocious look. The boy hit her back, but it was a ceremonial jab, nothing that would bring real pain. He continued to stare at Semerket, more from curiosity than fear, his obsidian eyes as black as those of the man he faced.

"A copper piece says you'll tell me," Semerket said, bringing out a piece of gleaming metal from his belt.

"Tell him!" said the boy's sister immediately.

"He's in the cemetery," said the boy. Eagerly he took the copper from Semerket. As he hurried away, Semerket heard the ensuing argument between the siblings, the boy's sister claiming half the prize.

Semerket trod the short, steep distance to the village cemetery and entered through its bronze gates. He had every intention of confronting Neferhotep about the beggars—who were not beggars at all, or else they would have known the secret sign—but as he walked through the deserted streets of the graveyard, there was no one to confront.

Each tomb faced the east, and in their courtyards were sycamores and flowering shrubs, gardens made exclusively for the enjoyment of the dead. Statues of the deceased inhabitants faced the sun from far niches at the ends of their respective courtyards, while small pyramids of brick crowned the vaults at the rear.

There was no sign of Neferhotep, and Semerket was beginning to doubt the schoolboy's veracity. But at that moment echoing voices came to him, carried on the winds that blew from the north. Stifling a sense of foreboding, Semerket followed the flow of words to a tomb near the center of the necropolis.

He passed through miniature pylons and into the courtyard. An old acacia tree, stunted from lack of water, grew in the center of the garden, while ivy crept around its base like a spider's web. Semerket gave a start when he saw the statue within the family niche. Hetephras herself stared back at him. The life-sized image had been freshly painted and the priestess smiled benignly, clad in her blue wig of vulture wings and linen sheath. To the side of the vault was another statue, that of Djutmose, her long-dead husband.

Suddenly Neferhotep's querulous voice echoed from a well in the center of the verandah. Semerket crept forward to peer into the hole. A steep stairway within, almost a ladder, led into a faraway crypt illuminated by distant wavering torchlight. He recognized the second voice as Foreman Paneb's. Straining to hear, Semerket bent farther into the shaft to listen.

"When will you make an end of this?" Neferhotep was saying. "You've done no work in Pharaoh's tomb for weeks. Now I hear you've put the rest of the team to work in Hetephras's tomb."

"We owe this to her, Nef. She shouldn't have died."

"Don't preach to me what I have said to you all along."

"Her tomb will be the finest in the cemetery. Maybe then, gods willing, she can forgive us."

"Gods! I'm sick of gods. A man has to look out for himself—"

Neferhotep's voice suddenly broke off in surprise. When he spoke next, the scribe's voice could barely contain his anger. "All the devils of Set! What are those?"

"What . . . ?"

"Over there—those pillars!" There was a sharp gasp. "Sweet Osiris, they're the ones from Pharaoh's tomb! You've stolen them—cut them out and brought them here! I can't believe it! Have you gone completely insane?"

"No one will notice, Nef."

"One investigation is not enough for you, now you want another?" Semerket heard the sound of pacing, and the light in the tomb wavered.

"Nef—"

Neferhotep's voice was a nagging irritant. "Well, I won't help you this time if you get in trouble. You've really lost all reason. And for what? Because of some simple-minded old woman—"

Paneb exploded in anguish. There was an aborted cry from Neferhotep and then sounds of choking came up the well-shaft. From experience Semerket could well imagine Paneb's hands around Neferhotep's throat, crushing the life out of the scribe.

Semerket was about to climb down the shaft to intervene, much against his will, when he heard Neferhotep abruptly sucking air into his lungs, gasping and coughing.

"Get out, Nef." Paneb panted, and his voice was low and angry. "Don't come down here again."

Neferhotep was sputtering. "You'll be sorry! I won't forget this!"

"I'm sorry for everything. Sorry for believing you when I did."

Neferhotep was rapidly climbing the well shaft. Semerket ran silently to hide behind the statue of Hetephras before the scribe emerged into the dying light of the courtyard, staggering. Neferhotep turned and screamed into the direction of the well, "And stay away from my wife! I'll bring you up on charges of adultery, both of you— see if I don't! I won't lift a finger when they stone you!"

The scribe lurched through the pylons and out of the necropolis. After a moment Semerket crept from his hiding place to the well shaft. The noises of construction resumed from within the tomb. Then, to Semerket's surprise, the sounds of sawing and hammering became mixed with Paneb's sobs.

THE WEEKS PASSED and gray clouds gusted over the desert, bringing to Egypt the scent of unaccustomed rain. Within the cemetery the new chamber that Paneb had created in Hetephras's tomb was finished, its curved ceiling supported by the four ornate columns purloined from Pharaoh's tomb. Satisfied that a sturdy tomb awaited his aunt's body, Paneb walked slowly through the burial chamber, holding a torch close to the walls to inspect every detail.

Now, he hoped, his duty to his aunt was discharged and life could resume its normal thrust. He and his team would go back to work in Pharaoh's tomb, and all would be well. But the sudden stab in his heart reminded him that Hetephras's terrible death had robbed the village of any peace it once had—of any it could have again.

In the flickering torchlight he instinctively reached for the jar of wine beside him and lifted it to his lips. A thick glob of bitter dregs filled his mouth. Gagging, he spat the mess back into the jar.

"Rami!" he called out automatically. "Bring more wine from the village!"

There was no reply, and Paneb dimly remembered that he had sent the lad home hours before. Paneb still had a long night ahead in the tomb, intending to apply fresh color to his uncle Djutmose's coffin and to the smaller coffin that was beside it, both of which had dulled over the years. He did not sleep well in his own house any longer, and actually preferred the comfort of his aunt and uncle's tomb during the long nights.

Well, he thought, wine would comfort him still further. Resolutely, he climbed the steep stairway up the shaft and went through the tomb's courtyard, past its ancient acacia tree, and out the cemetery gates. In his haste he did not notice he was being observed.

Semerket peered at the departing figure from behind the wall of an adjoining tomb. He intended to search Hetephras's vault; Paneb's refusal to be questioned—or even to emerge from his aunt's tomb for days at a time—made Semerket itch with suspicion. Once the foreman was out of sight, he quickly went through the pylons and into the tomb. Though he carried an unlighted torch for himself, he was surprised to see that Paneb had left a torch still burning in the crypt below.

"Hello . . . ?" he called into the shaft. Perhaps someone was there.

When no one answered, he quickly eased himself into the shaft and climbed down its stairway. A few steps and he found himself in the new room carved by Paneb and his team. Its walls were painted a vivid ochre, lending the light its special golden hue. As Semerket's dazzled eyes adjusted to the torchlight, the art on the walls revealed itself to him. He laid down his torch and flint and simply gazed.

Though all her life Hetephras had lived in a desert, the tomb-makers had ensured that her afterlife was verdant with painted sycamores and acacias, palm trees laden with dates, and swirling grape vines that grew up the lintels. Semerket felt himself transported into another world—which, he knew, was the exact purpose of the tomb.

That was how Paneb found Semerket—staring raptly at the paintings. The foreman's deep voice made him jump. "Well, now," Paneb said. He loomed large in the doorway, preventing any escape, and his lips were thin with suspicion. "People who go where they're not wanted usually end up badly." He took a step forward.

Semerket forced himself to smile. "Yes," he said, "it seems all my life I've gone into places I shouldn't—a hazard of my profession, I suppose."

"I don't much care for your 'profession,' " Paneb said. He slowly put the jar of wine down on the tiles, and his hands curled into fists.

"I apologize," said Semerket hastily. "The moment I realized that you weren't here, I should have left. It's just . . ." His words trailed off.

Paneb cocked his head.

Semerket indicated the tomb with a gesture. "It's just so beautiful." His tongue froze in his head again. He resorted to ineffective gestures to convey how impressed he was.

When Paneb spoke, he slurred his words. "Do you think she'd be pleased?"

Semerket nodded. The foreman, he realized, was drunk.

Paneb's expression softened a bit. He poured a bowl of wine and held it out for Semerket.

Semerket shook his head ruefully. "I mean no offense, but I can't drink it."

"You have a problem with wine? So did I, once."

"How did you deal with it?"

"I decided that everyone else had the problem—and that I was fine."

Semerket laughed out loud, caught by surprise. He was joined by Paneb's low rumbling chortle. Then they both stopped, surprised, and regarded one another with renewed suspicion.

"Was it over a woman?" Paneb asked, drinking. "It usually is."

"Yes," Semerket answered reluctantly. "My wife."

"What happened? Did she die?"

"No. She left me because I couldn't father the children she wanted."

Paneb looked at him sympathetically. "I began to drink when my wife left me, too. I was bedding too many other women, she said. I warned her at the time we broke the jar together, though, when you marry a snake you can't expect it to fly."

"At least not for very long," Semerket answered.

This time it was Paneb who laughed out loud. He took another drink of the wine and threw his arm about Semerket's shoulders. "Since you're so appreciative of our work here, let me show you something else you might like."

Paneb dragged Semerket to the far wall. A host of small figures were painted in several rows across the surface, each only a few inches high.

"Look closely," Paneb commanded.

Staring at the tiny people, Semerket gave a start when he realized that they were actually cunning portraits of the villagers themselves. In the wall's corner, the loveliest figure of all, a woman plucked at her harp.

"Why, it's Hunro!" Semerket said, impressed. "Exactly like her."

"Well," slurred Paneb with a dirty wink, "not like we men know her, eh? We have a legend around here, says a mosquito bit Hunro on her private parts—and she developed a permanent itch for it." His raunchy laugh boomed drunkenly in the chamber, but the foreman stopped when he saw Semerket's sober expression. "What's this? Sulks?"

"She's a married woman, Paneb."

The foreman poured himself more wine. "Don't tell me you haven't lain with her yet?"

"No."

"Then you're the only man around here who hasn't!" He peered closer at Semerket, swaying slightly. "Say—you really don't care for this sort of talk, do you?"

"I thought we could speak of who you thought might have killed your aunt. I've asked everyone else in the village for their opinion, but not yours."

Paneb stared at him.

"It was a foreigner," he said thickly, after a moment, trying to focus his eyes, "or a vagabond."

"Paneb—"

"A *foreigner* or a *vagabond*!" The foreman stood over Semerket, his wide mouth clenched in rage. Semerket knew Paneb was mere moments away from either attacking him again or passing out. But the foreman's expression abruptly changed with a new thought, and he leaned eagerly toward Semerket. "You know, if you like the work in here, let me show you some real craftsmanship!"

Paneb pulled Semerket up the well, out of the cemetery, and into the village, dragging him to his house. The first thing Paneb did was to pour himself more wine from a jar he kept in his larder. Then, putting a finger to his lips and winking, he beckoned Semerket to his sleeping area. Digging into a chest, he brought out an alabaster canopic jar from beneath some skins.

"Look at this!" Paneb handed the object reverently to Semerket, who took it in his hands. His host staggered about looking for a candle, for by now the sun was behind the mountain and the house was dark. He lit the wick inexpertly, his thick fingers clumsy with the flint. The fire caught and the candle flared.

The jar was topped with a bust of Imsety, the human-headed son of the god Horus who protected the deceased's preserved liver. Once again Semerket was astonished by the grace and delicacy of the workmanship. The glyphs were of inset gold and the god Imsety himself wore a cascading wig of carved lapis.

"My grandfather made it," belched Paneb. "He was famous in his time for these jars. Every pharaoh, every noble, the queens—they all had to have a set for their tomb."

"It's beautiful," Semerket said. "Did your grandfather leave it to you?"

The question was an innocent one, but Semerket instantly sensed that Paneb had tensed. "Amen-meses," Paneb answered, after a moment's hesitation.

"What?"

"A trader—a merchant—from Kush. Amen-meses brought it to me. He used to sell my grandfather's work down south—thought I might like to have it."

"He must be very old by now, to have known your grandfather." Semerket held the jar into the candlelight, but was actually staring at Paneb.

"Yes . . ." Paneb was weaving slightly, his eyes blanketed by the dark. Suddenly his entire face changed to distress. "I'm sorry . . . I . . ." he said uncertainly, lurching for the kitchen.

When Paneb had vomited out all the wine he had drunk, he sank to the floor, trying to curl up on the tiles. Semerket knew from his own sordid experience how uncomfortable the foreman would feel in the morning. Dragging him into the sleeping room, he laid Paneb down on his pallet, covered him with skins, and placed a jug of water beside him.

It was only then that he truly looked about the foreman's house, at the dirty plates left unwashed by the hearth, the overturned furniture and broken crockery. It exactly resembled his own home after Naia had left him. Semerket looked down at the snoring foreman, and felt a twinge of pity for the man. He was suffering badly, that much was obvious. It was not pleasant to see a person in so much pain.

But such unpleasantness did not prevent Semerket from seizing the opportunity that had been presented to him. Taking the candle into the kitchen, he retrieved the canopic jar from the niche into which Paneb had thrust it. He held the jar in the wavering candlelight, seeing again its perfect line and sinuous detail.

Turning it slowly in his hand, he noticed a small cartouche-shaped indentation that was incised into the alabaster, near its bottom. He knew that the sacred oval shape was used only to display the names of pharaohs, queens, and gods. He could not help but suspect that the complete cartouche, perhaps made of gold or silver like the rest of the inlaid glyphs, had been deliberately scratched from the piece so that its owner's name could not be read.

Semerket looked about the kitchen and found a fairly clean plate. Holding it above the candle's wick, he waited until a smear of carbon had collected, then wiped his finger across the soot. Holding the jar close to the candle so he could see, Semerket rubbed his finger lightly across the cartouche. Though faint, the glyphs once inlaid there were revealed.

Semerket mouthed their syllables slowly. "Twos-re." He had never heard the name before, but another sweep of his blackened finger across the cartouche enabled another glyph to appear. "Divine woman," it read, the symbol for a female pharaoh.

This was no leftover relic from Paneb's ancestor, Semerket realized, nor had it been made for sale to the Kushites. It was a queen's jar, and a ruling queen at that. Still, he had to make sure what he suspected was true.

Semerket strained, pulling at the lapis head. It refused to budge, so tightly were the two pieces wedged together. Inhaling silently, holding his breath, Semerket again pulled at the head, twisting it this time in his hand. The wig of carved blue stone cracked in half.

Semerket swore viciously to himself. The head came free, leaving a chunk of the stone wig attached to the rim of the jar. The room was instantly redolent of bay leaves and pine resin, so strong that he worried the aroma would wake Paneb. But the foreman's heavy breathing still rumbled from the sleeping room.

He set Imsety's damaged head down on the floor. Tilting the jar toward the candle, he peered within. As he had suspected, a resin-soaked, linen-wrapped object was inside, resembling a piece of rotting wood—Queen Twos-re's preserved liver.

From his experiences in the House of Purification, he knew that after the liver had been dried in natron and wrapped in linen strips, it was then placed in such a jar. A viscous resin mixture of juniper and bay had then been poured, boiling, over it. Semerket inserted a finger into the jar and felt the glass-like surface of the hardened resin. Judging from how strong its harsh medicinal scent was, he surmised that whoever Twos-re had been, she had not been dead for very long. Strange that he had never heard her name mentioned, nor seen any inscription or stele bearing her figure or cartouche.

The jar was stolen from a tomb, that much was clear to him. But who was the thief—Paneb himself or the merchant Amen-meses? Either way, Paneb had to have known that the jar was stolen. This in itself was a crime, though many nobles—even pharaohs themselves—collected the grave-goods of ancient dynasties as a pastime.

Semerket bent to retrieve the cracked Imsety head. Holding the candle so that the wax dripped onto its shattered edge, he glued the two pieces securely together. It would hold, but not forever. He was so intent on his task that when he felt the rush of softness about his legs, he gasped aloud, leaping and almost dropping the jar altogether. Sukis was looking up at him, obviously disgusted by his gutless reaction. She mewed in derision.

Fearful that Paneb would hear her, he put his finger to his lips, futilely attempting to hush her cries. Moving back slowly through the room in which Paneb slept, he returned the jar to the chest from which Paneb had taken it. He hoped that in the morning Paneb would believe that he himself had put it there, and that he would not look too closely for cracks or smudges of lampblack.

Semerket tiptoed from the room, returning to the hearth where the candle glowed. The steady drone of Paneb's breathing still rattled distantly, and Semerket roamed about the foreman's home, accompanied by Sukis. In the reception room, he found Paneb's tool sack. In it were copper chisels of every width, picks, pig-bristle brushes, wooden mallets for pounding. There was nothing made from the blue metal.

As Semerket returned to the kitchen, he heard Sukis's loud cry again. Holding the candle so its light swept the room, he saw the cat poised at the stairs that led into the cellar. Swiftly, she disappeared down into the dark.

He followed her; he would have to catch her and quickly leave. Looking about in the cellar, he saw the normal supplies—sealed jars of beer and wine, bits of broken furniture, extra linens, and sacks of wheat and hops. But there was something odd, too—the goods had been pushed deliberately against a corner wall. Paneb had piled everything, anything he could find, against that wall.

Semerket saw Sukis leap to the top of the heap, to look searchingly at the mud bricks. Perhaps she had located a rat, he thought. But the cat looked to him and wailed insistently.

As silently as he could, obeying some instinct (as well as the cat), Semerket lifted the sacks of grain and placed them against the opposite side of the little cellar. Just as he was about to move a chair that was missing its leg, he heard footsteps above. Sukis retreated behind some wheat sacks, ears flat against her head.

Semerket blew out the candle. Paneb had risen from his pallet and was tramping about the kitchen. In the dark, the foreman lurched into some crockery and swore dully as the dishes fell, crashing to bits on the tiles. Eventually he made his way to the rear privy. Semerket heard the powerful stream of Paneb's urine hitting the collection bowl. Groaning, the foreman finally returned to his sleeping room.

Semerket waited until Paneb's breathing again became steady. Though he would have preferred to linger, to find what was hidden beneath the rubble in the cellar, he could not find the flint to relight the candle. He cursed himself for his thoughtlessness when he realized that he had left it in Hetephras's tomb. In the lightless cellar, he just managed to edge toward the stairs to climb them one at a time. He slipped silently into the dark alley from Paneb's door, Sukis padding softly beside him.

HETEPHRAS'S FUNERAL took place on a day in midwinter. As soon as the sarcophagus came within sight of the village, borne on a sled and dragged by a white ox from Djamet Temple, the women of the village began to ululate shrilly, their eerie cries echoing through the canyon walls. As the catafalque drew near, Semerket saw that pepper had been thrown into the eyes of the ox so that the beast wept.

Behind the professional mourning women, who wailed and tore at their hair, stood the elders and their families, standing stoic and dry-eyed. Paneb wept openly, however, and many in the crowd went up to him to drape their arms about his shoulders and whisper comforting words into his ears. He seemed deaf to their appeals, the tears rolling steadily down his cheeks, and he could only stare in misery at his aunt's brightly painted sarcophagus. Hunro stood beside Neferhotep, wiping at her reddened eyes. For once the stoop-shouldered scribe stood straight. But he shed no tears, his face stony. Khepura stood on his other side, opposite Hunro.

Semerket peered at the head woman, trying to read her face. Whatever she was feeling, it was not mournful. Her eyes darted about, and she twisted and pulled at her wig, nervously trying to adjust it. Once she looked straight at Semerket and he ascertained immediately what she felt—it was fear.

At a sign from the priest the sled was pulled to the cemetery gates. Several villagers rushed forward to bear the coffin on their shoulders. Gradually they made their way into the courtyard of Hetephras's tomb and set her sarcophagus upright at the tomb's door, beneath the small brick pyramid, so that the priestess seemed to be a guest at her own funeral.

At that point the villagers brought forth their offerings—baskets of onions, whose sharp smell would remind Hetephras to breathe again in the afterlife; flat loaves of bread, jars of wine and honey, wreaths of sweet-smelling flowers. Queen Tiya herself had sent a beautiful chair of gilded wood. Taking a special lever made from the metal of a fallen meteor, a priest approached the sarcophagus and performed the act of opening Hetephras's mouth. Now that she could breathe and speak again, Paneb came forward to utter the ritual words, for he was her closest living relation.

"May you stand forever beside Osiris, Hetephras," he said, his voice hoarse, "in the fields of Iaru forever, in the house of eternity that we have made for you." Then he addressed the god of the afterlife. "Osiris, who created us, make her face to shine brightly again, raise her arms and fill her lungs with your breath." Then again he addressed the dead woman. "Open your eyes, Hetephras. Open your eyes."

Paneb's voice broke and he could not continue. It was Hunro who stepped forward in his place to utter the concluding prayer. "In peace, Hetephras, may you ever rest among those who did right."

Earlier in the day a great pit had been dug in the main avenue of the cemetery. The servants had filled it with coals and embers, and now it glowed hot. The ox was sacrificed. It was flayed, cleaned, dressed, and spitted.

The feast lasted long into the night. Hetephras's coffin was at last taken into the crypt, together with the grave-goods. Below, she was placed on the wooden bed next to the coffins of her husband and little son.

It was at that point that Semerket witnessed something strange. With many a grunt and heave, the men of the village rolled a huge stone wheel—the one he had seen in Ramose's workshop—into the tomb's forecourt, and painstakingly angled it in front of the tomb's door. It fit so snugly that not even a piece of papyrus could have been wedged through the cracks. Semerket looked about the cemetery in confusion. No such wheel blocked the doors of other tombs; Hetephras's was the only tomb that possessed one.

Semerket noticed that Sukis had perched on the rock behind him. Poor cat, he thought—did she know that her mistress was inside the tomb? He reached for her, to take her into his arms, but she backed away and leapt to a higher rock. She stared, eyes gleaming, at the tomb-makers as they continued to feast into the night.

SEMERKET WAS IN the potter Sneferu's workshop, again demanding to know when he might finish assembling the broken pieces of the pot Semerket had found at the phantom campsite. Sneferu apologized, saying that his official work had prevented him from attending to the matter.

"It seems you've taken a long time to perform a simple task," remarked Semerket, scarcely able to hide his irritation.

"If you'd care to take the pieces elsewhere . . . ?" asked Sneferu hopefully.

Semerket shook his head, "No, no . . ." He looked away.

Children suddenly went running past the shed in the direction of the northern gate, followed by groups of excited adults. Semerket turned to watch, his ears now catching the thin strains of rams' horns that blew from far down in the river valley. Sneferu rose from his pot-ter's wheel and joined Semerket outside the workshop. An incongru-ous smile of joy lit Sneferu's face.

"What—?" Semerket started to ask, but Sneferu was gone, joining the crowds to cheer at the village gates. Once again he heard the rams' horns blow, nearer this time, and the tomb-makers' voices rose to an even more excited pitch.

Semerket stood at the fringes of the crowd. Five chariots sped up the path toward the village, great clouds of dust churned from their wheels. The horses were among the finest he had seen, small red ones that soared like birds over the rock and sand, their legs a blur. Despite the steepness of the trail, the charioteers drove their teams at a har-rowing pace, seeming not to care that at any moment the horses might misjudge their footfall and plunge over the cliff's steep edge. But the steeds made no misstep, and the tomb-makers cheered; they knew this thrilling show was staged just for them.

As the riders drew near, Semerket saw that their leader wore a breastplate of overlapping gold discs, while on his head was a crown of woven leather. The men who followed him were also richly armored, though not so grandly. Khepura pushed her way through the crowd beside him, angling to get closer to the charioteers. Semerket reached out to grab her massive arm.

"Let me go, you fool! It's Prince Pentwere!" Khepura jerked her arm free and hurried forward.

Semerket was familiar with this son of Pharaoh, as all Thebans were. He was the firstborn child of Queen Tiya, and therefore the nephew of Mayor Pawero. Unlike his brothers, who were careful to remain dis-creetly in the background, Pentwere was a highly visible figure in the southern capital. The prince was chief of his own elite corps of chariot-eers. Often they could be seen on feast days performing feats of derring-do for the crowds, shooting at targets, thrusting their spears at one another in mock battle, and jumping back and forth from chariot to chariot. Thebans adored Pentwere above all the other royal family—for he was southern, his mother more royal than even Pharaoh, and he was as good-looking as a god.

But Semerket knew that Pharaoh had chosen another as his crown prince—also named Ramses, the firstborn son of his Canaanite wife,

Queen Ese. This prince was little known to the southerners, being confined to a life of duty and service in his father's court in Pi-Remesse.
Thebans grumbled bitterly that so fine a prince as Pentwere had been
passed over in favor of a middle-aged, sometimes sickly prince of the
north.

As Pentwere leapt from his chariot, the villagers gathered round to
hail him, and the prince held out his hands to grasp theirs and laugh.
He was every inch the folk-tale prince—tall, burly, chestnut skin
stretched taut across his high cheekbones, sleek and well-oiled.

Pentwere hailed Chief Scribe Neferhotep and Foreman Paneb as old
friends, who were careful to remain cordial to one another before the
prince. No trace of their recent disagreement was allowed to mar the
day. Surrounded by his handsome cohorts—all strong, muscular men
like himself—the prince clapped the tomb-makers fondly on their
backs. In a final gesture for the villagers, Pentwere's groom cast gold
pieces into the air. The tomb-makers and their children screamed for
joy as they ran to gather them up.

The gold was soon pocketed, and the crowd reluctantly returned to
the village. Neferhotep and the elders led the prince a few paces away
from the gates to confer with him in low voices. Semerket could not
imagine what they had to say to one another; he doubted whether the
finer points of tomb construction were in Pentwere's lexicon.

Semerket spied Hunro walking with the crowd back through the
village gates, her hips swaying languorously. Pushing his way through
the remaining villagers, he joined her.

"What's the occasion?" he asked, jerking his chin in the direction of
Pentwere.

"The prince often comes here to review the progress of his father's
tomb."

"And the others?"

"I don't know all their names, but the black one is Assai. Just look
at those shoulders! And that neck!" Her eyes were smoky with lust.
Then to Semerket's shock she began to jump up and down, making
sounds like a lovesick young girl. "Oh! Oh, look! They're coming this
way!"

Indeed, the royal party was progressing to where he stood. Hunro's
sharp nudge reminded him to bow low, arms outstretched.

"Well now!" Pentwere's voice was hearty. "So this is the clever man who solves the riddle of the old priestess's death! I especially wanted to greet you today."

"Oh?" Semerket said, looking up. "Why?"

Pentwere's black companion, Assai, was instantly offended that Semerket would question the prince so directly. But Pentwere ignored any breach of etiquette and answered Semerket carefully, so that all could hear. "My mother sends her regards, and bids you make haste in this matter. The gods grow impatient, she says."

"Tell your mother—and the gods, please—that I'm doing my best."

The prince regarded him with narrowed eyes and laid his arm across Semerket's shoulder. "How is the investigation coming? Do you have any leads?"

"Not really."

Semerket could not discern if the prince was displeased or simply indifferent to the news, but Semerket had the eerie sensation that behind Pentwere's bland eyes, for the briefest moment, he had caught a tiny flash of glee.

"I'm sure you'll have something soon," said the prince with royal condescension, then turned to regard the elders behind them. "I want you all to know that my mother, Queen Tiya, expects a quick end to this affair."

The elders bobbed their heads up and down in mute agreement. The groom then brought the prince a leather bag. Gingerly, he fished about in it, bringing forth a series of amulets and charms. The prince himself strung some of them around Semerket's neck, and placed the rest in his belt.

"More amulets?" asked Semerket.

"Mother thinks the one she gave you must not be powerful enough, otherwise you'd have solved the case by now. You know," Pentwere continued in a friendly tone, "my mother and I were very fond of the old priestess."

Semerket sighed, knowing what was coming.

The prince bent his head and whispered, "Have you ever considered that perhaps she was killed by a foreigner?" He looked solemnly at Semerket. "Or a vagabond . . . ?"

"I've considered it, yes."

"But you don't believe it."

"No."

"Well, I'm not surprised then that you have no leads. Poor tactics, I'm afraid, to concentrate your investigation here. How could you seriously believe one of her own neighbors killed her?"

Semerket became aware of the hostile stares directed at him not only by the elders, but also by the prince's men. Assai again was glaring intently at him.

"One," Semerket said firmly, forcing his tongue loose from his palate, "most victims are murdered by people who know them. Two, the priestess had gone to attend her shrines in the Great Place. Does it seem likely that a stranger wandered in and killed her in a place so tightly guarded? Three, she was blind. Though she was found on the other side of the river, I doubt if she could have made her way there on her own, do you? More than likely she was killed nearby, and her body thrown into the Nile." He paused. "Do you want me to go on?"

Pentwere frowned. "Have you any proof of these . . . allegations?"

Semerket shook his head. "No."

The arm around Semerket's shoulders was suddenly like granite, and in a moment of irrational panic he felt as if his breath were being slowly squeezed from him. "Then I would advise you," the prince said, a warm smile still brightening his features, "to either find some proof, or move on. The elders tell me that progress on my father's tomb slows because of you." The smile faded. "We can't have that."

It suddenly became clear to Semerket what was occurring. The tomb-makers had arranged for someone who outranked the vizier to remove him from the case, under the only pretext that would carry weight with the authorities—that work on Pharaoh's tomb suffered.

Seeing the elders' carefully expressionless faces, he also suddenly knew that guilt clung to them like the oily soot of temple incense. What they were guilty of, he didn't know yet, or even if their unknown crime had anything to do with Hetephras's death. What nerve they possessed, Semerket marveled, to defy so crafty a man as Vizier Toh, and how clever they were to enlist the royal family in protecting them. But he was nevertheless convinced that the tomb-makers would never have dared to prevent such an investigation on their own; someone had put them up to it.

Semerket bowed low before the prince. "I will keep the prince's wise words in my heart," he said. Semerket was sure it never occurred to Pentwere, being royal, that the dog would not obey.

SEMERKET JOINED QAR at the Medjay tower directly after his encounter with the royals. Qar, too, urged Semerket to find some evidence, and quickly, to keep the investigation alive.

"Once they pit the prince against the vizier," the Medjay pointed out, "court politics will kill it."

To the north, the royal party had disappeared into Pharaoh's unfinished tomb, ostensibly to conduct its inspection. Semerket turned to Qar. "You've been inside—what's it like?"

"What? Pharaoh's tomb?" Qar shook his head. "You've got it wrong—only priests and royals are allowed inside, and the work gang, too, of course. We Medjays only guard it—to make sure the likes of us can't get in."

Semerket made up his mind. "I want to see it."

Qar laughed loudly. "You can't! If you were caught, they'd expect me to execute you. Then we'd have all those priests over here again to drive your blasphemous stink out of it. I want to be spared that, if you don't mind—for I hate those fat, greasy priests."

"I need something . . . anything. It's the perfect hiding place, when you think of it."

"Hiding place for what?"

Semerket shrugged. "All the stolen treasure from your plundered tombs, I suppose."

Qar snorted derisively. "Pharaoh's tomb is the most public place in Egypt, Semerket, particularly now when it's almost complete. Every month there's some new inspection, some new ritual. Nothing could be hidden in it. Better to count on something real."

"Such as?"

"What about that brother of yours—the one who's snooping in the bazaars? Have you heard from him?"

Semerket shook his head, saying that he intended to make a secret visit across the river to consult with Nenry. He would wait, he told Qar, until Paneb and Neferhotep went again to Eastern Thebes in their "official capacity." He was resolved to know where the pair went, what they did there—and to whom they spoke.

At that moment a terrific screech from high above drew their eyes upward. A hawk was swooping down, dropping like a comet straight at them. At the last moment the bird drew up, but Semerket felt the rush of air on his cheeks as it dashed by. The bird fluttered manically around him in circles, chittering and squawking at him. It then perched tensely on one of the tower's crossbeams, staring directly at Semerket, a tiny thing of great loveliness, head cocked and large eyes alive with intelligence. When Semerket put out his finger to touch it, the tiny hawk chirped loudly and swooped off into the desert toward the Great Place.

Semerket and Qar looked at one another, speechless. Qar traced a holy sign in the air with shaking fingers. There could be no clearer omen. One of the gods who took his form as a hawk—Horus or Khons—had attempted to communicate with them. Semerket picked up his walking stick and Qar his spear, and both set off together in the direction the hawk had flown.

They had walked no more than a few minutes before they heard shouts. A furlong ahead, a party of Medjays came running toward them. Qar called back his greeting, and waved his spear.

The two groups met in a wadi. The leader, whom Qar saluted as his superior, walked directly to Semerket. His name was Captain Mentmose, he announced. Lean as a stick, rigidly erect and grizzled, he addressed Semerket solemnly. "Back there," he said. "Something you seek . . . or so we think."

Semerket followed the Medjays into the wash. His eyes scanned the Great Place, searching everywhere. In the pathway above them, a small chapel had been carved into the living rock. So well camouflaged was the shrine that he had never noticed it before. He pointed to it, asking Qar what it was.

"The shrine of Osiris," Qar said.

Semerket tensed. It was to this shrine that Hetephras had been going the day she was murdered. Far ahead, where the walls of the small wadi flattened themselves into the sands, a Medjay stood. They walked swiftly to see what he guarded.

At the Medjay's feet was a ball of broken raffia fibers, crushed and filthy, almost hidden between two small boulders. Semerket knelt to examine it. At one time it had been bright blue in color, but now sand and grit had turned it a dirty dun-colored hue. Something else had discolored it and Semerket leaned closer to see. The stain was dried blood, black and odious. Gingerly, he turned it over with his fingers. The thing was trimmed in foil-covered bits of wax. Gently he pressed the raffia out from the inside so that it might take on its original shape, and noted that the fibers had been woven to resemble the gentle swoop of vulture wings.

Even if he had not seen the painting on the wall of Aaphat's house or the small diorite figure the sculptor Ramose carved, he would have known he held Hetephras's ritual wig in his hand—the one in which she had been slain. Here at last was the piece of evidence that tied the murder to the area, the proof that Prince Pentwere had taunted him to find not more than an hour before.

Semerket closed his eyes, sighing; in that small sound was his unspoken prayer of thanks to the gods. After a moment he asked softly of the Medjay, "How did you find it?"

"It was odd," said the Medjay, leaning on his spear. "We come by this wash every day on our rounds, and never saw it there. But today, a stranger—"

Semerket and Qar tore their eyes from the wig to gaze at the man.

"A boy on a donkey. A prince, we thought, by the look of his robes, and by his side braid. We knew that a royal party was going to inspect the tomb today, and thought that perhaps someone had strayed from it. The lad never responded to our shouts, though, and we could never quite catch up to him. But he led us directly here—and pointed straight to these boulders. That's when we found it. But—this is the hardest part—" His voice grew quiet with soft dismay.

"The boy was not seen again," said Semerket.

The Medjay reluctantly nodded.

AS THEY TRUDGED from the wadi, they met the village elders and Prince Pentwere emerging from the royal tomb. From his broad smiles it was obvious that the prince was not at all upset by the "slowed progress" of the workers; nor had he noticed the theft of the four pillars now in Hetephras's tomb. The smile cracked a bit when he noticed the Medjays and Semerket standing directly below him in the wash.

"How now?" Pentwere's fine, burly voice rang out in the stillness. "What is this, a search party? There's no need—we know our way out!"

Fawning laughter broke out all around him.

"Look at the clerk's expression, my lord," grinned Assai, teeth gleaming in his handsome, black face. "He must be here to arrest us!"

Again everyone laughed at this jest. Only Semerket and the Medjays stood stern and silent before them. Pentwere's smile faded.

"Have you something to tell us, clerk?"

Semerket held out the blood-blackened wig in his hands. "Only that I have done what the prince advised me to do."

"What is that rubbish you hold there?" the prince asked.

"Proof."

Pentwere blinked. "That noxious blue weed? Proof of what?"

"That the priestess Hetephras was slain here. In the valley, my lord, not in Eastern Thebes. Not on the shores of the Nile, but here in the Great Place. This is the priestess's wig—we found it not a furlong from here. If you doubt me, see it for yourself in portraits throughout the tomb-makers' village. In every one of them she wears it."

Pentwere's eyes darted about in panic. Helplessly he turned to Assai. It was he who shouted down to Semerket, "How can that be called proof of anything, clerk? A bit of trash in the desert can be whatever you choose to name it!"

At that moment Paneb emerged from the royal tomb, closing its door heavily behind him. He came to where the others stood. It was a moment before the foreman took in the sight before him. His eyes traveled from the prince to Assai, and then down into the wash where Semerket and the Medjays stood. The elders waited breathlessly, and Paneb looked about in confusion. Then he saw the thing in Semerket's hands.

Paneb's eyes widened, and a half-scream choked his throat. He suddenly fell to his knees, wailing, "All of the demons from hell have come for me!" Then Paneb—who was known throughout the village for his fearlessness and hot heart—fainted in the sands.

The prince and his companions rushed in the direction of their chariots, not once looking at the foreman lying prone on the ground before them. The elders gathered around the twitching Paneb, throwing glances over their shoulders in the direction of Semerket. Their faces were no longer indifferent masks; they looked instead as if they stared into the very mouth of the Devourer itself.

LIKE THE RUMBLE of an earthquake, the news of the discovery of Hetephras's blood-stained wig spread from house to house. Overnight, gloom and horror descended. Where before the village had been a place of perpetual din, it was now silent and trembling in the bitter desert air. People locked their doors and huddled within their houses, waiting.

Semerket still trod the deserted main street and alleyways, seeking again to question the villagers, but he met no one. Knocking on their doors brought no answer, however loudly he pounded. Pricking his ears, he could sometimes catch furtive whispers in a nearby alley. Yet when he rounded the corner to catch the speakers, he found the street deserted, and from the corner of his eye he saw a door quickly shut and bolted.

Semerket waited. Finding the wig was the shock he needed to jar the tomb-makers from their smug self-confidence. But their confidence did not so much crumble as explode. The very night he found the wig, the village played host to another uninvited guest—one more frightening than Semerket. She arrived when the moon was at its most full. Some villagers later said they had seen a prowling hyena outside the cemetery gates that changed its shape into a woman's, passing through the village walls as though they were air. Others claimed to have seen a stain of clouds across the moon's face in the shape of a woman that descended as a swirling mist into the village, while still others had seen her only as a moving shadow on the walls, cast by flickering torchlight, silently going from house to house.

A servant's child was the first to see her. She woke on her pallet to find an old woman beckoning to her from across the room. She blinked, and when next she opened her eyes, the figure was bending over her. She could hear her sighs, the child said, as the old woman held out her arms to embrace her. As the child became more wakeful she realized that the woman's sighs and coughs were actually laughter, as if they came from the dry, parched throat of a mummy. The girl screamed, but the woman fled.

Soon the old woman's sighs turned to shrieks and wild gibbering in the night-filled streets of the village, rising and falling in mad crescendos. Some claimed to see mysterious lights parading past the cracks of their latched doors, or to hear the babbling voices of a great company of ghostly companions.

Within their homes the villagers clung to their husbands and wives, and draped their children with protective amulets and charms. Everyone knew the same awful truth—that somehow the heavy stone that had been rolled across the tomb's door had not been enough—that Hetephras had returned to her village.

STREET OF
DOORS

SEMERKET AND QAR DREAMED EVERY NIGHT of lionesses. Semerket, who had never before been frightened by the landscape of sleep, was now afraid to close his eyes for more than a few minutes. He discovered that by sitting up all night on the brick bench in Hetephras's reception room, he could wake more quickly when the lioness sprang, and so elude her fangs yet another night. Since that day when Prince Pentwere had bedecked him with amulets and charms, he had been prey to sharp, mysterious pains in his body, while his skull throbbed with headaches. It seemed at times that he felt a kind of suffocation enveloping him, as if his lungs could not breathe in enough air. During the day he went about his investigations red-eyed and grim, tired from his dream running, his temper short.

Qar, who had been trained by his sorceress mother to confront his nightmares, found his dream-spears powerless against the lioness. They fell short of their mark, or veered away at the last moment, or broke like straw against her. The only defense against her claws and teeth was to remain awake—or to run. Like Semerket, he dared not sleep for long.

Semerket one night woke from a dream where the lioness had lunged at him from behind a nearby tree. She had come so close to seizing him in her claws that she had managed to snag a few strands of his flying hair. He had wakened then, to find his scalp still stinging from where the dream lioness had pulled out his hair, and found the place shorn as cleanly as if it had been shaved. He felt his head in fearful puzzlement. But then the noise of Hetephras's door being latched caught him off-guard. Still terrified from the dream, he could not summon the courage to see who—or what—had been in Hetephras's front room.

Semerket gripped the charms and amulets around his neck given to him by Queen Tiya. They burned his fingers as if they had rested in fire, and seemed to have a weight that had not been in them before. Where they hung against his chest, the skin was chafed and red. In one gesture, without thinking, he tore them away, throwing them far to the end of the room where Sukis lay. She hissed and ran from the room to a wall in the alleyway, and from there leapt to the roof.

SEMERKET ENTERED THE House of Life at Djamet Temple through bronze-clad doors that rose six cubits or more. Situated next to Pharaoh's residence, the House of Life was a maze of gardens, reflecting pools, and pillared terraces. Within the House of Life were the books on mathematics, the natural sciences, moral precepts, official histories, and magic formulae that comprised the collected wisdom of Egypt, and it was to these he headed.

Semerket walked past the classrooms and lecture halls, glancing at the scribes-to-be who labored in them. Because the tomb-makers still huddled behind the locked doors of their homes, Semerket was taking advantage of his enforced idleness to find out more about the mysterious Queen Twos-re, whose liver—if it was truly hers—resided in the house of Paneb. He hoped to find a logical explanation why the foreman should possess such a relic. Try as he would, Semerket found it impossible to dislike the big man; he wanted to free his mind from the nagging doubts that somehow Paneb was involved in tomb robbery.

Semerket was directed to a librarian named Maadje. The man, slightly hunchbacked, sat on a bench with a papyrus rolled out in front of him. As Semerket neared, the librarian hastily rerolled the scroll, glancing up with irritation. Semerket noticed with distaste the rash of pimples that covered the man's face, and winced at his disagreeable scent.

"What do you want?" the librarian asked coldly.

"I'm looking for information on a Queen Twos-re."

Maadje reacted with a small but scandalized gasp, his eyebrows arching high. "Restricted section," Maadje said. "No one's allowed in there without permission."

Semerket was surprised. "Why should that be?"

"If I told you, there wouldn't be any need to restrict it, would there?"

Semerket sighed inwardly. Like many librarians Semerket had run across before, Maadje regarded the scrolls in the House of Life as his own property, to remain pristinely unopened and safe upon the shelves. He held up his vizier's seal hanging on the chain of jasper beads around his neck.

"Will this admit me?" he asked.

Sighing dolorously, the hunchbacked librarian rose to his feet, adjusted his kilt, and disappeared into the rear of the building. After he had gone, Semerket idly knelt to open the scroll the librarian had been reading. Images of the most outrageous sexual debauchery met his eyes. So exotic were the drawings that Semerket in his naïveté would have had difficulty even imagining the acts—let alone expecting to see them in a scroll belonging to the House of Life.

"Well?" Maadje called irritatedly from a distance. "Am I to wait for you until day's end?"

Semerket let the scroll roll shut. When he caught up to Maadje, the librarian pointed to a shelf full of scrolls located in a separate room. "In there," he said. He did not wait for any more questions, but scuttled quickly back to his papyrus.

Two other individuals were in the "restricted room." One was a Libyan, which Semerket discerned from the style of his beard—a bodyguard, by the look of him. He hovered near a very light-skinned gentleman, who squinted at Semerket with the pale eyes of a northerner.

Though the man might rank a personal guard, Semerket noticed, he was nevertheless dressed very simply, and his fingers were black with ink-stains. Semerket saw that the man was holding ancient building plans close to his face.

An architect, Semerket surmised. The man noticed him looking, and helpfully moved his scrolls aside so that Semerket could approach the shelves.

They nodded gravely to one another.

Semerket chose a scroll from the shelf that Maadje had indicated and opened it. He sat down on the floor and began to read, but as the minutes passed he became increasingly frustrated. The scroll had nothing to do with Twos-re, being instead a treatise about someone called "the great criminal of Akhetaton," someone who had supposedly ruled Egypt a couple of centuries before. He pushed the scroll aside, his mouth pursed in annoyance.

The man across the tiles squinted shortsightedly at him, and put aside his pens. "Might I help? I've become quite familiar with the arrangement of the scrolls here. If you'll tell me what you're looking for . . . ?"

"Well," began Semerket, doubtfully. "I need to find out about a certain Queen Twos-re."

"Really?" The man looked at him sharply. "May I ask why?"

Semerket spoke in vague terms. "I'm a clerk of Investigations and Secrets for Vizier Toh, and I've recently come across a—well, something—that refers to her. I need to know more, to make sense of it."

"Then you must be Semerket; Toh's mentioned you often."

Semerket gaped at the man, taken aback. It always surprised him to be known by others. Before he could ask his name, however, the man had seized the scroll Semerket had been perusing, and laughed. "Maadje's sent you to the wrong shelf, as usual. If you like, I can tell you what I know about her."

"You . . . ? You're a historian? I thought you were an architect."

The man was puzzled. "Architect?" Then he saw the plans that were laid out before him, and his voice became amused. "You think because of these plans here that I'm a . . ." He turned to the Libyan and laughed. The other man smiled as well. "Well, perhaps, but I also know a little history," he said. "Secret history, in this case."

"Secret?"

"Twos-re was not just any queen, you know—she was also a king."

Semerket remembered the glyph for "divine female" that he had found next to the queen's cartouche on the canopic jar. "She must have ruled quite a while ago, then. We haven't had a female king since Hatshepsut."

"She ruled just forty years ago, in fact."

Semerket was shocked. "But there is no monument to her, no mention of her at all on the temple walls. You'd think that with her reign's being so recent, one would hear at least a mention of her."

The man shook his head. "Her name was stricken from the official lists of rulers by King Setnakhte."

"Pharaoh's father?"

"He had her statues hacked to pieces, and her name obliterated everywhere it was found. Even her tomb was destroyed."

"What had she done to deserve so terrible a fate?"

"She had killed her own husband, so that only she was left to put on the red and white crowns. Even her nephews died mysteriously. But the gods were appalled by her sins, and they caused the Nile to fail in its flooding. Famine and plague broke out, and civil war ravaged the country. This was how Pharaoh Setnakhte became king."

"And she thought she could actually succeed?"

"Oh, there had been a precedent. Her own father had usurped the throne himself. Amen-meses was his name."

Amen-meses! Where had he heard the name before? He suddenly remembered—it was the name of the so-called merchant from whom Paneb had obtained the canopic jar that held the queen's preserved liver. Or so Paneb had said. It seemed strange, Semerket mused, that two names so accursed—Twos-re and Amen-meses—were linked to a foreman in the Place of Truth. The hair prickled on his head, and he felt exactly as he had when he was young, staying up at night to hear the ghost stories told by his parents.

At least the architect's tale explained to him why Twos-re's name had been hewn from the canopic jar containing her liver. How despised she must have been, that even her grave-goods had been defiled.

Semerket made the sign against misfortune. "At least we are spared such evil in our own day," he murmured piously.

The man and his bodyguard looked at one another cryptically. "Have we been spared?" murmured the man, looking off. He seemed to wrestle with himself for a moment, then leaned forward and whispered, "The tainted blood of Twos-re and Amen-meses is still alive in Egypt, Semerket, make no mistake, ready at any moment to—"

The architect abruptly ceased speaking when the librarian Maadje appeared, looking stricken. An imposing priest, tall and thin, hovered behind him.

"There he is!" Semerket heard Maadje whisper to the priest.

The priest entered the room, bringing his arms down to knee level and genuflecting elaborately. "Your Royal Highness!"

Semerket looked about, confused. Did they address the man who sat next to him? But he was an architect . . .

"Lord Messui." The man inclined his head to the priest.

"I had no idea this man was disturbing you. Maadje will be punished, for bringing him here."

"I was not disturbed," said the man. "If Maadje is to be punished, then let it be for having directed this gentleman to the wrong scrolls." He gathered together his pens and notes, which the Libyan stashed in a wooden case. With a nod to everyone in the room, coughing gently into a kerchief, he departed.

"Who was that?" Semerket asked the priest after a moment. "Why do you call him 'Royal Highness'?"

Messui looked at Semerket as if he were simple-minded. "That," he said with a scowl, "is to be our next pharaoh. If he survives."

"Survives?" Semerket started to ask.

But Messui was gone. Maadje whispered to explain to Semerket what the priest meant, smirking. "He's very sickly, the crown prince. Even so, they say he will be declared the official heir by Pharaoh. That's why he's come here incognito from Pi-Remesse. Queen Tiya has locked herself in her rooms because of it, they say."

"Really?"

"Oh, it's a great scandal at court! When Pharaoh married her, it was with the promise that *her* sons would inherit the throne, but instead he's going to name this son by his northern wife, Queen Ese, and she's just a Canaanite—"

"Maadje!" The priest Messui's voice came sharply over the shelves.

Instantly, the smelly little hunchbacked librarian was gone, leaving

Semerket to muse alone. As he rolled up the scrolls and replaced them on the shelves, his mind once again took up the story of the evil Twos-re and her equally despicable father, King Amen-meses.

What had the crown prince meant when he said that the blood of Twos-re and Amen-meses still lived? Some inchoate instinct told Semerket that the story of a Kushite merchant of the same name was a lie—that the merchant and the king were the same person. But if that were true, he reasoned, the logical extension of the thought was that the malignant spirit of Amen-meses still walked the pathways of the Great Place. And hadn't the crown prince himself just told him the blood of the evil pair still *lived* in Egypt—?

Again, Semerket felt his scalp bristle.

THE NEXT DAY, Semerket was in the village kitchens with Qar, looking for something they could eat without fear. They chose unpeeled onions with dirt from the fields still on them, cheese, and a loaf of bread pulled fresh from the ovens.

"Look what it's come to," Qar said to him in a low, dispirited voice. "Afraid to sleep because a lioness hunts us—afraid to eat because it might put us to sleep."

In any other mood, the irony of the observation might have amused Semerket. But he was too tired and too hungry to care. The morning was quiet. The tomb-makers had still not found the courage to leave their homes. Only the servants were up and about. Sukis wound herself about his feet, begging for scraps. Hunro's voice suddenly came to them from over the wall, raucous and angry. Sukis fled the kitchens. Catching Qar's eye, Semerket rose to peer through a crack in the gate.

Hunro was at the cistern, braying her anger to the few persons who had ventured out to draw their water. She was being forsaken—*again,* she said—because Neferhotep had forbidden her to attend the gala arrival of Pharaoh in Thebes, something she wanted to see just once in her lifetime. Yet here she was, imprisoned in this dreary hole of a place, guilty of an unknown crime she had not committed. It wasn't fair, she intoned, *it wasn't fair at all!*

"But *they're* going, oh yes," she said, pointing with her thumb at someone Semerket could not see. He shifted his position, straining to see who it was she addressed. Paneb and Neferhotep were striding up the path from the cemetery, conferring in low tones.

Hunro lunged at Neferhotep, claws out. A short, angry scuffle ensued, but Paneb and Neferhotep deftly grabbed her arms and hustled Hunro back into the village. She tried to wrench herself free, her mouth full of curses, but was caught between the two men like a mouse between two millstones. In a moment they had dragged her into the smoky maw of the village, her screams fading with her.

"If they're going across the river today," Semerket whispered to Qar back at the bench, "I'm going to follow them."

"See if that brother of yours has found any jewels in the markets," Qar reminded him.

Semerket slipped from the village at noon, long before Paneb and Neferhotep departed. It was a much shorter walk to the river than when he had first come to the village, for the burgeoning Nile waters now reached almost to the steps of the western temples. When he came to the place in the river where the ferrymen congregated, he waited in the shadows of a stable and folded his gray woolen mantle around his face.

The wharf was teeming with chattering Western Thebans anxious to be taken across to welcome Pharaoh Ramses III. Until that morning Semerket had not known of Pharaoh's return. Though normally Semerket despised crowds, they would be a boon to him this day—for if Paneb or Neferhotep happened to look in his direction, he could easily blend into the multitude.

Semerket paid a ferryman an entire gold piece to reserve his skiff, almost thirty times the man's normal fare. He wanted to be sure a boat would be available when he needed it, and did not count the cost.

An hour or so passed before he caught sight of his quarry. Paneb was a giant in the throng at the shore, easy enough to keep in sight. His broad face was implacable, but Neferhotep appeared uneasy. The scribe's eyes darted about and he kept looking behind himself to see who was on the causeway. Semerket heard his quavering voice rising tensely; Neferhotep was angry that no boat was instantly available.

At long last another ferryman gave them passage. Semerket sprinted to where his own skiff waited, and bade the man shove off. Inspired by the gold, or perhaps because he carried only one passenger, the ferryman quickly overtook the boat bearing Paneb and Neferhotep. Hunching his shoulders so that he appeared an old, frail peasant, and turning his face to the north so he would not be recognized, Semerket was at the eastern docks long before the tomb-makers landed. From behind a mooring stanchion he watched them disembark.

It seemed that all Thebes waited for Pharaoh at the quay. Though a Sed Festival had been proclaimed in Thebes the previous year to commemorate Ramses III's thirtieth year on the throne, tensions arising with the western barbarians had prevented his visit. Since then a peace treaty had been signed with the tribes, so there was no excuse for Pharaoh to spurn Thebes a second time. Word had been received a week before that the royal fleet was en route to the southern capital.

By now it was late afternoon and Pharaoh's fleet had not yet appeared. Paneb and Neferhotep mingled on the wharf for a time. Then, as the shadows lengthened, the two stepped into a quayside tavern called the Elephant's Tusk.

Semerket knew it for an awful place that reeked of stale wine and urine. Frequented by foreigners and fish-gutters and slaves, it was not a place Semerket liked to go—not without his knife—and he was surprised that the fastidious Neferhotep would consent to go inside such a hovel. But Semerket also knew that the Elephant Tusk possessed no back door, which would prevent the tomb-makers from eluding him.

Semerket slipped inside the tavern, bringing his cloak again around his face, keeping to the shadows. Paneb and Neferhotep sat at the rear, where it was gloomiest. It appeared to Semerket's eyes as if they had only stopped there for a cup of wine, for they remained alone and unspeaking. Semerket stepped back into the street, squatting beneath an ancient sycamore tree at the corner of the tavern.

Ra's barque was low in the west now, but the crowds were very thick, bright-eyed with excitement and dressed in their holiday best. All across the great stone wharves, pennants of azure and crimson undulated from tall spires, while the plating on Amun's temple doors was polished to new brightness.

The city's dignitaries and nobles took their places. A deputation of Pharaoh's sons was in its first rank, although there was no sign of the crown prince, whom Semerket had met in the House of Life. It was

Pentwere who led them, dressed for once in royal linen and not armor. Tall, thin Pawero next stepped forward; at his side was the smaller, rounder Paser. As mayors of the city they would be among the first to welcome Ramses back to Thebes.

When Semerket finally caught sight of his brother, Nenry, as expected, was hovering behind Paser in birdlike attendance. His face wore its customary mask of tics and grimaces, indicating to his brother even from a distance that he was overburdened with responsibilities.

Semerket called a nearby urchin to him and pointed out Nenry among the courtiers. "Tell him that his brother waits for him under the big sycamore." He gave the lad a copper and watched him dart through the crowds. The boy found Nenry without effort and pointed back to where Semerket stood. Nenry squinted in the direction of the tavern.

Semerket removed his hood and waved, but he could not tell if Nenry had seen him. Shouts coming from the lookouts atop Amun's Great Temple suddenly proclaimed that the masts of Pharaoh's fleet had at last been sighted.

From far up the river came the faint pulse of drums, pipes, and rattling sistra, beating out a steady rhythm for Pharaoh's oarsmen. As the music wafted to the throng along the shore, voices became more animated. Soldiers lit the bonfires on the street corners and priests placed balls of incense into huge censers so that pungent clouds soon enveloped the wharves like a low-hanging fog.

Cheers rose from a hundred thousand throats when the fleet rounded the bend in the river. The ships' lanterns had been lighted, and they blazed on the water across the Nile's entire breadth. The ships' riggings were strung with blooms, and every ship displayed the protective totems of its gods.

On the shores, temple choruses burst into chants of welcome. Though Semerket kept close watch on the tavern's doorway, expecting the tomb-makers to emerge, he could not help but be caught up in the spectacle played out on the river.

Rams' horns blew again when Pharaoh's venerable ship, *Horus-of-the-Morning,* pulled ahead of the other vessels. The dark green man-of-war was the same one in which Ramses had so triumphantly defeated the Sea Peoples some twenty-five years before. Though her bulwarks were scarred from battle and she listed to port, the ship was still a formidable instrument of war—like Pharaoh himself.

Sailors leapt to furl the *Horus-of-the-Morning*'s rectangular red sail in preparation for docking. As the warship slowly came round, the rays of the setting sun glinted on the bronze lion-head jutting from its prow. Its brazen jaws were clamped firmly around a glowering human skull—all that remained of the chieftain who had dared to lead his navies against Egypt. Grandparents hoisted their grandchildren to their shoulders to point out the hole in the skull's shattered cranium. Semerket heard their voices excitedly describing the splendid day when Ramses had clubbed the captive king to death with a granite mace in Amun's temple.

Another shout from the captain, and the rowers lifted their oars from the water. Towropes were cast to the dock, where they were secured around the stone stanchions. As the *Horus-of-the-Morning* was pulled into its slip and made fast against the bundles of straw that cushioned the stone wharf, Ramses III stepped from the vessel's canopied pavilion. Instantly the cheers doubled in volume, verging on the hysterical. Pharaoh majestically ignored the noise.

Semerket had never before seen the pharaoh at such close range, and stood on the trunk of the old sycamore to better view him over the heads of the crowd. It was easy to see he was the father of Pentwere, for he shared the prince's well-proportioned physique. Ramses had become gaunt with the years, Semerket noticed, and his head drooped under the heavy red and white crowns. Yet as he walked to the gangplank, his gait was anything but feeble.

Ramses was entirely what he seemed—a successful old warrior. Whatever majesty was in him came from the reflected glory of his office and not from the blood that flowed through his veins. Ramses III had not been brought up a royal prince; he was the son of the general Setnakhte who had acquired the throne almost by accident, rescuing it (Semerket now knew) from the grasp of Queen Twos-re. In the few times Semerket had heard Ramses speak from his Window of Appearances, he was wont to address his subjects as he did his soldiers. "Listen up!" were the words with which he usually began his rasping speeches—and people did. There were some, mainly southerners, who complained that his reign lacked dignity.

Pharaoh was even whiter-skinned than Semerket remembered. His lips were thin, his eyes pale, his nose a beak. Though others in his entourage were painted like statues, his face was barren of cosmetics. As a young man he had been red-haired, like most of the northern Ramessid kings, and the contrast between him and his chestnut-skinned Theban subjects was pronounced.

Semerket saw that the crown prince was beside him; this was indeed the same man he had met in the House of Life. Apparently the prince had slipped northward to board his father's warship downstream, so that he might arrive with him on this day of days. Clad in nondescript robes, he clutched a wax tablet and stylus in his hand. Now that Semerket saw father and son together, he noted the unmistakable stamp of Ramses III on the prince's features—the thin nose and lips, the pale skin.

Suddenly the whole purpose of Pharaoh's visit became clear to Semerket: just as the librarian Maadje had intimated, Ramses did indeed intend to cede his authority to his son within the holy capital, just as other far-seeing pharaohs had done at the end of their reigns, to ensure a smooth transition of power.

The crowds became silent as Pharaoh stepped aboard his royal carrying chair. Then Vizier Toh, more gnarled and bent than Pharaoh, brought him the scourge and crook and Pharaoh took them in his hands. In a radiating wave of prostration starting from the docks, Thebans knelt in an ever-expanding circle so that even those too far away to see him sunk in homage.

At a signal from the rams' horns, the first to rise were Pharaoh's sons. The twelve princes scrambled to hoist their father's chair upon their shoulders. The crown prince was not required to lift the chair, but preceded Pharaoh into the Great Temple. It was an honor not given to the other sons, and Semerket saw the humiliation that lurked behind Pentwere's eyes. Pentwere was used to being the darling of the Thebans—but now all eyes were focused on the rarely seen crown prince.

At that moment, Semerket was struck by the thought that none of Pharaoh's wives waited to greet him. He could remember other such occasions, when he had been much younger, when Queen Tiya had been very much on display. Now she was conspicuous by her absence. Semerket remembered Qar's words to him at Djamet, that Pharaoh "had a horror of women meddling in the affairs of men." He also remembered Maadje's words, that Tiya had locked herself away to protest Ramses's passing over her own brood of eaglets.

Pharaoh was borne by his sons through the Avenue of the Rams into Amun's Great Temple, accompanied by the chanting of priests, to spend the night within the god's sanctuary and commune with his celestial father. On the following day he would sail across the river to the fortress temple of Djamet, where he resided when he was in Thebes.

The nobles of the court followed Pharaoh into the temple, and after them, the city officials. From a distance, Semerket saw the mayors of Thebes, fat Paser and thin Pawero, hoisted onto the shoulders of their bearers. Pawero was rigid and dignified, never deigning to look at the crowds, but Paser smirked and shouted to the Thebans, who clapped their hands for joy to see him. They shouted his name and blessed him, and Paser kissed his fingers to his lips, waving to them as he disappeared behind the gates of the temple.

Though the day was not an official holiday, the Thebans nevertheless made for the pleasure houses and inns that lined the waterfront. The poor sat at the river's edge, laughing and singing together and generally behaving as if Pharaoh's arrival were a sanctioned celebration.

Semerket paced at the tavern's door, impatient for his brother's arrival. He gnawed at a thumbnail and went back inside, where he discovered that the tomb-makers had been joined by two other men. Their backs were to him, and he could not readily make them out in the gloom. He could only see that one was dressed in the fine linen of a noble, while the other wore filthy rags.

By now the tavern was full of strident Thebans whose noise made it impossible to hear anything the men said. A sudden tap on his shoulder made him spin around. It was his brother, mouth pursed in disapproval.

"I might have known you'd be in here." Nenry spoke loudly to be heard over the din. "I thought you said you'd wait out by the tree. Why are you all wrapped up like that, Ketty?"

Semerket made a gesture to quiet him and led Nenry into a corner of the tavern. "Keep your voice down," he whispered into his ear. "I'm following someone."

"Who?" Nenry whispered back, eyes wide.

Semerket pushed him to the edge of the pillar for a better view of the village's scribe and foreman. "Those in the far corner. The big one is named Paneb and the other Neferhotep."

Nenry peered into the gloom. "No," he said flatly. "Those are not their names."

Semerket blinked at Nenry's blithe denial.

"If you're going to follow someone," Nenry continued, "I really think you should know who they are. The big one is named Hapi and the little round-shouldered one calls himself Panouk."

Semerket's mouth fell open in amazement. He closed it and swallowed. *"What?"*

"I've seen them often at Mayor Paser's house. They're engineers." He turned to Semerket, smug, but a serving maid's passing oil lamp briefly illuminated Semerket's face in the tavern's gloom and Nenry's expression changed to alarm. "Ketty! Are you ill? What's happened? You're so thin!"

Semerket shook his head dismissively. "What do you know about them?"

"Let me think. I first saw the big fellow, Hapi, on the same day we found out your priestess was dead. He was in the mayor's private rooms, early in the morning, and he was covered in limestone dust from head to toe. I remember how embarrassed I was for him. Don't you think that when one stands before the mayor, one should dress for the occasion?" Whenever Nenry discussed proper attire, Semerket began to feel as if he were slowly settling into the ooze at the bottom of the Nile.

"But what do they discuss with Paser, Nenry?"

Nenry opened his mouth to answer, but stopped. A puzzled look came over his face. "I don't really know. It seems the mayor always has some errand for me to run the moment they . . ." Nenry's words trailed off. He looked sharply at his brother, and his voice became suspicious. "What don't I know, Ketty?"

Semerket rubbed his forehead. "I'm suddenly in the dark, as well. But I do know their names aren't Hapi and Panouk. And they're not engineers—they're tomb-makers." He indicated the other two men, the noble and the man in rags. "What about their guests—do you know them?"

Too many people had crowded into the tavern by this time, obscuring Nenry's view. "Give me your cloak," Nenry said. Draping it over his face as Semerket had done, he affected the unbalanced gait of a drunkard, lurching to the ditch at the tavern's corner as if to urinate. As he went past, he peered at the table where the four sat.

"The one to the left is nobody," Nenry said when he was again at his brother's side, "some awful beggar or criminal. His nose and ears are gone—there now, why do you look at me like that, Ketty?"

Quickly looking into the gloom, Semerket saw that it was indeed Noseless who sat with Paneb and Neferhotep—there could be no doubt. He quickly looked around the tavern for the beggar's two companions. If they were there and recognized him, he and his brother would be in danger. But though the tavern was crowded and smoky, he became fairly certain the other two beggars were not with Noseless.

"And the other one? The noble?"

"I know him, yes," Nenry said, looking at his hands. His face was beginning to contort again. "And so do you."

"I don't."

"Yes, you do, Ketty. It's Naia's husband, Nakht."

SOMEHOW HE HAD GOTTEN OUTSIDE. Pushing his way through the still-crowded avenues, he ignored Nenry's attempts to restrain him. He soon found himself at the end of the jetty where the deepwater harbor was dredged. Semerket sat on the pilings, staring out on the streaming Nile, breathing hard.

Nenry caught up to him. "Ketty . . ."

Semerket shot his brother a hate-filled look.

"Don't blame me," Nenry said, sitting beside him. "You were the one following them, not I."

Semerket's anger melted away. "You don't understand," he said with a sigh. "I'd thought I was finally getting over her. There was a whole day, once, when she didn't even enter my mind. But seeing Nakht . . ." He became silent.

The scents of pepper and cinnamon emanated from a nearby warehouse, while a recently laden ship in the berth next to them exuded the musty scents of corn and emmer wheat. The resulting effluence, mixing with the stale smell of bilge water, conspired to make Nenry a trifle nauseous. He glanced at his brother's furrowed expression. Always believing that it was his duty to cheer up people, Nenry cast about for something to beguile his brother from his gloom.

"Well," he asked, "do you want to hear about what I discovered in the bazaars? Isn't that why you wanted to see me?"

Semerket sighed. "I suppose."

"I did just as you said to do. Picture me, in the robe of a Babylonian merchant. I even covered my eye with a jeweled patch, if you can believe it, and spoke in that singsong way they have. 'Jewels,' I said. 'Royal jewels for my wives back in Babylon.'" He stared at his brother, who still continued morose. Nenry made his voice even more animated. "I winked at them, you know, so they'd understand what I meant. But they pulled out some rubbish even I could tell were fakes. 'No, no, no!' I said. 'Why do you slander my wives with this whore's trash?' I was so insistent they told me to come back the following day. Well, what could I do but return? Even though my wife was absolutely against it . . ."

This at last piqued Semerket's interest. "Why?" he asked, a trifle harshly. "What business is it of hers where you go?"

"Well, frankly, she thinks anything connected with you brings disaster. Not that I blame her—it usually does."

Semerket grunted, not being able to argue the point, and turned his gaze once more to the river.

His brother again took up his tale. "So the next day I returned to their stalls. But what do you think? The merchants said I should go away, that they didn't have what I wanted. Quite a different reception from the day before, let me tell you. What made them change their tune like that, do you think?"

Semerket continued to stare at the river. "Someone had tipped them off that we knew about the tomb robberies," he said dully.

Nenry's lips began to move spasmodically and his face contorted into a quivering mass of tics and spasms. *Tomb robberies?!*" The words were almost a shriek.

Semerket reached forward and put his hand over his brother's mouth. "Calm down. Do you want everyone to hear?"

Nenry pulled away. "You're going to have to tell me everything,

Ketty! If I had known these things about the jewels, I'd never have gotten involved. You know that. Tomb robberies!"

So Semerket related to Nenry all he had learned from the time he had begun his investigation—about finding the abandoned campsite within the Great Place and the ancient ear loop buried in the sands; of his suspicions concerning the tomb-makers and their odd, unfeeling reaction to the death of Hetephras; of being afraid to eat the village food for fear that it was drugged—or worse. He told him of the woman Hunro, and how she had hinted and teased of murky doings in the village. Semerket described the enmity of Paneb and Neferhotep, who nevertheless still worked in tandem, and how they often slipped from the village into Eastern Thebes, though it was forbidden for them to do so. He told of that day when he'd confronted the beggars outside the village temple, and now Noseless had shown up at the Elephant Tusk that very night . . . for what purpose he did not know. He told his brother, too—whose mouth by now was hanging slightly ajar—how the Medjays had discovered Hetephras's bloody wig on the sands of the Great Place, and how he suspected that the tomb-makers had enlisted the support of Prince Pentwere to confound and possibly stop the investigation. He related how he had found the criminal queen's liver in Paneb's house and learned about the mysterious merchant named Amen-meses who had supposedly sold it to him. Then he told of how the ghost of Hetephras haunted the village of the tomb-makers.

"I'm walking down a street of doors, Nenry," Semerket concluded, his head in his hands. "I search every house, open all the doors, and when I think I know everything there is to know, I go to that last door and pull it open—only to find an entirely new street, with new doors. The more I know, the less I know. And now, tonight, two new ones have opened—the door to Mayor Paser's house, and the one to Naia's." He sighed dejectedly. "The gods are dicing with me, Nenry. There is conspiracy here."

Nenry felt a sudden great surge of fear for his own position. "How can Mayor Paser have anything to do with this? For what purpose?"

Semerket stood up and headed for the main boulevard. "I don't know," he said tiredly. Always with his brother it was the same question—how did the situation affect his own career and standing in Thebes?

"Where are you going, Ketty?" Nenry said when they reached the main boulevard.

"Where you must not follow. Go home, Nenry."

Semerket was about to enter another door that night, one that had in fact opened weeks before on the day he had run into Noseless and his friends behind the village temple. He had to go through that door now, no matter how fearsome it was.

ALONE, SEMERKET FOLLOWED the streets that led into the foreign quarter of Thebes. Here lived the traders, mercenaries, and émigrés from distant lands who called Egypt their home. Many were exiles, banished to Egypt because of crimes they had committed elsewhere. Others were simple tourists who found Egypt too pleasant to leave.

Above the streets where Semerket walked were a profusion of galleries and balustrades, so close they seemed to touch. Where once they had been brightly painted, the balconies were now tattered and bleached with age. When a building fell, the rubble lay in streets fouled with heaps of rotting refuse.

The sordidness of the district was compounded by its other inhabitants, the vagrants, cripples, and mendicants who made up the Kingdom of the Beggars. Miscreants of every ilk loitered in the doorways, eyes staring after him as he passed. As he had done with Noseless and his accomplices back in the tomb-makers' village, he flashed them the secret sign of their kingdom with his fingers. This time the signal had the desired effect: seeing the sign, the beggars withdrew again into the dark alcoves and did not threaten him.

Soon he stood before the rotting gates of an abandoned temple. A foul place that good Thebans avoided, the building had been erected by the Hyksos hundreds of years earlier. Not many knew that it was the abode of a king.

Semerket waited at its pylons. He wanted to do nothing more than flee, but could not. Stiffening his resolve, he pounded with his fists on the rotting gates, crying, "Open up! I have business with the king!"

The black door slowly opened. A man immense as a god stood in the gloom. Semerket made the secret sign, and the giant returned the gesture. The man glowered beneath brows painted in the Egyptian manner, though he was bearded like a foreigner. Two curved knives crossed at his chest. He beckoned for Semerket to follow him.

In the temple courtyard, a strange silence reigned. The temple's sacred lake had silted up over the years, but was still connected by some long-forgotten underground viaduct to the Nile. Now it was an overgrown oasis of palms and reeds. Semerket followed the giant through the tiny forest, hearing the slither of asps and scorpions beneath the rot.

Within the temple proper, tiny oil lamps stuffed into the walls were the only illumination. Semerket became aware of hundreds of beggars that camped in the halls, waiting out the night. They seemed to shrink into the floor as he passed, occasionally moaning a curse when he blindly trod on a foot. He brought his mantle to his nose, for the place smelled worse than a privy.

The giant pushed open a screen onto yet another set of corridors. This hapless collection of crumbling hallways upon hallways reminded Semerket of the stories he'd heard of the people of Keftiu, whose god, imprisoned at the center of a great labyrinth, was a creature half-bull, half-man to which the people fed human flesh.

Almost upon that thought, the distant bellows of a demented and monstrous animal welled up from the dark. The bellowing became louder as they trod the dark hallways, and as he drew nearer Semerket determined that the lunatic ravings were made not by a beast, but a man.

The giant led him to a small anteroom adjoining the room from which the screams emanated. "Wait here," the man said. Semerket sat down on a crude chair, and found his buttocks poking uncomfortably through broken thatch. The screaming stopped abruptly. Familiar sounds drifted to him now: a very distinct tap-thump, tap-thump of some wheeled apparatus, followed by the plaintive bleat of a ram. Semerket found it impossible to sit quietly. He moved silently to the doorway and peered inside.

Three men with shaved heads, naked but for loincloths, held a bound man down on a table. A fourth, their leader, waited nearby. The bound man was gagged, but still managed to struggle and scream; it had been his cries Semerket had heard. The fourth man now approached the prone figure and placed his knee on the victim's chest, while the others held his head steady.

Their leader reached his long, thin arm over to a table of bronze instruments. He took up a small spoon, and turned it in his spindly fingers to catch the smoky light from the brazier.

Deftly, the thin man plunged the instrument into the victim's left eye socket, twisted it delicately, and plucked the wet, translucent orb from the gaping hole. He tossed the gleaming bit of flesh into a small basin. Blood sprayed geyser-like from the man's head, bathing his tormentors, but they labored on unconcerned for either the warm spray or their victim's screaming. A swift flash of the spoon, and the other eye was torn from his skull.

In that room was the Cripple Maker, Semerket realized, with his three assistants. Semerket tasted vomit in his mouth, but was too fascinated to even retch, for in the Kingdom of the Beggars, the Cripple Maker was as legendary as the Beggar King himself. An apostate priest trained as a physician, his special art was not in healing, but in creating appealing deformities with hooks and knives. Any painful alteration to a body, any new appalling deformity, would be tried that a more profitable beggar could be manufactured.

The Cripple Maker reached over to a brazier to take a glowing ember between his thumb and forefinger. Quickly, he plunged it into a gushing socket, and then repeated the procedure for the other wound. There was a hissing gurgle, the smell of burning flesh, and the man's bleeding ceased—as did his screams. A final convulsion and the man fainted.

The Cripple Maker spoke as he bandaged the man's eyes. In a surprisingly high, sweet voice, he prescribed, "Feed him a little opium paste tonight, and for three days after. No food; only broth. If there's no fever, he'll survive." The Cripple Maker sponged the drying blood from his own body with fastidious care.

Semerket could not see the person whom the apostate physician addressed. But a quiet voice now spoke from the gloom. "Send him to the Beggar King of the North, then, if he lives. The king must know that worse waits in Thebes for any more spies he sends into my realm."

"Yes, lord," the Cripple Maker said, his voice syrupy with pleasure. He was a man who enjoyed his work.

The other voice called out, louder, "Yousef!"

The giant who'd led Semerket through the halls put his head into the room. "Lord?"

"The other business—we'll attend to it now."

Semerket was so mesmerized by what he'd seen that he was unaware when Yousef returned to the anteroom to stand behind him, dragon's teeth in his tight smile.

"Careful," the giant said. "The poor fellow in there was guilty of seeing too much." He shook his head in mock sadness, "No more, though." But he laughed cordially, as if they were friends.

Semerket followed Yousef into the other room. The ironlike smell of freshly spilled blood clung to the air, and the place seemed overly warm. A sudden movement in the dark drew his attention. It was a ram, stolen from the sacred herd of Amun at Karnak. Its combed, white coat floated to the floor in soft, wavy skeins of wool, and its curved horns were enameled in rich gold. The ram pulled a miniature chariot made of inlaid citron wood from which a deep voice rose, "So it is Semerket who visits me?"

"It is I, Majesty."

"But you were in Babylon or Troy or some godforsaken place, weren't you?"

"Forgive me, Majesty, but you always know exactly where I am . . . as you know everything in Thebes."

A deep laugh rumbled through the room, and Semerket peered down into the chariot to find glinting back up at him the fierce eyes of the Beggar King. His neck was hung with heavy chains of gold and silver, and he wore a battered gold crown. Despite his kingly trappings, however, he was nothing more than a legless torso overhung by two muscular arms. His lower limbs had been long before taken by another Cripple Maker, before he had become king; the ram and chariot now served as his legs and feet.

"Are you investigating another crime, then?"

"Yes, lord."

"Does it concern a murdered priestess?"

Semerket concealed his surprise, asking in a quiet voice, "What can you tell me about it?"

The Beggar King slapped the reins across the ram's flanks and he began to drive the chariot about the room. "We had nothing to do with it, if that's what you mean. I have problems enough without slaughtering old women. Ah, Semerket—it's been many years since we've

talked, and much has changed. Times are hard in the south. Our empire has withered away over the years; only the north is rich today."

"Thebes seems prosperous enough."

"Not through the eyes of a beggar. When the great southern families are feeling the pinch, alms are scarcer, bribes leaner." He went on to
complain bitterly of his fellow Beggar King in the northern capital, an
even richer and more powerful monarch who had somehow wrested
control of the abundant inflow of foreign currency and goods that
came from across the Great Sea.

"He knows where we are weakest," the Beggar King said, "for he
sends his spies and agents here. One was apprehended in Thebes only
yesterday, this man on the table here." The Beggar King's stare was almost kindly as he regarded the barely breathing heap before him. "But
he has been punished so that he can never spy on us again. And because we are merciful, he'll be sent back to the north as a warning—if
he survives."

The Beggar King halted his miniature chariot at Semerket's feet.
"But these are our problems. Why have you come today, after so long?
What do you need from us?"

Semerket told him of the beggars who had come to the village of
the tomb-makers and how they had not known the secret sign he
made. Hearing the Beggar King's own story made him think they were
beggars from the north, somehow in league with the tomb-makers. Semerket said he feared it had something to do with tomb robbery.

"Robbery in the Great Place?" Even the Beggar King was shocked—
or envious—Semerket did not know which.

Just then the eyeless man made small noises as if he were waking.
The Beggar King moved his chariot to look at him. "Come, Semerket."

Semerket approached and bent to view the beggar. To his shock,
he recognized him. "He's one of those who attacked me at the village
temple!"

The Beggar King's eyes glittered redly. "Ask him your questions
then, Semerket; find out why he pollutes my kingdom."

Semerket whispered into the beggar's ear, "I am the vizier's man
from the tomb-makers' village, the one you tried to kill. Do you remember me?"

The man moved his head in the direction of Semerket's voice. Blood and tears oozed from beneath his bandages. With great effort he nodded his head.

"I hold your life in my hand," Semerket told him. "You can still live it out if you tell me the truth. Do you belong to the Beggar King of the North?"

The man again nodded.

"What is his connection with the tomb-makers in the Great Place? Why have you come here?"

The man's cracked lips moved as he tried to speak. Looking about the room, Semerket saw the basin of water. The Cripple Maker's instruments were still soaking there. Though the water was pink with blood and matter, he withdrew a sponge and squeezed a few drops over the beggar's lips. As the man attempted to speak, Semerket brought his ear to the beggar's mouth.

The beggar barely breathed the words. "The ship . . . is overturned."

Semerket and the Beggar King regarded one another in puzzlement. The man was delirious, Semerket decided.

"What ship is overturned? What do you mean?"

The man shivered. His breath came in shallow gasps, and he gasped for air like a hooked fish. Again Semerket squeezed a few drops of water over the beggar's lips. But they fell from the man's mouth to pool on the table. With a tiny groan, a faint exhalation of air, the man shuddered and died.

"Damn!" roared the Beggar King.

Semerket sighed and stood erect in the gloom. "There are more of his companions here in Thebes. I saw the noseless one tonight at the Elephant's Tusk—"

Instantly the Beggar King drove his chariot to the door, shouting to Yousef to take a party of men to the tavern and capture the beggar. After the giant had gone, Semerket approached the Beggar King.

"Do you consider me a friend?" he asked.

The king's eyes were suspicious. "I count allies, not friends."

"As one ally to another, then—don't be tempted to traffic in any treasure that should come your way. Already the Medjays suspect its loss. When they find the thieves and the missing jewels, all who have touched them will be punished with their lives. This I can promise you—even kings could fall."

. . .

THE NOTE READ:

> *Vital to see you. I'm at the stable near the public well. Come alone. I am not drunk. Please.*
>   *Semerket*

It was the next morning when Semerket, summoning all his will, went through the second door that had opened the night before. Standing in the small square onto which the gates of the nearby estate emptied, he waited until a serving girl emerged from the house, laundry basket on her hip. The girl would have been pretty but for her cleft palette, and she winced as he approached her, unused to strangers treating her with anything but revulsion. She hid her mouth with a free hand, and her eyes were frightened. Semerket made a gesture indicating that she should not fear him, and held out the piece of folded papyrus.

"Will you take this to your mistress?" he asked. "And make sure no one else sees . . . ?" He took a copper piece from his sash and held it out for her.

Seeing the shining metal, the girl's eyes became a great deal friendlier. She nodded her head and took the note from him, disappearing into the house. Casually, as if to prove he had no cares, Semerket strolled to the nearby stables where the families who lived on the square boarded their livestock: cows for milking and donkeys for transport and hauling, the occasional horse. He nodded to the liverymen who labored there but said nothing, and leaned against a hitching post.

Semerket forced his heart to calm itself. You will not fall to pieces, he told himself firmly. Today you will remain calm, unmoved. You will not—

"Semerket . . . ?"

Her low voice made him start, and he spun quickly in its direction. No matter the command to his heart, it now leapt rebelliously into his throat.

"Naia." His voice was barely more than a whisper.

She stood in the stable's doorway, slim and more beautiful than he remembered, and her familiar citrus scent was already in his nostrils.

She seemed absolutely unchanged, though she was dressed more richly than when she had been his wife. Gold discs hung at her ears and her head scarf was of rich wool that fell in long black sweeps to the ground.

It was then he noticed she carried something in her arms. He could not at first think what it was, but then heard the small whimpering sounds issuing from it.

Semerket's eyes became fixed and hard.

"I know your note said to come alone," Naia spoke quickly, seeing his expression, "but I couldn't leave him behind. He's only a week old, and I dare not trust the servants . . ."

When he sent her the note Semerket had never imagined such a scene. Indeed, he had been so careful not to imagine anything at all that his mind had been closed to all possible scenarios. He stood there, barely breathing.

"Semerket?" She took a step forward. "Semerket, say something!"

He swallowed. "I didn't know . . . I mean, no one told me . . ." Fiercely he tried to feel anything in his limbs, which had gone quite numb, tried to force his stupid tongue to work. Semerket took a long breath and spoke. "I mean—congratulations, Naia." To his astonishment his voice was calm and even.

Naia smiled in relief and walked to where he stood. Eagerly she held the child up to him, undoing the child's swaddling a bit so that he could see its face. "Isn't he beautiful?"

The child was indeed that, his skin the same pale, smoky hue as his mother's. He blinked up at Semerket blindly, and his dark eyes were large, like a calf's. Fine black hair covered his head, and his brow was high with promised intelligence. Before he could stop himself Semerket lifted a finger to touch the child's hand, a thing of perfect softness.

The child looked at him gravely, and clung to the finger with a strength that surprised Semerket. Though Semerket's face remained expressionless, he was thinking silently to himself, I will crawl into the earth and die here, now, right on this spot.

But in that same surprisingly clear voice he had used a moment before, he instead asked, "What is his name?"

"There's a tradition in Nakht's family that they are descended from Pharaoh Huni—so that's what we call him, at least for now."

"Huni." Semerket pulled his finger away, and the child closed its eyes and turned its head, making sucking noises. Semerket looked then upon his ex-wife. "I don't need to ask you how you are, Naia. You're beautiful."

She smiled, pleased. Then her brows drew together in concern. "Oh, but Ketty—! You don't look well at all. Something ails you!"

What was he to say? He could not tell her that the food he ate might be poisoned or drugged, or that he was afraid to sleep at night because death lurked in his dreams. So he said, "I'm fine. Really."

"What are you doing here, Ketty? Your note said it was vital."

He looked about the stable, trying to phrase what he had to say. "It's a long story. I'm investigating a crime, a murder—"

She put her hand to her mouth in happiness. "Are you back with the courts, then? Ketty, that is good news."

"Naia—"

"It's just what you need to get your life going forward again."

"Naia—"

"You don't know how I've worried about you—"

His voice was more severe than he meant it to be. "Naia, stop!"

She was instantly silent, her eyes growing large.

"I'm here because I suspect your husband is involved in it."

She continued to stare at him, silent, with the same terrible expression on her face, cradling the child closer to her breast.

He spoke rapidly. "Naia, I saw him. Last night. Nakht met them— the men I was following. Naia, they're bad men. There's one, a beggar—without a nose—who even tried to kill me once. He's dangerous, Naia. Another is a foreman from Pharaoh's tomb, and the scribe— there's been a murder of a priestess, and we think there's tomb robbery going on in the Great Place, and now Mayor Paser . . ."

He stopped. It was all coming out wrong, a great incoherent jumble. Naia was still looking at him with the same wide-eyed expression. She thinks I'm mad, Semerket told himself.

"Naia . . ." he said helplessly.

"What do you want from us, Semerket?" It was the coldest tone she had ever used to him.

He blinked. "I need to know what's going on."

She shook her head slowly. "And so you come here today, out of nowhere, and expect me to inform on my own husband." She sat on a bale of straw as if her strength had failed her. "I thought . . ." She sighed and did not continue.

He sat next to her, trying to explain. "Naia, if Nakht is involved in this, the consequences will be terrible for everyone. You know the law in Egypt. Your entire family will be punished. Everyone will be at risk— you, your servants. Even that child in your arms."

Her mouth opened in astonishment, and her dark eyes sparked with fear and indignation. "And you think to make me do what you ask— by threatening my baby? Oh, Semerket! No! *No!*"

She fled the stable. Semerket caught up with her by the well and reached out to catch her arm. It was the first time he had touched her in months, and the shock of it was electric for them both. She stopped, breathing hard, but did not turn to look at him.

Semerket spoke in a low voice. "I did not come to threaten your child, sweetheart—I would kill anyone who did that. I came here to help you, help your husband, if he will have it."

She was silent for a moment, still refusing to look at him. Then she spoke in a tiny voice. "What do you want me to do, Semerket?"

"Go to him. Tell him that however he is involved, whatever he has done, it can still be undone. The best way would be for him to tell me what he knows."

The child at her breast began to wail, and the sound seemed to galvanize her into movement. "The child must be fed, Semerket." She hurried to her gate and pulled it open.

"Will you tell your husband . . . ?" he called after her.

But she was already through the door of her house.

THE MOON WAS a sliver that evening. Only the black silhouette of the Gate of Heaven against its blanket of stars served to guide him from the temple landing to the tomb-makers' village. Strange that he should be relieved to see the torches atop the village ramparts. Had his life become so lonely that he looked forward to the company of people who hated him?

He went through the smaller southern gates into the darkened enclosure of the village. Though the hour was early by tomb-makers' standards, the village was deserted. Doors and gateways were firmly bolted against the night and whatever lurked in it.

Semerket stepped slowly through the dark corridor of the main street, advancing toward the priestess's house, his fingertips brushing against the walls on either side of him. He felt about with his foot, careful to avoid the jars and brooms that waited outside the doorways.

As he inched forward, he gradually became aware of another noise. Every time he took a step forward, he heard a distant echoing step behind, as if someone tried to match exactly the pace of his footfalls. He turned to peer into the dark, but all he saw were the distant torches at the southern gate.

"Yes?" he called into the darkness. "Who's there?"

No voice answered him, but when he stepped forward again, the faint echoing noise came again to his ears. Suddenly the image of a slashing lioness rose in his mind, and he saw beside it the evanescent figure of Hetephras, blood-spattered and grisly. He broke into a run, heedless of any pots or brooms lurking in the corridor ready to trip him.

Semerket streaked to the door of Hetephras's house, shaking and breathless. Swiftly he pushed the door open and slid its bolt into place, then waited with his ear pressed to the wood, listening. When Semerket heard no other sound, he forced himself to take deep breaths. Gradually the fear within him subsided.

A small voice spoke to him from the dark. "Do you believe she is really here among us?"

Semerket twisted around, a gasp caught in his throat. Hunro was sitting on the tiles of the front room, a shawl pulled over her shoulders against the chill. She held Sukis in her lap. Companionably, the cat ambled to where Semerket stood, to twine between his legs.

Calming his racing heart, he bent to stroke the cat's fur, all the while watching Hunro. She seemed small and afraid, not at all her usual bold strumpet. Her face was bare of paint, and her robe was a simple one.

He took a step forward. "I've seen how remorse can so eat away at the guilty, they see ghosts and demons everywhere."

Hunro shivered, holding her head in her hands. She had forgotten to drench herself in sandalwood fragrance, as was her custom, and Semerket was suddenly struck by how infinitely more attractive she was when barren of all emollients and paints and goddess's garb.

Semerket brought his finger to her face and stroked her cheek. He was surprised to find it wet with tears. "Aren't you afraid that Hetephras might be waiting here in the dark?" he asked gently.

She ignored his question, but her breathing was ragged. "I came here to tell you that I'm leaving tomorrow. I have my jewels." She pointed to a small alabaster chest on the tiles. "I'm going across to the eastern city at first light. I wanted to ask if you'd help me find a house there, somewhere where they can't find me again. They'll make me come back if they know where I am."

"Hunro . . ."

"If you won't help me, I don't know what I'm going to do. I've no one else to ask."

The words slipped out before he had even thought about them. "Yes, I'll help you," he said.

Hunro looked at him in wonder. "You will? Truly?"

He nodded. Quite simply, she was the only person to whom he felt close. But that was not the main reason. Why shouldn't one person get what she wanted out of life, he asked himself.

Semerket saw the heat in her eye that kindled when he answered her. She was parting her lips and leaning in so closely that he could feel the warmth of her body. As she tilted her head, their lips met and her breath was flowing into his. He groaned, trying to pull away, but found he could not.

Suddenly he heard the same soft footsteps that had trailed him in the corridor, now stopping outside the door. Snapping his head up sharply, he gazed into the dark. He sensed that Sukis had gone suddenly feral, her back arching and her ears flat against her skull. He put a finger to his lips, warning Hunro to be silent, and he tiptoed to the door, listening. No longer afraid, for the sounds were distinctly human, he pushed it open.

Of course, he should have suspected who it would be. "What are you doing out there, Khepura?" he asked loudly.

The head woman gaped for a moment like a hooked fish. "I heard sounds coming from Hetephras's house tonight," she said at last, somewhat defensively. "I had to see for myself if *she* was here."

Semerket knew he was supposed to think Khepura had come looking for Hetephras's ghost. But it was more than likely, given Khepura's
ability to scent out such things, that she knew Hunro was behind the
door.

"She isn't." Semerket was as unspecific as the head woman, and his
black eyes were hidden in the dark.

"I thought I heard more than one voice," Khepura said innocently.
"Are you not alone?" Khepura bent her head to peek past him. Semerket thrust his body between her and the rooms behind. Behind him he
heard the soft noises of Hunro retreating into the distant kitchen.
Khepura heard the sounds as well.

"I'm not alone," he said.

"Oh . . . ?"

"The cat is here with me."

"Oh."

She flashed him a lewd smile. "Good night, Semerket," she said, and
in those innocuous words she somehow implied that a universe of
shamelessness existed behind the door.

Repulsed, he backed away from her, and at that moment Khepura
saw the alabaster box that Hunro had brought with her. It sat on the
tiles, iridescent in the starlight. There was no doubt she recognized it,
and the same knowing smile became wider on her face, as if all her suspicions had been confirmed. Chuckling softly to herself, she turned
and retreated down the alleyway. For such a hefty woman she moved
with a certain grace, Semerket thought, elephantine though it may
have been.

Semerket once more refastened the door and joined Hunro. He noticed that Sukis had relaxed her stance, but nevertheless stood alert
and wary.

"She knows you're here," he told Hunro.

"What of it? After tomorrow I'll be free!"

"She saw your box of treasures on the tiles."

Hunro's face became momentarily panicky, and she ran to the reception room to gather up the small chest in her arms, cradling it as
Naia had cradled her infant. Then her face grew savage. "That hog—I
hate her! She's half the reason I want out of here—always spying on
me, telling lies."

"You have to hide them," Semerket said. "You can leave them here with me, if you want."

He saw the involuntary flash of distrust that lit her eyes. She clung to the box even more tightly. "N-no," she answered. "There's a place in my house where I keep them, behind a loose brick. Only I know where they are." Then her voice again took on its customary light-hued purr. She began to speak about the kind of house she wanted for them in Eastern Thebes. "And when you come home, you'll lie upon our bed and I'll rub your feet," she said, "and our neighbors will sensibly hide behind the gate."

He was astonished. "Hunro," he began awkwardly, desperation beginning to make his tongue once again unserviceable, "when I said I'd help you, I didn't mean . . . what I want to say is . . . I'm bad luck for any woman—a terrible risk. You'd only end up cursing me."

Hunro merely smiled confidently and brought the alabaster box under his nose, as if the mere sight of the treasures hidden within it would smother any protests he might have. She lifted its lid and when Semerket saw, speech indeed died in his mouth.

There, in front of him, were the royal jewels he and Qar had sought—the ones Nenry had vainly searched for in the bazaars—rings, loops, bracelets, amulets massed together in the box, a medley of colors that flashed brilliantly even in the dark. From their workmanship alone Semerket would have recognized them as royal jewels. But more than this were the telltale glyphs of inlaid gold and silver and ivory and electrum, each proclaiming them to be the property of pharaohs, queens, and princes from Egypt's distant past, names as legendary as the gods' own.

In enthralled wonder he picked up a jeweled heart scarab, holding it high to read its inscription by the feeble starlight. The name of Pharaoh Hatshepsut leapt out at him from the scarab's golden belly. Hurriedly he picked out other pieces. Cartouches of Thutmose, Amenhoteb, Nefertari flashed at him in rapid succession. But the most damning of all was the name of Queen Twos-re inscribed on a magnificent cuff of gold inset with cabochon rubies, the largest piece Hunro possessed. Semerket had beheld its like once before—the cuff exactly matched the ear loop he and Qar had found beneath the campfire ashes in the Great Place.

"Hunro—!" he gasped.

"I'll get a good price for them, won't I, Semerket? They're good quality, aren't they?"

"Where did you get these?"

She refused to meet his eyes. "I told you—from the men on the tomb's work gang, mainly. I make them give me the jewels for . . . for what I do for them. You're not going to be jealous, are you? I've always been honest with you about it. But after tomorrow, I'll never—"

"This one—who gave it to you?" He held up Queen Twos-re's ruby-studded bracelet.

"Paneb."

"And this?"

"The lapis ring? It was from Aaphat, I think."

"And this?" he asked, holding up a pectoral of gold and carnelian shaped like the snake goddess Meretseger.

"Sani gave it to me . . . Semerket, why are you looking at me like that?"

He shook his head, trying to find the words. "Hunro, do you know where these come from?"

"Yes, of course. The men purchase them with their wages. They come from a merchant. Amen-meses, I think his name is."

"Have you seen this man yourself?" His voice was so sharp that she backed away from him, confused and frightened.

She shook her head.

"Has anyone here in the village seen him—anyone other than Paneb and his men?"

"I don't know . . ." Her voice was faint. "Semerket, are you saying that my jewels aren't worth anything? That I can't sell them?"

He shook his head sadly. "I'm saying that if you even tried to sell any of them, you'd be arrested. I doubt you'd even go to trial before they'd tie a noose around your neck."

Her eyes grew wide. "Semerket, I don't like your jokes."

"These are *royal* jewels, Hunro—they came from *royal* tombs. There is no merchant. Amen-meses was a king, a man who stole the throne of Egypt for himself years ago. The name is probably a code word for where they got the jewels. Maybe they came from his tomb, I don't know. But they didn't purchase them from any merchant, that much I know. These jewels are stolen."

Her mouth opened, but she could only stare at him. Then she seized the jewels and began stuffing them back into the alabaster box.

"I don't care," she muttered. "They're mine now. You're mistaken." Her hands shook so that she could barely grasp the jewels in her fingers. The lapis ring went flying across the tiles.

He retrieved it for her, and gently placed it in her palm. Her hand was icy, and she stared off into the dark as if into an abyss.

"Hunro . . ." he began. "Nothing's changed. You can still go live in Thebes. Come with me to the vizier tomorrow, and tell him how you obtained the jewels—"

Alarm blazed in her eye. "No."

"He'll reward you. You'll have a pension, a house, whatever you wish. Hunro, listen to me! Once the authorities get involved, it will be over."

She was shaking her head, shame and desperation in her glance. "Semerket, if I tell the authorities, everyone in Thebes will know how I—" Her feather-light voice broke from stress. He leaned forward to comfort her but she recoiled from him, pressing herself against the wall, clutching the alabaster jewel box. "They'll know how I got them."

Semerket suddenly understood the extent of Hunro's misery. She had been the butt of so many cruel village jokes for so long, she had come to believe them herself. Even her lover Paneb told lewd stories about her. The village men had traded her among themselves, plying her with bits of stolen jewelry. She had behaved like a wanton because she saw it as the only way to leave behind a life she abhorred. Just as Semerket had been condemned as a follower of Set since he was a boy, never permitted to be anything else but what the name implied, so had Hunro been condemned for a role that others had thrust upon her.

"Suppose I do tell the authorities," she whispered. "What will become of those men who gave me the jewels?"

His sober gaze confirmed what she suspected.

"Semerket, I've known these men almost all of my life!"

"I cannot alter their guilt and neither can you," he said. No matter how gently he might put it, in the end it came down to one thing: "Hunro, if you don't want to die with them, you must do what I tell you."

Her lips were trembling. "I can't . . . I can't destroy everyone I've ever known."

"They've destroyed themselves."

She was shaking, and a light sheen of sweat had broken out on her forehead. She abruptly bent and vomited onto the tiles. When she had finished retching, he helped her to the bench. Her breathing came slower, then, and she leaned her head against the brick wall, silent.

"What are you going to do, Hunro? What are you thinking?"

"Thinking?" She rose to her feet then, as if every joint in her body ached, and turned to him wearily. "That I wish I'd never met you."

SNEFERU WAS SEATED at his potter's wheel. The light in his workshop's doorway darkened and he glanced up to find Semerket and Qar standing there.

"Gentlemen," he said, his voice uncertain. "What can I do for you so early in the morning?"

"Have you managed to repair Hetephras's jar as you promised?"

He nodded. "Well, some of it, as well as I could. Some of the pieces were missing. I had to use raw clay to fill the holes. I hope that's all right."

"Bring it to me," Semerket said.

Once again Sneferu's heart jumped in his chest, both from Semerket's sober expression and from the unfriendly tone in his voice. He darted a worried look at the pair, then disappeared into the recesses of the workshop.

Semerket and Qar exchanged glances but remained silent. Semerket had gone to the Medjay's tower at dawn to tell him of all that he had learned in Eastern Thebes, and of the clay pieces he had found in the Great Place so long before, the ones that he had taken to Sneferu to reassemble. Finally, Semerket had described to the Medjay every jewel that Hunro possessed.

"They're robbing the very tombs they built," Qar remarked in wonder. "Yet it makes sense it would be the tomb-makers. Who else knows the Great Place so well?"

Qar and Semerket had agreed that they would force Sneferu to divulge the name of the jar's true owner—who was surely one of the tomb robbers. Later, they would confiscate Hunro's jewels. It would seem a terrible betrayal to her, of course, but Semerket would ensure she received the credit for exposing the conspiracy. At least it would save her life.

Sneferu reentered the workshop carrying the jar. "I'm surprised you found this jar in Hetephras's house, Semerket," the potter remarked timidly.

"Why?"

"It's not hers."

Semerket exchanged a quick glance with Qar. "Really? That's a relief—I'd hate to have Hetephras longing for it in her present mood. Whose is it then?"

Sneferu hesitated, frightened by the way Qar and Semerket were studying him—like owls watching a vole, he thought. He felt a tremor of fear run up and down his spine. "I—I made it for Sani."

"The goldsmith? Khepura's husband?"

Sneferu nodded, looking at the pot doubtfully. "Perhaps Khepura loaned it to her before she was—"

They were abruptly interrupted by rising screams at the village gate. One voice rose hysterically above the others.

"It's Hunro!" Semerket said to Qar.

Qar thrust the jar into Semerket's hands and left the workshop. He pushed through the teeming crowds to the square with Semerket fast behind him. Hunro was indeed screaming and sobbing. She fell to her knees when she saw Semerket, hammering the ground with her fists.

"They're gone. All of them gone," she said. Tears streaked her face and her hair was a wild, haunted thicket. Hunro clung to him, gasping. "The jewels—they've been taken, Semerket."

Semerket went numb. If the jewels were gone, so was the evidence he and Qar had planned to use against the tomb-makers. Only the pitiful, cracked jar in his hands remained—hardly enough to convict anyone. He turned to Qar, who was gazing about the square in anger, as if he could pick the thief from among the gathering crowd.

The boy Rami emerged from the throng, followed by Hunro's husband, Neferhotep. When he saw that his mother was at the center of the mêlée, Rami ran to her.

"Mother, come away. People are looking at you. Don't do this." He attempted to pull her to her feet, but she was helplessly limp in his grasp, continuing to cry and moan. "Mother, please," he said again, glancing around at the curious tomb-makers. "You're embarrassing me."

Neferhotep slunk through the crowd. "Get up, you whore," he said to Hunro between clenched teeth. "You'll not shame our family any further."

Hunro blinked, startled by his harsh words, but it was at that unfortunate moment that she saw Khepura push her way through the crowd, accompanied by Paneb. The head woman stopped in front of her, smiling with thin contempt. Khepura leaned past Paneb to whisper something into Neferhotep's ear, and everyone heard her tiny cackle of joy.

Hunro shook herself loose from her son and screamed at the head woman. "Thief! Robber! Give me back my jewels! I know it was you who took them!"

"I didn't steal your whore's rubbish!" Khepura protested, eyes wide. "By Amun, I will lay myself in my tomb if I am lying!"

"I know you did!"

The crowd itself broke the stalemate. "Let our good god decide," they shouted. "Bring out the oracle!"

The tomb-makers erupted in cheers, all but the elders. Neferhotep was speaking in fierce low whispers to Hunro, commanding her to drop her accusations. Rami pleaded with his mother to please, *please* take back her words. Paneb, too, urged Hunro to calm herself.

"What are they talking about?" Semerket turned to Qar, whispering.

"They're speaking of the statue of Amenhoteb—the pharaoh who founded this village over three hundred years ago. He is the judge they use for such disputes."

"A statue?"

Qar only nodded, eyes fixed on the villagers. They shouted that Qar must choose the god's bearers, according to their ancient custom. The Medjay quickly pointed to various men in the crowd, six in total. Rami stood apart, trembling and red-faced.

The men chosen by Qar sped inside the sanctuary, returning within moments bearing a god's sedan chair on their shoulders. Seated within it was the limestone figure of the first Pharaoh Amenhoteb. Wearing his striped nemes crown, hastily rouged and anointed, the graven pharaoh stared sternly at his village.

The men brought the statue to where Hunro stood. For a moment she hung her head. But when Qar abruptly pushed her forward, she caught her voice. "Act, my lord," she implored the statue, "to restore my loss."

For a moment nothing happened. Then the six bearers began to sway on their feet and their eyes fluttered. The men on the chair's right unexpectedly dipped in unison, as if they intended to pitch the statue onto the ground. The crowd gasped, striving to keep themselves from the god's gaze. The chair righted itself, only to pitch forward when the two lead bearers fell to their knees. Cries from the tomb-makers rose again. But the lead men leapt once more to their feet, turning the chair around, to run headlong in the opposite direction. The villagers fell away before them, yelling.

"What's going on? Tell me!" Semerket demanded.

Qar leaned back to whisper in his ear, "The god is pressing down upon the shoulders of the bearers, to indicate which direction they should take him."

The bearers seemed to be confused. Round and round they turned, so that Amenhoteb's oracle could gaze his fill at all his villagers. Then the bearers stopped, their feet suddenly rooted to the ground. For a long while they did not move. Then they turned in Khepura's direction, rushing headlong at the head woman.

Qar prodded Semerket. "Now," he whispered.

The statue teetered forward, so that its inlaid obsidian eyes could glare down upon her. Khepura flung her arms over her head and opened her mouth to scream. But at that precise moment the statue was shifted slightly to stare at another beside her. The bearers sank to their knees then, and made no other move.

The good god had found the thief.

Hunro put a fist in her mouth to stifle her scream—and the other villagers backed away from the accused, leaving him alone at the circle's center. Semerket seized Qar's arm.

It was Rami.

The youth fell to the ground. Hunro ran to him and held his face in her hands. "Did you do it, truly?"

Reluctantly the boy nodded.

"I drop the charges," Hunro cried instantly.

Qar stepped forward, saying the god had made his judgment and that the charges remained in effect. "But," he said, "if Rami produces the stolen items, we will forgo his punishment. If not, the stick shall be brought and his father shall beat him according to the law."

Hunro stroked her son's head, pushing the hair from his eyes. "Rami," she said, "please. You must do this thing."

Rami smiled weakly at his mother, and shook his head. "I'm sorry, Mother, but the jewels are gone," he whispered. "I don't even know where they are." He dropped his head and refused to look at her.

"Let a stick be brought!" shouted Qar.

A branch, thick and pliable, was cut from an acacia tree in the temple garden. When its thorns had been shaved away and the leaves removed, Qar deemed it serviceable. He brought it to Neferhotep.

"Take it. Whip him until he confesses where his mother's jewels are."

Neferhotep exchanged glances with Khepura. Semerket watched them closely. Neferhotep's voice rang clearly out over the crowd. "I cannot."

"It is the law!" Qar thundered.

"I cannot whip him. Rami is not my son."

A chorus of gasps erupted from the tomb-makers. Their faces wore expressions ranging from shock to glee. Hunro put a hand to her throat where a blue vein throbbed.

"I have concealed my shame from the village long enough," Neferhotep continued in the same clear voice, though he affected a grief-stricken stance. "It is the cuckoo's egg that has hatched in my house. Paneb is the father of Rami. My wife is an adulteress. Paneb must punish his own son."

Semerket instantly realized the full import of Neferhotep's words. Hunro was to be denounced as an adulteress and arrested. The jewels were gone; now the chief witness against the tomb-makers would be put away as well.

Paneb's roar of rage caught everyone by surprise.

"You bastard!" he shouted at Neferhotep. "You've made me do terrible things in your time—but you can't make me do this!" Paneb rose to his full impressive height. He seized the acacia branch from Qar, and his knuckles were white as he gripped it. The branch hissed through the air as he charged forward.

Neferhotep ran. He broke through the crowd of tomb-makers and sped down the hill to the village gates. "Stop him!" he implored the villagers as he passed. "Somebody make him stop! He's a crazy person!"

No one intervened.

Paneb caught Neferhotep by the gates, bringing the branch across his shoulders. Neferhotep screamed like a hare caught in a hyena's jaws and tripped, rolling in the sands, trying to protect his face.

By this time Qar and Semerket had caught up to the big foreman. They clung to his arms, but he continued to lash at Neferhotep until sweat dripped from his brow. In desperation Qar threw himself between Paneb and the scribe. Neferhotep immediately seized his chance and leapt again to his feet, fleeing through the gates and into the village corridor.

Paneb flung Qar aside as if he were a child, running after Neferhotep for the entire length of the village's main street, kicking aside the pottery and refuse at the villagers' doors. Dogs barked after them, feeding the confusion and tumult. Neferhotep reached his house just as Paneb caught him. The scribe flung himself through his door, sliding the bolt behind him.

"Come out of there, Nef!" Paneb roared, pounding on the door. "I've killed before—what's another death to me? I'm damned whatever happens, thanks to you!"

It was Qar, accompanied by other Medjays, who subdued the foreman, clubbing Paneb over the head with the butt end of his spear. Paneb fell, stunned. The Medjays bound him then with ropes, thrusting a pole through his bonds. They carried him away on their shoulders as if he were a trussed antelope. Qar gave the orders to also bind Rami. When this was done, father and son were taken to the prison in the Medjay headquarters at the edge of the Great Place.

Semerket and Qar could not speak. Finally, turning to Qar, Semerket whispered. "What in hell just happened here?"

LATER THAT AFTERNOON, the news was brought to them that Hunro had been arrested by a women's delegation headed by Khepura. She was taken, struggling and cursing, to be imprisoned in the cell located at the back of the village. The jewels were gone, and so, too, was their chief witness, just as Semerket had foreseen.

Qar was at last moved to action. "It's time to take back control of this," he said.

That evening the sound of tramping feet caught the tomb-makers unawares. Realizing that men and not spirits made the noises, the villagers crept from their houses to gawk from their doors. In the corridor they saw a cadre of Medjays walking two abreast. Captain Mentmose led them, their spears held at the ready. At one of the alleys the Medjays turned.

Moments later the villagers heard loud knocks on some distant door. From over the walls came Khepura's surprised screams, followed by angry shouts from her sons. The tomb-makers stared at one another with frightened eyes. They began to gather in the corridor, afraid and silent, just as the Medjays reemerged into it.

To their dismay they saw Khepura's husband, the goldsmith Sani, being led away in manacles. The Medjays unceremoniously prodded Sani toward the northern gate. Sani's face was so fearful that he appeared almost unrecognizable to his neighbors. The Medjays roughly shoved aside any of the tomb-makers who stumbled in their way.

Khepura's screams of anguish erupted into the corridor, pursuing the Medjays down its entire length. "Sani!" she screeched. "Sani—!" But the Medjays continued to force the goldsmith ahead of them, using the points of their spears. Khepura collapsed in the corridor, shrieking her husband's name again and again, surrounded by her sons. "He is a good man," she wailed. "Bring him back to me!"

Qar looked back into the village corridor. Half-expecting to see an angry mob, he saw instead families huddled together in their doorways, their expressions resigned, as if the thing they feared most had at last come to claim them.

As Sani was led away by Qar, Semerket slipped from Hetephras's house and out of the village. The wind was sharp and only starlight illuminated the desert. Rain clouds massed on the horizon. From deep in the Great Place Semerket heard the chirping yelps of a jackal pack on the prowl. Squinting in their direction, he saw their dark forms frolicking together on the distant sands. Every so often they would stop, dig for rodents and grubs, and then move on, grunting to one another.

The hackles on his neck rose; jackals were the dogs of the cemetery, the companions of death.

He walked swiftly down the trail to the village jail cell. It was nothing more than a deep pit lined in mud brick, over which a small bronze grate was locked. The villagers had posted no guard, and he approached the grating unobserved. Kneeling beside it, he heard a small pebble drop to the cell's floor far below. The pit must be at least five cubits deep, he surmised.

"Hunro," he whispered into the cell.

He heard a small movement, but could see nothing below. "Semerket?" Her feathery voice came back to him through the dark.

"I've brought you a cloak, and some bread. Watch out now—I'm going to drop them to you."

He pushed the cloak through the grating. Then he dropped the loaf of bread to her, though he had to tear it in half to fit it through the grate.

She was touched. "You're good to remember me, Semerket," she said.

"We've arrested Sani. He's going to be tortured if he doesn't tell us what he knows, Hunro. Paneb's already in custody. The day after, and every day after that, the Medjays will arrest another member of the work gang until one confesses."

There was no reply from her at first. Then he heard her muttering into the dark, "Horrible . . ."

"I want you to know that I'll save Rami if I can. But you must warn him, Hunro, that his only hope is to confess. It will be to his advantage if he does. Will you tell him?"

It was a moment before she spoke again. "If I see him again, yes. Thank you, Semerket."

"Tomorrow at first light I'm going to Djamet to see the vizier. He'll order your release."

She was silent. He thought she must be weeping again, but when her voice reached him it was surprisingly calm.

"Goodbye, Semerket," she said.

Reluctantly, he stood up and brushed the dirt from his knees. As he adjusted his woolen mantle about his shoulders, he happened to look in the direction of the Great Place. Six pairs of gleaming yellow eyes stared back. The jackals stood very near to him, bold and unafraid. He made a threatening gesture at them and stamped his foot. The jackals turned and fled down the trail, stopping occasionally to return his stare.

The desert wind rushed at him from over the dunes, grit-laden and chill. Shivering, he trudged to the village kitchens to fetch his evening's meal from the servants. Lost in his thoughts, fearing for Hunro, he pushed open the door without thinking who might be behind it.

Khepura and her sons sat in a tight circle, surrounded by their neighbors. As she wept, her sons bent over her, begging her to be brave. Other tomb-makers murmured words of comfort, saying they knew in their hearts that Sani would be home soon, that the Medjays could not possibly keep him in jail for very long . . .

Khepura moaned that she feared her husband would be beaten by the Medjays—that he was not young—that he could not possibly survive such treatment. At this last, she broke into fresh wails.

Semerket came through the gate and the tomb-makers instantly were silent, dropping their heads to glare at him from hooded eyes. Semerket cursed his luck to find himself surrounded by resentful villagers. His only course was to brave it out and hope there would be no confrontation.

Semerket nodded to them, refusing to meet their gaze, and headed for the hearths. He directed the attending servant to give him a jar of beer, and asked another woman to fill a bowl with greens and cheese. Semerket was on the point of leaving, but as he turned from the hearth he found that Khepura was standing directly behind him, blocking his exit, her expression malignant.

"It was you who had my husband arrested," she muttered accusingly.

"No," he said firmly. "The Medjays arrested him."

"You were behind it."

"Blame yourself, Khepura—he wouldn't be in jail had you not taken Hunro away."

"Sneferu told us about the pot, how you tricked him into repairing it. Do you think we don't know what you're trying to do to us—making innocent people into criminals so you'll look good to the vizier?"

Semerket felt his face redden with anger. He wanted to laugh at her words, to fling accusations at her. So they were innocent people, were they? He knew in his heart that Khepura had something to do with the disappearance of Hunro's jewels, even though Rami had taken the blame. Hot words began to bubble to his lips, his tongue freed of its usual sluggishness. It was all he could do not to tell her—tell them all—that though the villagers may have slipped through the noose by their timely theft of Hunro's jewels, he would soon tighten it again.

But he saw her four strong sons glowering at him, ready to spring if their mother gave the word. Semerket placed his jar of beer on the hearth, beside his bowl of greens. Turning to them, forcing his voice to remain calm, he only said, "If your husband is innocent, Khepura, then you needn't be afraid."

"He *is* innocent. It's *you* who are guilty." Her invective came pouring out like molten lead. "I know Hunro was with you last night. I know what went on, don't think I don't. I could have you imprisoned on the very same charge of adultery if I chose. I'm head woman here and it counts for something—though you think you're so much better than us."

The flush of anger again surged through him. The unguarded words came spilling out. "You couldn't arrest me, Khepura," he said, "because you know your own husband is guilty of the charge. Tell me this—did Sani ever bring you jewels from a tomb, as he did Hunro?"

Khepura gasped, and backed away from him. Her sons erupted in violent protests. Semerket immediately rued his words, though he could not deny the pleasure they brought him. Hurriedly he turned back to the hearth for his food, wanting to leave before the villagers jumped upon him. But his beer and the bowl of greens and cheese were gone. Irritated, he called to the servant. After searching the kitchen for a few moments, she located his meal at the end of a long wooden bench.

He left the kitchen, returning to Hetephras's house. Sukis greeted him at the door and wound herself around his ankles, enticed by the aroma of his meal. The yellow cat followed him into the house. Placing the beer and bowl on the brick bench in the reception room, Semerket looked about for a candle. The moment he went into the kitchen, Sukis leapt brazenly atop the bench and seized a piece of cheese.

"Spoiled Sukis!" he said, making a hissing noise from the door to shoo her away. She jumped from the bench and sat, tail erect and twitching, her eyes following him. He went to find a candle. There was none in the kitchen, but he remembered that a fresh bundle of them was in the cellar. Downstairs, he groped about until he found them.

Once again in the kitchen he pulled his flint from his sash and managed to light the wick. He sniffed at the beer. Again the servants had overflavored the brew with herbs. The bowl of lettuce and cheese had a bitter scent as well. A tiny warning bell rang in the back of his mind.

Before he could even give thought to the suspicion, however, he heard a small retching sound coming from the reception room. He held the candle high and beheld Sukis walking stiff-legged on the tiles, struggling to reach him, coming toward him with a comical mincing strut. Strange hacking sounds erupted from her throat and Semerket saw foam bubbling from her jaws. She was trembling.

Semerket rushed to the cat, trying to take in what was happening. She fell on her side, gasping, but then seemed to overcome her initial spasm. "Sukis . . . !" he said aloud. He would have taken the little animal into his arms but at that moment she emitted such a horrifying wail that he inadvertently backed away, frightened. The cat's eyes bulged from their sockets. Her spine, to his horror, was arching inward as if it would snap in two. Her wail grew louder still, and the cat's mouth pulled into a wide, macabre grin.

He looked around helplessly, panic rising, not knowing what to do for her. Suddenly there was nothing to do at all; with a choking noise, Sukis died. Her eyes became fixed, slowly withdrawing again into their sockets. The terrible spasm relaxed its hold, and her spine straightened. Her body again became soft and pliable. But she was still.

Semerket gazed down at the cat. If Sukis had not stolen the piece of cheese, he knew, he would have been the one lying on the tiles, back bent, foam on his lips. His eyes misted as he bent to stroke her yellow fur.

Gathering up the cat's body, he wrapped it in a cloth, laying it at the side of the room. Later, he promised himself, he would have Sukis preserved and placed beside Hetephras in her tomb. Then he took the bowl of food and the jar of beer into the far privy and poured them both down the hole.

Semerket returned to the room where Sukis's body lay, and opened the front door. He stared into the sky. The dark ledge of rain clouds on the distant horizon stretched over the far desert. Semerket suddenly needed human company; he craved it. He thought at first he would go to Qar's tower, to inform him of what had happened. But then he remembered that Qar was at the Medjay headquarters on the other side of the Great Place. He had only a vague idea where the quarters were located, knowing only that they were in some abandoned tomb on the western side of the valley. It was too dark a night, he thought, to attempt a run across the steep and winding trails of the Great Place, for there was no moon . . .

He lifted his head, gazing again into the sky . . . *There was no moon!*

He suddenly knew—the tomb-makers were going to rob another crypt.

THE TOMB-MAKERS EMERGED from one of the village's alleys, turning north toward the Great Place. Semerket waited for them, concealed behind the temple wall. He was astonished to see that they carried torches, the light spilling brilliantly upon the pathway. The men seemed blithely nonchalant at being so visible in the night-shrouded valley. Even their knapsacks, laden with their copper tools, pealed merrily into the night as they ascended the high trail. They seemed not in the least worried they might attract attention.

In the circles of torchlight, Semerket saw that the scribe Neferhotep led them. Behind him was the master painter, Aaphat, and his two assistants, Kenna and Hori. Only these four remained of the chief work gang, where once there had been seven. The goldsmith Sani, the big foreman Paneb, the lad Rami—all were confined in the Medjays' jail. Surely four men would not be enough to break open a tomb, Semerket thought, to strip it of its treasures, and then bury it again in a single night . . .

He became uneasy. Perhaps they were not going to rob a tomb after all. They certainly made no effort to muffle their footsteps. He crept on the trail behind them, at a distance of some fifty cubits, careful to cling to the dark crags. At no time did they turn and look behind to see if he followed them. No doubt they believed he was dead from the poisoned food they had given him.

A trio of Medjays accosted the men, emerging from out of the dark, demanding to know why they traipsed through the Great Place at such an hour.

Neferhotep's thin, reedy voice rose nasally. "We're going to Pharaoh's tomb, where else?" he replied in aggrieved tones. "Now that you've taken our best men, we've no choice but to labor nights to complete it."

The Medjays allowed the tomb-makers to pass and returned to their towers across the valley. Semerket heard the tomb-makers' mordant snickers. Their smugness made him suspect that Neferhotep and his men had deliberately made themselves noticed in order to divert the Medjays from their real purpose. But as he followed them again along the high pathway, he saw that the men indeed descended into the valley where Pharaoh's unfinished tomb waited.

Though there was no moon, the night was almost silver-hued, starlit from above and infused with the ambient hues of distant Theban hearths. He saw Neferhotep take a large wooden key and insert it into the cedar door at the tomb's entrance. Before the scribe closed the door on them, Semerket saw him turn to sharply survey the valley. Semerket pressed himself against the cliff wall, barely breathing—and saw in the light spilling from the doorway that Neferhotep was searching for someone, or something. After a moment, Neferhotep pulled the tomb's door closed.

Semerket crossed the wadi, taking up a position on a low escarpment, and settled in to wait. An hour passed. Another. His legs were cramped and the desert air was frigid. He grew nervous and uncomfortable, unable to wait quietly. Throwing aside caution, he crept down the side of the cliff and crossed the wadi to the door of the tomb, one silent step at a time.

He fully expected the door to be locked. When he pulled on its handle, however, it swung silently toward him, perfectly balanced in its jamb. Semerket was careful to open it only a tiny fraction.

No one waited there. Summoning his resolve, Semerket took his first step inside the tomb of Pharaoh Ramses III. Torches lit the tomb at various intervals down its long, descending corridor, and it took a moment for his eyes to adjust to the brightness after being so long in the dark. Semerket heard no voices, nor any sounds that indicated the tomb-makers were at work.

They had gone to the far end, he reasoned, into the distant burial chamber itself. He listened, cocking his head in that direction. Again, silence. Fighting down his urge to flee, he forced himself forward.

The tomb's entryway stood at the top of a long staircase that descended into the mountain. At his left was a large wooden workman's chest stained with paint and battered from long use. Inside were various tools—saws, axes, picks, chisels, hammers. Out of long habit he quickly ascertained that none of the tools was fashioned from the blue metal that had killed Hetephras. A few torches were stowed deep in the chest as well, and he quietly removed one. It would both provide light, should he need it, and be a dependable weapon for his defense. A nearby jug was filled with the sesame oil and salt that would provide a smokeless light. He filled the torch's cone, but did not light it.

Semerket counted the steps down to the first passageway, twenty-seven in all. On the lintel above were paintings that the master artist, Aaphat, had recently completed—a pristine sun disk flanked by images of the goddesses Isis and Nephthys.

The torches that the tomb-makers had lit were located great distances from each other, illuminating only a few lengths of the corridor at a time. Much of the time Semerket walked in long patches of shadow before he came again into light, able to view only a portion of the tomb's painted figures. Those he did see were formal and terrifying, as befitting the tomb of a god.

As he crept along, Semerket noticed that the entire angle of the tomb began to diverge very slightly to the right. In all this time he heard no voices—no sounds at all. Ahead, leading to what he supposed would be the burial chamber, the torches stopped. Only primordial black lay beyond. The tomb-makers did not labor in the distant burial chamber, as he had first thought; they had reached this wide gallery and seemed to have vanished.

He took a step forward into the dark, heading toward the burial chamber, but abruptly stumbled over a heavy object at his feet. In the dim light he saw that a series of baskets had been placed in the hallway, at least seven laid out in a line before him. They were filled with what seemed like flat, oblong pieces of metal. He reached for one, to examine it beneath a flame—but at that moment voices came to him from the tomb's entrance.

Semerket fled into the darkened corridor ahead, hiding behind a large square pillar that supported the curved roof of the long gallery. From the sound made by their feet he surmised that there must be three individuals. The men stopped at the place where the tomb angled, and turned into an anteroom. Semerket peeked around the corner of the pillar.

The unmistakable profile—or lack of one—of Noseless the beggar met Semerket's gaze. The ragged man scrutinized the floor of the anteroom, then spoke to his two cohorts, pointing. "It's there," he said in his pronounced Delta accent. "Lift it up."

The torchlight eerily projected the beggars' wavering shadows onto the wall in front of Semerket. They hovered together, straining at something in the floor. Semerket heard the scrape of stone. Then, one after another, he saw them descend into the floor itself.

He waited until he could no longer hear their voices, then stole into the anteroom. In its floor a ragged hole gaped wide, filled with soft torchlight rising from a room below. Crude steps had been hacked into the short shaft that led down. He heard other voices then, recognizing Neferhotep's distinctive whine.

The tomb-makers were in a room below. He returned to his hiding place in the darkened gallery to wait. Within a few moments he heard noises coming back up the shaft. The four tomb-makers and the beggars emerged from the hole. Noseless and Neferhotep came last, conversing together.

"—how many?" asked the scribe.

"Twenty, at least," said Noseless.

Neferhotep exclaimed in dismay.

By now the two were in the anteroom. Noseless grabbed a torch from the wall and began walking down the hallway toward Semerket's hiding place. The light grew brighter and Semerket held his breath, heart thumping.

"Seven in this part of the tomb, and the ones below. What's really needed is an ox-cart."

The beggar and Neferhotep passed directly by the large, square pillar that shielded Semerket. The passing light of their torch clearly illuminated him. But the two men were staring at the baskets of metal discs on the other side of the corridor. Had they turned their heads a fraction to the left they surely would have seen him. Semerket edged around the pillar, facing the northern wall. A painted harpist plucked out a tune on the wall in front of him.

"Just how are we supposed to keep the Medjays away with that many of you in the valley?" he heard Neferhotep demand shrilly.

"Send them to hell with the vizier's clerk, for all I care."

"I can't poison them all."

"Why not?" snorted Noseless. "By the time anyone figures out what's happened, it'll be too late, won't it? In the meantime, we'll move these out tonight, and return for the rest tomorrow . . ."

With many a grunt and curse, the men hoisted the baskets to their shoulders. The tomb-makers and beggars slowly made their way up the sloping corridor to the tomb's entrance. As they retreated, they extinguished the torches that lined the walls. Semerket peered up the slanting corridor. The men were now at the distant cedar door. Neferhotep doused the last torch, plunging the tomb into darkness, the blackest Semerket had ever known. The scribe pushed open that door and the men silently exited.

Then Semerket heard the most terrible sound of his life—the tomb's cedar door being locked from the outside. He was sealed inside Pharaoh's tomb!

Terror claimed him.

Semerket plunged rashly into the darkness, swiftly ascending the causeway to the door. He reached the steps, counting them as he went up. At the twenty-seventh riser he stopped. Edging forward by inches, he placed his hands on the heavy door and pushed. There was not a fraction of movement.

Fighting his hysteria, muttering to himself to remain calm, Semerket moved his hands along the door's face, searching for any kind of bolt or mechanism that he could release from inside. But the wood was as smooth as polished stone. Semerket slid to the ground, panting.

Locked in a tomb . . . ! Sternly, he told himself that reason and logic would see him through the crisis. His mind raced. Surely the work gang would return in the morning to continue their tasks. Yes. They would be coming back. Upon that comforting thought his heart calmed a bit. Of course he would not be imprisoned in the tomb forever. He would merely wait until the workers came in for the day, and then sneak out when their backs were turned.

Light was what he needed, he told himself. It would cheer him, and he could put his imprisonment to good use by exploring whatever was beneath Pharaoh's tomb. He reached into his belt, praying to the gods that he had not forgotten his flint.

The flint was there. He struck it, holding it close to the torch. The flame caught on the first strike. With light again flooding the tomb, his panic began to ebb.

Semerket retraced his steps down the twenty-seven stairs, then went from gallery to gallery. He located the point where the tomb angled to the right, and turned into the anteroom. Holding the torch close to the floor, he looked for any sign of a door or passage, brushing away the limestone dust that carpeted the area. His fingers suddenly detected a slight crevice. A limestone wedge, shaped to cover a hole about a cubit in diameter, was clearly discernible. He pried it open to reveal the shaft that connected the two areas.

He dropped the torch to the floor below, a distance of some six or so cubits. Swallowing his fear, Semerket lowered his legs into the pit. The shallow footholds allowed him to slowly, if precipitously, climb down. Step by step, clinging with toe and finger, he at last reached a level surface. Semerket breathed raggedly, glad to be on even ground again. He seized his still-burning torch from the floor of the room and held it high above his head.

And then he saw.

The glint of gold was everywhere. Hammered masks of the gods, vases, cups and goblets, inlaid chests, necklaces, pectorals, ear loops— riches piled higher than his head, in a space as big as Hetephras's entire home. Semerket's mouth gaped open. He became dizzy with the spectacle, and had to sit.

Semerket remembered the conversation he had had with Qar, the day they had found Hetephras's blue wig not more than a couple hundred cubits from this very room. He had surmised that Pharaoh's tomb would be the perfect place to hide the treasure. But the tomb-makers had gone one better, secreting it in this hidden room beneath the tomb. They could come and go as they wished, innocent to all eyes, observed by the Medjays, the inspectors, even Pharaoh himself and never be noticed. He had to compliment them on their devious cleverness.

Semerket's wits returned, and he walked about the room, gazing at the piles of treasure. As a child he'd read the fables of peasants who stumbled on the cache of gods and wizards, but his paltry imagination had never conceived anything on the scale of what he saw at that moment.

Wicker baskets were heaped in the room, each brimming with oddly shaped metal discs like those he had seen above in Pharaoh's tomb. Semerket fished out one of the haphazard, oozing shapes. He ran his tongue over it, on the off chance that it could be brass, but there was no sharp acid reaction. The disc was surely gold.

Somehow the precious metal had pooled like water, then solidified. From the remote edges of his mind he remembered Qar's story of how robbers sometimes found it more convenient to burn a tomb's contents entirely, and then collect the melted blobs of congealed gold and silver from beneath the ashes. The unbidden memory of the boy in the Great Place astride the donkey came to him, and he heard again his words—"god-skin is made there."

Semerket gazed at the baskets, realizing that the disc he held in his hand was perhaps a cup that had once touched the lips of a pharaoh or a queen, or a sacred vessel that had held sweetmeats offered up to a god. Semerket looked at the rows upon rows of baskets that lined the walls of the room, filled to overflowing with the melted globules—and only then did he perceive the true extent of the theft, the waste, and the wantonness of the destruction that had accompanied it.

Semerket suddenly hurled the thin paten of gold across the room. It smashed into glinting bits against the wall. How could they have done it? These things had been made by their grandfathers, uncles, and fathers. Now they were gone, and forever. Were the tomb-makers so immune to their own artistry that they no longer saw it, melting it down because it was easier to carry away? But then he remembered Paneb, so proud of a jar crafted by his grandfather. Undoubtedly, it too had been part of the spoils, claimed by the big, angry foreman in a fit of sentimentality. Semerket felt his heart soften toward Paneb—at least one of the tomb-makers wanted a treasure for more than its mere value in the marketplace.

Semerket tipped his torch to inspect the rest of the room, and the light revealed a doorway at the room's rear. Curious, Semerket crossed to it, and emerged into another hallway. He stared in shock.

This was no hidden cellar—but an entirely different tomb! It stretched into the dark in both directions, for what length Semerket could not imagine. Qar had told him that Ramses' tomb above had been pierced thirty years before by the fathers and grandfathers of the present tomb-makers. Seeing how this tomb thrust forward, he could tell that the two tombs had collided, the roof of this forgotten tomb intersecting with the floor of Pharaoh's newer one, forcing the builders to re-angle it. That explained why it diverged to the right.

Semerket raised his torch to the walls to see if he could determine who was the tomb's original owner. Though he could clearly see the shapes of the figures that had once graced the walls, they had been carefully hacked away, leaving only their ragged outlines.

Semerket slowly walked the length of the corridor. Everything had been deliberately stripped from the walls. At the very end of the tomb, however, he discovered a bit of mural that still survived. On it was the small head of a pharaoh, recognizable by the uraeus of asps the king wore on his brow. Whoever the pharaoh had been, he was an immoderately handsome man, if the portrait was at all lifelike. Seeing the king's strong, even features reminded Semerket of someone he had met recently . . . who? Perhaps it was only a trick of his memory; he shrugged away the thought. Fortunately, a cartouche had been overlooked by the desecrators. The hackles on his neck rose when he painfully deciphered the faded glyphs within it—"Amen-meses," he breathed.

He was in the tomb of the accursed usurper, the father of Twos-re, the queen whose name had come up more than once in Semerket's investigation. Semerket suddenly realized how despised Amen-meses must have been to warrant such terrible desecration. The obliteration of his name from even his tomb ensured that the rogue pharaoh's immortal life was forfeit. No doubt his daughter's tomb, wherever it lay, had been identically stripped.

The oil in the torch was almost spent. Semerket retraced his steps through the room of gold and climbed the incised, rugged ladder to Pharaoh's unfinished tomb above. He once again took his place behind one of the large pillars in the grand gallery. Soon the torch sputtered and died, and he settled down to wait for the reappearance of the work gang. He knew that on the next night the beggars would return—the moon would still be dark—to remove the remainder of the treasure. But where were they taking it? And why?

The answers to these questions were immaterial. Because as soon as he could slip away in the morning, he planned to go directly to Vizier Toh. The thieves would be stopped in their tracks.

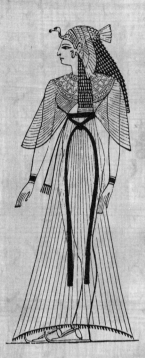

THE SEERESS OF
SEKHMET

As Semerket had known they would, the tomb-makers returned at dawn. They strode past him, unaware of his presence, going down into the burial chamber to continue their work. When he was satisfied they were not coming back, he slipped up the main corridor and out the entrance—the door now thrown open to the rising sun—and climbed the cliff to the trail above the tomb.

Within an hour he was snaking his way through Djamet's makeshift bazaar. Hundreds of stalls had sprung up outside its walls since Pharaoh had returned. A flash of his vizier's badge to the guards at the Great Pylons, and he was admitted at once into the temple.

It was not so crowded within the gardens. Nevertheless a horde of nobles, priests, and craftsmen swirled around him, intent on their morning duties. Though acrid smoke from the morning sacrifices hung over the temple compound, the paved walkways in the garden were perfumed with the scents of nearby citrus trees and jasmine vines.

At the inner temple doors Semerket approached a guard. "The vizier's quarters—where are they?" he asked, knowing that Toh had abandoned his offices at the Temple of Ma'at to be near Pharaoh when he was in Thebes. Again Semerket held his badge for the soldier to view.

The guard told him. "But if you're looking for Toh," he added, "he left before dawn for Erment, with his garrison."

Semerket's expression was such that the guard quickly added, "But he'll be back in a week or so! He went to inspect the new Buchis bull!"

Semerket had been aware of the prior Buchis bull's early death, a horrifying omen of catastrophe. The bull was considered the earthly manifestation of Pharaoh Ramses III's power, and his replacement was a task entrusted only to the highest official, which explained Toh's unexpected departure.

"Perhaps his scribe, Kenamun, can help you if it's so urgent," the guard said.

Kenamun . . . yes. He would know how to get in touch with Toh by the quickest method. Semerket nodded his thanks and stalked through the dark halls, the polished basalt tiles gleaming beneath his rough sandals. But some time had passed since he had last been inside the temple, and he grew confused. He recognized the wall of blue faience tiles . . . but did he take the left or right hallway?

A familiar voice caught his ear, and across the courtyard he glimpsed the lean figure of Mayor Pawero. The mayor did not exhibit his usual hauteur, instead amiably chatting with some other person, even laughing uproariously. Semerket was intrigued; never before had he seen the Mayor of the West so relaxed and approachable. He moved down the hallway to better see who the other person could be.

It was Mayor Paser.

Semerket could not have been more surprised. What had become of their famed distaste for one another, their ill-concealed enmity? Had the stoat and the cobra become lovers?

Semerket approached them stealthily, hoping to overhear their conversation. Unfortunately Pawero shifted his weight at that moment, and spied Semerket. The Western Mayor flinched when he realized who it was, and the color drained from his face. Seeing his colleague so undone, Paser turned to see what disturbed him.

They leapt apart like guilty children, Semerket thought.

"You!" Pawero said, barely able to speak. "But you're supposed to be . . ." He swallowed, unable to go on.

Paser shot an alarmed glance at the tall mayor. Instantaneously he took up the Eastern Mayor's words. ". . . supposed to be at the tomb-makers' village, we thought." The tall mayor nodded dumbly in agreement, his face still pale.

"Why are you here, Semerket?" Paser asked.

"The vizier—I've come to see him."

He saw the quick glance between the mayors. "Have you solved the murder of the priestess, then?" Pawero asked faintly.

Semerket studied the pair of them through narrowed, critical eyes. Something about them was not authentic. He shook his head gravely. "I merely came to get my pay from Kenamun, lords."

Instantly, the two mayors' spirits lifted. Paser even smiled. "Do you mean you've already gone through all that silver I gave you?"

Semerket smiled. "Wine costs dearly these days, Mayor," he said, winking.

Paser guffawed, but his eyes remained coldly appraising. Pawero, on the other hand, had become once again his rigid former self. Without another word he fled, rushing to his chambers, occasionally looking back at Semerket and shuddering.

"He's heard of the disturbances in the tomb-makers' village," Paser explained. "You can't blame him for believing you to be the cause, Semerket."

"They caused it themselves," Semerket answered shortly, then added, in a tone less harsh, "Excuse me, lord, but I must find Kenamun. Can you tell me where the scribe might be found?" Paser pointed down a hallway. Semerket stretched his hands at knee level, and left the mayor there.

Kenamun was at a table, writing upon a scroll. When he saw Semerket enter the room, his eyes widened, and Semerket noted how he turned the papyrus over. Semerket fancied for a moment that the vizier's scribe, too, was not happy to see him.

Quickly he told Kenamun of finding the gold in the forgotten tomb in the Great Place, of how the tomb-makers had attempted to kill him, and that somehow he felt it was all connected to the murder of Hetephras. He asserted that Hunro's arrest and the theft of her jewels had effectively stymied his inquiry. "I want her freed," Semerket demanded, "and placed under the vizier's protection. And tonight, a squadron of men must be dispatched to capture the beggars who plan to remove the treasure."

Kenamun's face paled. He paced back and forth in shock. "Oh, my . . ." he said raggedly, thinking quickly. "I could certainly order the woman's release—that's no problem—but I've no authority to obtain a military escort for you."

"Who has that authority?"

"In the absence of Vizier Toh, only Pharaoh, I'm afraid." Kenamun shrugged his shoulders helplessly.

"Then we must go to him," Semerket declared.

Kenamun appeared horrified by the suggestion. "One simply can't demand an audience with Pharaoh, Semerket. There are intricate ceremonies, a thousand rules—"

"Surely, such a treasure as I've seen piled in that tomb should be enough reason to go around them!"

"You don't understand—it's not that simple. No, we need someone who has immediate access to him." Kenamun thought for a moment and then nodded to himself, as though coming to a decision. "Wait here," he said. As he hurried off into a hallway, he warned over his shoulder: "Do not speak of this to anyone, do you understand?"

Semerket nodded his head, albeit reluctantly.

The scribe returned a few moments later. "We're very lucky," he said breathlessly. "Tiya, the Queen Mother, has consented to see us. Once you tell her your story, I'm sure she'll prevail upon Pharaoh to send some men."

Semerket followed Kenamun through hallways leading to the southern part of the temple. Only then did he realize that he was actually being taken into Pharaoh's private residence. An unornamented cedar door served as the only entrance, unmarked and modestly sized. The single pair of guards did not challenge their entry; Kenamun seemed well known to them.

The palace was vast by Egyptian standards, but not so huge as those Semerket had glimpsed in Babylonia and Syria. The residence was built of stone, unlike most homes in Egypt, which were constructed from mud bricks. Kenamun led Semerket up a staircase to the second floor, entering a narrow passageway pierced by thin slits. Gazing through them, trying to regain his bearings, Semerket focused on the view of the temple gardens below and the sacred lake beyond. Only then did he realize where Kenamun led him.

Semerket stopped. "But this is the bridge into the harem!"

"Where else would you expect to find the great wife of the king?" asked the scribe.

Semerket dutifully followed him over the bridge and through the doors of the women's apartments. They entered a small, airy chamber. No one rushed to greet the two men, nor were any of Pharaoh's wives in evidence. Semerket felt a momentary pang of disappointment.

He contented himself to examine the room. The walls were decorated in bright murals; on closer inspection, Semerket was disconcerted to find these depicted scenes of embarrassing intimacy. On one wall Pharaoh played a game of senet with a naked girl. The wall opposite showed Ramses with his arm draped about a concubine's slim form, his fingertips casually grazing her breast, while she extolled his erotic prowess with an upraised fist.

The soft noise of a footstep caught him by surprise and Semerket turned in its direction, every nerve taut. Tiya was there. She was not clad in the same severe garments as she wore the first time he had met her. Instead, her robe's sheerness caused him to blush.

"Semerket!" Her splendid voice was at once low and tender and warm, and her skin was the color of the golden jasper beads around his neck. "You have been much on our minds since that day we met in the vizier's chambers."

Semerket fell to his knees. She came forward then and lifted him by the hands. Her perfume rose in his nostrils and to his shame he found himself staring at her dark, hennaed nipples beneath the fine lawn of her bodice. She looked at him sharply. "But where are the amulets and charms I sent you?" she asked. "Didn't you receive them? Pentwere said he'd placed them around your neck himself. If he lied——!"

He interrupted her pretty distress. "Your son did indeed give them to me, lady, but I removed them because of . . . of strange dreams they sent me."

Tiya wagged a finger at him. "That's because of the powerful prayers and incantations I said over them. You should never have taken them off. No wonder Kenamun here says you're in trouble now. It explains much to me."

Queen Tiya's clucking tone was so oddly reminiscent of his own mother's that he felt absurdly comfortable in her presence. But then he found himself staring again at her heavy breasts beneath the sheer muslin bodice, and he hastily dropped his eyes.

"You have the good sense to be ashamed, I see," she said, stroking his face. "You're all such naughty little boys, aren't you, never doing as you're told. But thank goodness for that! Where would I be today if my own sons didn't need me as much as they do?"

Tiya grazed his cheek with her nails, and when she smiled at him he saw the tips of her even, white teeth. Her fingers continued to travel upward, lingering for a moment at the spot in his scalp where his hair had been so mysteriously shorn. "Come," she beckoned to him, "sit beside me at the window, and you will tell me everything that has happened in the tomb-makers' village. Kenamun says it's very serious. We will listen, and then decide together what's best."

He allowed himself to be led onto an enclosed balcony above the gardens of Djamet. The queen indicated that he should sit next to her on a couch by the grated window. Kenamun was given a small footstool to sit upon, somewhat farther away. The scribe, reticent to join their discussion, seemed content to merely listen.

As he spoke, Semerket became aware of the Queen's sinuous movements—how she absently traced a finger across the line of her brow, or played with the tassel on her golden belt. And even when she stretched her shoulders indolently, he was aware of how closely she listened. She frowned and made soft moans of horror at the thought of her ancestors' tombs being plundered, at how close he had come to death at an assassin's hands. When he paused in his narrative, she put sharp questions to him that demonstrated her keen insight and understanding of the situation. Kenamun must have briefed her well, he thought. He then told the lady of how Hunro now languished in the tomb-makers' jail, accused of adultery, because she had helped him.

"That's also why I've come," he concluded, "so that she can be rescued from prison to testify against her neighbors."

The queen smiled at him. "Are you in love with her?"

"She is another man's wife, lady," Semerket said, dropping his eyes.

Tiya put her hand under his chin and raised his face to hers. "Semerket, you should know that it's useless to try to hide anything from me."

Semerket was suddenly ashamed, though he did not know why.

"She is the first woman since my wife to make me . . . feel something," he answered her tentatively. "If that is love——"

She laughed delightedly. "Spoken like a man. Why can your sex never be truthful about its feelings?"

"Does it matter what I feel?" he asked with some urgency. "She's in danger. And the beggars come tonight to remove the treasure from the Great Place! There is no time to lose, Great Lady!"

The sound of faraway rams' horns pierced the little room. Tiya's face changed, becoming for a moment hard and set. A maid—or perhaps one of the lesser wives—crept to whisper something in her ear. She shook her head, saying nothing.

"I'm told that Pharaoh has concluded his conferences," Tiya announced to Kenamun and Semerket. "This morning my son Pentwere has organized a duck hunt in the southern marshes. I will make arrangements for you to join us, Semerket."

Semerket was appalled. There was no time for such frivolity. "Your Majesty——"

She held up a hennaed palm, her voice low. "There's a reason I ask you along. These days the red and white crowns are heavy on his brow. Another blow like this and . . . well . . ." She sighed tragically, implying that Pharaoh was too frail a man to burden with such news.

Semerket spoke without thinking. "Once the crown prince is named co-ruler, I'm sure it will be easier——"

Tiya visibly started, her tawny eyes grew wide, and her mouth stretched into a sudden grimace that exposed her sharp teeth. She seized Semerket's arm, her nails making red crescents in his flesh. "Who told you that? Where have you heard such a lie? Spit it out, stupid! No one has yet been named a co-ruler. Least of all that——"

Kenamun rose from his stool and cleared his throat loudly. Tiya looked at the scribe then, and instantly shut her mouth. She lay again on the couch, breathing deeply. When she had calmed herself she looked resentfully into Semerket's eyes. "Pharaoh has no need for a co-ruler. He is a mighty bull, a soaring falcon."

The traditional words sounded flat and lifeless in her mouth. Semerket said nothing. The crescents she had left on his arm began to ooze thick blood. Tiya pretended a fascination with the weave of her robe.

"I'm just an old woman," she said, "too protective of her husband,

I suppose. But I'll help you, Semerket, despite your cruel words."

Tiya was suddenly full of plans and details for the proposed duck hunt, as if nothing had happened. He would share her pleasure barque, she told him, and Pharaoh's mood would surely improve after a few successful kills. "Then I will ask him for an escort to accompany you to the village. I must find the perfect moment to put the question to him. But you must remain silent, for now, for I am the only one who knows how to handle him."

Suddenly, as if a spell had been lifted, the harem was full of activity. The lesser wives appeared from their rooms, yawning, and eunuch guards were everywhere about.

Swiftly Tiya gave Semerket instructions about when he was to appear at the temple wharves. Kenamun would stay by him, allowing none to approach. He was not to leave Semerket's side, she emphasized. Who knew what dangers lurked, or where? Hadn't they already tried to kill Semerket once?

Bowing low, Semerket left the queen at the grated window. As he went through the doors that led to the stone bridge, Kenamun hurried after him, saying, "An extraordinary woman, the great wife, is she not?"

Semerket merely stared at him. All the way over the stone bridge he felt the sting where her nails had dug into his arm.

AT THE SAME MOMENT, many furlongs away, the servant Keeya stood at the outside fire pit, carrying a basket of trash. It was filled with the usual detritus of Theban living—bones from the week's meals, fish heads, rags too worn for further service. She searched about for the flint and the palm-fiber kindling.

It was midmorning and her mistress had gone to Sekhmet's temple to visit her uncle, the high priest. Merytra was often at her uncle's temple these days, Keeya thought. And when the woman returned, she was invariably moody and withdrawn. At such times, Merytra often locked the servants in the small cellar where the three of them slept at night. In the dark, next to the sacks of musty-smelling grain and jars of fermenting beer, they heard her walking on the floor above, sometimes treading in circles. Often they heard her softly chanting to herself. Keeya suspected their mistress had become possessed by a demon.

The flint was in a small niche within the mud-brick wall. As she stretched for it, she felt a paving tile move unsteadily beneath her feet. It was slightly raised above the others.

She thought little about it, and bent to shift the tile back into its place. But still it was loose, as if it pressed on something beneath. Keeya lifted the tile, and beheld what was tucked into the hole beneath. She only just managed to stop the scream that threatened to escape her.

Swiftly she replaced the tile. When her mistress returned home, she said nothing, waiting for Nenry to return for his noon meal. As soon as the scribe, loaded down with papers and scrolls, wearily pushed open the gate, Keeya approached him.

"Master," she said. "Will you take a moment to look at something?"

Nenry was about to put her off, for Paser had left him alone with the morning's work that day—surveyor reports, taxation schedules. For some reason the mayor had rushed off at the last moment to attend a duck-hunting party with Queen Tiya, of all things. But the maid's expression was so serious that whatever protests Nenry harbored were stilled. Nenry followed her to the fire pit.

Keeya lifted the tile. In the hole were the remains of an infant, a female. It was painted red and glyphs were drawn upon its tiny palms, on its feet and forehead. They were not ordinary glyphs, but primitive symbols from an ancient time. Various amulets and charms were placed all about the little corpse. The infant's stomach had been slit open, and within it, among its dried and desiccated viscera, was a waxen doll. A knife protruded from the baby's chest, and around its eyes a small bandage was tied.

"Gather the others," Nenry said, his voice terrible.

Merytra was lying atop her bed, for it was her custom to nap while her husband ate his noon meal—an arrangement that suited them both, for it kept their daily interactions to a minimum. She was therefore surprised to see her husband suddenly appear in her doorway, the servants close behind him.

"Why do idiots disturb my rest?" she asked resignedly, as if she addressed the gods to fathom their purposeless ways.

Nenry swiftly crossed the room, grabbing her by her hair. He threw her, screaming, against the wall.

"Witch!" he yelled. "Sorceress!" He almost began to weep, but

stopped himself, firmly banishing his tears. "Seize her," he told his servants. "Bind her tightly. Then take her into the cellar."

Merytra was too shocked to speak. Not until the servants laid their
hands upon her, tying her hands together, did curses and hot oaths
begin to pour from her. But her husband and servants were deaf to her
threats and promises of punishments. Merytra had to take what satisfaction she could from seeing how they shrank from touching her, as if
she were a thing of scales and horns.

In the cellar, Nenry waited, refusing to look at her while they tied
her hands and feet to a chair facing a workbench on which the evidence
of her black magic was neatly laid out. Seeing her husband and servants
so aloof and judgmental, Merytra began to struggle against her bonds,
raging that they must unloose her at once—that she would tell her
uncle—that Nenry would lose his position—that she would sell the
servants to a brothel!

They allowed her to scream and rage until she was spent. It was
their impassivity that finally stopped her. She became quiet, and no
longer pulled at her ties.

"How could you do this to me?" Nenry asked. "Didn't I provide for
you? Didn't I give you all that you cherished?" He stared at the terrible
wax doll he held in his hand, skewered with a golden needle. Then his
eyes fell upon the baby's corpse. Seeing the pitiful child, its belly ripped
open and stuffed with the awful charms, he moaned softly.

"Let me go, you fool," Merytra blustered. "When my great-uncle
hears how you ruined the spell—"

With a cry Nenry lunged at her, striking her so viciously across the
mouth that blood trickled down her chin.

"You've ruined me," Nenry said savagely. "I am destroyed."

"Trust you to get it wrong." Her voice was suddenly pleading.
"Don't you see I worked the magic to protect you?"

Nenry merely shook his head, gesturing toward the baby's desiccated, red-painted corpse. "This child—is it ours?"

She rolled her eyes at his stupidity. "Of course not. How could I hide
a pregnancy even from you? I bought the child from a prostitute at the
city gate. She was going to leave it there anyway. I held my hand over
its mouth, until it—"

She was cut short by her husband's muffled wail. Nenry raised his hand; only the purest self-restraint kept him from striking her again. He held out the waxen figure to her instead, saying, "And this—it's me, isn't it? You've cursed me to my death."

"Calm down, Nenry. I swear it isn't you."

"Who then?"

"It's your brother, of course. That's his hair in the wax. Who else could it be?"

"Semerket?"

She spoke in an offended manner. "I had to do something. He was involving you in things he shouldn't—and you know it. When I tell you whose idea the curses were, you'll thank me for what I've done. The very highest in this land want your brother dead, and all his friends. Do you think I'd let that happen to you? I've worked too hard to lose everything because of your gullibility."

"But who could possibly want him dead?" Nenry asked scornfully.

"The seeress of Sekhmet, that's who. And her magic is the most powerful in all Egypt."

"Who—?" He had never heard of such a person before.

"Don't tell me you don't know who she is! You, who even labored in Sekhmet's temple once. Well, that doesn't surprise me, you've always had your head buried in the sand—"

"Who?" He raised his hand again.

Her words were rapid. "She is the king's great wife—Queen Tiya!"

Nenry had sense enough to believe her. In a kind of daze he told his valet to get his cloak and walking stick ready. He was going across to Western Thebes, he told them. "He must be warned," he muttered, more to himself than to anyone else.

But his wife laughed jeeringly when he said this. "Better to stay at home, you fool. There's nothing you can do for him. It's too late. Great-uncle told me himself. The lioness goes abroad today. Today your precious brother dies!"

From the shelf where the knives were kept for the slaughter of fowl and the filleting of fish, he took a long carving knife, and handed it to Keeya.

"Keep sharp watch on her," he said. "If she tries to escape, or begins to rave, or utters a curse—slit her throat."

Keeya did not flinch. Then, strangely, she embraced him. "The gods go with you, my lord. Now go save your brother, for you are both good men." She kissed his cheek.

The last thing he saw as he left the cellar was Keeya standing before his wife, the long, bronze knife gleaming in her hand. Once outside his house, Nenry ran. All the way to the docks he kept repeating his brother's name like a talisman, calling on all the gods he knew.

"Semerket—!" He said the name aloud, and in it was every prayer he could muster.

THE FLEET OF pleasure barques had departed Djamet at midmorning, sailing down the temple canal to the Nile. At the river the boats turned south, and the sailors hoisted small square sails to catch the winds blowing sharply from the desert. The rowers stowed their oars then, allowing the brightly painted craft to sail before the breezes.

Semerket sat with Tiya beneath the wooden canopy of her barque, clad as always in his fringed kilt and gray woolen cloak. He had never owned the traditional hunting clothes of white, pleated linen that the courtiers wore. When he had gone fowl hunting it had not been for sport, but to bag an evening's meal.

His thoughts were interrupted by a shout from another craft. Prince Pentwere's boat was rapidly gaining on them. Semerket noticed that the prince's inevitable comrade, the black-skinned Assai, reclined with him beneath the canopy.

"Mother!" Pentwere shouted across the water to her. "Fine day for a kill, what?"

Semerket looked at the sky, saw the gray rain clouds on the edge of the desert, and wondered what the Prince could mean. At any moment it seemed that a storm might engulf them. But at her son's words, Tiya emitted a laugh of silver, tinkling bells.

"A splendid day!" she said. "You couldn't have chosen better. The gods are with you, Pentwere."

Pentwere turned his bright-eyed gaze upon Semerket. "Look, Assai—it's our friend the clerk! Do you suppose he's found more wigs in the desert to show us?"

Assai sniggered at the gibe. But his eyes were cold, and he pointedly refused to look directly into Semerket's face.

"No wigs, Highness," Semerket replied.

"How goes the investigation? Have you found the priestess's murderer yet?"

"Not yet."

Pentwere and Assai looked at one another and broke into raucous laughter. With a look of disgust, Semerket turned away. He had little patience for spoiled princelings and their humorless jokes. He studied instead the boats that made up the hunting party. There were at least thirty or forty vessels, he surmised, each trimmed in flowers and streamers, the morning sun glinting on their gilded wooden canopies.

The sun's flash off a gilded stern suddenly smote his eyes. Pharaoh's gold-trimmed yacht was pulling next to them. Pentwere and Assai genuflected, and Tiya, too, inclined her head. Semerket saw on her face a look of . . . what? Irritation? Panic? To Semerket's dismay, the king's sailors furled the yacht's sail so that his boat paced the queen's.

A raspy voice called over the water. "What an unpleasant surprise, madam, to find you here. Pentwere, you know I wanted no females along."

It was Pharaoh himself who spoke. Glancing over at the prince's skiff, from his kneeling position, Semerket saw that Pentwere had gone ashen beneath his chestnut skin.

"Father—"

"Don't blame the boy, Ramses," Tiya interrupted her son smoothly, stretching lazily on her seat beneath the canopy. "I invited myself along. I thought a picnic among the reeds would suit me."

"Picnic, madam? This is a hunt. Haven't I created gardens and lakes enough for your picnics? And who is that with you—your lover?"

It was a moment before Semerket realized that Pharaoh was pointing his stick directly at him. Semerket hid his face, cringing. The last thing he needed at that particular moment was to be accused of being the great wife's paramour.

"Don't be absurd, Ramses," Tiya answered irritably. "Do you think I'd take a peasant as my lover? Marrying into your family was low enough for me."

Pharaoh's pale eyes glittered. "Who knows how low you would go, madam."

"He's Semerket," Tiya went on in a languid tone, ignoring Ramses.

"You remember, surely—he's the investigator of the priestess's murder. Toh appointed him."

"You there—" Pharaoh spoke directly to Semerket. "Raise your head so I can see you."

Semerket hauled himself to his knees.

"Hmmph," said Pharaoh doubtfully. "Toh calls you the terrible truth-teller. Is it true you called my wife's brother Pawero an idiot?"

"No, Your Majesty."

Pharaoh frowned. "That's what Toh said you called him. Who's the liar here? Speak up."

Semerket sighed dismally. "I didn't call him an idiot, Sire. I called him a pea-brained old pettifogger."

Pharaoh's short staccato laugh rang out across the river. "Ha! Perfectly true!"

Instantly the entire river around them was filled with hoots as courtiers aped Pharaoh's harsh laughter. Semerket glanced at the queen from beneath lowered lashes. She had flushed dark crimson, and Pentwere and Assai were again staring at Semerket with loathing.

"Toh was right about you, I see!" Pharaoh said, smiling gleefully. "After the hunt you shall sail back to the palace on my yacht, Semerket. Do me good to hear someone talk sense for once."

"Why?" Tiya spoke up. "You never heed it."

"That, I suppose, madam, is your subtle reference to our disagreement concerning the succession."

"It is my subtle reference about honoring the promise you made at our marriage."

"I do what's best for Egypt, madam—not your family."

Tiya's eyes shone, and she looked about the small fleet as if seeking a face. "Where is the crown prince? Pentwere specifically invited him along on the hunt. Is he ill?" Her lips drew into a delicate sneer. "Again?"

"He attends to Egypt's business, madam—which is none of yours."

Before any more could be said between his parents, Pentwere interrupted from his own boat. "I could help you attend to Egypt's business, Father. Test me! Set me a task. Name anything and I'll do it." Though he was a man of almost twenty-five years, his voice at that moment sounded thin and bleating. "If you'd only give me a chance . . ."

"What?" said Ramses with a slight frown. "And deprive the Thebans of your circus tricks at festival time? I couldn't be that cruel. Stick to amusing the crowds, my son; it's what you do best." Pharaoh turned to his coxswain and pointed ahead. "On!" he commanded. Instantly his sailors let out the sail. It billowed tightly in the winds, and Pharaoh's yacht sped forward. With many shouts, the courtiers again let their boats free. Queen Tiya's vessel, being crewed by her ladies, was slow to catch up.

The hunting fleet separated in the papyrus marshes. The queen chose a small lagoon far away from the hunt in which to moor her vessel. She had been silent after Pharaoh left them on the Nile, fuming to herself, but when her boat reached the reeds her mood improved and she became talkative, almost gay. With her own hands she raided the wine stowed at the stern, and pried the clay seal from a jar. From a gem-encrusted goblet of pure gold, Tiya treated herself to a long swig.

"Oh," she sighed in contentment, "but that's good. It's from my family's estate. They say our grapes are as fine as those in Osiris's own vineyards. Will you take some?" She poured another splash into the goblet.

Semerket had tasted only beer the entire time he had been at the tomb-makers' village, and the thought of wine was a torment on his tongue. The queen saw him hesitate, and she withdrew the cup.

"Ah," she said, and her face was gentle, her many-textured voice filled with pity, "but didn't my steward Nakht tell me once—what was it? Yes, I remember now—that you have a problem with wine. He told me how you'd hammer on his door at all hours of the night, drunken and angry, wanting to take his wife away from him, in fact."

"He told you that?" Semerket's voice was low.

She withdrew the cup. "I don't think I shall offer you wine after all. I don't want to tempt you to bad behavior."

At the mention of Naia, Semerket's mood had intractably darkened. He reached for the goblet. "Nakht has misinformed you," he said shortly.

She appeared to hesitate, but her lips quivered as though she suppressed a smile. Tiya let him take the golden cup.

Semerket drank. The deep crimson flowed over his tongue. Tiya had been correct—the grapes that had produced this vintage indeed must have been grown in the heavenly fields of Iaru. He rejoiced in the wine. It was both tranquil and exultant at the same time, a reminder to him that Egypt had once been a place of order and respect. . . . As he drank further he found wisdom in the wine, too. He held out his goblet to taste of wisdom again, and again the queen poured.

Her ladies came from the stern then. They sat beside him and placed a wreath of flowers about his head. They drizzled roasted barleycorns over him, and one of them took up a harp and sang softly. He laughed. "What?" he asked. "Are you going to sacrifice me?"

But the maids only smiled and bade him hush, so as not to disturb the hunters. The morning passed in the hum of dragonflies, the distant shouts of the courtiers, and the cries of wild birds. Again he held out the golden goblet and again it was filled.

As through a mist, Semerket saw one of Tiya's maids run a red signal flag up the mast. A few moments later, very close by, he heard the sound of oars. He struggled to peer over the boat's gunwales. The time for Tiya's picnic had arrived, for Ra's solar barque was almost at its zenith. He heard the queen call out, "Pentwere! Is everything ready?"

The prince entered the lagoon alone, paddling the skiff himself. Semerket was dimly surprised to see that the glowering Assai was not with him. "Everything is just as you want it, Mother," the prince called out. "They're coming now."

"Wonderful," she exclaimed. Tiya moved to cling to one of the gilded lotus columns that bore the boat's canopy. She called out across the lagoon, "Nakht, steward of all the king's palaces! Welcome!"

A distant voice barked out to her. "Hail, Tiya! Queen of kings!" Semerket, raising his head, saw Nakht entering the lagoon. Semerket snorted at the sight of him, immaculate in his starched, white hunting habit, the picture-perfect nobleman. Semerket thanked the gods for the excellent wine he had consumed; even the presence of Naia's idiot husband could not disturb him.

"Hail, Paser, vizier of Egypt! Welcome!"

Semerket blinked, overtaken in befuddled surprise to see the fat mayor of the Eastern City, Paser, enter the thicket of reeds. What was he doing so far from his bailiwick? He noticed how the mayor's skiff listed to one side under his weight, and Semerket chuckled immoderately.

"Iroy, high priest of Egypt!" Another boat entered the lagoon. Semerket had seen the man before, and he tried to remember where. In the warmth of the marsh his thoughts oozed about in his mind like thick clay. He closed his eyes to concentrate. The answer came to him slowly—the man was Nenry's father-in-law, or uncle . . . something . . . And he was the high priest of Sekhmet, not—what had Tiya called him? "High priest of Egypt."

Semerket sat up, removing the garland of flowers from his brow. The maids tried to pull him back to lie upon the deck again, but he brushed away their hands, trying to make his mind work. A grain of fear crept into his soul. The titles the queen called out to the men were not correct; it was as though they had been secretly promoted during the night . . . as though all their superiors were suddenly dead and out of their way . . .

"Hail, Tiya, queen of kings!" Another boat had entered the lagoon. Semerket recognized the whining voice of Neferhotep even before he saw him. The fear, which had been a trickle, now surged through Semerket's veins.

But why, he asked himself, why *should* he be so filled with terror? He knew the explanation was tantalizingly near, just within reach, and he closed his eyes to concentrate—but with the wine pounding in his skull, the white, harsh sunlight searing his eyes . . .

"Is it coming together for you, Semerket?"

His eyes flashed open. Tiya stood over him, the dazzling sun flaring behind her head like the coronet of a goddess. He blinked, and in a trick of sunlight Semerket saw the red fangs in her dimpled smile. In that moment of absolute clarity he realized that his nightmares had become reality—that the lioness had at last caught him in her grip.

Tiya bent down to him and he winced, closing his eyes, expecting her to slash his throat with her fangs just as she had tried to do a hundred times in his dreams. But her face was kindly and her voice was as beautiful as ever.

"Why?" he whispered up to her.

"You found us out, Semerket," she murmured.

I didn't find you out! he wanted to shout at her. The killer of Hetephras still is free! But he knew now that they were far from concerned with whoever had killed the old priestess. It was something else. What had he stumbled across to make the most powerful personages in Egypt converge in a marsh, with him the cynosure of their attentions?

Concentrate, he told himself fiercely.

There could be only one answer: the stolen treasure in the tomb. What else could it be? Yet this too made no sense. What need had these persons in the lagoon for more riches? With the exception of Nefer-hotep, they were among the wealthiest people in the nation. So that was the wrong question. He must ask himself, instead, what was worth more to them than gold?

He exhaled, suddenly knowing the answer. There could be only one: power.

Semerket stared across the lagoon, and saw his suspicions confirmed in their faces. Nakht, Paser, Iroy, Pentwere, even the queen herself—they were using the stolen treasure to finance their own schemes. Only days before, Semerket had told his brother that he sensed conspiracy afoot.

What kind of conspiracy did they plan, how far was its thrust, and against whom? The wine in his blood was no longer a hindrance to perception; instead it allowed his mind to freely assemble disparate facts and odd pieces of information into a suddenly coherent whole.

Semerket heard the distant prattling voice of the librarian Maadje in his mind, gossiping away to him in the House of Life. "When Pharaoh married her, it was with the promise that *her* sons would inherit . . ." But Pharaoh had reneged on his agreement, instead choosing his pale-skinned son of the foreign-born Queen Ese as his heir. Then he heard that same crown prince speaking: "The tainted blood of Twos-re and Amen-meses is still alive in Egypt, Semerket, make no mistake . . ."

Rising unbidden in his mind, he saw again the tiny portrait of Pharaoh Amen-meses in the tomb beneath the tomb. Semerket stared across the lagoon and saw in Prince Pentwere's face, and in the softer lines of his mother's, the same fiercely handsome features he had seen in the portrait . . . and Semerket visibly flinched.

Tiya was the most royal woman in Egypt; Semerket had heard that description of her all his life. He had never stopped to question it, nor wonder how she earned such a distinction. But what other reason had Ramses for marrying her in the first place? It was a time-honored tradition for pharaohs not born in the Golden House to marry the daughters and granddaughters of the previous line, to bolster their own claims. The criminal Twos-re was alive in Tiya—Semerket saw that clearly now—the ferocious woman who had slain her husband in the pursuit of power.

And there it was, the thing he had so unwittingly uncovered, from a clue found in the deliberately obscured past—the thing they were so afraid of his knowing. The accusation rose to his lips:

"You're going to kill Pharaoh!"

Tiya gasped slightly, backing away from him. For a moment her eyes were full of panic. She spoke angrily to the men in the lagoon. "Didn't I tell you he should be feared? But he was only a drunken sot, you insisted, incapable of finding his own backside, much less—"

"Don't say anything more, Mother!" Pentwere pleaded suddenly from his boat.

From across the small lagoon he heard Nakht speak reassuringly to the prince. "Oh, this Semerket would never tell, Your Majesty," he said in his clipped, aristocratic tones. "Our plan is safe."

"Don't be so sure, Nakht!" Semerket yelled.

Nakht replied as if he spoke to a trained baboon. "But if you told, Semerket, Naia would be put to death along with us. It's the law. You let her know yourself, didn't you?" A cordial smile broke out on his blandly handsome face. "And thank you—if you hadn't warned her when you did, we'd never have guessed how much you knew."

The priest Iroy could not contain himself any further, and spoke up impatiently from his boat. "Can't we end this now? We all know the real reason he won't tell—he'll be dead. It's why we're all here, isn't it, to see him die?"

"Iroy!" chastised Tiya. "Don't be crude."

The scribe Neferhotep's thin, supplicating voice penetrated the glade. "Might I remind the august queen that we have very little time? Tonight the treasure must be moved north with the beggars, to the generals of the armies. I agree with the reverend high priest—kill him now." His tone went from wheedling to bitter. "I've waited six months to see it happen."

At Tiya's signal, her maids lunged forward to hold Semerket fast in their grip. The queen's eyes were blank and pitiless. "Turn him over," she said curtly.

The women roughly tossed Semerket prone onto the deck, so that his head hung over the side of the boat. Though he struggled, they held him fast. He could see his own face perfectly in the smooth, green water below—black eyes wide, mouth open in fear. He raised his head to see if any of the men in the lagoon could be reasoned with. But the conspirators were leaning forward in their skiffs, staring avidly.

"Goodbye, Semerket," smirked Nakht. "I'll be sure to tell Naia how you begged for your life at the end."

Scornful laughs broke out among the men. Tiya silenced them with a gesture. She knelt beside Semerket, speaking in grieved tones. "I shall inform Pharaoh of your terrible accident," she said. "How you became so drunk you fell overboard. We did our best to save you, but what could we do? My maids and I are only feeble women."

Then her voice was in his ear, words meant only for him. "You've resisted my magic until now, Semerket, but today you won't escape its power." Her lovely voice took on a mystical quality. "Look into the waters, Semerket. Stare deeply. See how at my command I make them roil and churn."

Semerket stared. As she spoke the waters indeed began to heave below his face. His reflection shattered into pieces. A black mass took shape beneath the waters, coalescing, rising from the river bed, lunging upward—

"Now—" Tiya said, triumphant, "see how you *die!*"

The thing crashed through the surface of the water. Semerket felt it seize him, dragging him headfirst into the lagoon. The surprising coldness shocked the remaining wine fumes from him. He fought blindly, eyes closed, scratching and kicking at whatever pulled him down.

In the suddenly silent world, all he heard were his own terrified grunts and the explosions of bubbles around him. His back hit the spongy mud of the river bottom, and he forced his eyes open to see what held him in its grip. But the mud rose in dirty clouds around him, blocking his view. Semerket exhaled his last breath into the Nile. For a brief moment the water cleared—and he saw at last the thing that had pulled him in.

It was Assai.

All sleek black muscle, the prince's favorite was smiling even under the water, his hatred for Semerket radiating as brightly as the golden dagger in his hand. Assai slashed out at him. With both hands Semerket seized Assai's wrist, just stopping the knife's descent into his throat.

Abruptly Assai twisted free, lunging at Semerket as he did. The water was filled with sudden red. Semerket's forehead was slashed open, and the cold water stung the wound like hot coals. Assai slashed at him again; Semerket avoided the blow by kicking away, plunging downward into the slimy river mud. At the last moment, through the black clouds of silt, he saw the gold dagger streaking at him.

With a powerful kick, Semerket made for the open waters of a far lagoon, weaving through the clumps of reeds with Assai in pursuit. He broke the surface and gasped for breath. Glancing behind, he saw a line of bubbles heading straight for him. Gulping a lungful of air, he sank down and peered through the water. Beneath the surface, Assai was swiftly swimming toward him.

It was clear that Semerket could not outswim the stronger Assai. He cast about in his mind for a way to escape, desperation making his heart beat like a temple drum. As Assai bore down, Semerket exhaled so that he could sink rapidly to the bottom of the lagoon. Raking his fingers across the slimy river bottom, he churned up the silt. Flailing his arms about he distributed the mud into a screen that, he hoped, would hide him from the black warrior. Though now he could not see Assai himself, he shot off obliquely to the side of the lagoon, toward another thicket of reeds.

He permitted himself a moment to glance back, and saw Assai break through the cloud of black mud, heading in the direction where he had last seen Semerket. Assai stopped, hesitating, then swam to the surface of the lagoon.

Unable to stay down, hungry for air, Semerket rose swiftly upward to once again feel the sun upon his face. He noisily gasped the air into his lungs. As Semerket knew he would, Assai instantly spied his location. Assai lunged powerfully in his direction, his long arms pulling him swiftly forward in rapid strokes. Semerket sank into the water again, swimming frantically for a reed copse in front of him. He dug his fingers again into the river bottom and the ancient silt rose in thick clouds. Again Semerket veered, hidden by the wavering screen. He broke through the swirling mud into clear water, and saw a thick mass of rushes in front of him, not more than a few cubits away. Caught in their leaves, not far from the water's surface, was a sunken yacht of great age, a rotting and splintered hulk. It would perhaps hide him from Assai, he thought. Though once again his lungs were aching for oxygen, he swam underwater toward the ghostly wreck.

His lungs were giving out. Desperately he skimmed the surface for air, then sank back down. Twisting his body, he saw the flash of Assai's linen-clad form only a few cubits away, bearing fast upon him.

Panic seized him, and he kicked swiftly for the reeds. He felt his foot strike something solid, and realized that it was one of Assai's arms. Assai seized his ankle in a strong grip, but he kicked out, freeing himself, and swam swiftly away.

A hole gaped in the side of the yacht's hull. Semerket dove through it, hoping that he could hide within the black gloom of its interior and then escape through its rear hatch into the thick reeds beyond. Almost through the hole now, he felt Assai's hands grasp his leg again. This time they held him firmly. No matter how he struggled and kicked, Assai's grip remained merciless.

By this time flashes of light were sparking at the backs of Semerket's eyes. He had to breathe, had to inhale. His lungs shrieked for air, but Assai held him fast. Twisting around, Semerket saw Assai's grin in the dark water. Semerket's lungs were afire. Unable to prevent himself, he opened his mouth to breathe.

The water scalded his lungs, and he choked, but only for a short time. He felt blackness overtaking him. Through the few cubits of water above him, a pinpoint of distant light danced overhead, the sun. Though his rebellious body still feebly struggled to save itself, a strange calmness began to overtake him. He felt a sublime sense of release transfusing his limbs, cascading through his body. Fighting the descending torpor, he forced himself to summon one last bit of strength, and pulled against the rotting wood of the wreck. The cedar broke jaggedly in his hands. He pulled again, and felt Assai's grip loosen. One final kick—and he was through . . .

But by now the black was all around him, and within him too. He felt himself drifting upward. And the pinpoint of sunlight—the last thing he saw—burnt itself out.

HOUSE OF
ETERNITY

WINDED FROM HIS CLIMB FROM THE RIVER, for he had run almost the entire distance, Nenry caught his breath at the southern gate of the tomb-makers' village. He was momentarily astounded by the bright colors of the houses within its narrow main street. Ketty had never told him of the village's odd beauty, or how it was in reality two buildings, each with their own huge roofs. Yet the strangest thing about the place was the silence that so profoundly enveloped it. It seemed a gathering place for phantoms.

Nenry stood at the gate, hesitating. "Hello . . . ?" he called into the corridor. No one hailed him. Tentatively, he stepped inside. At the first door, he tapped lightly.

"Is anyone there? Can you help?"

Silence again met him.

"Please," he pleaded, "I'm looking for my brother—Semerket. Is he here?"

Only quiet.

Knocking on a few of the other doors produced the same result. Nenry was beginning to feel undone by the place's eerie stillness. But at that moment he heard the cries of many people. The voices did not come from within the village, but from outside.

He retraced his steps down the main street and out the gates. The shouts were louder here; they came from the western side of the village, and Nenry followed the noise.

Around the corner he found a horde of villagers gathered at a far clearing in front of a red cliff face, streaked and veined like a slab of meat. Nenry surmised that some celebration or local religious rite was occurring. Perhaps Semerket was among those assembled, he hoped, and he set off to see for himself. He reached the edge of the crowd within a few moments. So intent were the villagers on what was transpiring in the clearing, they did not turn to acknowledge him, nor even seem to notice that a stranger was among them.

Through their crowded forms, he glimpsed a contingent of grim-faced women shouting angry accusations at someone. Apparently the person had behaved shamelessly in some fashion and was undergoing some sort of trial. Despite his urgent need to find his brother, Nenry paused, fascinated. He pushed himself through the villagers, and saw that in the center of the clearing was a woman, hands bound behind her. Tall and oddly beautiful, she was not gagged, and Nenry was shocked to hear the words she hurled at her accusers. Never in his life had he heard a woman swear so lustily as she did. The woman was threatening them with all manner of punishments if they did not release her at once, and Nenry was surprised to hear her use the name of his brother, Semerket, as a form of threat.

"Wait until he gets back—you'll see. He's gone to the vizier himself, to get troops. You'll be lucky if you're not all thrown into Djamet prison."

"Semerket—?" Nenry said aloud, pushing his way forward to the woman.

When the hundred or so villagers at last noticed Nenry standing before them, draped in the various insignia of his office, they drew back guiltily. Even the woman in the clearing ceased her invectives.

In the awkward silence, he made a gesture of greeting. "You speak of Semerket—he's my brother. I'm looking for him."

"Oh, thank the gods!" the bound woman exclaimed.

The rest of the villagers were uncertain about how to proceed. The woman shouted to Nenry, "You must help me! I'm to be stoned for what I know about them—about what they did. Your brother said he'd get me out of here if I told the authorities. Oh, please, my lord—you've got to do something, or else I'm a dead woman!"

Nenry swallowed, glancing nervously at the villagers. "I'm sure," Nenry began, gesturing ineffectively, "I'm sure if Semerket said—"

A rotund, intimidating sort of woman suddenly broke free from the others and pushed her way to where Nenry stood.

"Your brother isn't here," said the fat woman forcefully. "And you're not wanted, either."

Nenry snapped his head in her direction. The woman reminded him so much of his wife with her rough, intemperate tongue that he was filled with sudden wrath. "How dare you speak to me in that fashion," said Nenry. His tone was low and dangerous, for once, surprising even himself. The woman became flustered, looking around to the villagers for support, but they still hung back.

"You're trespassing," she said, still defiant, though her voice was not as certain as before. "This village is off-limits to all but—"

"You are addressing the chief scribe of Eastern Thebes," Nenry interrupted. "What is your name, woman?"

"Her name's Khepura!" the bound woman shouted from the clearing.

"Damn you, Hunro—!" the big woman sputtered.

"Quiet!" shouted Nenry. To his surprise the woman fell silent. He turned in the direction of the woman whose name was Hunro, saying, "Release that woman. Instantly. If my brother said he'd take you from here, then he had good reason. We'll go together to find him."

"Thank you, my lord . . . thank you!"

When none of the villagers moved he started forward to untie her himself, but Khepura, mad rage again claiming her, cast about in desperation. She bent suddenly to grasp a rock from the pathway. With a scream she hurled it at the woman in the clearing. The stone struck the side of Hunro's head with a thud that resounded through the canyon. Hunro fell to the ground like a marionette whose strings had been unexpectedly cut, blood spurting from her scalp.

Nenry had been so near to her that his face and cloak were spattered. In a kind of daze he whirled around, meeting only the flat, expressionless faces of the villagers. Their eyes were hard and filled with a frenzied hatred. Nenry had been on the verge of chastising them, but his mouth clamped shut when he saw their insensate expressions. Instinctively he realized that his own life was now also at stake. He watched helplessly as the villagers bent to retrieve rocks from the ground.

Hunro staggered to her feet, and looked about at the villagers. She approached one of the men. "Aaphat?" she asked incredulously. "Will you really do this to me? After what we were to one another?"

The man looked awkwardly at the ground. It was his wife, suddenly enraged, who threw the next stone. It caught Hunro on the shoulder. "You can't do this," Hunro muttered; "it isn't fair."

Then the rocks began to rain down on her from all sides. The sickening thuds of stone smashing against bone and flesh filled the canyon. The tall woman fell and did not move again. Not until her body was an unrecognizable mush did the villagers cease throwing their stones. At the end, the woman lay half-buried in rock.

Nenry stared aghast, expecting the villagers now to turn upon him. But the feral light in their eyes had burnt out. Not even glancing at him, the villagers turned and trudged back to the northern gates of the village. They were oddly lethargic, as if they were dead to the world around them. Nenry stood in their midst, hysterical half-sobs emerging from him. He searched their faces, but it was as if he were invisible to them. Whatever threat from authorities he represented was simply ignored. When all of them had disappeared into the village, the gate was closed and Nenry heard the bolts slide into place.

It was this noise that freed him at last to move. He felt the bile rise in his throat. He had to get away from there. His entire world—indeed, all of Egypt—had been upended. What had happened, he thought, that everyone's rage should suddenly break out, first with his own wife and now here in this distant village?

As Nenry ran, he never noticed that he was now in the center of the Great Place. He darted in and out of the protruding crags, following the serpentine path at the top of the cliffs. Nenry might have run into the western desert had it not been for the two black Medjays who intercepted him as he came hurtling around a boulder. Bracing themselves, they caught him in their arms as he flew past.

Seeing the insignia of the Eastern Mayor's office around Nenry's neck, the Medjays did not instantly arrest him as a trespasser in the

Great Place, nor prod him in awkward places with the points of their spears. Instead they allowed Nenry to pour out his tale—how he had crossed from Eastern Thebes just an hour before, only to see a woman stoned to death at the tomb-makers' village, when all he'd done was to ask after his brother, who was in terrible danger, Semerket was his name—

"Semerket?" Medjay Qar interrupted, staring at the man whose face was indeed a parody of his friend's, though it was fraught with frightened tics and twitches.

"I have to warn him!" the man pleaded.

"Why?"

Nenry blinked. Should he trust these men? Perhaps they were also involved in the plot that threatened Semerket's life. Finally, simply because they were Medjays and black-skinned, he felt he could tell them the truth.

"He's in danger from Queen Tiya," he said, "something to do with what he's discovered here. Today she plans his death. I have to warn him."

Qar addressed the other Medjay. "Thoth, go back to headquarters and tell the captain to take some men into the Place of Truth. See what has happened. If they've taken matters into their own hands—"

"Too late," muttered Nenry, "too late."

"What about you, Qar?" asked Thoth.

"I'm going with this man to Djamet. If there's a plot against Semerket for what he knows, we'll all be next."

Qar seized Nenry by the arm. As they walked swiftly down the limestone-strewn path in the direction of the temple, a sudden gust of fierce wind caught them. Qar sniffed the air, and turned with a worried glance to the west. A black ledge of clouds hung at the fringes of the Great Place.

A distant flash of silent pink lightning threw the crags behind them into sudden soft relief. Nowhere but in the deserts surrounding the Great Place was there to be seen lightning of such a hue, Qar explained to the numbed and silent Nenry.

"But it can kill you just as quickly as the other kind," he added. The Medjay held the copper head of his spear to the ground.

They had reached the crest of the cliff and Nenry stared ahead to the ribbon of blue that was the distant Nile. The horror of what he had just seen was at last claiming him and he began to shiver uncontrollably.

A wall of wind caught them there at the crest. Wrapping their cloaks about themselves, accompanied by the acrid smell of the approaching storm, Qar and Nenry walked swiftly down the path that would take them to the Great Temple of Djamet.

HE VAULTED TO the surface of the lagoon. Vomiting water from his lungs, he sucked in the dank air. Though it stabbed like cold fire, he filled every part of his chest with it. Only then did Semerket open his eyes.

Panic was his first reaction. He lashed out blindly, feeling Assai's hands still clutching him. But it was only a tangle of wet leaves that had wrapped itself about his arm. Assai was not there.

Semerket gulped more air into his lungs and sank again into the waters, searching, expecting Assai to loom from the green water at any moment. But the water revealed nothing. He was alone. Taking another gulp of air into his chest, he swam down the few cubits to the wreck caught in the underwater thicket. Assai was snagged by the neck of his linen habit, pinned by the jagged cedar planks of the yacht's hull. Pentwere's favorite twisted and turned frantically, hacking at the linen with his curved knife. In his hysteria, his movements were ineffective, and the water was fast becoming red with the wounds he inflicted on his own flesh. Still the wreck would not release him.

Assai shot Semerket a desperate, pleading look. Fighting down every instinct he had, Semerket watched in horror as the man slowly drowned before him. Assai's movements became even more wild, his eyes bulging in his skull. Finally, Semerket heard a bubbling scream of the most profound rage as Assai exhaled for the last time. Unable to watch his death struggles any longer, Semerket kicked toward the surface.

There, hidden in the reeds, he waited until no more foam appeared from below. Shaken, he twisted in the water, trying to get a notion of where he was. Semerket sensed that the murderous plotters were very near. Sure enough, he spied the red flag atop Queen Tiya's barque snapping above the reeds in a lagoon a short distance away.

Something human touched him. He spun, heedless of the splash he created and the short scream that erupted from his lips. But it was only Assai's outstretched arm. Semerket's eyes were drawn beneath the water to the body that hovered just below the surface. Once Assai had ceased his struggle, the sunken yacht had let him go. His would-be slayer's mouth was open in an appalling grimace, filled with the silent echo of his final scream, and his eyes stared straight up at the sun, unblinking.

Semerket knew he had to leave the reed thicket quickly. The blood seeping from Assai's self-inflicted wounds and his own forehead would be sure to draw crocodiles, even though they preferred the open waters to these reed marshes. And, too, the conspirators in the lagoon were sure to come looking for their companion. As if conjured by his thoughts, Pentwere's plaintive voice rose from behind a nearby screen of reeds. "Assai?" the prince called out. "Where are you?"

Semerket seized Assai's body by the neck and dragged it to a distant clump of weeds, hoping that the corpse would blend in among the shadows and rotting vegetation. The longer the favorite's body remained unfound, the more time Semerket would have to leave the reed copse and head for safety.

A sudden large splash roiled the lagoon, as if someone had jumped from a skiff. More splashes were coming toward him, and Semerket sank out of sight. Staying below the surface, he swam as far as he could through the clumps of reeds. Above him were the hulls of the cabal's hunting boats, the largest of them being the queen's. He surfaced silently at her boat's stern, pressing himself below its overhanging deck. His black, glistening hair allowed him to blend in with the dark water.

He started when he heard a piercing wail: Pentwere had found Assai's body. Watching through the tall grasses, Semerket saw that the prince had caught his friend in his arms and was holding him, pleading with him to live, to breathe again, begging the gods for mercy.

Semerket saw in the distorted reflections on the water that Tiya stood at the prow of her boat.

Paser's nervous voice came from the other side of the lagoon. "Your Majesty! If Semerket is alive—"

"Shut up!" the queen hissed.

"But he will tell everything!"

Tiya turned on the fat mayor then, and the boat rocked with her steps. "Is this the kind of counsel I can expect when you're vizier? You should be giving me advice, not pointing out the obvious!"

Semerket heard the oars of Iroy, Nakht, and Neferhotep as they pulled nearer in their boats. Pentwere's demented shrieks still echoed in the far lagoon.

"If Semerket has tried to reach Pharaoh, Majesty—" Nakht began.

"Impossible!" snapped Tiya. "Ramses is clear on the other side of this misbegotten swamp. That clerk couldn't get there so fast. Surely the crocodiles will take care of him—"

"Crocodiles avoid these reeds, Your Majesty," Iroy pointed out.

"I don't care! He's not with Pharaoh, I tell you!"

"But it's simply a matter of time, isn't it?" Paser said. Semerket could imagine him, his fat face hanging in dispirited folds. No doubt he was seeing ahead to the terrible death he would suffer if he were captured. Since he was not royal, there would be no silken cord for him, no private suicide as was accorded to nobles. His execution would be a hideous public spectacle. "We must flee," he said, his voice cracking, "and go into exile."

"Yes," agreed Nakht. "Syria. Or Libya. Later, when we can return—"

The queen's laugh interrupted him. "Oh, what fine brave men I have around me," said Tiya scornfully. "If we were to reach India itself, Pharaoh would still find us."

"Are you saying we've lost?" It was Paser again, his voice moving up a notch.

"No," said Tiya firmly. "Our only hope is to go forward with the plan—tonight."

"But, Majesty—! We're not ready!" Neferhotep's distinctive whine filled the lagoon. "The treasure is still in its hiding place— the generals have not yet received their gifts of gold—"

Tiya did not speak at first. Below the deck of her boat, hiding, Semerket waited. "The treasure truly departs tonight?" the queen finally asked.

"Yes, Divine Majesty." Neferhotep accelerated his whine to an even keener pitch. "But it will take many days to reach Pi-Ramesse, and many days after that for the beggars to convey it to the generals."

"Then the generals will simply have to wait for their rewards."

"But who will protect us from our enemies?" asked Paser. "You can't expect Pharaoh's northern family to sit idle, particularly after the crown prince has been killed."

In the water, Semerket winced. So the plot included even Prince Ramses! He should have guessed as much—how else could Pentwere rule if his chief rival for the throne were not eliminated?

Tiya considered. "We will make Djamet into a fortress and barricade ourselves in it, until our own armies reach us."

The men in the lagoon fell silent. Though Semerket could not see them from where he was hidden, evidently they acquiesced, for Tiya quickly issued her instructions.

"Paser, you will return to Eastern Thebes and collect the men of Sekhmet's temple garrison. Bring them to Djamet for our defense. Iroy, you will return with Paser. Prepare the works of sorcery. Distribute them to our enemies, so they may know they are bewitched. In particular, you must ensure that Pharaoh's guards realize they are under my control."

Paser and Iroy murmured agreement.

"Nakht, you and Neferhotep will go into the Great Place, to send the treasure north with the beggars."

"And you, Majesty?" Nakht asked with a cough.

Semerket could hear the lioness's fangs in the queen's voice. "Why, I shall merely await Pharaoh's pleasure in the harem, arrayed in Asian silks and bathed in perfume from the shores of Punt. What else is there for me to do?"

"But . . ." began Paser.

"Yes?" Her multi-stringed voice plucked a fierce note.

"It's a wise plan, a perfect plan, Your Majesty. But what of the crown prince? Who will . . . that is to say . . . be honored with the task of . . . ?" Semerket heard the queen call to her son. Pentwere still moaned and sobbed beside Assai's corpse. "Come away, my son," she said to him. "We will build a mighty tomb for your hero—but later. There are more important things to think of now."

Semerket sank beneath the water, silently swimming away through the adjoining pools and thickets, leaving the conspirators far behind. When he knew he was far enough from Pharaoh's hunting fleet to remain unseen, he pulled himself from the Nile.

The winter winds were bitter against his wet skin. Looking to the south, across the inland sea of reeds, he saw that the sails of the hunting fleet were spread widely among the marshes. The hunt was still in progress. His head began to throb, and he raised a hand to his brow. When he brought it away, it was bathed in red. Until that moment he had forgotten that Assai had slashed it open.

What should he do . . . ? He knew he should try to warn Pharaoh now, while the conspirators still caviled in the lagoon, but the king was too far away. Going around the marshes on foot would take hours; if he tried to swim to the fleet, he would no doubt become hopelessly lost in the thickets, or fall prey to a lurking crocodile. No, the best thing to do was try to warn the authorities in Djamet.

To the north, Semerket saw a massive bank of dark clouds at the edge of the deserts, with soft flashes of lightning illuminating them from behind. A rare Egyptian rainstorm was developing. He had no time to lose.

Semerket began his long run to the temple.

THE WINDS FROM the desert storms bore down upon Djamet Temple. Outside, in the makeshift bazaars, the vendors' awnings were torn away from their stanchions. Merchants scrambled to lash down their wares before they went crashing. Unnoticed in all the furor, Semerket stood at the wall of blue faience tiles within the temple's main building. Though others were shouting that such winds were surely omens of terrible catastrophe, Semerket silently thanked whatever god had sent them—for the longer they gusted, he knew, the longer Pharaoh would be detained in the marshes and away from danger.

Semerket had no way of knowing the extent of the conspiracy, so was unsure of whom to trust. He could not go to the army captains—Queen Tiya had declared the army to be under her control. Whether she spoke the truth was immaterial; Semerket could not risk exposing himself to anyone he once considered friendly, not until he knew the number and names of those plotting to assassinate Pharaoh.

He hid in the shadows of a column, pondering his dilemma. At that moment he happened to catch sight of Mayor Pawero, hurrying along the corridor. An army of servants followed him, and Pawero hurled quick orders to the chamberlains to lower the wooden lattices at the doors and windows where thin curtains billowed wildly.

"The holy fires must be snuffed out!" he heard Pawero command. "If a spark catches on these screens, the entire temple will be set ablaze."

Semerket instantly made for Pawero's offices. Since the Western Mayor was Queen Tiya's brother, Semerket was certain that he was also a member of the conspiracy. He thought back to their encounter that morning. Pawero had seemed oddly furtive at being discovered in cheerful conversation with his rival Paser.

Then it came to him; the two mayors' famed loathing for one another was a sham. Their enmity was nothing more than an attempt to deflect attention from their shared goal—to see Tiya's son on Egypt's throne. And if Paser had been promised the vizierate, Semerket now wondered, what was to be Pawero's reward for his part in the conspiracy? As the blood uncle of Pentwere he certainly would be first among the advisors to the young king, ranked above any vizier. In addition, he would probably be elevated to the rank of Prince of the Blood. Semerket shuddered, considering what flowed in that blood—Pawero, too, was every bit the descendant of the accursed Amen-meses and Twos-re.

Semerket realized that Tiya and her brother had probably long planned to divide the rule of Egypt between themselves. Tiya's son Pentwere, captivated by his favorites and the cheers of the mob, would be easily convinced to divest himself of the more onerous responsibilities of ruling, leaving his mother and uncle to administrate. Semerket saw ahead to the Egypt brother and sister would rule, with arrogance and hauteur the centerpiece of their governance. How they would relish it, he thought, when all the kingdom groveled before them, convinced as they would be that the rightful heirs of Egypt again held the scourge and crook in their blood-stained hands.

Pushing aside the curtain at Pawero's door, Semerket entered the mayor's office. The room was dark, the only light coming from a small opening in the high stone roof. Semerket stepped into the gloom, looking sharply for any lingering scribe or clerk. His luck held, for the room was empty; the rare storm had claimed everyone's attention.

Rapidly he crossed the room to tables strewn with papyri. Glancing at them, he saw that the documents were all blandly innocent of treasonous plots, being transcriptions of court cases, lists of goods that had been delivered to Djamet as tribute, taxation records, and so on.

If incriminating documents did indeed exist, he pondered, where would the mayor hide them? The office was replete with rows of shelves, each stone cubicle in them containing several scrolls. He quickly scanned their leather identification tags—none purported to contain anything other than lists and schedules like those he had found on the table.

Semerket spied a door at the far end of the room, difficult to see in the dark. Pushing it open, he discovered a chapel of sorts. A variety of gods and goddesses crowded together, each in their own small niche. Devotional flames had been left burning before them, and the room was warm and bright from their glow. Pawero was famed, after all, for his religious fervor and his ostentatious display of piety.

Semerket remained unimpressed; Pawero was simply another criminal who cloaked his sins in pompous devotion. Semerket turned to leave, but as he stepped through the door, his foot kicked something across the room. The thing, whatever it was, bounced lightly off the wall. He looked down and saw that the floor was littered with at least five or six crumpled balls of papyrus. Curious, he knelt to examine them.

"The land is in desolation," he read, after smoothing out the paper. He recognized the handwriting. Pawero had written the words, and recently too, for a set of still-damp reed pens and a pot of ink were in the corner of the room. Blank rolls of paper were piled neatly beside them.

Many of the words on the papers were struck through with lines, and other words had been altered, as if Pawero had toiled to find just the right phrases to use. "Heaven has hardened its heart against Pharaoh, and the gods have extended their hand to another—"

Semerket exhaled. Here was evidence of treason indeed!

His heart beat rapidly as he unfolded the other pieces of paper, all drafts from some larger document. Though the phrases came to him in a random fashion, cadged from the pieces of papyrus, he was able to develop a sense of the document's entire intent:

> . . . *gods have extended their hands to the great Prince Pentwere, passing over those ahead of him* . . .

Semerket's breath caught in his throat; Pawero was attempting to justify the overthrow of Pharaoh as a directive from the gods. How convenient it must be, Semerket thought bitterly, to so easily discern heaven's mandate.

Now we must flex our arms in order to snatch Egypt from her violator. He and his minions will flee like tits and sparrows before the falcon. We shall take back the gold, silver, and bronze of Egypt, which he has heaped at the feet of his Asiatic harlot . . .

"Asiatic harlot." Semerket whispered the words aloud, sensing the wintry influence of Queen Tiya in them. Pharaoh's devotion to his northern wife, the Canaanite Queen Ese, was being singled out by her southern rival as justification for the rebellion. From this, Semerket inferred that the letter was probably intended for the heads of the southern families. He saw how carefully Pawero and Tiya played on old prejudices toward Egypt's one-time colonies. And the hypocrisy! At the same time brother and sister accused Pharaoh of squandering the riches of Egypt on his foreign-born wife, they themselves rifled the tombs of Egypt's royal dead, not even sparing their own ancestors.

All the gods and goddesses have manifested their oracles (Semerket read from another ball of crumpled papyrus) *and have pronounced their judgment: Get the people together! Incite hostilities in order to provoke rebellion against their lord! Proclaim the new dawn in Egypt!*

The final pieces of paper revealed a list of some fifty names, which Paser had methodically annotated. Semerket had no way of knowing if they comprised a list of conspirators, but it was likely. The names ranged from those of well-known generals to the overseer of the treasury, from the royal magician to the keeper of the king's cattle. Even the names of the two librarians in the House of Life, Messui and the crook-backed little Maadje, appeared on the list. Apparently, from the notations next to their titles, they were responsible for retrieving the forbidden volumes of magic that were hidden in the House of Life. Semerket, perhaps more than anyone, could well imagine the kind of harm the queen intended with the spells found inside the books.

Most of the names, however, were minor ones—butlers and cooks and scribes who labored in the Djamet workshops. At first glance he might have omitted them from his consideration, but then he realized that though they were not illustrious or powerful folk, these men were probably the most dangerous conspirators on the list. They were the "mice," the little ones who possessed the attribute of invisibility, able to come and go from the palace at any hour without being noticed. In all likelihood they were the ones who smuggled such letters as these to their intended recipients.

After reading through the list a second time, Semerket began to notice another phenomenon he had not at first apprehended. In the annotations beside the names, Pawero had systematically marked that such-and-such a person was the "brother of Pharaoh's wife of the second class, Hathor," or that someone else was the father or uncle of "Pharaoh's wife of the fourth class, Ipet," and so forth. In fact the term "Pharaoh's wife" occurred so frequently on the list that Semerket suddenly comprehended that if these were indeed the names of the conspirators, then the plot must have been hatched in Pharaoh's harem itself!

It was apparent, then, that not just Tiya but all of Pharaoh's southern wives were behind the conspiracy. He suddenly felt the chill lagoon waters on his skin, remembering what Tiya had said as he lurked beneath her skiff . . . what was it? "I shall await Pharaoh's pleasure in the harem . . ."

The truth smote him like an axe: Pharaoh's murder would be attempted in the last possible place anyone would think to look— where not even the king's personal guards dared follow. It was clear to him, as well, that Tiya meant to accomplish the deed herself. The lioness was ready to spring once again. This time, however, an eagle was her prey.

He shook his head in dismay. He knew that he should not be surprised—there had been a precedent, after all. Tiya's grandmother Twos-re had slain her own husband, and for the same reason.

Carefully Semerket folded the bits of paper and hid them in his sash. He slipped from the chapel, silently retracing his steps to the curtained doorway that led into the outer hall. His next task, he knew, was to find the crown prince and remove him to safety. Above all, the proper succession in Egypt must be guaranteed. Pentwere would never be proclaimed king as long as the crown prince was alive. More than even the safety of Pharaoh himself, the survival of his heir was paramount.

Semerket sped along the black tiles of Djamet, rushing through the many-columned halls whose blue roofs were spangled with golden stars. Though the winds had become calmer, Semerket glimpsed through the open courtyards the dank gray ridge of clouds that had moved in over the Nile valley. Servants were still at work, cleaning up the debris left from the winds. Occasionally, they gave him a stricken glance as he sped by, shocked by his blood-stained forehead and muddy kilt. Fortunately, none challenged him. Semerket noticed for the first time that his vizier's badge was missing—probably at the bottom of the lagoon, he assumed glumly, lost during his watery struggle with Assai. He prayed that no one would stop him.

Where to find the crown prince? The acres of the temple complex were a warren of offices and workshops, storage bins and grain silos. So huge was it that it was boasted that the entire population of Western Thebes could crowd within it in times of war. The prince might be anywhere in such a place. Semerket emerged from a side door into the temple grounds, uncertain where to turn. He had gone no more than a furlong before he heard a cry.

"Semerket!"

At the far end of the courtyard he saw two men furiously waving to him. Semerket goggled at them, amazed.

"Nenry," he said faintly. "Qar!"

His brother and the Medjay ran to him. "Semerket—thank the gods you're alive," Nenry said. But then he stared aghast at his brother, at his slashed forehead and fouled appearance. "You *are* alive, aren't you . . . ?"

"You knew I was in danger?"

Nenry nodded. "When I discovered that the queen planned your death today," Nenry said, "I rushed across the river to save you."

"Save *me*?" Semerket looked at his brother with an odd expression. Nenry nodded again.

"Well, why not?" Semerket said after a moment. "It's the second time you've done it."

The brothers stood for a moment, tongue-tied and awkward, unable to speak. Semerket glanced over his brother's shoulder at the Medjay.

"There are many things you both should know," he said.

THEY WALKED SWIFTLY through Djamet Temple's compound. Above, the slate-colored clouds lent a frail piquancy to the remaining sunlight. Nenry, flashing his emblem of office, asked one of the temple guards where they might find Prince Ramses. They were directed to a small rear building where two soldiers stood guard. Nenry, suddenly quaking, asked if he and his associates might be announced to the crown prince "on a matter of some urgency." A moment later they were ushered inside.

The prince was making notes upon a papyrus at a wooden table. Scrolls were piled high around him, while models of temples and civic buildings crowded the small room still further. The brawny Libyan bodyguard stood behind the prince, just as he had in the House of Life, arms folded.

As before, Prince Ramses wore no wig or insignia, and his garments were ink-stained. He coughed slightly, bringing a kerchief to his lips. As they entered, he squinted shortsightedly at them and rose to his feet.

"Majesty," began Semerket, kneeling, "I doubt if you remember me—"

"I do. You're Semerket, the one who sought to know more about Queen Twos-re. Have you found what you needed?"

"More than I cared to," said Semerket grimly.

The crown prince did not question the meaning of his words, looking instead at Semerket's companions. "Who are these friends of yours?"

His brother and the Medjay had also knelt. "This is Qar, a Medjay who guards the Great Place—and this is my brother, who is . . . was Mayor Paser's chief scribe."

"They are welcome. But what is so urgent, Semerket, that you must see me immediately?"

Semerket crept forward. "Highness, there is a plot against you and your father. You are in much danger."

The crown prince sat back down at the table, astonished, and began to unconsciously roll up a scroll. The Libyan bodyguard seized his armor and without comment began strapping it to himself.

"Queen Tiya," Semerket continued, "has used black magic and treasure stolen from the tombs in the Great Place to make your half-brother Pentwere the new pharaoh. It is not a small plot, Majesty. I've come across this list made by Mayor Pawero—there are more than fifty names on it."

Semerket fished the folded papyri from his sash and handed them to the prince. Ramses brought them close to his eyes as he read the documents, slowly, one after another. When he was finished, his face was paler than before.

"But . . . but am I still the crown prince?" Prince Ramses asked in a small voice.

"We pledge our lives," Qar said.

The prince put a hand to his forehead, the full import of the plot becoming clear to him. "My father!" he said abruptly. "I must go to him! If he's in danger—"

"No, Majesty, you must not," Semerket said firmly. "It's not safe in Djamet. We believe that some members of the army have gone over to the traitors. You must go into hiding until we know who's loyal to you."

"That is cowardly."

"But sensible." Qar said adamantly. "Others must fight for you now, Highness. And you must stay alive so they have something to fight *for*."

The crown prince rose and paced to the doorway. "But if it's true, all of this, where in Thebes *will* I be safe? I'd rather take my chances here, with my father."

Ramses had asked the one question for which they had prepared no answer.

"There is one place I know," Semerket said reluctantly, "and an army for us, too . . . if we dare use it."

They stared at him.

Semerket looked at the prince. "Your majesty," he asked, "can you make this sign with your hand?"

Semerket held up his fingers and formed the secret sign of the Beggar Kingdom.

THE BEGGAR KING spoke privately with Semerket. Nenry, Qar, the crown prince, and his Libyan guard waited at the rear of the room.

Nenry cast his eyes over the place, examining its crumbling walls and bizarre ornaments. Strange as the old Hyksos temple was, however, stranger still was the legless man in his miniature chariot, with his stained robes and battered crown of acanthus leaves, the one who now spoke to his brother.

Semerket never ceased to amaze him. How did he even know such ruffians? Nenry cast a surreptitious glance at Prince Ramses, who seemed unperturbed to be in such bizarre surroundings, amid such odd people. But then, reasoned Nenry to himself, the prince must be inured to meeting strange personages, everyone from foreign ambassadors to professional assassins. A lifetime at court prepared one to be fazed by nothing. Unconsciously, Nenry straightened his shoulders and made his features as blandly unassuming as the prince's.

But Nenry flinched when the Beggar King muttered a surprised "Hmmph!" at something Semerket whispered to him. From his chariot, the king peered closely at the crown prince, running his red-rimmed eyes over Ramses in cold appraisal. Then the Beggar King inclined his head to him, one potentate to another. The crown prince nodded as well.

"Yousef!" the Beggar King shouted suddenly.

The tallest man Nenry had ever seen entered the room. The giant and the prince's Libyan bodyguard eyed one another uneasily.

"Bring a chair for His Majesty—*the crown prince!*" The Beggar King raised his eyebrows at Yousef significantly. Prince Ramses sat gratefully in the proffered chair, taking out his kerchief to wipe his face.

The Beggar King drove his chariot to where the crown prince sat. "Semerket was prudent to bring the son of Pharaoh to us. You will be well protected here."

"Thank you," said the prince, remembering to add "Your Majesty." All the way from Djamet, Semerket had attempted to prepare his companions for the surreal spectacle that now confronted them; in particular, he had stressed the Beggar King's wish to be addressed as a fellow monarch.

The Beggar King laid his whip again on the ram, and moved his chariot to where the Libyan stood. "Is this Your Majesty's bodyguard?"

"He is."

"His weapons will be restored to him. We want you to know that you are in no danger from us." The king's face became abruptly and utterly filled with rage and he banged a fist down upon the chariot's frame. "To live in such times!" he said in a scandalized voice. "When a Pharaoh can be murdered by his own wife and son—what infamy!" He waited until he was calm again. "Yousef."

"Lord?"

"I want two hundred strong men and women, dressed in beggar's rags, and armed. Assemble them in the forecourt in twenty minutes' time. Be ready to ferry them to Djamet."

"Yes, lord."

When the giant had departed, the Beggar King's countenance was grave. "I fear, gentlemen, that even two hundred of my beggars will not be enough if the army has gone over to those traitors."

Semerket spoke up. "Then we must bring Vizier Toh and his troops back from Erment."

Quickly, paper and ink were brought to the crown prince so that he could compose a letter to Toh informing him of the conspiracy and pleading for his quick return. With any luck, the prince told them, Toh was camped in the vicinity of Thebes, for he had been gone only a single day.

It was decided that Medjay Qar would take the letter personally to Toh. The Beggar King volunteered a horse to ensure the speediest of deliveries. Despite the gravity of the situation, Semerket smiled to himself—from what stable, he wondered, would the beast be filched?

They agreed that Nenry would accompany Yousef into Djamet, there to await the arrival of Toh. Semerket knew that if he himself were seen by any of the conspirators, he would be instantly dispatched. Nenry was somewhat known among the temple acolytes, and he could excuse his presence by saying that he waited for Paser. If the opportunity presented itself, he must force himself into Pharaoh's presence to warn him of the danger.

"In the meantime, I will go into the Great Place," Semerket continued, "to prevent the treasure from being moved to the north."

"No," insisted Nenry. "I know you, Ketty. You're only doing it so that you can arrest Nakht. You're too weak from loss of blood. You'd not survive it."

"There's no one else, Nenry," answered Semerket. "I'm the only one who knows where the tomb is, and how to enter it. I'll go to the Medjays first for their help."

Qar, Nenry, and Semerket stared soberly at one another. "That's it, then," Qar spoke crisply.

When they were gone, the Beggar King spoke soothingly to the suddenly trembling crown prince. "Don't fret, Your Majesty. My beggars will rescue your father. For if they don't, they know the Cripple Maker will be waiting for them."

THE THUNDERHEADS, which had earlier confined themselves to the edges of the desert, now flattened and stretched wide across the horizon, obliterating the setting sun. In the darkness a series of thatched reed boats and other small craft crowded with beggars were secretly launched from the poor quarter of Eastern Thebes. The boats were sent across the Nile in ones and twos, to avoid detection by the river sentries.

When the beggars were safely across the Nile, Yousef dispersed them to various locations around the pylons of Djamet——alongside the canal, at the base of the twin colossal statues of Pharaoh, and some, the brawniest of them, clustered near the massive gates. Yousef positioned his army so casually that the gradual infusion of beggars into Djamet's outer courtyard went unnoticed even by the temple guards.

At Yousef's signal, the beggars settled down to take up their usual evening activities. They threw bones with one another, shared songs, or laughed at jokes. Some lit fires in small braziers and roasted a bit of game. To the inhabitants of Djamet, the beggars seemed as indolent and indifferent as on any other night of the year.

Nenry noticed the smell of rain from the southwestern deserts that permeated the courtyard. A moment later a cataclysmic shock of thunder shook the ground so profoundly that even the massive stanchions bearing the blue and crimson pennants quaked. Intermittent raindrops began to bounce on the granite pavement. Rain was such an infrequent visitor to Thebes that many of the younger beggars had never before seen it. They raised their heads, and held out their hands. The sky was suddenly lit from horizon to horizon by a silent flash of lighting. Nenry, saying nothing, gripped Yousef's arm, for in that burst of light he had seen Pharaoh's hunting fleet turning from the river into the temple canal.

Yousef made a signal to the beggars. Heads turned. The beggars were treated to the sight of the boats struggling up the canal in the increasing rain. Their sails hung sodden on their masts, and the flowers that had been strung in their rigging were withered and dripping.

Panic ensued at the docks. Boats thumped into one another in their haste to moor nearest the temple. A few were swamped in the mêlée, and their listing hulls became impassible barriers so that even Pharaoh's yacht was forced to moor a distance away. Dripping courtiers swore at each other, and small fights broke out. Armies of servants came running from the temple to hurriedly divest their masters' vessels of dead ducks and hunting sticks. Pharaoh was left to fend for himself as his courtiers went running for cover. Even his bearers could not penetrate the chaos at the wharf, and the king was forced to walk the long avenue into Djamet, his mood darkening with every step.

As Pharaoh passed some distance away, muttering, Nenry turned to Yousef. "I must try to reach him," he said. Yousef nodded. Nenry hurried inside Djamet, and crept to the audience hall where his sovereign stood glowering.

Ramses hurled his sopping wig to the floor; it scurried across the shiny black tiles like a water rat. He stood dripping, fuming at the commotion around him, as servants ran to fetch towels. As Nenry pushed his way through the throng of hovering courtiers, Ramses spied Pawero in the crowd. The pharaoh pointed a condemning finger at him.

"You!" Ramses said loudly. "Is this how you manage my estate? No fresh clothes—no braziers to warm me! I count for so little, it seems, to you proud southerners!"

Pawero was caught short. "I humbly apologize, Great King. The servants are indeed lax. I will see that they are beaten—"

"I will see *you* beaten, sir. Being my wife's brother won't save you. Where is that woman, anyway?" The pharaoh turned in irritation to scan the courtiers.

"She and your son have not yet returned, Your Majesty." Pawero's tone was obsequious and mollifying.

"Good. I didn't want to see them anyway. It's that truth-teller I want to talk to. What's his name . . . ?"

Tiya's rich voice suddenly broke through the din in the audience hall. "Do you mean the clerk Semerket, my lord? Have you not spoken with him yet, then?" It seemed an innocent question to all around her. Only Nenry, cringing at the back of the hall, heard the edge in it; Tiya was unsure whether Semerket was alive or dead, whether he had reached Pharaoh in secret.

The queen had possessed the foresight that morning to take with her a cape infused with beeswax. She now stepped from its folds to emerge as dry and composed as always. Other than a little dew on her wig, no other traces of the rain were to be seen on her. Prince Pentwere skulked behind his mother, also wrapped in a slicker, his eyes swollen from weeping.

As Pharaoh was stripped of his hunting habit, he turned on his wife. "It's a sad day, isn't it, when one finds out the gods don't exist?"

"Whatever can you possibly mean, Ramses?"

"I prayed the waters of the Nile would swallow you up, but you're not even wet."

Nenry saw the flash of cool hatred that sparked in Tiya's eye then, but in front of he courtiers she became all consideration and comfort. Taking a towel from a servant she began to rub Pharaoh vigorously. "You talk such nonsense at times," she said lightly.

Pharaoh's eye lighted on Pentwere. "A fine day you picked for a hunt, sir," he called over to his son. The prince said nothing, staring at his father with strangely burning eyes. Momentarily astonished, Ramses turned to Tiya and asked, "What's the matter with him? Has he been bitten by a rabid ape?"

"Assai is missing. He fell overboard."

"Missing? Assai? Are they searching for him?"

"Of course."

"Well," said Ramses grudgingly, "they'll find him." An unholy light shone in his eye, and the old man could not resist a final jab. "But if they don't, perhaps your son might bed with a woman now and again. Millions recommend it, you know."

There were small gasps from the courtiers. Pentwere cast off his slicker and his fists tightened. Tiya shook her head at him, so slightly that she might not have done it. Pentwere reluctantly dropped his red gaze, muttering, "Yes, Father."

Tiya finished toweling Ramses. "There. You're dry. Go to your rooms now for a warm bath. I shall send my masseuse to you."

"I have my own masseuse!"

Tiya took a breath before she continued. "Well then, afterward, come to the harem and your wives will beguile you. We'll make sure all your cares slip from your shoulders. You'll see."

No one but Nenry, out of all those assembled, seemed to think her words betokened anything other than the queen's usual forbearance toward her irascible husband.

"Well," said Ramses, somewhat mollified. "Perhaps," he said, "perhaps. Send Semerket to me, first, when he's found. A rare fellow of good sense, he is."

"Really?" sniffed Tiya. "Rather too fond of wine for my taste. But when he comes here again—if he does—I will know what to do."

Satisfied, Pharaoh indicated to Pawero that he should assist him to his apartments.

"Your Majesty!" Nenry found his tongue and called desperately after the king. "Please! I must see you! A matter of state!"

Tiya furiously overrode him, chastising Nenry before the courtiers. "Later, you idiot! Who was that?" She glared at him. Nenry cast down his eyes, not wishing to be recognized as Semerket's brother. He crouched in the shadows. "Can't you see how tired and ill he is? He has no time for business tonight! Come back tomorrow." She called out to a chamberlain, "I want no one to disturb you. Do you understand? *No one.* Pharaoh must have his rest." The man inclined his head, and fell in line behind Pawero, accompanying Pharaoh into his rooms.

Tiya, surrounded by her ladies, ascended the stairs that led to the harem. Halfway up, the courtiers heard the queen suddenly chuckle to herself, the tinkling sound of little bells, enjoying a joke that only she heard. Moving with her usual feline grace, she went to prepare herself for Pharaoh's arrival.

Nenry stared after her in panic. He had failed to intercede with Pharaoh. Moving numbly through the throng of milling courtiers, he wore a dazed expression. Having been so sharply rebuked by the queen, he was given a wide berth by the others. Disfavor at court, apparently, was contagious. He moved swiftly down the hall and out the temple gates to rejoin Yousef.

"I wasn't permitted to speak to him," Nenry almost wailed. "And she's inveigled him into the harem!"

"That's not our only problem," said Yousef. He nodded in the direction of the Nile. Barely seen at the end of the canal was a large warship. It had arrived only a few moments before, Yousef said, while Nenry was inside the temple. Armed soldiers were streaming down its gangplank. Nenry gasped, for he recognized their uniforms: it was the garrison from Sekhmet's temple.

Mayor Paser and High Priest Iroy stood at the rear of the ship. Iroy was the first to disembark, leading a gang of slaves who carried his supplies into the rear of the temple. Paser was next off, following the soldiers as they marched in formation to the Great Pylons.

At the gates, one of the guards challenged their right to enter. Paser gave orders to his captain. There was an abrupt shout from one of the temple sentries, a flash of copper, and the sentry fell to the ground clutching his side. When he was dragged away, a stain of red melted into the wet paving stones.

The sentry's commander came running to where Paser stood, profusely apologizing for the man's stupid behavior. The commander gave the order to the rest of his men to withdraw from this and every succeeding gate within the temple. They were to be replaced by the men from Sekhmet, he said. This was such an odd command that the men at first seemed hesitant to leave.

"Go to your barracks," commanded the guard captain. "And wait there for me. New orders have come in." Soon every guard had been replaced by a man from Sekhmet.

Paser stood at the outer pylons, congratulating himself on the smoothness of the guards' transition—an entire temple complex had been delivered into his hands with only a single death. "Perhaps I should have been a general," he thought. As he was preening, he heard a member of the Sekhmet garrison mutter in disgust.

"Horus's balls!" the soldier said. "I thought the beggars were bad across the river. But here—look at them—just like rats from the sewer!"

Paser looked about the glistening temple square for the first time that night, and beggars indeed lurked in every niche, behind every statue, under every tree. The mayor's lip curled. When he was vizier, as the queen had promised, he would throw every last one of them to the crocodiles. What a relief never to rely again on the favor of the poor and humble. Those days were over at last. He would be a different man when he was vizier—for then he would be a noble, something else Queen Tiya had promised. Paser sniffed, preening again, glad to be beneath the pylons and out of the rain.

Lightning scalded the courtyard. In its lingering flash something struck the fat mayor as odd. The man that huddled in a distant crowd of beggars looked so ridiculously like his simple-minded scribe, Nenry. A certain cast of feature, a vaguely reminiscent tilt of the head . . .

The Eastern Mayor looked again, but it was now too dark to see across the courtyard.

"Ridiculous!" Paser said, chuckling to himself. Nenry was of course safely on the other side of the river with that awful wife of his.

ONE OF THE BEGGARS who had crossed the Nile into Djamet did not accompany the rest of them to the temple. Instead, when his skiff touched the western side of the Nile, he slipped quickly away, alone, throwing off his beggar's rags and climbing the pathway that led into the Great Place. Following Qar's precise instructions, Semerket found the Medjay headquarters without becoming too lost even though the rain had begun to fall and no stars served to light his way.

The headquarters were located in an abandoned tomb bordering the Place of Beauty. The command post was no more than three rooms in length, arranged in a descending row of square stone boxes. Generations before, Qar had told Semerket, tomb-makers had painstakingly carved out the rooms before discovering a deep rift of quartz that cut diagonally through the mountain. Deemed unsuitable for further digging, the unfinished tomb made an excellent, if rough-hewn, headquarters and prison for Captain Mentmose and his gang of Medjays.

Medjays surrounded Semerket now in the first room, where arms and armor were stored in niches carved into the walls. He had gathered the soldiers together as soon as he arrived, soberly telling them of the plot against Pharaoh's life, and of the stolen treasure he had found hidden in the tomb under the tomb. Before he could even ask for their assistance, however, one of the Medjays spoke against him.

"What hope is there against an army?" asked the Medjay in disgust. "They are thousands and we are not even twenty. We'd be throwing our lives away, and for nothing!"

"He's right," agreed another. "I say that we join up with Queen Tiya. Who wants a northerner as Pharaoh anymore? Good riddance, I say. Let Pentwere rule."

The Medjays had always regarded him as an interloper, Semerket knew. Despite his friendship with Qar, the other Medjays had shunned him. To them, he was a man of Eastern Thebes, appointed by the vizier, sent to do a job rightfully theirs. The fact that he had discovered such a terrifying plot against the state did nothing to endear him to them. Semerket intuitively knew that some of them, no doubt, had thrown in their lot with the tomb-makers long before.

"Queen Tiya and her men have perpetrated the most terrible crime in the history of Egypt," Semerket said, "and it was done under your watch."

He saw fear and shame rise in some of their faces, defiance in others. If the stolen treasure indeed left the Great Place, and should the theft be discovered and prosecuted, the most lenient sentence the Medjays could look forward to was a term in a Sinai copper mine. The Nubian policemen were foreigners, hired mercenaries, and harshly treated when they failed in their duties.

"Tonight they mean to move the treasure to the north," continued Semerket, "again under your noses. It may be that Tiya will succeed, I don't know. But I mean to stop them, whatever the cost to me—with or without your help."

Semerket began to fasten a breastplate to himself. For a moment none of the Medjays moved. Finally, Captain Mentmose reached for his own armor, and began fastening the straps. One by one, the others prepared themselves for battle as well.

"We'll hide behind the crags, across from Pharaoh's tomb," said Mentmose. "When they come out, loaded down with treasure, we'll attack."

"I'm sure they won't venture into the valley until they think you Medjays are sleeping," said Semerket. "We must go into the village, in the meantime, to free Hunro."

A silence fell on the room. Suddenly the Medjays were busying themselves with adjustments to their swords and rebuckling their armor. Foreboding crept up Semerket's spine.

"What . . . ?" he said.

"Did not your brother tell you?" Captain Mentmose whispered. The Medjay regarded him for a moment. Then, taking a deep breath, he spoke. "Hunro is dead, Semerket. She was stoned to death earlier today by the villagers, in the field behind their temple that they use for such things. We arrived too late to stop it."

Semerket looked up and out the door at the black rain falling in the Great Place.

"Tell him the rest," said Thoth loudly. He was the Medjay who had wanted to join up with Tiya.

"Quiet!" commanded Mentmose.

"What?" Semerket asked, so faintly that it might have been a sigh. His eyes were blacker than the Medjays had ever seen them.

Glancing defiantly at his captain, Thoth took a step toward Semerket. "They told me she called your name at the end. Even at the last she was convinced you'd save her."

THE RAIN BECAME HEAVIER as Semerket and the Medjays made for Pharaoh's tomb. Thunder echoed in the Great Place, loosening rocks and pebbles so that they cascaded onto the pathway from cliffs above.

"Listen for any rushing water," Mentmose warned them. "Keep to the high paths."

A sudden flash of silent pink lit up the valley. The pungent smell of scorched air permeated the pathway where they walked. They trudged in blackness, slowly, on the limestone paths, careful to keep away from the slick edges. Mentmose led the way.

Semerket followed in a slough of misery, barely noticing the oozing mud that sucked at his sandals and made him stumble. He was thinking of Hunro, and how he had failed her so utterly. She had been the only villager who had been friendly to him, the only woman to have engendered a spark of feeling in him since Naia. Because he had urged her to betray her neighbors, she had been killed, and horribly.

Semerket groaned aloud, sinking into further agony. I've failed every woman I've ever known, he thought. No one is safe around me . . .

He had driven away his life's love, Naia, being unable to give her a baby, the one thing she wanted most. The dullest of sewer dredgers could father a child, he moaned to himself—but even that was beyond him.

His heart sank further as he considered the task ahead of him that night. If he stayed, disaster would no doubt be the outcome of the evening's venture. Crowding upon that thought, he suddenly heard again the mocking voice of Queen Tiya in his mind. "You told me he was a drunk, unable to find his own backside . . ." Her exact words were lost to him, but he realized now that he had been given the investigation into Hetephras's murder only because he was not expected to solve it.

A terrible thirst suddenly seized him, a fever on his tongue. He looked furtively over his shoulder to see how many Medjays followed him. Gradually, Semerket let them pass him until he was at their rear. He would leave, he decided, go back into the city. He had only to hang back a little more, slip down one of the trails, and make his way into Thebes. He craved an inn with a friendly serving maid and a jar of red that never emptied. A few jars of wine, and then he would be able to deal with the memories of the entire stupid panoply of his stupid wasted life—

"We're here," Mentmose said.

Semerket was caught short. They were on the other side of the wadi, across from Pharaoh's tomb.

Though the rain was far from torrential, already small rills of water were beginning to snake down the cliffs of the Great Place, to form fast-flowing brooks on the desert floor. Mentmose and the Medjays took up their positions, hiding in the outcroppings of the cliff, melting into the mountainside. Even when another flash of pink lightning brightened the canyon, Semerket could not see them.

Sodden and miserable, Semerket settled down beneath a rocky outcropping. He was grateful that it afforded some minuscule protection from the wet. A few seconds later another heart-stopping peal of thunder resounded through the Great Place. He pulled his mantle up, soggy as it was, and settled in to wait.

He could not discern whether hours passed or only moments. The steady drip of water and the endless pervasive dark were always the same. It was too late to decamp for Thebes, he knew. At any rate, it was better to die on the sands of the Great Place, he thought, in the service of something bigger than himself, than on some tavern floor. As he waited for what the night would bring, a leaden torpor enveloped him.

Semerket awakened with a start. Something had disturbed him— the sound of a wooden key being inserted into the tomb's door. He stared across the wadi and saw distant figures disappearing into the cliff-face . . . or imagined that he did. Then he heard the distinct thud of the door as it shut behind them. Yes. The beggars were there. He wondered if the other Medjays had seen them. A few minutes went by, and then the door of the tomb opened once again—

Torchlight flooded into the valley, shining from inside the tomb. Semerket crept forward to observe, amazed by their boldness. Beggars clustered at the tomb's entrance, baskets of treasure already strapped to their shoulders. The scribe Neferhotep directed their endeavor. Semerket could hear the whining tones of his voice, though in the patter of the rain his words remained indistinct. The beggars began to move into the wadi, trudging to the north.

They were already leaving! He looked about wildly, searching for the Medjays. Now was the time to attack! Why were they hanging back?

Across the wadi, emerging from the rear of the tomb, quite distinguishable in the firelight, a group of Medjays appeared—carrying baskets of treasure. Semerket's heart sank; as he had suspected, some of the Medjays were indeed in league with the conspirators.

Semerket groped his way to where he had last seen Mentmose. Heedless of the stones that he dislodged, he climbed a crag leading to an upper ledge of rock. A streak of distant lightning scarred the sky and allowed him to see Mentmose sitting quietly on a ledge above, asleep.

Semerket's veins were infused with sudden fury. Damn him! The captain was allowing the beggars to get away, accompanied by his own men! He climbed the last few cubits to the ledge, scrambling to where the man dozed. "Mentmose—!" he hissed. He reached forward, touching his shoulder. Even at his touch Mentmose did not wake. Semerket nudged him again, and the captain merely slumped to his side, as though he might tumble from the cliff. Semerket reached out to grab him. When he brought his hand back, it was covered in something slick. The ferrous smell of it told Semerket the rest of the story—the captain was dead, struck from behind.

Before he could register the enormity of what had happened, a clipped, aristocratic voice cut through the dark from behind him. "I don't believe it," Nakht said. "Are you some kind of god or devil that *doesn't—ever—die?*"

Semerket immediately attempted to leap down the cliffside, but he was checked by Nakht's sword at his throat. "Not quite so fast, Ketty. I'm afraid the treasure must leave as scheduled, and we can't have you spoiling the party yet again." Semerket glanced down; even in the dark he could see that the blade was covered in blood. It was Nakht who had killed Mentmose.

"Naia always said you had a rare talent for survival," remarked Nakht with a small sneer. "Since I was only ever privileged to see you drunk, I never quite believed her."

The pressure on his throat eased a bit as Nakht called across the wadi, "I've got him!" Lightning blistered the valley again.

"You'll not get away with it, Nakht."

The aristocrat's laugh bellied out across the canyon. "Naia also said you weren't exactly a sage when it came to expressing yourself. She was correct there, too."

"We know the names of all the conspirators—Pairy the treasurer, the master of the stables, Panhay, the librarians Messui and Maadje, Kenamun—all fifty of them."

He heard the tip of Nakht's sword strike the ground, as if the man's arm suddenly had lost its strength.

"What if you do know the names?" Nakht's attempt at bluster would have succeeded but for the slight quiver in his throat. "By tomorrow, Ramses will be dead, and Egypt will have a new pharaoh."

"There may well be a new pharaoh, but I can tell you that it won't be Pentwere."

"You're so sure—"

"I am sure. The crown prince is hidden far from Djamet, and safe. You'll never find him."

He could not see Nakht's expression. But there was a sudden cry of rage, and Semerket heard the slash of the blade as it came down. He instantly rolled to the side, and the sword clanged against the stone ledge where he had stood. Not waiting for another sword thrust, Semerket pitched himself forward, over the stone lip, falling blindly down into the dark.

It was no more than a cubit or so before the sloping face of rock caught him. A thin coat of slurry now layered the cliffs, and Semerket slid down to the valley floor, head over heels, accelerating as he plummeted. He attempted to grab at any stone or boulder in his path but they, too, were slick with mud. The slope ended abruptly some distance above the wadi floor. He pitched forward into space.

Semerket landed in a pool of water. From the stinging sensation on his forehead, he knew his wound had again torn open. Amazingly, it was his only major injury. He stood shakily, testing his limbs. No broken bones—all seemed intact.

A cry from above echoed through the canyon. "Get him!" shouted Nakht. "He's in the wadi!"

Semerket ran. He had no idea where he went, for in his fall from the cliff he had lost all sense of direction. He splashed through the newly created brooks and pools, following the bend of the valley floor. He turned his head to see if anyone followed him, but the patter of the rain and the cascades of water from the cliffs above prevented him from hearing anything else. Suddenly he was on his face. Something— or someone—had tripped him. When he tried to rise, rough hands held him down.

"We've got him!"

The voice belonged to the northern beggar, Noseless. He was pulled to his feet by many hands, and his arms were pinned behind him. Though he struggled, he could not free himself; there were too many of them.

Accompanied by a surge of mud and gravel, Nakht worked his way down the cliff, half sliding, half leaping to join them.

"He's a snake, this one," said Nakht, "always slithering away to hide behind some rock."

"Well," said Noseless, fingering the knife in his belt and walking confidently toward Semerket, "he won't be slithering away again." The beggar assumed a wheedling stance, hunching his shoulders, and whining in mock piteousness, "A tiny dablet of cash, kind sir? Some silver? A piece of copper? What about *this* piece—?" Noseless whipped the dagger from his belt, and looked back to his beggars to see if they enjoyed the joke.

Neferhotep came running to them from the tomb. "For the gods' sake, quit talking and kill him this time!"

"He says they have the crown prince hidden away," Nakht said, his voice edged with uncertainty. "Maybe we should force him to take us there—"

"Don't be a fool," said the scribe. "Semerket'd never tell, you know that—he's that stubborn. Kill him *now,* I say."

After a moment Nakht leaned toward him, his clipped voice low and gloating. "Well, it seems you're out of luck at last, Ketty."

They circled him. Semerket knew he had only moments to live, and for the first time in years he actually found his lips forming words of prayer. "Help me, Mother Isis," he prayed silently. "Not for my sake, but for Egypt's. These men shouldn't be allowed to live."

They forced him to his knees and shoved his head forward to bare his neck. In the dark, he heard a sword unsheathed. He waited for the icy blow, not breathing. He thought of Naia. Of his brother. Of Pharaoh. Semerket closed his eyes, leaning back into his heels, and faced death for the second time that day.

But the blow never came.

A sudden blast of cold wind hit his face instead. From down the length of the black canyon there came a growing roar, sounding like some huge animal, unleashed. The sound grew louder, accompanied by explosions of canyon walls as they collapsed. Even in the darkness he could see the line of white foam—the frothy edge of an immense wave of water speeding at them from far up the canyon.

The last thing he heard before the wall of water hit him was the screams of the men in the wadi. Then the churning desert sea engulfed him. Dense with mud, sand, and grit, it hurled Semerket forward on its curling spume. Patches of his skin were instantly rubbed raw, for the water was like emery dust. His head broke the surface, and he saw beggars and Medjays crushed against the cliff walls, screaming. The baskets of golden discs, heaped on the desert floor, were instantly overturned and buried by the waters.

Semerket felt himself carried along by the infant river in an almost leisurely fashion. Though he was jolted painfully as he was hurled against submerged boulders and canyon walls, he found that by simply allowing the water to flow where it may he was in no immediate danger of drowning. He almost laughed aloud, thinking how ironic it would have been to escape a watery death in the Nile only to find it in the middle of a desert.

The clouds were fast clearing from above, and the blanket of stars behind them suddenly shone through, silvering the Great Place with their light. He saw that an overhang of rock was just ahead; as he passed under it he reached up, feeling with his hands, searching for a handhold—a branch, a crevice, anything. The waters tore at him, though, defying him to escape them. It was hopeless, he decided. Just as he was about to drop again into the torrent, his fingertips brushed something warm and living—another hand was reaching for his.

Semerket almost let go from shock. He raised his head and found himself looking into the face of the young prince who had so long ago told him that god-skin was being made at the campsite.

"Hang on to me," said the boy.

He reached, but the waters pulled savagely at him.

"I'm too heavy for you—I'll only pull you down with me!" he told the boy. "Save yourself!"

"Don't be afraid," said the prince, grinning. And, strangely, Semerket was not afraid. He stretched his arm as far as he could reach, grasping the prince's fingertips.

Then he was atop the ledge of stone, and safe.

THE GATES OF
DARKNESS

HE AWOKE ON A PALLET OF SOFT DOWN. THE brightness of sun on whitewashed walls stabbed like knives in his head. Squinting, Semerket saw a room that was very neat, very orderly, except that there seemed to be two of everything—from his newly washed kilt and mantle, hanging from pegs in the wall, to the jug of water on the tiles beside him. It was a moment before he realized he was seeing double.

The sound of cheerful humming floated to him. A young woman knelt before a chest, not knowing he was awake. Semerket studied her as she withdrew a linen towel. If he concentrated very hard, he discovered, he could force his eyes to focus. The woman's long black hair had a blue sheen, almost as blue as the strands of beads in her ears, glimmering like the wings of beetles.

"I know you," he said aloud, surprised.

She looked over at him, smiling. "I am Keeya, and, yes, you know me, my lord. I serve your brother. He'll be relieved to know you're awake."

He was in his brother's house across the river in Eastern Thebes. "How long have I been here?"

"Three days."

"*Three*—?"

"Lay your head down, my lord," Keeya told him firmly. "The physician says you are not to move, not until the iris in your left eye is equal in size to the one in your right—though your eyes are so black, I can't see how he tells the difference."

"How did I get here?"

"Medjay Qar brought you. He says they found you high in the mountains of the Great Place, the morning after the terrible rains. A young prince stood beside you, he said, and called them over. When they reached you, the prince was gone. You were so still, he said, they thought you were dead. They don't know how you managed to survive the terrible flood."

Semerket brought his hand to his forehead and felt a bandage. "Where is Nenry?"

Keeya dropped her eyes sadly. "Alas, my lord, he is at the House of Purification. We are in mourning in this house."

He sat up then, despite the girl's admonitions. "My brother is dead?"

She put a finger to her lips. "No, my lord. Please lie back down or the physician will be very angry with you. Your lord brother has accompanied his wife's body to the embalmers."

"His *wife*?" Semerket wrinkled his brow, and pain shot down his face from his wound.

Keeya moistened the linen rag and brought it to his face. "An accident in the cellar," the girl said, and there was an odd spark of satisfied reminiscence in her eye. Idly she brought a hand to her ear, lost in thought. Then she shook her head slightly, and her blue earrings sparkled in the light. "A knife," Keeya said, her eyes hooded. "It was very sad."

He sat up again to question the girl further, but the pain in his head was so great he could only wince and lie back on the pallet.

"Do you see why the physician says to remain quiet?" Keeya asked archly, drawing the blanket over him again. "And he is a very great physician—from the palace!—so you must do as he says. Really, you would not wish to go outside into Thebes today. It's not a happy place." She poured him a bowlful of water and held it to his lips.

"What do you mean?" he asked after he had swallowed. "What has happened?"

"Why, soldiers are everywhere! There have been so many arrests, they say, that the forecourt in Amun's Great Temple has been turned into a prison just to accommodate them."

The thing he had been unable to remember rose suddenly in his mind to smite him. The conspiracy!

"Pharaoh!" he said. "What has happened to him? Tell me!"

"Ah, my lord, it's very tragic. Who would choose to live in such times? The stories they tell are unbelievable."

"Just tell me, Keeya!"

"From what your brother says, His Majesty's wives surrounded him in the harem. Queen Tiya took a dagger and . . ."

The pounding in Semerket's skull overwhelmed him, and the sudden roar in his ears drowned out the serving girl's words. He slipped again into unconsciousness.

WHEN SEMERKET NEXT WOKE, it was afternoon. His brother sat cross-legged on the floor next to him, dressed in the dark gray robes of mourning. Nenry seemed anything but mournful, for he was conversing in low but energetic tones with two scribes who wrote quickly as he spoke. When Nenry saw that his brother was awake, he dismissed the scribes with a gesture. They backed out of the room, bowing as they left. "Welcome back, Semerket," he said.

"Who is Pharaoh now?" his brother asked.

The question seemed an odd one to Nenry, and he blinked. "Why, Ramses III, of course."

Semerket gave a start. Had he dreamed the conversation with Keeya? "But your serving girl said . . . at least, I think she said . . ."

"He was wounded, Ketty. But he is still alive—and asking for you, by the way." Nenry could not resist a smug grin.

"Me?"

"You're a hero! The blackest conspiracy in the history of Egypt was thwarted because of you."

Semerket dismissed his brother's words. "Tiya and Pentwere . . . ?"

"In custody—though Pentwere is trying to convince everyone that the conspiracy was all his mother's idea. It won't save him, though. Ramses is like a lion in his wrath."

"And the rest of them . . . Paser . . . Pawero? Iroy?"

"All in the Djamet prison awaiting their trial—along with almost everyone whose name was on that list you found, together with their households. All yesterday and today, soldiers have been raiding their estates and taking their families and servants into custody. Over a thousand men and women, I'm told, all locked into Amun's temple."

The image of Naia rose in Semerket's mind. She would be among the thousand, and probably terrified. "Nenry, you have to help me." Semerket struggled to sit, though his head still pounded and again his vision became blurred. "I have to get Naia away from there, somehow—"

"Lie down, Ketty. Though I can't have her released, I've seen that she and her child have their own cell, and that the temple cooks should prepare her meals. She'll eat as well as the priests—which is to say better than Pharaoh."

With a relieved sigh, Semerket lay back down. Then he turned alarmed eyes once again on his brother. "How is it you can give such orders? Are you trying to protect me—?" He stopped speaking when he saw the odd expression of wonder on his brother's face.

"Ketty," said Nenry, swallowing. "I've the most incredible piece of news . . ."

Semerket stared at him. Never had he seen his brother so rapturous. "Well?"

Nenry took a shaky breath. "Yesterday the vizier proclaimed me the new Mayor of Eastern Thebes."

Semerket decided that he was hallucinating again and settled back down into the bedding to wait out his mind's spasm. But when he opened his eyes again his brother was still sitting there with the same expression of wonderment on his face.

"I didn't know you had another son to sell, Nenry."

Nenry did not sputter his usual protests, nor did his face fill with its usual tics and grimaces. "My son is playing in my courtyard at this moment, Ketty," he said with calm dignity. "His adoption by Iroy has been invalidated. I became mayor because of my 'exemplary courage' in helping to put down the rebellion. Anyway, I was Paser's scribe and knew about ruling the city. It made sense to everyone."

"You're a widower, too, I hear."

"Y-yes . . ." Nenry said, and Semerket was relieved to see his brother's face fill again with its customary grimaces. "Merytra, er, had an accident in the cellar. Terrible. Blood everywhere. Poor thing."

"A knife was involved, Keeya said."

"Yes—the servants were the only witnesses to her . . . clumsiness." Nenry could not long endure his brother's black gaze, and he wailed, "She would have been put to death anyway, Ketty! For colluding with her uncle and the queen. At least I'm spared any scandal at the start of my term."

"I understand, Nenry."

And Nenry truly did see understanding in the black depths of Semerket's eyes, even approval. After that, Nenry eagerly told his brother of his night at Djamet.

The night of the rains, he told Semerket, Paser and Iroy had come to the temple and replaced all the guards at every gate with men loyal only to them. "Luckily," said Nenry, "I had already arrived with Yousef and the beggar army. I went back into the barracks to rouse the soldiers against the conspirators, but what I saw there—" Nenry shuddered, remembering.

"What did you see?"

"It was like something out of an old folk tale of wizards and bewitched palaces. On every barracks door, Iroy had scrawled symbols of bewitchment in human blood—how he got it, the gods alone know. He had strewn amulets and charms everywhere. When I opened the doors, I tell you, brother, it was the eeriest thing I'd ever seen. All the men were *dormant*. They couldn't move, could barely even breathe, though there wasn't a mark on their bodies. Who would believe that magic could be so powerful?"

Semerket remembered the terrible dreams that Tiya had sent and how perilously close to death they had brought him. He swallowed. "Go on," he said.

Before Nenry could continue, however, they were interrupted by Keeya. Gravely she led a physician into the room, followed by three of his servants. Semerket noticed how the young woman fleetingly touched his brother on the shoulder as she left, how Nenry's face flushed with pleasure when she did. He suddenly knew the truth between them, the thing that Nenry was too shy to mention. Thebes would have an intelligent and kindly first lady, he thought.

"Good afternoon, sirs," the physician said, scanning Semerket criti-
cally. "I shall be glad to report to Pharaoh that our patient has revived."

Semerket was surprised to see by his insignia that the man was actually one of Pharaoh's own doctors. The servants placed the physician's
box of instruments and medicines beside the pallet. The physician sat
next to Semerket, cross-legged. He snapped his fingers and a servant
handed him a stick. The doctor held it in front of Semerket's face, commanding him to stare at it as he moved it up, down, and sideways.

"Have you experienced any pain in your head?"

"No."

"Any double vision?"

"No."

The physician regarded Semerket doubtfully. "Please, Lord Mayor,"
he said, "I have interrupted your tale—do continue." He began to
undo the dressing on Semerket's head.

Nenry again took up his narrative. "At any rate, Yousef and I knew
that we would have to fight our way into the temple if we were to save
Pharaoh. Yousef gave the command soon after the Sekhmet garrison
came, so that they barely had time to settle in.

"I tell you, Semerket, I could hardly believe it myself." He laughed
raggedly, remembering. "A beggar who only a moment before had
been dying of leprosy—to see him suddenly leap forward to stave in a
guard's skull—or the beggar woman who without warning thrust a
dagger into a soldier's throat—nothing could have been more surprising to the soldiers."

Nenry told how he had slipped through the mêlée to run through
the temple crying that there was a riot in the courtyard. All the
Sekhmet guards deserted the palace doors, and came streaming to the
temple's entrance.

"It was a scene out of hell," said Nenry, "the rains streaming down,
blood on the tiles everywhere. But then, from out of the dark, another
army appeared from the south. We all stopped fighting then, even the
Sekhmet guards. We just looked at each other—we didn't know who
these men were. But then we saw old Vizier Toh borne in his chair,
with Qar riding beside him. We knew that the old man had come
to save us. The moment he had received the crown prince's message
he had embarked with his men to Djamet, Qar told me later. From

then on, it was a fight from room to room throughout the temple."

As they suspected, Prince Pentwere and a couple of his warriors had gone looking for the crown prince, swords drawn, fighting their way to where his offices were. What they did not expect to find was the giant Yousef and his brawniest warriors waiting for them. A scuffle ensued in which a disbelieving Pentwere and his men were taken prisoner. Pentwere's showy swordsmanship may have dazzled the crowds on festival days, but it was no match for the underhanded tactics of Yousef's men.

Nenry himself stormed up to the harem with his own contingent of beggars. "It was just as I'd seen in the barracks," Semerket's brother said. "All the guards were bewitched, frozen stock-still at their posts, not even aware that we had come into the hall. We broke open the doors—not one of them moved to stop us. Tiya had bewitched them all so that they would not come to Pharaoh's aid."

The physician at this point emitted a gentle cough. "If I may continue from here, Lord Mayor?" he asked. "Pharaoh himself told me what had happened prior to being rescued. Perhaps you care to hear his story?"

"Please," said Nenry in such a regal tone that Semerket rolled his eyes.

The physician was making a poultice of honey and herbs for the new dressing, and continued to work while he spoke. "His Majesty was taking his ease in the harem, as was his habit in the evenings," he said. "I believe he was listening to one of his wives playing a harp. At some point, the commotion of the battle came to him from below. He rose from his couch then, to speak with his guards—but was surprised when his wives clung to him, preventing him from leaving. They were afraid for their lives, they said, and he must protect them. It dawned on him—gradually, he said, not suddenly—that his wives were actually forcibly holding him there. They clung to his arms so he couldn't move, and encircled his legs with their bodies to prevent him from walking. He wasn't so much fearful, he said, as irritable—which, if you know him, is His Majesty's usual reaction to anything unpleasant.

"It wasn't until Tiya approached him that he realized something was very wrong indeed. She was carrying the books of forbidden magic that she'd taken from the House of Life, and was chanting a spell from its scroll. She showed him a waxen doll and Pharaoh, horrified, saw that it was of himself. Tiya told him that it contained fingernail clippings and hairs from his body, and even his seed that his wives collected after he had coupled with him—"

The brothers stared at the physician, aghast.

"Yes," the physician nodded. "Tiya had compelled every one of his southern wives to join the conspiracy—not that they needed much urging. They had planned his demise for months, they informed him. They had written secret letters to their brothers and fathers, who were the army generals and captains of the south, saying to rise against Pharaoh. Oh, gentlemen, the women were very well organized! But by then your brother and his men were at the door, causing some of the wives to panic. Pharaoh managed to wrench himself free and stagger to the door just as it fell open. But even when Tiya saw that all was lost, she was determined to kill her husband. She took out a knife and stabbed Pharaoh along his abdomen . . ."

"Yes! I saw it happen," agreed Nenry. "Thank the gods it was only a scratch. After all her planning and evil-doing, she failed in the end."

The physician wrapped Semerket's head tightly with a fresh bandage. He coughed in a rather embarrassed fashion, dropping his voice so that his servants could not hear him. "Forgive me, Lord Mayor, but I'm afraid that Queen Tiya accomplished exactly what she sought to do."

The brothers looked at the doctor then as if they had not heard him correctly. "Beg pardon?" said Nenry.

The royal physician barked a command to his attendants; they withdrew from the room to wait in the courtyard. "What I tell you, gentlemen," the physician whispered, "is a state secret—though it can't remain one for very long."

Semerket, feeling chill, spoke harshly. "Well?"

It was a moment before the physician spoke again. "What you must know is this: When I examined Pharaoh's wound that night, it seemed nothing very severe. I bandaged it as I would any other superficial cut. But when I changed the bandage again yesterday, the wound had enlarged and was even putrefying. Nothing seemed to stanch the flow of blood at the site. Suspecting the worst, I demanded at once to see Queen Tiya, who by then was in Djamet's prison. She admitted her final evil to me—the knife's blade had been coated with venom from the pyramid adder, Egypt's most toxic serpent. No one has ever survived its bite. It may take weeks for the victim to die, but die he will—and so will Pharaoh."

The men found it difficult to look at one another after such devastating news. Semerket swallowed, asking in a small voice, "Does he know?"

The physician nodded. "And that is why you must get well, Semerket—why you must tell me the truth about your condition. Ramses calls for you daily. Your name is his only comfort, he says, for you are the only one among all his subjects who truly loved him. You saved his throne, and his heir is safe because of you. He wants to thank you in person, before . . ."

"*Thank* me?" Semerket asked, stunned. "But he's lost his life because of me. If I had only discovered the truth a single day earlier . . . !"

"But Pharaoh certainly doesn't believe that," the physician said incredulously. "He'll make you a rich man, exalt you above all others—you have only to name your reward."

But Semerket shook his head. "No," he said. "I want nothing. I deserve nothing. I've failed."

"YOU CANNOT REFUSE Pharaoh's gifts."

Two days had passed and Semerket still could not stand without dizziness. Now he was bowing his head before Vizier Toh, who had come to see him in his sickbed.

"Pharaoh is generous," Semerket said, "but I cannot accept his gifts. I have done nothing to deserve them."

A look of exasperation crossed the vizier's rubbery features. "I will not argue with you," he said testily. "I will keep the gold he has sent you at my estate, against the time when you will want it—as you inevitably will."

"Great Lord!" protested Semerket. "I have no need for such riches. I would feel a hypocrite to accept them."

"It is not your needs I am thinking of," Toh lashed out at him. Seizing his staff of office, he rose from his chair to stand over Semerket. Semerket felt the old man's rheumy gaze boring into his neck.

"You must understand, Semerket," he said firmly, though his voice was softer, "that it is Pharaoh's needs I am considering, not yours. My friend—the companion of my youth—is dying. He needs to demonstrate his gratitude to you in any way you will let him. You cannot be so cruel as to refuse him."

Toh's words moved Semerket to shame. "If the king truly wishes to reward me—"

"He does."

"Then wait until I have at last completed the task that you set me so long ago—to find the murderer of the priestess named Hetephras."

Silence fell in the room.

"You have two days, you stubborn man," Toh said, sighing.

"I will need only one."

"And then, by the little brass balls of Horus, you will appear before Pharaoh—and you will be grateful for whatever he gives you—or I myself will cast you into prison alongside the conspirators. I don't care if you're a hero or not. Pharaoh will not be disappointed—not anymore."

SEMERKET STOOD WITH Qar in the cellar of the house that had belonged to Paneb. The two men watched, silent, while a squad of Medjays cleared away the sacks of grain, the fetid jars of beer, and all the other trash that Paneb had so determinedly heaped against the cellar's mud-brick wall.

Semerket had known, always, that some terrible thing would be found behind the tangle of hurled belongings and moldy foodstuffs. He had sensed it when he explored the cellar that night so long before, together with the cat Sukis. At the thought of the little beast, he felt his skin prickle—he suddenly remembered that it had been she who had led him to the cellar, where she had stood atop the pile of trash, mewing. Semerket put his hand to the bandage on his forehead. Sukis . . . why should he feel so despondent over the death of a cat, when so many people had died?

"Semerket—are you all right?" Qar asked, putting his hand on his friend's shoulder to steady him. "Do you need to sit?"

Semerket shook his head.

Only a few of the original Medjays who had guarded the Great Place were still on duty. All the others had perished in the flood. Qar was now promoted to captain, a reward for his loyalty to Pharaoh. The new Medjays who labored in the cellar had been hastily conscripted from units throughout Thebes. But their duties would no longer include the policing of the tomb-makers; Vizier Toh had permanently assigned an army regiment to the Great Place. From that time forward, the tomb-makers would be forever overseen by them, never again left unguarded.

A day before, the bodies of Neferhotep and Hunro had been recovered. Qar had ordered the corpses, which were damaged almost beyond recognition, taken to the House of Purification. Though he could have prevented it, he allowed Neferhotep to be mummified. As Qar told Semerket—he did his duty, but was no lion. As for Hunro, Semerket himself had volunteered to provide a tomb for her afterlife. He had no wish to see her buried next to a man whom she had so detested and who had engineered her terrible death.

Another division of soldiers labored in the Great Place, attempting to recover as much of the stolen treasure as possible. But the wild river that had washed through the canyons of the Great Place like a gigantic purge had scattered the gold far through the ravines and gullies. Even the furtive tomb of the accursed Amen-meses had been flooded, being built so low into the mountain. What desecrators from other times had overlooked, the sands, rock, and grit that had broken through its weakened doors destroyed. The gesso coating on the limestone had peeled away to mix with the churning waters, congealing like rock around the treasure that remained. Months would be needed to recover it all.

But for now, the Medjays had finally removed the last bit of trash from Paneb's cellar. Qar and Semerket stared at the brick wall that had been revealed.

Semerket began tapping at the bricks, pushing on them to see if any of them could be dislodged. Qar did the same, and for many minutes they worked in silence.

"Here, Semerket!" said Qar. He had found a loose brick at the wall's farthest corner. Carefully he drew it out. Semerket brought a candle near. The flame's light revealed a large niche that extended almost a cubit into the earth beyond.

And there it was, just as he had known it would be: a long object wrapped in a cloth. Qar gingerly removed it from its hiding place and handed it over to Semerket.

It was a moment before Semerket could find the strength to uncover it. Because his legs and hands were shaking, Semerket was forced to sit down on the nearby stairs. The gash in his forehead throbbed. Breathing deeply, summoning his resolve, he at last unwrapped the object.

He stared for a moment.

Semerket abruptly laid the thing down, and thrust himself into the room's corner, bringing up bile. Qar went upstairs, returning with a jug of water, and Semerket rinsed his mouth.

He looked at Qar sideways, and nodded. "I'll see them now," he said.

Paneb and Rami, tired but wary, faced Semerket and Qar in the village kitchens. They had been brought at Qar's command from the Medjays' jail, where all the village elders were crowded together. He had brought the two of them, father and son, to these kitchens because he could not endure Khepura's continuous weeping and wailing in the jail cell.

Semerket spoke to the point, without greeting. "Who first came to Neferhotep with the idea of robbing the tombs? Was it Pentwere, Paser? Who?"

Despite the fact that he had lost everything, Paneb was still all dissimulation. "You make no sense, Semerket, as always," he said, eyes indignant.

"What had they promised the tomb-makers? Gold, treasure? Freedom to leave the village—what?" His voice became harsh. "It must have been something worthwhile, Paneb, to have killed Hetephras over it."

Paneb's head snapped up, startled. "She was my beloved aunt!" he said automatically. "How can you accuse me of . . . A foreigner or vagrant—"

Semerket reached for the object he had found in Paneb's cellar, and unwrapped it. It was an axe from the Hittite nation. Into its haft of carved citrus wood was fitted a blade of rarest blue metal, the hardest known on earth. Yet the blade was nevertheless damaged, for a chip was missing from its lethally sharp edge.

"Do you want to tell us about this weapon, Master Foreman?" Semerket asked softly.

At the sight of it, Paneb buried his face in his arms, shaking his head.

"What about you, Rami?"

The boy looked in horror at the axe, and then turned pleading eyes on the foreman. "Paneb——?"

"Leave him alone!" Paneb shouted, rising to his feet, his chains ringing. His face was ravaged by anguish. "He and I know nothing——*nothing!*"

Paneb fell silent when Semerket brought out a tiny wedge of blue-black metal from his sash. Holding the Hittite axe's blade so that Paneb could see, he fitted the two pieces together so that not even the faintest trace of light shone between them.

Paneb stared. "Where . . . ?"

"A gift from Hetephras," Semerket explained. "From the House of Purification. The Ripper Up found it when he pulled her brain from her skull with a hook."

Paneb's eyes rolled into his forehead and he began to teeter on his feet, as though he would faint. His breath came in large gulps.

Semerket and Qar caught him, staggering beneath his weight, and placed him in a heap against the wall.

"Get him some wine," said Semerket.

Qar brought a jug from the storeroom and held it to Paneb's lips. It was a moment before the vapors hit him. He recoiled a bit, stiffening, but then drank gratefully.

"Do you want to know what I think happened?" Semerket asked gently. Paneb only looked away.

"She was murdered on the first morning of the Osiris Festival, correct? At dawn, she had to make the offerings at the shrine. It's a hard walk from here——I know; I've walked it. Rami was supposed to accompany her. Isn't that true?"

"Y-yes," the boy muttered. "But I overslept that morning. She left without me."

"She left without you, yes, but you hadn't overslept. In fact, you were somewhere else entirely. Would you like to tell me where?"

His low voice and genuine compassion seemed to confound the boy. The resentment in Rami's eyes slowly dissipated. He only shook his head and stared at the ground.

Sighing, Semerket began to speak once again. "There was no moon the night before——I checked the records. Earlier that evening you had robbed a tomb, one that was located near the path that Hetephras would take. You must have been late in leaving it, if I'm guessing correctly? But you never expected her to actually show up—not with Rami in the tomb beside you."

Semerket saw that Paneb's face was growing ruddier by the moment, and that tears were welling in his eyes.

"Say that I'm wrong!" challenged Semerket harshly.

But father and son remained silent, heads bowed in shame.

"Hetephras discovered you. It's as simple as that. And you killed her. Your 'beloved aunt' got in your way, and you cut her down. She was murdered by the man she had taken in as a child. You had no more thought for her than for a dog. With a couple of blows from your axe it was done, over."

"It wasn't like that," Paneb said harshly. Rami cradled his head in his hands. Qar and Semerket stared at one another. Qar looked suddenly old, thought Semerket. His own head throbbed and he could only imagine what kind of ancient mummy he himself resembled.

"Tell me what it *was* like . . ."

Paneb shook his head.

"If you won't save yourself," Semerket said, staring straight into the foreman's gold eyes, "will you not save your son here?"

Their eyes met. Semerket nodded, a promise. With a great sigh, Paneb regarded Semerket with both loathing and respect. "All right," he said.

Semerket leaned forward. "Tell me first, Paneb—what could the old lady have seen that morning?" he asked. "Why did you have to kill her? She was *blind.*"

"I—I was in a panic. We'd just come out of the tomb, to find her there. She just kept saying, over and over again, 'I see you! I know who you are!' Who could tell what she really saw, what she meant? All the men were looking to me to do something." He swallowed tightly. "I had a Horus mask in my hands, I remember, from the tomb. I went to her and raised my axe. It was the only thing I could think of doing to silence her. But when I raised it, she looked up at me as if it were the happiest moment of her life. I almost couldn't do it then. But . . ." Paneb wiped his eyes with the heel of his hand.

"And then you cast her body into the Nile," Semerket prompted.

Paneb nodded his head, breathing heavily to fight back more tears. "We thought if the crocodiles would take her, she'd go directly to heaven. That's what the priests say, anyway." He wiped at his nose. "Then we heard that her body had been found on the eastern side of the river. Even that was a blessing, we told each other, because then Paser would find a way to cover it up." He raised his head and stared at Semerket. "But then you came to the village."

"Yes," Semerket said bitterly. "Sent to make a hash of everything. I was a drunk, who couldn't even find his own backside. 'A vagrant or a foreigner did it,' you all said."

Paneb nodded. "If everyone told you the same story, we thought, you'd go away to look for a make-believe stranger. It was Neferhotep's idea."

"Did they get to him first? Was it Nef who brought up the idea of robbing the tombs?"

Paneb's face became flushed with anger, and he nodded. "Yes. He said we could help build a new era in Egypt, get our empire back. We'd all be made into nobles, he promised, with estates. The queen had promised him—and we believed it."

"But you two fell out. I heard you fighting that day in Hetephras's tomb. You almost killed him then, didn't you?"

Paneb again nodded. "Because he kept pushing. Every tomb was to be the last one, he said, but it never was. Nef told us that Queen Tiya was protecting us through her spells and enchantments. But when Hetephras died, it changed everything. I didn't believe him anymore. I began to hate him, for what he'd brought upon our village, for what I was forced to do. We were artists—we didn't need titles or riches. That was his dream, not ours."

Semerket looked at Rami then. "Did you take your mother's jewels, as Amenhoteb's oracle said?"

Rami nodded unwillingly.

"Why?"

"Because Neferhotep and Khepura came to me the night before. They said my mother was a . . . that she was a bad woman, and that everyone would know she was one because you had convinced her to tell the authorities how she got the jewels. I knew where they were hidden."

Semerket sighed, once again sorry for the role he had played in Hunro's sad life. "Where are the jewels now?"

The boy shook his head. "I don't know. I gave them to my fa— to Neferhotep."

That was all Semerket asked. At his gesture, Qar took them once again to the Medjay jail. Semerket was left alone in the kitchens to consider what they had said.

It was all a terrible family tragedy, he thought—two of them, in fact. One lone murder of a minor priestess in the desert had destroyed a family of artists, and another family living in a palace. In the end, family was the center of everything that was both good and bad in this world, he thought.

Before he left the village, Semerket went a final time to Hetephras's home to retrieve the body of her cat, Sukis. He had promised the old lady's spirit—promised himself, really—that the animal would be mummified and laid beside the old priestess in her tomb. But when he searched the house, the cat's body was missing. He found the cloth that he had wrapped Sukis in after she died—but no corpse. Puzzled, he sat upon the stone bench and wadded the cloth in his hands. From its folds a small metallic object of bright silver clattered to the ground.

It was a small figure of a god. He stared at it. The thing was so small it fit in the palm of his hand, an image of a boy—a prince. On the side of his head was a braided sidelock, while his lips were twisted into a mischievous smile. The cartouche at his feet bore the single name of "Khons."

Semerket remembered how the nieces of the weaver Yunet had told him that the moon god Khons was Hetephras's special patron, the god whom she most adored. In addition to the moon, Khons was also the god of time—and of games. And he looked remarkably like the prince whom Semerket had met in the desert, on his very first foray into the Great Place. "God-skin," he had told Semerket, "is made there." It had been the first indication of what the solution to the priestess's murder might be. He was the lad who had pointed out Hetephras's battered wig to the Medjays . . . and the one who had pulled him to safety from the raging torrent.

Semerket fled quickly from Hetephras's house. All the way back to Eastern Thebes he said nothing, nor did he speak a word to anyone at his brother's home that entire evening. He simply kept looking at the tiny silver figure, shaking his head and shivering.

"HAVE YOU CONSIDERED what your reward will be, Truth-Teller?"

Keeping his word to Toh, Semerket had returned to Djamet to meet with Pharaoh Ramses III. They met on a palace terrace overlooking the Nile. Ramses reclined on a couch, his midsection tightly bandaged. On one side of him stood the crown prince; on the other was Vizier Toh. The usual throng of courtiers and servants was kept far away that day.

Since the rains, spring had appeared quickly in Egypt. The hills and cliffs around Djamet were brushed with the bright tints of wildflowers, while the fields next to the river were hazed with a faint fringe of green, emmer wheat thrusting up in the good black earth. Though it was the season for life renewed, on that terrace in Djamet Temple it was death that made a home. Pharaoh's bandages were soaked with his blood, and his breathing was labored.

"I have considered it, Majesty."

"Then you will allow me to reward you?"

"Your Majesty, I will."

"Name it then."

Semerket took a breath and began. "There are three prisoners, family members of the conspirators, that I beg you to pardon—the wife and child of Nakht, the steward of your harem, and the boy Rami, son of the tomb-maker Paneb."

"Never." The word cut like a knife. Semerket instantly sensed the old man's righteous, unquenchable wrath against those who had betrayed him. "I will never forgive them. Never."

Semerket dropped his head. "You said to name what I want, and I have."

A terrible silence reigned.

"Is he always so pig-headed?" muttered Pharaoh at last, looking askance at his vizier.

"I've found it's easier to ask the Nile to flow backward, Your Majesty," Toh sighed, "than to ask such a man as this to change his mind."

The crown prince stepped forward hurriedly and knelt before his father. "May I remind my father that I am alive because of this man's intervention. I would ask Pharaoh to at least know the reasons for his request."

"Well?" growled the king, sitting back down on his couch. "Speak them."

Semerket took a breath and began, silently asking the gods to free his tongue. "In exchange for his confession," he said, "I promised Foreman Paneb that I would save his son."

"This Paneb," said Pharaoh, slowly. "Not only was he the killer of the priestess, but he was also the foreman of the team that rifled so many tombs. A strange candidate for such a favor."

Semerket raised his head. "It is in memory of the boy's mother that I also ask. Hunro was my only friend among the tomb-makers. She, too, died at the hands of the conspirators, Your Majesty, because she helped me."

"Hmmph. What about this other woman, then—this wife of Nakht? Why do you plead for her?"

"I was once married to her, Great King."

The pharaoh snorted. "And she left you for that traitor? Then she is guilty of the crime of bad taste, deserving nothing less than death!"

"She wanted children, Pharaoh. I could give her none. The fault was mine."

He saw Pharaoh's eye begin to harden.

"I still love her, Your Majesty," he added, "more than my life. Even when she went to live in another man's house, I could not stop loving her."

There was a terrible silence. Semerket's head ached from the strain of speaking so many words, and he fell again into obeisance, resting his forehead on the cool tiles. The pharaoh stared at him, like an eagle stares at a hare.

"This is my judgment," Pharaoh said at last.

Instantly a nearby scribe took up a stylus and wax tablet.

"Naia, the wife of the traitor Nakht, and Rami, the son of the traitor Paneb, are spared execution."

Semerket's breath gusted from him in relief. "Thank you, Great King!"

"Do not thank me so soon, Semerket. I am not yet finished." He turned again to the scribe, directing him to continue writing. "They will be exiled, never again to step foot in Egypt or drink from the waters of the Nile. They will be sent as indentured servants to Babylon, and there live out their days."

"Pharaoh—!" protested Semerket.

"Do not ask any more for them, Semerket. My gratitude has limits."

"What—what, then, of Naia's child?"

"Let her take the child with her if she wants, or let her give it away. I care nothing for infants. Now go and bid your farewells to this Naia of yours, and the lad, too; a ship carrying our new ambassador leaves for Babylon this very day."

A spasm of pain gripped Pharaoh, and he grimaced, clutching his side. The crown prince called sharply for a physician, and courtiers began to scramble about like alarmed ants. During the fracas, Semerket slunk away.

Once Semerket had departed the terrace, the crown prince hurried to him. They stood at the top of the stairs that led into the main room of the palace. "Don't blame my father overmuch, Semerket."

Semerket shook his head. He was still in shock, unable to speak.

"Though he doesn't say it," the prince continued, "this business has truly shaken him. He had convinced himself he was beloved, you see. Then to find out that everything he believed in was a lie—well, that is why he needs you in his last days. You risked your life to save his, and it comforts him to have you near. Please come back. You remind my father that he counts for something in at least one person's heart."

"But Pharaoh is loved . . ."

"A pharaoh is feared. He is worshipped. Adored. But loved? Semerket, I am under no illusions; the red and white crowns are far more wonderful things to see than to wear." Prince Ramses laid his hand upon Semerket's shoulder. "You and I will talk together in the days ahead; I do not forget my friends."

Semerket bowed until the crown prince had returned to his father, then went downstairs into the main room of the palace. To his surprise, he spied the immensely tall Yousef, lieutenant to the King of the Beggars, standing amid a group of his fellows at a far wall. They all were clad in their best, most outlandish garments, cadged undoubtedly from many a Theban noble's waste heap. The beggars waited in front of a niche that held a silver vase filled with glorious new lilies. Almost hidden in the beggars' midst was a miniature chariot drawn by a ram.

The Beggar King was clean, for once. Semerket was forced to admit that legless as he was, the king exuded a regal air that many blood-born nobles might envy. When he saw Semerket approaching, he hailed his ally gleefully, flicking the reins against his ram's backside and driving to where Semerket stood.

"Semerket, savior of the kingdom! Man of the hour! Friend of kings!"

Semerket scowled at his compliments. "I can't believe you're here, Majesty. Have you become respectable at last?"

"My brother the pharaoh himself commands me to attend him. At one time or another," he smirked nonchalantly, "everyone wishes to meet me in person. They say he will even request a favor of me."

"What sort of favor?"

The Beggar King shrugged.

"Pharaoh and his advisors are being very mysterious," said Yousef.

"But of course I shall grant it, whatever Pharaoh asks," said the Beggar King. "We are brother sovereigns, after all."

At that moment the palace chamberlain came to murmur to the king that he and his company were awaited on the terrace. With their joyful farewells ringing in his ears, Semerket headed again for the temple pylons. From the corner of his eye he noticed that the vase of silver in the niche was missing.

Ah well, Semerket thought—it's none of my concern. He had sadder things to think about; he was going to the prison at Amun's Great Temple, to tell Naia that Egypt was no longer her home.

SEMERKET STOOD AT the docks. It was noon. Rami, hands bound behind him, stood at his side. A fast river transport in the royal harbor made ready to depart for the north, and last-minute crates and bales were being stowed on its decks. It was a new ship of shallow draft but wide beam, constructed in the manner of Phoenician vessels, with a keel and ribs. This meant that the ship was capable of voyaging not only upon the river, but also out on the salt seas beyond—something most Egyptians in their keelless boats dreaded.

The new ambassador to Babylon had already gone aboard, along with his gifts for Babylon's king. As they waited for Naia to be delivered to them, Semerket looked over at Rami. Though he affected an adolescent's disdain, Semerket could tell he was terrified, and that he probably blamed Semerket for his misery. The lad had lost everything because of the man beside him—his home, his parents, even the girl he was to have married.

"Rami," Semerket said, "I'm sorry how everything turned out. I wanted you to live in my brother's house with me, in Thebes."

"You?" the lad spat. "I'd rather live with hyenas."

For a while you did, thought Semerket, but he did not say it. Firmly he placed his hand on Rami's shoulder, looking deeply into his eyes. "Anyway, I'm sorry," he said. "Truly."

The boy said nothing, dropping his gold eyes sullenly, and went quickly aboard the ship. He would not stand any longer beside Semerket.

In despair, Semerket gazed down the wide avenue that bordered the wharves. In the distance he saw Naia walking in the company of temple guards. The baby squirmed in her arms, made fretful by the noises and sharp smells of the docks. He embraced them both when she arrived, without speaking, and they stood together for endless moments, saying nothing, oblivious to all and everything around them.

All too soon the impatient captain yelled to them from the deck that Naia was to come aboard instantly. Semerket snarled an epithet in his direction.

"We can't put it off any longer, my love," Naia said. She was robed in a simple sheath of mourning gray, and wore a head scarf of the same plain material. She should have been dressed as a queen, thought Semerket bitterly, not a servant.

"I will come for you," he said to her, taking her free hand.

"You cannot."

"I will. You know I'll do it."

"Oh, Ketty, why do you always make things harder than they need to be? Let us say goodbye here in Thebes, and forever. Put me out of your mind."

"I won't. I can't."

She was suddenly very angry. "You are a cruel man!" she said in a wail.

The child began to wail too, and Semerket stood looking helplessly at them both. "How can you say that, when you know I love you so?"

Naia looked at Semerket, and there was a strange light in her eye. She kissed the child desperately then, as if she would crush the baby to her. "What I need to take with me now," she told him, "is the knowledge that you are not suffering. You don't know how much I need it. It will be the only thing to give me strength to endure—the next thing I must do."

He did not like her strange tone, nor the odd, determined glint in her eyes. Before he could speak his fears, however, she abruptly thrust the child into his arms.

"Take him," she said.

When Semerket could only stare, she cried again, harshly, "Take him!"

Semerket was shocked into taking the now-squalling Huni, and held him to his chest. He could not speak, for again his tongue was lifeless in his mouth.

"I want him raised as an Egyptian, by the best man I have ever known and ever will. He is *our* son, Semerket—remember that. Though Nakht fathered him, the gods gave us a child in the only way they could. It doesn't matter how we got him—he is *ours*. I bore him, and now you must rear him."

"Naia!" He was aghast.

"That's why you must be happy here in Egypt for me. For if you are not—if you mope and pine for me, and drink yourself sodden—I will know our son cannot be happy. Can you do that for me?"

He forced himself to nod.

The captain yelled at them again, threatening to send down guards to forcibly drag Naia aboard. Reluctantly, Semerket and Naia moved to the gangplank.

Semerket looked at her helplessly. "Naia . . . the only thing I can think of now is that flower you saw, after we were first married, in the eastern deserts. Do you remember it?"

"The strange purple flower, high on that cliff. Yes, I remember. I joked that I wanted it for my garden."

He was weeping now, unabashedly. People on the docks stared. "I could have climbed that cliff. Why didn't I?"

"Oh, Ketty—it doesn't matter."

"Every day since I met you, I've looked for your face in all the women I see. None of them is alive to me—only you are alive. But I know now I'll never see your face again, anywhere."

With a cry she turned away and hurried on board, not once looking back at her husband and child. The crew was quick to drag the dripping anchor stone to the ship's deck, and the rowers thrust their oars into the Nile. The ship turned, bow heading to the north, and the river god caught the vessel in his arms and gently pushed it forward. The rowers changed positions, and dipped their oars again. The ship increased its speed, and sailed swiftly past the docks and into the center of the river.

Semerket, with his child in his arms, watched as it disappeared in the bend of the river. But even when he could no longer see the tip of its mast, he did not move. He was thinking, instead, how perverse the gods were. Where once he had despaired of ever having a son, he now had Naia's.

And he was the unhappiest man in Egypt.

QUEEN TIYA OPENED her eyes and saw the old man at the cell's door.

"Toh!" she said in surprise.

"Greetings, lady," the vizier said. "The pharaoh in his mercy has decreed that you are to live."

"I don't believe it." She had no modesty. "Why should he show me mercy now when all my life he has humiliated and bedeviled me?"

"Who knows? Perhaps he grows sentimental in his old age, lady. He has sent this wine to you as a gesture of his goodwill. Will you drink some?"

"No doubt it is poisoned."

"If you think so, then I will drink some with you." He poured a bowlful.

"You drink first, old man!" she commanded.

Toh raised the bowl to his lips and took a sip.

"All the way down!"

The vizier of Egypt continued to drink until there was no more. He poured out a second bowl.

Tiya seized the bowl and drank greedily. "That's fine stuff," she said. "I've only had water since they put me in here, and brackish at that. Not even beer."

Toh smiled and took his leave, telling her that she should be prepared to move from her cell. When he had returned to his chambers, he put a feather down his throat to vomit up the wine, along with the oil he had swallowed earlier to prevent the powerful sleeping herb from taking effect.

When she awoke, Tiya was no longer in the chilly cell in Djamet's dungeon. She gazed around the unfamiliar room, at its barbarous friezes and strange colors. The queen lay on a flat, hard table, with no pallet beneath her. When she tried to rise, she found that she was quite naked, and that her arms and legs were strapped tightly to the table.

A strange animal sound came to her through the gloom. Twisting her head, she saw that a ram had made the bleating noise. Strangely, it was reined to a miniature chariot. Craning her neck to see, she found herself staring into what appeared to be the red eyes of a man—a horrible legless creature with a crown of battered acanthus leaves on his head. Tiya uttered a small cry.

"We are honored, madam," the legless thing said, "to entertain you today in my kingdom!"

With a snap of his fingers, four other men drew forward, dressed only in scant loincloths. At that moment Tiya saw the braziers of charcoal that were placed nearby, each containing a set of hooks and knives, all glowing a bright orange.

"May I now introduce you, madam, to the finest surgeon in Thebes?" asked the king gallantly. "Cripple Maker, meet Lady Tiya."

"A pleasure, great lady." The man's sickly syrupy voice made her recoil more than the cruel instruments he held in his hands.

"She was a queen of Egypt once," the Beggar King said. "But that was not enough for her. So today she is given a new kingdom to rule— mine. Make of her your finest creation, for the queen of the beggars deserves the very best. But mind that you do not kill her in your zeal, for the pharaoh has promised that she may live. And he is a man who keeps his word."

Tiya's famed voice of many strings rose up in a crescendo of short, sharp screams.

• • •

PHARAOH GRIMACED as he rose from his couch and clutched his side. Irritably he waved away the slave who would have assisted him. He pulled aside his hand, and revealed that his freshly changed bandages were again soaked in blood.

Already he wears his mummy wrappings, Semerket thought to himself. As the crown prince had requested, he had returned again to Pharaoh's side, leaving Huni in his brother's house in the care of Keeya. Semerket shuddered to see the blood, and dropped his eyes to prevent Pharaoh from reading his mind. But it was too late; the king had seen him staring.

"Yes," Pharaoh said. "My wife has won her battle."

"A hundred years," Semerket muttered the ritual phrase automatically.

"A hundred!" The old ruler's laugh was sharp. "I would give all I have for one."

With difficulty he walked the length of the terrace to gaze at Eastern Thebes across the river. Semerket followed at a discreet distance, avoiding the drops of blood that trailed Ramses. The fires in the city's hearths gleamed like facets in a thousand rubies. The entire horizon was aglow with them.

"Do you remember the Egypt of my father, Semerket?" The old man's hand shook as he reached out, as if to clasp the rubies to him. They shimmered just outside his touch, and the hand fell slowly back. Still, the fingers clenched and unclenched, unused to not holding what they sought.

Semerket kept his silence. In his mind Pharaoh was addressing a contemporary. What good would it do to remind an old man of his age? Ramses was not much interested in Semerket's reply, in any case. The words poured from him in pained gasps, a confession. A valedictory.

"Egypt was cast adrift. Every man was a law to himself. Anyone could murder whomever they chose, high and low. So many years of misrule and discord before him . . . generations of civil wars. My father took up the red and white crowns that had fallen in the dust. But he was an old man when he became Pharaoh. The gods gave him only two years. Then it was my turn." He pointed to the black mass of the distant temples. "I found the gates of Karnak stripped of their plate and jewels. Amun's barque had even sunk in the Sacred Lake, it was so rotten. This was my inheritance."

Pharaoh stared into the night, the hard, bitter line of his profile limned by torchlight.

"My father had given Egypt back its government. I vowed to give it back its place among nations. And I was young, and strong as the Buchis bull. It was sunrise in Egypt, I told the people."

Ramses pulled a kerchief from his pectoral and wiped at the flecks of spittle at his mouth. In the flame's light, Semerket saw the tinge of pink. Pharaoh saw it, too, and quickly closed his hand around the cloth. "And for a while I thought I had succeeded. Yet I was forced to marry Tiya, to assuage the pride of these ludicrous, arrogant southerners. I had to promise to make her firstborn my heir. It seemed that only I saw the evil in them both. I should have had her quietly killed, but I felt sorry for Pentwere. He was so attached to her. And what real harm could she do, I thought. She was only a woman, after all. And then the other children came." He looked at Semerket with bitter irony. "Though I am worshipped as a god, Semerket, I am Egypt's biggest fool."

For the only time in his life Semerket wished that fulsome words of flattery and praise could bubble spontaneously to his lips, words of reassurance and hope, empty though they might be; for the only time in his life Semerket wished he was his own brother.

But his tongue was a block of wood in his head as always. So unused to saying any words but those of the stark truth, his throat actually hurt from the effort to find sweet and temperate ones, full of comfort and lies. In the end, Semerket could only reach out to the old man in a gesture of fleeting spontaneity. He wished to draw him near, so that Pharaoh's pain might be eased. But the majesty of Pharaoh overwhelmed him. How to comfort a living god? Semerket's hand stopped, only to fall uselessly to his side.

Ramses regarded Semerket with grim amusement. But then he was seized with another abrupt spasm of pain. He dropped to one knee. Semerket caught him, and led him to a bench where he could regain his breath, holding him as the spasm slowly subsided. Pharaoh's bandages were now soaked completely in red.

It was Pharaoh who moved away first, sitting up straight and dignified on the bench beside Semerket. After a time, the king spoke again. His voice seemed strengthened.

"For a while it seemed I had succeeded in my dreams for Egypt. I planted the entire land with trees and greenery and I let the people sit in their shade. A woman of Egypt could travel freely wherever she wanted, and no one molested her, not even foreigners. I sent to Lebanon for cedar to repair the sacred barque. I replated the temple doors. I built new . . . or so I thought."

Then Pharaoh turned and regarded Semerket with an expression of absolute bitterness.

"And then in this Year of the Hyenas you came into our lives. You were the one, Semerket—the terrible truth-teller—who opened all our eyes at last. Until you came, everyone thought the rams' horns blew paeans of praise for me. But you told us it was a dirge they played instead. Thanks to you, I realize now it was not a triumph I led—but a funeral procession." His breath came in gasps at the end.

Pharaoh and Semerket watched through the long evening together, saying nothing, as one by one the fires of Egypt's hearths went out.

"I wish . . ." Semerket began, and stopped.

Irritation again lit Pharaoh's eye. "Yes? What is it you wish for? Everyone wants something from me in the end. Well, gold chains I have offered you in plenty. These you have all refused. What could you possibly want, I wonder?"

Semerket dropped his head. "I wish that it had not been me."

The living god of Egypt was startled, and for an instant his face became a shattered mask of woe. He collected himself swiftly.

"Nonsense. It was the fate the gods gave you . . . and me." Though he spoke crisply, Pharaoh reached out tentatively and draped an old, sinewy arm across Semerket's shoulders. It was an arm unaccustomed to such familiarity and it lay there stiff and immobile.

Feeling Pharaoh lean on him, a great dullness fell upon Semerket's heart. As he gazed out into the blackness of Thebes it seemed to him that Egypt had been plunged into an eternal night.

ABOUT THE AUTHOR

Brad Geagley has worked for many years in the entertainment industry, mainly as a producer. All of his assignments—from documentary television shows to virtual reality attractions—heavily emphasized his writing abilities. History was Geagley's first love, however, particularly that of ancient Egypt. He became a full-time writer in 2001 and is currently at work on his second Semerket novel and on stage plays. He lives in Palm Springs, California.